Forget

Forget

Baleigh Whitworth

Chapter One

Tae's Pov.

They say only time tells us when we leave this world, whether it's sickness or just natural cause of death, I knew I was dying and slowly at that. I was weak I never let anyone in because I knew if I did one day I'd be gone from this world and I don't want them to miss me because I know how it feels. I feel it every day the same with my dad.

I was afraid of dying, I wanted to live and see the world, go on journeys and explore places I've never been, but I couldn't, I had to stay right here in Anderson, South Carolina, but then I met someone, someone who changed up everything. He was kind, had a good heart, but I was too afraid to let him in and he knew that and he knew my ways so, he played the game.

"Blondie let's go!" My dad calls out as I finish wetting my hair for school. "It's your first day you don't want to be late."

I quick pace down the hall to where my jacket lays on the couch. "It's not even that late dad."

He tosses me a granola bar while grabbing his keys. "I know that, but as the coach I have to be extra early you should know that by now. Do I have t-"

I cut him off. "I know, the early bird gets the worm."

I roll my eyes at him and he nods at me while flicking the light off in the kitchen, we head out of the house and into my dad's pickup truck. Over the last three years it has been rough on my dad and I, first with Georgie leaving for college and mom dying it really hit hard on us.

My mom was beautiful, she was such a sweet woman and we miss her so much every day. She was my best friend so was my dad's, their marriage was like the perfect couple you wish you could have, but no couple is ever perfect. My mom hid cancer from me and Georgie until I turned thirteen, that was the time when it hit her hard.

I was upset at her for not telling me, but I could understand why she had done it, three years ago on March fifth my mom had died from leukemia, it ran in the family. I never really understood cancer until about a year later after my mom died, I was diagnosed with leukemia, I was scared out of my mind but there was nothing I could do but take medicine and hope for the best.

I had found out that I have had it ever since I was little but it was nothing too serious until I grew up, now I'm in my junior year of high school and I can gladly say I made it through. Hopefully I can live another year so I can graduate.

"Are you nervous?" My dad cuts me out of my thoughts. "My little girl is growing up on me."

"Oh, dad stop it," I cringed looking at him as he fake cries.

"First Georgie now you another year and you'll be off to college.

I sigh out and look out the window. "That's if I even make it through another year."

"Tae," he warns me I knew he didn't like me saying that but it was true.

We didn't know if I was going to live for another year, nobody would know. I just have to make the best of my life until it ends.

"I'm sorry it's just I'm nervous and I didn't mean to say that I was just thinking-"

He cuts me off. "I know it's alright I know how you feel."

I stay quiet while looking out the window again, biting my lip.

My dad sighs out while parking in the back of the school. "Look, I know it's hard but we can get through this. Happy thoughts alright?"

I nod and he lays his enormous hand over my head and shakes it a little. "Make the most of this this year will be fun I promise."

"I hope so," I tell him and he nods for me to get out.

My dad follows me out of the car and we make our way to the entrance of the school.

"Nervous?" I ask him while smirking.

He gives me a look then shakes his head. "Nah not me."

I raise my brow at him and he gives me another look but then sighs.

"Yes, only because of Mrs. Hyde she kind of makes me nervous," He explains and I do a double take looking at him.

My jaw drops as we enter the school. "You like Mrs. Hyde?!"

"Shh be quiet," He covers my mouth with his hand and I couldn't help but laugh at him.

He acted like a school boy that was shy, Mrs. Hyde was the school's guidance counselor aka my best friend since I didn't have one, she was the only one that knew about me being sick in the school except for my brother and my dad. She wasn't like any other counselor.

"Have a good first day!" my dad kisses my cheek while making his way to the gym where his office is.

I sigh out making my way to the office to get my schedule and keep repeating what my dad told me.

Have a good first day...

Chapter Two

Keaton's Pov.

Senior year was all about having fun and living life as it goes, but not for me. I had to take it step by step, I had my future planned out for me as for everyone else they were too busy partying and doing whatever the hell they wanted. Most of the part of my life is having fun, but also to work on my studies and scholarships.

Football was my life; it ran the entire family. My dad made me join when I was around the age of twelve so I basically had to stick with it. I didn't mind though; over the years I began to love football and so did my best friends.

A hard shove on my back caused me to clear my thoughts and turn my head to see my best friend Reece. "What's up? Last day of our first day of school is here! Look Mandy's boobs have gotten bigger this year."

"You're such a pig Reece!" Winnie's screeching voice appeared as she comes into view.

She hugs up on Landon who's already wearing his school's jock jacket on, he rolls his eyes clearly annoyed by her and I start to wonder why he's even dating her in the first place.

"You're just mad that she got bigger ones than you so shut it," Reece snaps while leaning against the locker beside mine.

I quietly snicker while taking out my books and shoving my book bag in my locker before closing it with a bang.

Winnie gasps. "Hers are fake unlike mine that are natural as melons."

"Oh, bite me," Reece bites back causing Winnie's face to turn red and her red plump lips form into an aggressive smile.

"Come here then." Reece looks at me wide eyed and takes off down the hall with Winnie chasing after him.

Landon laughs. "She's killing me man."

"Tell me why you date her again?" I sarcastically say while he shakes his head.

"I love her, but damn she's a handful."

I nod. "Damn right."

"You coming to tryouts today?" He asks playfully hitting my chest.

I hit him back. "You know it, mom and dad making me go anyways."

Lydia Brock walks past me, but not without brushing her arm against mine seductively, before purring out. "Hey Keaton."

"Hey," I say without looking at her which caused her to scoff but I didn't care I was tired of her trying to get with me.

No means no and that's it. I didn't want a girl that flashed her skin out of her clothes I wanted a simple girl, a chase, one that was hard to get, but none of them seemed to be eye catching to me. A girlfriend wasn't in my vocabulary right now, I thought it would be easier to just focus on my studies and football.

Until I seen Coach Lambert walking down the hall with a girl I couldn't recognize, they resembled each other a lot and seem like they were close as she was holding onto his arm. She seemed nervous, her shoulders were tense and her bottom lip was between her teeth while smiling up at coach Lambert.

"Hey, who's that?" I hit Landon's arm catching his attention while pointing towards the mysterious girl.

"Who's what now?" He says confused as he looks through the crowd trying to find out who I was pointing to until he figured out. "Oh, that's Coach's daughter."

"He has a daughter?" I was shocked, he never told us anything about him having a daughter.

Landon nods. "Yeah, but she's weird. She doesn't talk to anybody except for the teachers."

I give him a look before looking back at the girl to see her alone, Landon pats me on the back interrupting me from checking her out he gives me a look, but I ignore it while looking back to see her gone.

"Let's go," Landon says nodding his head to class. "Quit checking her out it's not gonna happen."

I laugh. "I was not checking her out."

"Mhm."

I push at him causing him to go forward a little as we walk to our class for the next hour, I huff as I enter the boring class of history and take a seat in the front beside Landon. Graduates from last year told me about this class and told me I didn't have to worry about failing because all the teacher did was give out an assignment as he sits down in his chair on his phone. Senior year was looking good so far.

Chapter Three

Tae's Pov.

Friendships. One word to describe many of the thing's kids had these days that I never had; I was too afraid. I sat in Mrs. Hyde's big Rolly chair waiting for her to get out of her meeting so we could start our nice talk we always have every day of every single year I've been in high school.

Our lunchtime I usually isolate myself from making any new friends or getting my food dumped all over me by students passing by. The door of Mrs. Hyde's office clears my thoughts as it opens revealing the sweet smile of Mrs. Hyde.

She closes the door silently before turning around, putting her hand against her hip. "Why aren't you at lunch?"

"Pshh go to lunch and eat by myself when I can eat with you? Who would miss an opportunity to do that?" I tell her clearly trying to distract her so she wouldn't make me go to lunch.

She sighs. "Anyone would, Tae, I think it's time for you to get out of your shell a-"

She stops herself before causing us to both laugh at the same time at the fact that she was trying to get me to make friends, she leans under her desk and takes out a brown bag that usually has a sandwich with chips in it.

"Here you go."

I smile graciously while taking the bag. "Thanks."

"How was your summer? Was it fun?" She asks as she props her legs on the table leaning back watching me.

I bite into the sandwich before answering. "If you call getting needles stuck in your arm and getting x-rays done is fun, then yeah my summer was exciting!"

"Alright fine, I'm sorry, how are you holding up?" She leans forward while letting her feet down giving me a concerned look.

"Good I guess I'm just bored all the time," I state sitting the brown paper bag back down on the desk not suddenly feeling hungry anymore.

She shrugs. "Well, you don't do nothing Tae. You should do a sport that'll cheer you up."

"My dad and doctors will kill me if I played in a sport," I exclaimed laughing. "Besides, I don't think they'll want Ms. wheezy on their team."

"Then why don't you just help your dad out on the field, it must be pretty hard with him coaching the boys and all," She insisted and I give her a bored look.

"My dad wouldn't let me."

She shrugs. "It wouldn't hurt to try."

"Whatever, I think I'm going to class now," I tell her, standing up brushing the crumbs of sandwich off my lap.

Mrs. Hyde stands up with me. "Wait, class doesn't start until thirty minutes."

"Exactly, I'm going in early," I say, causing her to laugh while shaking her head at me.

"Alright, I'll see you kid."

I grab my book bag before saying. "Later!"

I walk along the quiet long halls of the dreaded school with a sigh, my thoughts were stuck in my mind like gum stuck in someone's hair. Maybe Mrs. Hyde was right, maybe I could help my dad at least it'll give me something to do other than just sitting in the library till my dad was done with practice.

I walk in my precalculus class dreading an hour of listening to the teacher talking nonstop of shapes and numbers. I sit down at my normal table and begin writing down what's on the board to get a head start, one thing I know about Mr. Pine is that he loves when people are on time.

Students start arriving once the bell rings indicating to get to class, an hour later I'm on my way to my locker putting my things up for another lectured class. By the end of the day, I'm already exhausted and weak. I walk to the nurse's room to find nurse Pattie helping a girl that had a huge blood stain on the back of her pants.

My heart sinks for her knowing how embarrassing that can be, but I wait on the table as the girl walks into the bathroom with new jeans in her hands.

"Well," Nurse Pattie sighs out before turning around in her chair and noticing me. "Ahh Tae how are you?"

"I'm fine, how are you?" I say back suddenly feeling awkward being back in this room.

"I'm doing great."

Memories flooded my head of me in this room everyday secretly taking my medicine while everyone goes about their day, the girl with the blood-stained pants came out of the bathroom wearing her new jeans, she smiles brightly and thanked nurse Pattie for the pants and makes her way out of the office.

Nurse Pattie turns around with a big pill in her hand. "Alright, you ready?"

I nod, taking out my stress ball out of my book bag giving it a squeeze as Nurse Pattie hands me the pill and I gulp it down with water, I sigh in relief as she smiles at me and I put the stress ball away.

"That wasn't bad, was it?" She asks while taking the gloves off her hands before washing them.

I shake my head. "Nope."

"I'll see you tomorrow. I'd also take it easy tomorrow as well, I seen where you came in looking tired just don't rush yourself," She explains and I nod at each word she says.

"Yes ma'am," I saluted her, causing her to laugh as I jump down from the table.

I tell her bye once more before leaving her office and heading to finish off the rest of the day in boredom, I walk down the halls passing students as they frown from being tired on their first day. I smiled to myself as I enter the classroom catching Mr. Hollis giving me a blank stare.

"Hello Mr. Hollis," I greet him.

"Tae, why am I not surprised that you have my class again for the third year?" He lifts his eyebrows at me.

I shrug innocently, taking a seat in the far back. "Because you're my favorite."

I hear him chuckle. "How could I forget? Don't tell anyone, but you're my favorite too."

I smile at him hearing the school bell ring, indicating to get to class and that lunch is over. Students file in and I watch seniors, juniors, even freshman's taking a seat in the class. Every year I chose this class because one; it was easy, and two; it was easy.

I roll my eyes as the most dreadful part of the class was seeing the stoners kids enter the classroom with the 'popular' people entering in right behind them, did

I mention they were acting like a fool while walking in?

Most of the class had hooligans like; Reece Paul, Landon Barnes, and Keaton Davis. Which includes the 'popular' people.

I hated how this school split everyone up just because of their looks, and of course, the one and only redhead of the school with a smile plastered on her face enters the class and takes a seat beside me like she always does.

Winnie Adams, the school's perfect ex cheerleader, rumors say she and her best friend, Lydia Brock broke up. *But really who's keeping up?*

Just like every day she sends me a smile and in return I ignore it, it was fake, everyone was fake, plus I couldn't allow myself being involved with someone like her, I couldn't.

"Alright class, cell phones need to be put away and if you're sitting next to your boyfriend or girlfriend, I suggest you move," Mr. Hollis starts the class off.

"I don't need another couple being excused from the class because the guy couldn't keep his fingers out of her," He mumbled clearly letting us hear which causes the immature class to laugh.

I sigh, sitting back in my seat as Mr. Hollis continues with his lesson. *Agriculture.*

It seemed like forever until class was over, it was like every year, every question Mr. Hollis sent us Keaton Davis would be there to answer.

Stupid jock.

For three years straight, never noticed someone like me, he sat in front of the class like the perfect guy he is.

It's not like I didn't like the guy, it's just that I didn't like how he was fake.

I just couldn't wait till I become a senior so people like Winnie Adams and Keaton Davis could leave and be off to some rich prick college.

Chapter Four

Waking up in the morning at five was something my dad and I did every day, we'd do our morning walk then get ready for the day, it felt weird that Georgie wasn't here to do it with us since he usually is.

Ever since Georgie left for college, things weren't the same. The morning walks stopped and dad making us breakfast stopped.

It was the little things that mattered to me most changed.

I put my joggers on with a shirt to go over it, I pulled my hair into a ponytail putting a headband to finish the look. I knew it was sketchy for me since we had to walk in a fast pace, but I wanted to do normal things like normal people to make myself forget.

Which wasn't easy with the wheezing.

"Blondie! You ready?" I stand at the doorway of my room meeting my dad at the top of the stairs.

I pose for him. "How do I look?" He smiles at me.

"You look beautiful," He tells me and I smile at him. "Now are you ready to get your butt kicked during this walk/jog?"

"Only losers say that," I said and he scoffs.

"Whatever," He waves me off before turning around and walk downstairs to finish getting ready.

My smile fades as I catch a glimpse of Georgie's room cracked open, I take slow steps toward the room and as I enter my whole body begins to feel cold.

Ever since Georgie left, it was never the same. My dad's goofiness was just a cover up to me so I wouldn't know if he was sad about him leaving.

Georgie might've been my brother, but he was my best friend.

The room was still in its place and I smile at the picture he left on his desk top of me and him, it was him holding me on his back with us both smiling and I knew exactly who took this picture.

Mom.

Georgie leaving was the worst thing I could have ever felt besides my mom dying. I take a deep breath, placing the picture back in its place.

Shutting his bedroom door with a sigh, I turn around jumping from my dad leaning on the wall.

"Dad! Don't sneak up on me," I hold onto my chest as I feel my heart pump.

He holds his hand in surrender. "Sorry."

I walk around him going back to my room to find my tennis shoes, I was trying to get away from the Georgie conversation since he caught me in his room.

I put on my sneakers one by one feeling my dad's eyes on me as he leans on my door frame in his tracksuit.

"I miss him too," He murmurs.

I close my eyes. "Can we not?"

"What? I was just trying to make conversation," He tries to make amends.

"I know, but when things get sad between us it gets weird and when it gets weird-" He cuts me off.

"You cringe, I know," He rolls his eyes.

I nod before getting up from the bed. "Yes, now that we got that settled, race you outside!"

I hit his stomach before running out of my room and racing downstairs, and outside I'm at. I wait a few minutes, hearing the creaking sound of the door letting me know my dad made it.

I give my panting dad a smirk. "I'm fine." He pants out.

We start our walk down the neighborhood and as we make it to the park, I stop leaning down on my knees wheezing my lungs away.

I felt a hand on my back. "Are you okay?" I hear my dad's voice throughout the ring in my ears.

"Yeah," I pant, standing back up.

I looked at my dad who was looking far off at the park with his hand over his eyes.

"Is that Keaton Davis?" I hear him mumble to himself.

I squint from the sun shining in my eyes. "What?"

I look around trying to find that stupid jock and I wish my dad was lying when he said that was him, it was for sure Keaton, he was with an older man.

Keaton was doing pull ups on the monkey bars while the older man which looked like to be his dad, was yelling in his ear.

"Davis!" My dad yells making Keaton and the other guy turn their heads.

"What?! Dad, no," I panicked looking for a place to hide.

I see my dad shrug. "What? Keaton's nice, you'd like him."

Yeah, okay.

I roll my eyes while sighing as I watch the two walks towards us, I prayed that the ground would turn into one big whole and suck me into it.

"Coach Lambert, hi," Keaton greeted, shaking my dad's hand.

"Good to see you Randy," My dad shook hands with the man beside Keaton.

"Good to see you too, Bo," Randy told my dad who nods.

I felt a push on my back and noticed my dad's hand on it.

"This is my daughter, Tae," I put on a fake smile as I shake hands with Randy.

This couldn't be anymore worse.

My eyes catch onto Keaton's as he sends me a gentle smile.

"You go to the same high school as my son, don't you?" Randy asks with a smile.

I nod. "Yeah."

Before he could say anything else I hear Keaton. "She's a junior."

I awkwardly smile. *How did he know? Did he even know who I was?*

If this could get any weirder, then it has.

I looked at the time on my phone seeing that if we don't head back home right now, we would be late for school. I hit my dad's arm, grabbing his attention to show him the time and he excuses us to head back home.

That was the last time Keaton and I were ever going to be associated with each other, and I was going to make sure of it.

Chapter Five

Tae's Pov.

Jumping out of my dad's car didn't seem too promising when I was trying to make it on time to my class, the second day of school I was already late.

Great.

I cursed myself while walking down the halls of the school, I walked in the empty classroom making myself look like a complete fool. All the attention was on me when it was supposed to be on the teacher.

"Ms. Lambert, why are you late?" Mr. Pine asks, lowering his glasses to the tip of his nose.

"I'm sorry sir, won't happen again," Hearing the class snicker, I groan to myself looking around as students watched me with amusement.

Mr. Pine fixes his glasses on his face. "Well, I'm afraid there are no more seats in the class, you'll have to do-"

"She can sit beside me Mr. Pine!" I hear Winnie's voice cut in.

I looked around for the redhead and spotted her in the back where she always is, Mr. Pine nods his head for me to sit down and I drag my feet taking myself to sit beside 'Ms. perfect'.

Winnie sends me a pearly white smile which I ignore.

"I'm Winnie," I hear her whisper.

I turn my head towards her and nod. "I know."

"Oh, cool," She seemed peppy and I awkwardly nod before turning away.

An hour goes by of me almost falling asleep during class and with Winnie shaking me, I found it weird that she cared that I fell asleep but I shook the feeling off.

One class turned into another as the long day was almost to an end and all that was left was lunch, nurse, then Agriculture.

My feet lead me to Mrs. Hyde's room where she was waiting by the door.

Her smile never once left her face as she fed me lunch.

"What?" I said with a mouthful of food.

"I talked with your father this morning about you helping him."

I nod. "Yeah, I changed my mind about doing that."

"Why?" She looked at me like I had grown a third head.

"Because I don't want to be helping snobby rich boys," I scrunch my nose at the thought.

Mrs. Hyde stands with her hands on her hips. "You're doing you and your dad a favor."

"Yeah, I'm doing him and I a favor by not messing with boys."

She rolls her eyes. "You're so stubborn, just do it!"

"But-" She cuts me off.

"You better be on that field with your daddy this afternoon."

I throw my head back letting out an aggravated sigh. "You're no fun Mrs. Hyde."

"No, I'm hip!"

I stand up quickly. "Yeah, and I'm leaving."

I hear her laugh as I walk near the door. "Oh, come on Tae, I'm playing."

"I'm not, I have to get to class before the bell rings." She nods before letting me leave her office.

I walk into another boring class filled with a bunch of smelly kids and dumb people, throughout the day, I found it easy to take a bathroom break during class to speed up the time. By the end of the day, I'm making my way to the nurse's office with a frown.

By now you'd think I'd be used to taking medicine, but unfortunately, I'm not. Plus, the pills are huge. I knocked on the closed door of nurse Pattie's room, which she opens with a smile letting some coughing kid out.

"Afternoon Tae, how's it going?" She starts off.

"Nothing much," My conversation is quick with her as my nerves start to act up again, seeing the pill she has in her hand.

She hands me the stress ball I always use, and I take the pill from her hand and water and tilt my head back swallowing the pill, squeezing my eyes shit in the process.

I let out a heavy sigh once I'm done and I earn a smile from her.

"I need to ask you a few questions and I'll send you off, alright?" I nod as her question and she brings out the old clipboard she always uses.

She sighs before looking up at me. "How's your breathing?"

"Normal I guess," I shrug.

"You guess?" She jokes and I roll my eyes.

"My dad and I did our morning walk this morning and I had a little bit of trouble breathing that's all," I explain, she nods.

"On a scale of one to ten how bad was it?"

"Maybe... 5?" I question it.

I've always had trouble breathing, but never something severe.

She nods. "Okay, I'll send this off to your doctor to make sure he knows, when is your next appointment?"

"I'll have to check my calendar," I tell her.

"Okay, well just be careful and make sure you don't walk too fast," She instructs and I salute her before grabbing my bag and heading off to my last class of the day.

Walking to class usually goes by fast because I quick paced there, but when there's Mandy Moore and Lydia Brock life just never gets worse. Strutting the halls is the 'popular' girls which sounds too cliche but it's true.

Walking past them is like choking on a bunch of perfume and dying from it, I never understood their friendship when Lydia was the one that was controlling and Mandy was just the lost puppy right behind her.

Rumor has it that Mandy lost her voice in beauty camp when she blew a guy too hard and it ruined her talking pipe, but who's keeping up?

"Party at my place, everyone's invited!" Lydia's baby like voice screeching throughout the halls.

I enter the empty class of Agriculture seeing Mr. Hollis waiting for me with a smile.

"Can you believe that? Lydia's throwing a party on a school night?!" I exclaim, over aerating a bit.

I hear him laugh. "Tell me why you hate her so much?"

"Because, she's a fake plastic rat!"

"Oh yeah, right," He agrees and I nod.

"She gets under my skin when she tries to act nice to people like me," I roll my eyes while taking a seat.

"And who are you exactly?" I give him a blank stare as if he didn't know.

Oh, he knew.

"An outcast," I mumbled, taking out my binder for the class.

I hear him 'hmm' at me and went quiet as students filed into the class, I slumped in my chair waiting for class to begin and humming everyone out.

"Boys and girls listen up, this afternoon we'll be on the topic about saving the turtles," At his statement everyone laughs and I roll my eyes at their immaturity.

"Mr. Hollis and his cliche topics," Reece comments with a smirk causing all the girls to giggle.

Mr. Hollis didn't seem fazed by his smart remark, in fact, he shot one back at him.

"Mr. Paul and his STD's," Mr. Hollis' face went from a sarcastic smile and then a frown.

Reece's face falls and the class goes silent, I smile at Mr. Hollis and wanted to so bad high five him, it felt good that someone told that prick off.

Maybe this year won't be so bad after all, I mean with all the back talks STD boy brings and me being amused because Mr. Hollis' claps back.

Chapter Six

Tae's Pov.

At the end of the day, I wasn't too happy. I remembered I had to help my dad with helping the football team and I have to remember to thank Mrs. Hyde for that every day. Sitting outside of my dad's office didn't take long as I hear his loud footsteps appear along with a group of guys heading into the locker room.

I swear if I see one shirtless boy I'm out of here.

"You know, Mrs. Hyde is something else," My dad said amusedly.

I raise an eyebrow. "Oh yeah, and why is that?"

"Because she told me that you wanted to help me with the boys and I just can't find that to be true."

"Oh, it's true alright," My sarcastic Ness didn't go unnoticed by him.

"How I know that's not true is because you think guys are gross," He explains while taking a hold of his gym bag and cones.

I nod. "You're not wrong."

He rolls his eyes but nods his head to follow him anyway, I was really hoping him to deny me helping him since he knew I didn't want to. I follow him outside with a frown, we stop at a bench that had a clipboard and a water jug laid on it, he hands me the clipboard and I give him a confused look.

"What am I supposed to do with this?" I ask him, holding up the clipboard.

He taps the clipboard. "Since you'll be helping me. I'll need you to take the boys names before practice, it's just tryouts I'll need you to help me pick my good players as well."

"Bu-"

He cuts me off. "No buts. Mrs. Hyde said you wanted to help so here, you are helping me, wait- I forgot something."

I raise an eyebrow as he turns around grabbing a string that was attached to a whistle and ties it around my neck.

"There you go!" He cheered while clapping his hands. "Go on take names."

I roll my eyes playfully at him as he pushes me to stand in front of a bunch of teenage boys, some small and some tall. I awkwardly looked down at the paper and back at my dad as he gives me a thumbs up.

"Uh Bailey Adams?" I call out shyly as I feel all eyes on me and they all look around for the person I called out.

"He's not here," A voice called out and I exes his name off the paper.

I look at the board before looking up. "Landon Barnes?"

A blonde tall guy with chubby cheeks raised his hand. "Here."

I nod before checking his name and call out different names, it seemed pretty easy and I thought that I could do this without no problem. All I had to do was brush off the weird looks that the guys were giving me and that was it. I was going to be fine.

"Keaton Davis?" I call out again looking around as my eyes fall upon the stupid jock I was dreading to see.

His eyes latch onto mine for a moment before he raised his hand slightly. "*Here.*"

I nod before checking his name off and calling out the last name. "Reece Paul?"

"Present."

"Alright boys, this is my daughter Tae, you should respect her as much as you should respect me understand?" My dad hollers out causing me to jump.

"Yes sir," they all say in sync as they walk off onto the field to stretch.

"I don't think is a good idea," My dad mumble to me while watching the boys.

I look up at him. "Why? I did fine just now."

"I know you did, but I just have a bad feeling about this."

"Dad, I'm gonna be alright, I'm not going to be doing any runni-"

He cuts me off. "That's not what I'm saying. I'm worried about the guys."

"Okay, wow thanks but I'm not that pretty," I joked but he wasn't playing.

"Seriously Tae, I just don't want any of the guys to pick on you," He says, and I send him a reassuring smile.

"If they haven't messed with me before they won't mess with me now."

He nods before hollering out at the boys to file in a line, while the guys were trying out, I couldn't help but begin to feel dizzy in the hot sun. I think I blacked out when I felt arms around me and I was on the ground, I look up to see my worried dad talking but I couldn't hear.

Finally, my hearing started to form and I hear my dad shout. "Tae!"

"Davis! Come here quick," I hear him shout as I was spacing in and out.

"Is she alright coach?!" I hear Keaton's muscular voice asking in worry, I almost scoffed but I was too busy spacing out.

Such a suck up.

"Can you please take my daughter to the nurse, I'll end tryouts early today," My dad sits me up while instructing the stupid jock to take me to the nurse.

If I wasn't so dizzy, I would complain about it.

"Yes sir," Keaton nods.

As he goes to grab me my dad pulls me back. "I'm trusting you with my daughter son, don't do anything you shouldn't."

"I'd never."

"Alright then," My dad hands me over to Keaton who which I wrapped my arm around this neck with him holding me up by his arm around my waist.

Walking into the school along with the school's golden boy would be something that I would never do if I wasn't weak, I had no idea why I was acting like this and it scared me.

"The nurse is still here after school?" I ask him, raising up to look at the side of his face.

He turns his head at me. "Yeah, she stays just in case one of us gets hurt while practicing."

I think about it for a moment and nod. "Makes sense."

I see nurse Pattie who runs to me and takes a hold of my face in her hands.

"Would you please lay her down on my bed, dear?" She asks Keaton who nods and does what he's told.

I watch Nurse Pattie bring out her thermometer and a bottle of my medicine, my eyes float back to Keaton who was impatiently biting his fingernails staring at the bed I was laying on.

I was confused as to why he was still here, but maybe that's what he was supposed to do.

Nurse Pattie obviously knew by my facial expression that I wanted him out of the room while she was talking to me.

"Could you step out for a minute?" She asks him sweetly and he nods not saying a word, walking out of the office.

She turns back to me. "He's such a sweet boy."

I ignore her while she checks my pulse and other vitals, I was nervous to see if there was something wrong with me but I already know. *Cancer.*

"Looks like you were just dehydrated," She states and I let out a breath. "I'm going to give you another dose of your medicine because we don't know for sure if it's just dehydration."

I nod letting her do her thing, a couple of minutes later and she was all complete, she let me lay down for a bit for my dizzy spell to go away and then I could wait in the office for my dad or just wait here.

I sit up from the bed and carefully walk out of the office, I fixed my shirt that was wrinkled and noticed a presence sitting in the seats in front of Nurse Pattie's office.

Keaton.

He stands up once he notices me. "Hey, you good?"

"Yeah, I'm fine," I cross my arms, looking away.

He sighs, running his fingers through his hair, "well damn, if I had known you had cancer, I would've gotten you here faster."

My heart drops at the sound of him saying cancer, my head turns to him so fast that I could've caught whiplash.

"What?"

"You have leukemia, right?" He raises an eyebrow.

How-

"How did you-"

He cuts me off. "My mom had leukemia a long time ago so I knew your symptoms, plus the medicine Pattie gave you is the same my mom took."

I could honestly say that I was in complete shock.

He had found out my secret.

But to him it really wasn't that hard for him to find out because of his mom.

I walked around his figure quickly trying to avoid the conversation, I didn't need his pity and I didn't want him to say anything.

"Tae! Wait!" I hear him call out but it only made me walk faster.

I hear his shoes screech from running and he ends up in front of me stopping me from my walk.

"So, no thank you for helping you get to the nurse?" He gives me a smile, holding out his hands in a shrugging motion.

Did he just seriously ask me that?

I should knee him in the balls right now.

"Thank you," I continue my walk but I didn't get too far when he stops me again.

"So why don't I see you around much?"

I give him a one- sided look. "Maybe because you don't look."

"No, I'm saying why don't I see you around like lunch and adviser-" I cut him short.

"Why are you talking to me?"

His eyebrows furrow.

"You've never talked to me, we've went to the same school for four years and you've never spoke a word, why now?" I ask him.

He holds his head down. "I'm sorry, you just seem..." He pauses trying to come up a word that won't offend me.

"Anti-social, I know, let's let it stay that way," I demand.

"But how about we get to know each other?" He tries to make amends and I walk past him while rolling my eyes.

"I'm good, thanks," I smile fakely at him seeing that he was walking beside me.

He shakes his head laughing. "Is this because I found out about you having cancer?"

I stopped dead in my tracks. "No, this is about you having nothing to do with an outcast like me until you find out there's something wrong with them, I suggest you leave me alone – and please don't tell anyone about this."

When he doesn't say anything, I take that as my cue to walk away from him, God I hate that stupid jock.

"Okay, I won't tell on one condition," He makes me stop dead in my tracks again.

I turn around with crossed arms. "Are you seriously blackmailing me? You do know that I'm the coach's daughter and I could easily-"

"Do what? Tell him that I threatened you about telling this little secret of yours just to have a nice lunch with my friends and I?" He cut me off with a sarcastic remark. "I'm sure he'd believe you when I'm his best player."

My fist clench by my side. Why is he doing this?

"Tae! I'm so glad you're okay," My dad's worried face comes into view.

I was crushed into a hug and only to see Keaton's smirk. "I'm okay, just dehydrated."

"That's good," He holds his chest while breathing out. "I was beginning to worry."

He turns around to Keaton. "Thank you, I owe you big time."

Keaton then sends him a polite smile. "It was no problem; you owe me nothing when I just made a new friend." He wiggled his eyebrows at me and I so wanted to run to him and rip them off.

Chapter Seven

Tae's Pov.

Sitting on a stool in the kitchen staring at my phone screen, trying to convince myself to give Georgie a call but my finger never presses on his number. I haven't spoken to Georgie since he left for college, my dad has had a few talks with him but I knew that if I had picked up the phone and spoke with him, you'd never get the phone away from me.

Words couldn't explain how much I missed the rascal, when he was here, he actually made our house feel like a home since mom died.

"Call him" I jump, setting my phone down on the counter and twirl the chair around seeing my dad.

"What?" I try to play dumb.

He gives me a bored look. "Call him, he misses you."

"Yeah, but then I'll just miss him more once he gets off the phone," I whine, slipping myself off the stool.

"You have to stop making excuses for yourself-"

I cut him off. "I'll call him after school, how does that sound?"

He nods. "Alright, but you actually better do it."

"Yes sir," I salute to him before walking upstairs to get dressed.

As I walk into my room, I look at my calendar and remember the doctor's appointment I had. Seeing that the doctor's appointment was this weekend, I almost jumped in excitement that I didn't have to hang out with Keaton.

After thirty minutes of getting ready, I was finished. Walking downstairs with a fresh faced, brushed teeth, and an okay looking face I was ready for school. Seeing my dad run around the house with his gym clothes on I laugh, standing at the bottom of the stairs.

"Where are my keys?" He panics and I smile at him before walking over to his key hanger and lift it up with my hands making it jingle.

He sighs, snatching the keys out of my hand. "Thank you."

"You seemed stressed," I observed and he shakes his head in denial.

"Just a little worried about our first game that's all."

I shrug. "The boys will do good; they win every year."

"Are you complimenting the team?" He jokes and I roll my eyes.

"I'll admit they're good but I still don't like them," He nods at my statement.

"Grab you a bagel on the way out," He instructs and I make my way over to the bag that holds the delicious bread.

Walking outside of the house and into my dad's pickup truck, we leave for another dreaded day for school.

I find my dad staring at me then looking back at the road which annoyed me and I finally say something.

"What is it?" I knew he wanted to tell me something.

"What's up with you and Davis?" I scrunch my nose in disgust at his question.

I look out the window. "Nothing, he just won't leave me alone."

"Maybe that's because he likes you," He tells me.

I cringe. "Ew dad, that's gross. He only asked me to sit with him and his friends at lunch, that's all."

"Okay," It seemed like he didn't believe me but I didn't care.

I don't like that stupid jock and neither does he like me.

After the conversation my dad and I had, it was silent till we got to school. He had dropped me off in the drop off center and I walk into school just like any other day.

My feet carried me to my locker, opening it up, I slide my book bag into it and take out my books I need for Mr. Pine's class.

I roll my eyes as I feel a presence beside me, I slam my locker door seeing that it was Keaton.

Of course, it was.

"What?" I asked annoyed.

I then see his goofy smile. "Did you think I was going to *forget* about yesterday."

"I was hoping," I made my way to move down the hall but with the jock beside me.

Before he could say anything, I cut him off.

"Is this some bet you're trying to pull?" I look his way and his face grows confused.

"What?" He asks.

I hold my books tightly. "I've seen too many movies about this and I'm not going to be one of those girls."

I sound like an idiot and hopefully he thinks I'm one too and leaves me alone.

"Are you trying to make me look hot, take my virginity? Huh, it's not going to happen-" He cuts me off short.

"Calm down Tae, you're not a bet, I swear," I watch him hold his hands up in the air in surrender.

I nod my head and noticed that we were stopped in the middle of the hallway.

He huffs out a breath before saying. "I just want to get to know you, you seem like the realest person in this school except for my friends."

I roll my eyes at the mention of his friends.

"You don't need to get to know me."

His smile appears. "Why? Do you have a disease or something?"

I give him a blank stare and then he noticed what he had said.

"Oh shit, I'm so sorry, Tae," His eyes were filled with guilt.

"Yeah actually, it is because of that, if I want to die in peace then let me," I glare at him before walking off leaving him in the middle of the hall.

I roll my eyes as I walk into Mr. Pine's class, here's to another boring day.

By the time lunch time comes, I start regretting ever coming to this school.

I walk into Mrs. Hyde's office, clearly trying to avoid Keaton.

Maybe my little outburst made him rethink ever asking me to have lunch with him and his friends.

"What are you doing?" Mrs. Hyde asks me as she witnesses me staring out of her blinds and out in the hall.

"Nothing," I tell her, feeling relieved that nobody was in the halls.

I turn around jumping when I see Keaton sitting in my spot and Mrs. Hyde sitting in her rolly chair.

My eyes go wide as I watch a smirk appear on his face. "What is he doing here?"

"You are having lunch with me," Keaton stands up, having me to look up as he walks closer.

I look around him at Mrs. Hyde and glare. "Are you approving of this?!"

"Yes, simply because you need friends and especially ones like Keaton," Mrs. Hyde states.

I look at her like she's grown two heads. "You can't be serious."

"Oh, she's serious," Keaton butts in and I send my best glare.

I huff out in annoyance and stomp out of Mrs. Hyde's office or should I say traitor.

I look back at Keaton. "Come on if you want to get to your precious lunch."

His smirk grows and out he comes from the office.

"Bye Tae," I hear Mrs. Hyde's mocking voice from behind me as Keaton and I walk to lunch.

If she was my age, I'd so flip her off.

"Why are you so keen on getting to know me? You've literally never spoken to me a day in your life," I try to get him to answer.

"Well, when you're so busy with trying to keep straight A's and play football at the same time, you don't notice anything and especially when 'someone' doesn't talk and stays in the back all of the time," He explains in sarcasm and I cross my arms.

"And I have a good reason for that," I tell him look away from his stare.

"What's the reason then?" He asks and I shake my head not saying a word.

We get to the cafeteria, and I stop at the door looking through the small windows of the doors.

"Please Keaton, I don't want to go in there," I plead, now staring at his eyes.

He shakes his head. "It's not as bad as you think it is."

"Oh, yes, it is," I defend myself, but he shakes his head at my stubbornness and nods his head towards the cafeteria to follow him.

I sigh out in defeat because I know he's going to win the situation.

I was expecting everyone to stare as we walked in like the cliche thing our school does, but no one seemed to care that the weird quiet girl was following the school's golden boy, in fact the only one that did care was Lydia Brock as she stands up giving me a cold stare.

Keaton leads me to 'his' table and three of his friends stop their conversation just to stare at Keaton and I.

"Guys, this is Tae," He introduces me and Reece's mouth pops open and out falls a half-eaten grape.

Landon freezes in his spot and Winnie, his girlfriend, sends me a smile and a little wave.

Keaton sits beside Landon and that only leaves me to sit beside Winnie who looked like she was about to jump out of her seat in excitement.

"Guys, introduce yourselves, don't be rude," Keaton instructs and they all cough in awkwardness.

This was too awkward for me; I'm really tempted to get up and-

"I'm Winnie, but you probably already know that," The redhead beside me states and I nod but smile.

Her smile fades as she turns her head at her boyfriend who wasn't saying anything but staring down at his lunch tray, she elbows him in the arm catching his attention.

"Oh! Hey, I'm Landon," He jumps but states as Winnie gives him a glare.

I send him a small smile, which was awkward.

"And I'm Reece," The boy in the middle states, his eyes longing on mine for a little longer than expected.

"This is the crew," I sit back in my seat feeling the most uncomfortable situation I've ever been in, while listening to Keaton talk about how great his friends were.

"I hear you like to read," Keaton says again and I raised an eyebrow.

"Just because I'm a so called 'nerd' doesn't mean I like to read," I tell him, suddenly over this whole lunch thing.

He shrugs. "Well, do you like to read?"

"Yeah," I look away, knowing he was right in the first place and I was just being a brat about him being right.

"Winnie here..." He pauses, nodding off toward Winnie who smiles. "Her dad owns a library, maybe she can show you around."

"It'll be fun," Winnie cuts in.

I give her a small smile and a nod; I could tell the girl was trying to make amends with me but clearly, I was being too stubborn.

But half of me wondered, what did Keaton really want with me?

But the real question was, why were they acting so nice- well two of them at least.

After lunch, I had to make a trip down to the nurse's office just like every day. I didn't understand the reason why behind Keaton wanting to get to know me, I mean I was just like every other outcast.

Maybe he felt bad that I have cancer and he was just being nice because of that. I didn't need his pity.

By the end of the day, I didn't have much strength to do much, I could tell by what nurse Pattie said to me and said to take it slow. I stood outside of the school with my phone in my hands and Georgie's number was tempting me.

I finally press his number with my thumb while biting my lip in nervousness, butterflies swarm in the pit of my stomach as I hear the third ring, but then I grew sad when he didn't pick up.

"Hey, Tae," I hear Keaton's low voice.

I turn around with my phone near my ear as I try to call Georgie for the second time, plus, I just wanted an excuse not to talk to this hooligan.

Getting Georgie's voicemail again, I sigh while hanging up.

Seeing that Keaton was walking my way, I put my phone in my back pocket and try making my way to my dad's pickup truck.

"Hey! Wait up!" I hear his laughter right after causing me to stop in my tracks and having the urge to roll my eyes.

I turn around. "What?"

He stands in front of me in all his glory with his famous jock jacket giving me the brightest smile.

"How was lunch, did you like my friends?"

"Winnie's sweet," I shrug, looking around for my dad not really into the conversation.

I then hear him chuckle. "What about Reece and Landon?"

I give him a blank look and he nods in understanding.

"Reece can be a dick," He gives in.

"Really? I totally couldn't tell," His eyes roll at my sarcasm reply and I do the same.

His friends were douches.

"Alright, I get it," He tells me. "What are you doing this weekend?"

"Are you seriously about to ask me to hang out with you? I already had to spend a twenty-minute lunch in hell with your friends, what more could you want?" I exclaim.

I seriously didn't know what he wanted from me.

"I'm just trying to be your friend, Tae," He defends and I roll my eyes. "I don't understand why you hate me so much; you don't even know me."

Breath Tae.... Just breathe.

"Whatever, I got to go," I tell him, pointing at my dad who's exiting the school.

Always the right timing.

"Hang out with me this weekend," He begs, holding onto his back bag on his shoulder.

I wince. "Can't. Got a lot of homework to do, sorry."

"Well, Keaton can come over and you can do homework together," My dad cuts in and I give him a cold stare.

Keaton smiles. "That sounds like a plan Coach Lambert."

"B-But he's not even in my grade," I try an excuse but obviously it backfires.

My dad shrugs, and I groan out while hearing Keaton's laugh.

"Put your number in and I'll send you a text to see when's a good day when we could hang out," Keaton tells me before handing me his phone.

Giving him a blank stare, I snatch his phone, putting my number in but so badly wanting to put a fake one in.

I just wish this kid would leave me alone.

Handing him his phone back, his hand ever so slightly touches mine causing me to recoil in shock.

"Bye Tae," Keaton says, waving sarcastically at me and I so badly wanted to flip him off.

"Bye Davis," My dad says from the driver's side of his truck.

Keaton waves bye to my dad and waits for me to say something to him with a smile on his face, I roll my eyes but sigh in defeat.

"Bye jock," I tell him causing him to nod his head and walk off.

Walking to my dad's truck, seeing my dad's eyes on me with a goofy smile plastered on his face I wanted to just open the door when the truck starts moving and fall out of it.

Chapter Eight

Keaton's Pov.

"What the hell man? Tae Lambert, the antisocial freak," Reece raises an eyebrow at me as he asks me.

Landon and Reece sit back on my couch in my garage where I spend most of my time working out. Beers are in their hands watching me as I do pull ups on the pull up bar.

"Would you back off me?" I laugh out. "And if my dad walks in here and sees you guys drinking that shit, he'll beat both of your asses."

Landon sits up. "Wait- you don't mean to tell me Keaton has a little crush, does he?"

I stop and give him a glare. "Hell no."

He smirks before leaning back. "Okay."

"I don't even know her enough to like her, and if I did what's the big deal?" I ask them and they both shrug.

"Oh, come on, don't be pussy whipped like Landon," Reece exclaims. "I thought you we were going to be different."

I roll my eyes at Reece's immaturity.

"I'm not like that anymore," I say, finishing with pulls up and go to sit on the bench and grab my weights.

"Like what? Like me?" Reece sits up and I let down my weights.

I roll my eyes not really in the mood to get in an argument right now.

At one point, I was like Reece. I partied, had one-night stands, and didn't give a shit about life. It all changed once I got into eleventh grade. My parents found out that I was an underage drinker and decided to help me and push me to become this perfect golden boy that everyone thinks I am.

My dad and mom have a reputation to keep up, so me drinking and basically being a fuckboy, didn't look good on them. The thing about Reece, he doesn't have any help like I had, he didn't have someone to push him and make him do better.

He wasn't forced to live in this tiny world where if you do one thing wrong, everything is down the drain.

No fights, no drinking, no one night stands, and no partying.

Reece didn't understand the way I had to live life, but Landon did. Winnie was always so understanding and Landon is lucky to have her. Everyone in Anderson was fake, everyone had a secret or they were hiding behind this mask.

I was one of them.

Tae's *different.*

She let me know right off the bat she hated me. I didn't understand, but I'm curious to know. Yeah, she had a secret and it was just about her disease, and I don't understand either why she wanted to keep that a secret, but I'm gonna find out, I'm going to break those walls down and get to know the real Tae, not the sick one with barriers around her.

She seemed like the only real person at Westside.

"It's not like that, Reece."

"Then what is it? Because you're so intrigued with that girl and she doesn't give a shit about you," He spits, squeezing his empty beer can trying to scare me.

I nod. "Yeah, I know that. She's not like all the other's girl in school that drops their panties anytime they get a chance."

"What the hell. Where did our Keaton go? Because the Keaton I used to know didn't care about freaks like that," He stands up, throwing the beer can across the garage causing it to bounce off the door and onto the floor.

I clenched my jaw waiting for the slam of the door that was about to come. After Reece's dramatic outing Landon raises an eyebrow at me.

"I honestly don't know why he's so pissed," He speaks up. "I wasn't trying to-"

"Yeah, I know, you were joking with me."

"If you do like her, just be careful, she doesn't seem like the types of girls you usually go for," He tells me and I nod.

Tae's Pov.

"How come I never knew about this place until now?" I ask myself, not realizing I said it out loud.

I skim my fingers over the books that were placed on the shelves and my eyes scan over the thousands of books around me.

"Because it's old," Winnie states, and I nod. "I didn't think you were going to actually come with me."

"Well, when a crazy redhead girl keeps knocking on my door and won't stop until I agree to come, what was I supposed to do?" I hear her laugh out as she follows me down the isle of the many books.

"Sorry about that," She laughs out and in the corner of my eye I see her shake her head.

"How'd you know where I lived anyways?" I look back at her.

"I see you and your dad walking every day and I seen you guys walk into your home," I try to ignore the fact that she sounded like a total creep and nod.

"So, where's your dad," I ask her, referring to when we walked in and I saw nobody at the front.

She gives me a small smile. "He passed away."

My heart drops.

"Winnie-" She cuts me off.

"Don't apologize, I'm used to talking about it now," She explains and I look away from her stare.

"It's good to talk about your loved ones passing, even though it hurts."

I ignore her trying to keep my emotions down.

"My mom owns this place now. My dad built this for her when they were younger," I awe at the story.

"They must've been really in love with each other for him to build her a library huh?" I crack a smile causing her to nod.

"Yep, they were. My mom won't even redo any of the parts in this place. I'm surprised it hasn't been run down yet," She jokes.

I smile. "It seems good to me."

After a few long seconds she asks. "So, what's your favorite genre?"

"That's a hard question, but romance," I tell her.

I knew I seemed the type to not like romance but I was a sucker for romance in the books.

"Mine too! Oh my god, I'm a sucker for romance," She gushes with a little blush.

"You're dating Landon, right?"

"That's right, our one year is soon," She tells me. "Actually, it'll be on our first game."

"That's cool."

"Do you have a boyfriend?" Her question almost makes me laugh.

Almost.

I snort. "No."

"Why not? You're so pretty," She asks, her face was in shock.

"Thank you, but I don't want one," I shake my head at the thought.

"Keaton seems to be smitten by you," She tilts her head on the shelf near me.

I roll my eyes. "He's annoying."

"He's really not that bad," She tries to make me believe but I'll believe that when the school loses their first game.

Which never happens by the way.

Never.

Chapter Nine

Tae's Pov.

"Hey guys," Keaton's voice rang in my ears as Winnie and I headed out of the library with empty hands.

I was really hoping I didn't have to see him.

"Hey," Winnie says, squinting as the sun sets down on us.

"Find something you liked?" He looks at me when he asks but it was clear he was talking to both of us.

I give Winnie a look causing her to speak out. "No, but maybe next time. Shouldn't you be with the boys?"

"I was, we just decided to call it a day," He replies.

"Lucky you," Winnie tells him causing him to chuckle.

His eyes caught onto mine as he stops laughing. "Mind if I take her?"

"Nope. She's all yours," Winnie winks at me and I raised an eyebrow. "I have a Landon to find."

She walks off to her car to meet up with Landon and I watch her drive off. I hear Keaton cough, trying to catch my attention.

"Did she talk your head off like she does with us?" He jokes, but my face never once did crack a smile.

"Are you supposed to take me home?" I ask him while raising an eyebrow.

He nods. "Then let's go."

Before I could walk off to God knows where because I have no idea what the dude's car looked like, Keaton pulls me back causing me to roll my eyes.

"I am supposed to take you home, but not just yet. I wanna take you to my favorite place," He explains and I cross my arms.

Oh please, this is every guy's line.

He'll probably end up taking me to some stupid pond and spill his guts to me. Blah blah.

"Why?"

And there goes him smiling again. "Because if we're going to become friends, we gotta know each other, right?"

I sigh out as I had to follow him to God knows where, he was ahead of me while I dragged my feet behind him.

He turns around. "You coming?"

"Not like I have a choice, do I?"

"Nope," He cheekily remarks and I so badly want to trip him up.

"Where's this place at anyway?" I hear myself ask.

We were walking further and further from the library.

"Just up here," He nods toward wherever he wanted to go.

"This better not be some pond or a tree house," I mumble under my breath.

Keaton suddenly stops and looks back at me, smiling, he says. "It's something better."

He looks up causing me to mimic his actions.

In front of me I see a big blue sign 'Greenhouse Cafe' I catch Keaton staring at me, in which I give him a blank stare.

"Really? A diner is your favorite place?" I ask him and he shrugs.

"Yeah, so?"

I sigh. "Okay, let's go."

I just wanted to get this over with.

Keaton opens the door for me which I give him a curt nod, walking inside the diner I've never been too, I look around seeing it was an old fashion modeled diner, which I liked to my dismay.

"Keaton Davis!" I hear a muscular voice.

I turn my head seeing a body builder man, an apron around his neck and a smile appeared on his face as he walks closer to Keaton and I.

"Tommy, hey, what's good man?" Keaton greets the tough looking man who shakes his hand.

The man named Tommy shrugs. "Nothing much, just working my ass off."

"Tommy, what did I say about cursing in my diner?" A petite woman with brown hair glares at Tommy as she gets onto him.

"I'm sorry baby," Tommy looks back at her with adoration in his eyes, makes me want to melt.

The women 'hmps' in triumph and walks off to take everyone's orders.

Tommy turns back around to us and smiles. "That's boss lady right there." He tells us and I crack a smile.

My smile catches Tommy's eye and he looks at both of us with a questioning look.

"Is this your girlfriend?"

"No!" Keaton and I both exclaimed causing Tommy to hold his hands up in surrender.

"Sorry. Take a seat and Ally will be with you shortly," Tommy instructs us and I pick a booth to sit in.

Keaton takes a seat in front of me, sitting back in the seat.

"Does he own this place?" I ask him.

He nods. "Him and his wife."

"He doesn't look like someone that'd own a place like this," I tell him, letting out a laugh.

He chuckles but nods. "He did it for Ally."

"Who?"

"His wife," I hear him say and I nod in realization.

"It seems like you come here often," I state, tapping my fingers on the table watching him sit up in the booth.

"Yeah, this place was here before I was even born," He explains and I watch intensely as he smiles at the memories going through his head.

"Don't tell me, I'm the first girl you took here," I mimic his voice, joking.

He rolls his eyes playfully. "If I'm being honest, you're not."

"I feel flattered," I tell him in sarcasm.

As he goes to say something, the same petite woman that got onto Tommy comes to our table with a smile.

"I hope I didn't interrupt something," She looked apologetic.

I smile at her as I hear Keaton. "Nah, your good."

"How's it going player?" She leans her arm on the top of the booth as she lifts an eyebrow. "Finally, someone settle you down?"

Why does everyone think Keaton and I are a thing?

"We're just friends," Keaton corrects her.

"I knew it, I told Tommy you were always going to mess around," She sounded like she was joking.

Let's just hope so.

"Once a player always a player," She states looking at me and I nod.

Keaton's mouth opens. "Hey, Tommy was a fuckboy."

"Was," Tommy cuts in as he moves around with a mop in his hand.

Ally smirks at Keaton but couldn't hold on to it after a while and goes with a smile.

"I'm just messing with you, what would you guys like to drink?" She laughs out.

"We would like two flat house burgers with a coke," Keaton tells her and I slap the menu down on the table in confusion.

"Okay, sit tight and your food will be here in a little while," She gives a smile before leaving me glaring at a smiling Keaton.

"What?"

"You're unbelievable," I tell him, aggravated.

He shrugs innocently. "What did I do?"

"Nothing," I wasn't going to try to fight with him.

I sit back in the booth with a frown and I watch Keaton soak in my annoyance at him, he looked like he was enjoying me being irritated at him.

Stupid jock.

I count to ten in my head before calming down and start a conversation.

"You guys act like family," I state.

"Who?" He raises an eyebrow.

"You, Tommy, and Ally," I say in a 'duh' tone.

"We basically are, I grew up with them, and they know what happens at home and shit, they get me," He lets out, I don't even think he realized what he said.

"Plus, Ally can't have kids, so they're like my other parents," He adds and I nod.

I don't say anything, besides I didn't know what to say.

"So, tell me about you," He tries to get me to open up.

I give him a blank stare. "No."

"Oh, come on Tae, I just told you something about me."

"Yeah, about this stupid diner, that I didn't want to come to," I snap at him.

He looks away before looking back at me. "You didn't have to come."

"You were my ride," I glare at him only for his smirk to grow.

"You have a phone. You don't need me, you wanted to come here with me or you would've called up your dad to come get you," He says, and I give him a dumbfounded look.

"You know what, I'm over this," I tell him while rolling my eyes and getting up from my seat.

I head out the door of the diner with Keaton calling name, I make my way to the library where I was at in the beginning and take out my phone to call my dad.

"Tae, stop!" He calls for me but I ignore.

As I hear the third ring my phone gets snatched out of my hand and I turn around with a glare seeing Keaton ending the call.

"You are the most annoy-ingest boy I've ever met and I've met some annoying people," I state, pointing my finger at him.

"And you're stubborn. I'm glad we got that settled," He rolls his eyes and I gasp.

"Then leave me alone if I'm so stubborn, why deal with me? I never asked you to get to know me and I'm pretty sure nobody is forcing you to either," I exclaimed, putting my hands on my hip. "Or... you're doing this to win a bet!"

"Shut the hell up with that bet shit, that's so cliche and immature of me to do," Keaton snaps, causing me to jump.

"I don't know how or why you have this wall build up, and why you keep trying to push me away," He starts off. "I was trying to do something nice because I'm not like the other guys at our school, I'm not a prick, I just wanted to make a new friend."

I stay silent for a while.

"Just take me home," I tell him but demand.

He holds his head down in defeat but nods, he walks back into the diner to pay for our meal that we didn't eat and he comes back out with his head down, staring down at his keys.

We both walk in silence until he stops at a black Jeep, I hear a click letting me know that the car was unlocked. I sit in the leather interior seats with my arms crossed, I look in the corner of my eye to see Keaton driving with one hand and his other on the door with his hand in his hair.

His jaw was clenched letting me know he was mad, but he had to look at this in reality. I wasn't trying to do this on purpose, I was doing him a favor and deep down in me knew the Keaton was a good person, but I just couldn't get myself attached.

I tell him my address after a while and he gets there in about twenty minutes, he parks on the side of the sidewalk on the road and I turn to him.

"You gotta stop with this whole getting to know me, because it's never going to happen," I tell him truthfully. "Get to know someone else."

He nods, not saying a word. I give him one last look before getting out of his fancy Jeep and shutting the door while at it. I walk inside my house without looking back and shut the door behind me.

My dad stands in the kitchen, chopping a cucumber while listening to mom's old DVDs. He sees me and gives me a smile and I stand across from him.

"Did Keaton drive you home?" He asks, trying to hide his smile.

I nod. "Yep."

"Where'd you go?" He asks again and I sigh.

"To eat but then we argued and he took me home," I explained not afraid to tell him what happened.

He nods and shrugs. "Couples fight."

"Keaton and I are not dating," I roll my eyes, leaving my dad downstairs when I walk upstairs.

"Oh yeah, you are coming to the game with me," He stops me in my tracks and I turn around giving him a confused look.

"What? You never make me go to them," I complain.

He nods before popping a cucumber in his mouth. "I know, that's why I want you to go. Support the team."

I sigh out in aggravation and continue my destination upstairs, once I get in my room, I fall face first on my bed.

Chapter Ten

Keaton's Pov.

I slam my locker shut before getting tackled by Reece, He laughs as he sees my unamused face.

"Are you still mad at me for walking off yesterday?" He asked, squeezing my shoulders.

"Nope, I'm over it. Just not in the mood today," I tell him, looking around the halls for the dirty blonde girl.

Reece sighs. "Is this about Tae? What happened?"

"Nothing," I shrug him off me.

"Hey star boy," Winnie greets me with Landon's arm over her shoulder.

I give her a small smile. "Hey."

"Oh, so Winnie gets a smile and all I get is a pouty look?" Reece complains and I shrug back at him, couldn't help but smile.

"That's because he likes me more," Winnie smirks at Reece who glared at her.

Reece leans on the lockers looking off in defeat, I laugh at the two.

"You ready for the game tomorrow?" Landon asks, hitting my chest playfully.

I nod hearing Reece sigh. "I know I am."

"We all know you are; you wouldn't stop talking about all summer," Winnie says, rolling her eyes at the memory causing me to nod.

Reece bits his lip in anger. "What was that ex cheerleader?"

Winnie moves forward to hit him but Landon pulls her back.

The cheerleading topic was a sketchy subject for Winnie to talk about, she was once a cheerleader and best friends with the slut of the school that is head cheerleader.

Lydia Brock.

Lydia took her place after she sabotaged Winnie by putting drugs in her bag and Winnie got in shit load of trouble after the incident, you would wonder why Winnie didn't try to prove to them that she was clean but it was no use.

They wouldn't have believed.

"Reece, cut the shit," I demand, shaking my head.

"What? She started it," He defends and I shake my head at him.

Looking back at Winnie, she looks away from us with a frown.

Her posture gets straight and she smiles at something afar, I look at where she was looking to see the dirty blonde I was looking for. I see Winnie wave at her causing Tae to quickly look away and walk into her class.

Winnie frowns and is quick to turn her head at me. "What'd you do?"

"Nothing," I defend, shrugging.

"Mhm," Reece chuckles.

"What did you do Keaton?" Winnie growls and I hold my arms up in defense.

"I was just trying to get to know her and she got offended which caused us to argue." She smacks her forehead and I roll my eyes at her because I knew she was going to give me one of her lectures.

"Boys are stupid," She mumbles before walking off.

Landon gives me a look before waving her off.

"Girls are stupid," Reece says, rolling his eyes.

"Shut up Reece," Landon snaps, causing Reece to walk off.

I raise an eyebrow. "What's his problem?"

"I don't know, he's always like this before games."

I nod. "He needs to watch his mouth or one of these guys will beat his ass."

"I have a feeling one of us will," Landon mumbles causing me to laugh.

We head to class and I yawn before the day has even started, sitting down in my first class I couldn't help but think why Tae didn't want to get to know me or let me get to know her, it seemed like she was afraid, but of what?

"Mr. Davis!" Mrs. Nolan yells causing me to jump from my thoughts and my seat.

I look around to see everyone staring at me. "What?"

"The answer Mr. Davis," She demands and I sit up in my seat.

"Uh, I don't know, I'm sorry," I tell her and she gives me a pointed look and goes back to the lesson.

"Dude, what's up?" Landon whispers from behind me and I shrug.

"I told you I'm not feeling it today," I whisper back, keeping my eyes on the teacher.

"Mhm," He mumbled, not believing a word I said.

Hell, I didn't believe myself either.

After the first class of the day, I was already slumped and wished I could go back to my old ways just for right now and skip school. By lunch, Tae was nowhere to be found, but I knew she wasn't going to come, she was probably in Mrs. Hyde's room eating lunch like she always does.

Going through the lunch line I felt hands wrap around my arm causing my head to snap towards the brown-haired girl.

"Keaton, I've been looking everywhere for you!" Lydia purrs, leaning into me trying to seduce me.

I give the lunch lady my money before shrugging Lydia off of me as a response, I heard her huff and I hear the cafeteria lady laugh. I give myself a pat on my back for not caving in like I usually did with Lydia, she was nothing but all talk.

Lydia was a player; she knew the game and how to play it. She is worse than me when I was in that phase, she knew how to steal a guy's heart and rip it to shreds. *I would know.*

I sat my lunch down on the table, catching the attention of Landon and Reece.

"What's up man?" Landon greets me with a bunch of food in his mouth and I take a bite of mine.

I take a look at Reece to see him typing away on his phone with a smile on his face, I raised an eyebrow but didn't say a word.

"Nothing much," I sigh out, taking another bite of my food.

"Where's Winnie," I add, looking around for the crazy red head.

"I don't know, lemme' text her," Landon replies, taking out his phone sending Winnie a quick text.

Reece looks up at his phone and up at me. "You do know the game is tomorrow, right?"

"Yes, and you keep reminding me," I smile sarcastically, sitting back in my seat.

"And he's already lectured by his dad," I roll my eyes at Landon's statement which was true.

My dad spent every minute forcing me to practice during the summer for the first game, when he heard that some people were going to be watching me for scholarships that's when he flipped his shit with excitement.

"As he should, what was that with Lydia I just seen?" Reece asks with a smirk.

"Why are you suddenly all up on me?" I ask him.

He sits up causing Landon to raise an eyebrow studying us. "Since you're suddenly all up on that girl, Tae."

"Not this again," I exclaimed.

"Seriously Keaton, like today in class. You weren't paying attention at all and Lydia fucking touched you and you suddenly reject the chick?"

"That has nothing to do with Tae. First of all, I don't have to be perfect all the damn time and last time I checked I was done with Lydia," I defend myself.

What the hell was this dude's problem? Why was he suddenly up my ass about everything. The game this, the game that.

"Now if you'll excuse me, I have someone to find," I excuse myself, sending Landon a curt nod and Reece a blank stare.

"The freak," Reece coughs out in sarcasm clearly trying to let me hear.

"Dude chill," Landon shoots him a glare and I leave the cafeteria, but not before I dump my trash in the bin.

The hallways seemed peaceful when students were piled in and running to their classes, my footsteps were echoed by the halls and as I look down at the half-lit hallway. Making my way around the corner, I finally reach my destination of the guidance counselor's room.

I check the time on my phone, seeing that it was a minute until the bell would ring, I stood by the door waiting patiently for that bell to ring. Wouldn't be my first time waiting on that bell.

The sweet sound of the loud alarming bell rang through the halls causing the doors of the classrooms to open and the lunchroom as well. I hear the door of Mrs. Hyde's office start to open and out comes the dirty blonde I've been awaiting to see.

As she looks up at me, her face turns into a surprised one but then goes blank, if I knew she would've walked off the minute I tried to speak I would've stopped her, but that would be too easy.

She walks off without letting me get a word out causing me to sigh out in annoyance, I watch her retreating form turn the corner disappearing from my eyesight. I lean my head back and groan before getting poked at.

I opened my eyes seeing the crazy redhead. "Where the hell have you been?"

"The library," Winnie innocently states and I roll my eyes at her nerdiness.

"We missed you at lunch."

She rolls her eyes. "I'm sure y'all did."

She looks back to where Tae left and looks back to me. "She won't talk to me either."

"Yeah..." I trail off as we start walking to our lockers.

"She'll come around, Keaton," She states and I nod giving her a small smile.

I stop by my locker while unlocking it quickly grabbing my books and slinging by book-bag over one shoulder.

"Well, I'll see you later," I tell her.

"You'll actually see me at practice," She states and I nod.

"See you!" I yell out as I walk further and further away from her.

I get to my class on time sitting down for another lecture, I sigh out in boredom letting my daydreams carry me throughout the hour.

****

Walking towards the locker rooms never seemed to bore me, football distracted me from what happens at home. I don't really talk about what happens there, the only person who does know is Winnie. Getting ready and putting my gear on, I wear a sleeveless shirt with some basketball shorts while walking outside, the sun light beams on my face causing me to squint my eyes.

Landon and Reece haven't arrived yet, only a few guys and I stood outside. I do my stretches so I could get done before everyone else even though I knew I would have to do them over, my eyes scanned over the field and latching onto Tae's form walking towards the bench that had the water jug and cones.

My perfect chance would be now to talk to her, so I take the chance and jog to where she was standing. She had her hair tied up in a ponytail with the same clothes she had on today. She doesn't notice me until she turns around with her hand in her hair playing around with a few curls.

"Hey," I didn't know what to say and I wanted to punch myself in the face for just saying hey.

Clearly, she wasn't amused. "Keaton, I told-"

I cut her off. "I know you told me to leave you alone, but I just can't seem to stay away from you."

"Okay, maybe this will help..." She trails, grabbing a cup and fills it with water from the jug and turns back to me.

Oh shit.

I raise an eyebrow but it quickly fades into a shocked expression as she splashes the water in my face getting the top of my hair wet and my shirt.

"Tae! What the hell are you doing?" Coach Lambert screams out causing everyone's head to turn.

Tae rolls her eyes. "Leaving, that's what."

"No, you're not. You don't even have a ride home, what the hell was this all about?" Her dad asks, pointing at me.

I stayed silent, watching the dirty blonde get yelled at.

"He wouldn't leave me alone, which this obviously didn't work," Tae explains and I hold my hands up in surrender.

I watch her dad sigh in annoyance. "Go ask if Mrs. Hyde can give you a ride home."

Tae scrambles up her things before sending me a look and walking off the field, Coach watches as she walks off then looks back at me.

"I'm sorry about that, Davis," He apologizes.

I smile. "It's fine Coach, I got the message loud and clear."

I walk away, standing in my spot on the field. Landon and Reece walk out of the locker rooms just in time for them not to see the show.

"Boys, you missed the show," Bailey Adams announced causing me to roll my eyes.

"What?" Reece questions, looking off towards me.

Bailey looks back at me. "Some chick got pissed at Keaton and splashed water in his face."

"Was it Tae Lambert by any chance?" Reece smirks at me.

"Yeah, why?"

"Nothing," I roll my eyes at Reece, looking away from the laughing boys.

It really wasn't that serious; it was just water and not a lot of it. They were making a big deal about nothing. But the only thing that was a big deal was the way I was feeling, why did it hurt a little when Tae's angry with me?

Chapter Eleven

Tae's Pov.

After being lectured to death in the truck from my dad, he lets me out in the drop off zone in front of the school and I make my way inside. I hated days like these, everywhere you looked was someone who had paint on their faces and cheerleaders wearing their uniforms getting ogled at and football players wearing their jerseys for the game.

Football games were famous in this school, they took it way too seriously when it was only high school football. I get it, some of these boys were trying to get in or already got a scholarship, which were lucky to get. People would kill to get in the colleges that the good football players get in.

I did want to go to college, I really did. It all changed, even if I still do want to go to college, I'd never be able to go, I'd never make it. I'm dreading to go to the doctor's because I'm afraid of what they're going to say, was I healthy enough? Was I cured? The second question is absurd, the doctors would laugh in my face if I'd ask them that, heck, I'd probably even laugh.

I make my way to the nurse's office just so I can get it over with I wouldn't have to go during the day, which I don't really have the energy for. I knock twice hearing the sound of Nurse Pattie telling me to come in.

I open the door, hearing the sound of music playing in the background, which I found oddly strange. I furrow my eyebrows as Nurse Pattie turns around in her rolly chair giving me a giddy smile.

"Hi Tae, what are you doing here this early?" She checks the time while asking.

"I just wanted to stop by to take my medicine so I wouldn't have to take it this evening," I explain, sitting on her table as she nods.

"That's not a problem," She smiles.

She opens a bottle of the medicine I always take and handed me two pills with a cup of water. I thank her before downing the pills with water.

"Are you going to the game?" She asks, I nod while frowning.

"My dad's making me go."

"Aww, they're not so bad, I'm going with my fiancé," She explains, causing my eyes to go wide and I choke on my water.

"What?!" I exclaimed. "You're getting married?"

"Yes, he asked me last night," She tells me.

"Can I see the ring?" I throw the cup in the trash, watching Nurse Pattie pull off her gloves showing me her big diamond ring.

"Congrats Nurse Pattie," I awed at her and she smiles.

"Thanks darling."

"I'll see you at the game," I tell her before exiting her office.

I sigh out, waiting on people to pass by, my eyes latch onto Keaton who walks down the hall with his books in his hand with his famous jersey on, the number twelve was written on the front, I look away before he could see me looking and may think I want to talk to him.

Walking towards my first class with the drag of my feet really told everything. I didn't want to go, but I manage to pick up my feet and carry myself into Mr. Pine's class for the next hour listening to his boring lecture.

After his class came another, then another, then another, Lunch finally came around the corner and I was glad, my stomach growls begging for food and as I pass the lunchroom my stomach growls even more at the smell of delicious food.

I stop in the middle of the hall seeing my dad walking around the halls with his gym clothes on, I give him a confused look and in return he smiles.

"How about we go to lunch together?" He asks and I shake my head.

"I'm not going in there," I state, pointing the opposite way towards the lunch room.

"No, I meant let's leave and come back."

"Let's go," I ordered, snapping my fingers causing him to laugh.

We pass by the front office on our way out, I couldn't be happier getting out of the school just once, don't get me wrong, I love school, but sometimes it can get tiring and sometimes I just need a break. My dad unlocks his pickup truck and I hop in without any hesitation.

"Where do you want to eat at?" My dad asks as we drive off and away from the school.

I hum before speaking. "McDonald's?"

"Oh, you know it," He laughs out before driving off to our local McDonald's.

Walking into the little restaurant and ordering our food didn't take long, I found a place for us to sit as my dad gets the big tray that carries our food and carefully places it on the table.

I open the cheeseburger that was wrapped with paper and take a bite.

"Tomorrow's your doctor's appointment, right?" My dad asks as he takes a sip of his drink.

I nod, not saying anything because my mouth was full of food.

My dad nods before picking at his food acting like he wanted to say something, I sigh out, sitting back in my seat and roll my eyes.

"What is it?"

"We still haven't talked about why you threw water in Keaton's face," I groan, sitting up with my head in my hands.

"I'm serious, Tae. That was totally not like you," He adds.

"I know, it was immature of me to do, but what would you have done if someone you don't like stalks you around and won't leave you alone?" I ask him, raising an eyebrow.

He shrugs. "The kid wants to be your friend."

"And I clearly explained to him that I don't want friends."

"I'm worried about you..." He trails and I give him a look of confusion.

"Why?"

"Because you're sixteen with no friends, that's not good. You're a teenager, Tae, you should be going out and having fun with your friends," He explains and I pick at my food not feeling in the right mood to eat anymore.

"You know the reason behind me not wanting friends, dad. Please, just let me do my thing, okay?" All I want is for everyone to leave me alone and let me be.

"Alright," He holds up his hands in surrender. "But don't say anything when Georgie comes back home and makes fun of you."

"I think I'll live," I laugh out.

After lunch, dad and I drove back to school and I went along with my classes. The day seemed to go by faster since I got back but maybe it was all in my head. By the end of the day, I was in Mr. Hollis's class sitting in the back by myself, that was until Winnie sat beside me.

I was really hoping that I could avoid seeing her. And Keaton.

"Hey," Winnie whispers.

I try to act like I don't hear her, but I couldn't help this bubble feeling guilty eating at me, I turn my head towards giving her a small smile and earning a bright smile back. I suddenly felt better however, there was still this guilt feeling of me not saying hey back.

Just then, Landon, Keaton, and Reece walks in causing me to slump in my seat with Winnie eyeing me carefully.

"Are you coming to the game tonight?" I hear Winnie's chirpy voice ask.

I nod, not looking anywhere near her. "My dad is making me attend it."

"I'm glad you're coming; I was hoping you would."

I continue to look somewhere other than at her, my eyes found their way to Keaton who was staring back at me, usually I was the one looking away first, but to my surprise Keaton turned away. Mr. Hollis clears his throat at the many students that were blabbering about either drama or the game.

"Since today is Friday, I'll let you guys off the hook for today and let you guys have free time-" He couldn't even finish his statement before kids rumbled around the room to their friends, sitting in their seats, talking about the same thing they were talking about when they entered the class.

Chairs scrape the floor catching my attention, Keaton, Landon, and Reece move their chairs around the table to themselves talking amongst each other. I roll my eyes at the fact that the class interrupted Mr. Hollis.

I stand up and out of my seat, walking towards Mr. Hollis who already knew I was coming his way. I send him a bright smile before sitting down in his chair earning looks from the students. Mr. Hollis stands up straight from sitting on his desk and walks to his white board writing the assignment for next week.

"I was going to ask if you're going to the game, but I forgot, you're the outcast and you don't interfere with other kids," Mr. Hollis jokes but it was true.

I shrug. "I'm going."

Mr. Hollis looks back at me with a surprised look as I twirl around in his chair.

"Since when did you decide you want to go to the games?" He asks, looking back at the white board concentrating on what he was writing.

"Since my dad is making me attend," I retort, earning a pointed look from Mr. Hollis.

"They aren't so bad."

I sigh. "Yeah, but I just don't want to go you know?"

"I'll be there. You can hang out with me," He states and I smile.

"Are you bringing your wife and kids?" I asked him excitedly.

I loved his two kids to pieces, Andy and Angie were twins and both looked just like their mom, Mr. Hollis's wife, Jenny, is a sweetheart. I met all of them at a family greeting at the school four years ago.

"Yes, they'll be there," He nods.

I stop swirling the chair, already feeling dizzy. "Good."

"You alright?" Mr. Hollis asked, raising an eyebrow and I sit up holding my stomach.

In the corner of my eye, Keaton's head pops up staring at me, I nod at Mr. Hollis who gives me a worried smile. During the hour of class, I kept getting stares from the golden boy and Mr. Hollis and I spoke about how his family was doing.

The bell rings signaling that school was over and it was time to leave, I get up from Mr. Hollis's chair and make my way in the back to get my things. I notice Winnie was already gone from her seat, probably with Landon. I sling my book bag over my two shoulders while taking a hold of my book for agriculture.

Heading out of the class, I couldn't help but feel eyes on me as I walk to my locker to put my things away. I look around seeing that the cliche group were surrounding Keaton who was slamming things in his locker while eyeing me a few times.

I shut my locker before locking it, making my way down to the gym where my dad was *always* at. A couple of guys open the gym door for me as they make their way out of the gym, I give them a smile out of thanks and make my way to my dad who was speaking to a boy who looked to be a freshman who had sweat dripping down his face.

"Alright, Coach, thanks," The boy had said to my dad, giving him a smile before taking his things and leaving.

My dad turns to me giving me a smile. "I'm so nervous for this game, you don't even know."

"Don't be. You guys win every year," I try to pep him up.

"I know, I'm just glad you're going to be there, it makes me feel so much better knowing you're in the bleachers watching and cheering for us," He tells me. "And not at home by yourself not associating yourself around people."

"Hey, I'm good at that," I defend.

He laughs before taking a hold of his gym bag. "I know."

"We don't have to stay here the whole time until the game starts do, we?" I ask him as I watch him make his way out of the doors.

He nods, looking back at me. "Yes, I am the Coach, Tae."

"But I don't want to stay here longer than I already have to," I complain, feeling the need to go home.

"I would just have to turn back around and come here then go back home after the game, it's a waste of gas," He explains and I huff, following him outside and onto the field.

"What time does the game start?" I squint my eyes while asking, as the sun shines bright in my eyes.

"Six thirty," He answers and I drop my book bag on the ground before sitting on it not even caring if I broke anything inside.

More men came out of the gym doors, walking towards my dad and I with cameras and the famous football, two of the men with the camera's go up the bleachers and onto the top fixing the cameras making them stand up.

"Where are the boys, dad?" I ask him.

He looks up at me from his clipboard. "Eating."

They must be in the cafeteria; I sigh out from being so hot. My dad must've seen me fan myself and nods his head toward the school.

"Go inside while we get ready out here, Mrs. Hyde should be in her office so stay in there until the game starts."

I salute my dad before hopping up from my bag, I go to grab my bag but my dad takes it before I could walk off with it.

"I'll take it to my truck, don't worry."

I nod giving him a smile and walk inside the gym back doors and out of the gym and into the halls of the school, I could hear the rumble of the guys who were in the cafeteria eating and probably making a fool out of themselves.

Me being nosey, I walk to the doors of the cafeteria, looking in the small long windows seeing the football players laughing as they eat, I hear footsteps causing me to walk away from the doors of the cafeteria and look down the hall, seeing the stuck-up cheerleaders heading in the lunchroom.

"Move bitches, is Keaton in there?" I hear Lydia push her way through the crowd of cheerleaders and smiles as she sees Keaton.

I roll my eyes at her before turning around and dashing off towards Mrs. Hyde's office.

I walk in her office without knocking, already knowing nobody was there. Mrs. Hyde sits up in her seat giving me a knowing smile, knowing that my dad sent me here.

"I'm surprised I didn't see you today," She states and I laugh.

"I know, I went out with my dad for lunch."

"That's sweet," She nods for me to sit.

I sit down in front of her. "I'm so sick of hearing about this game."

"Get used to it. Our football games are the talk of the school," She explains and I nod.

"They're good, we get it. They don't have to keep putting it into our brains that they're good," I tell her and she laughs.

"How are you?" She asks and I raise an eyebrow.

"I'm good..." I trail.

"I'm serious, how are you?"

"I'm good," I repeat, feeling suspicious that my dad had talked with her about me.

"What was that incident I heard about with Keaton?"

I groan, leaning my head back. "It was just water, besides I just wanted to show him I mean business about leaving me alone."

"Mhm. That boy seems very fond of you."

I stand up. "Okay, I'm leaving."

"No, wait, Tae."

I hear her pleads of me calling me back but I ignore her, I shut the door before turning around and suddenly bump into someone.

"Shit, I'm sorry," I apologize, looking up and my face turns sour.

Keaton stands in front of me in all his glory, I contemplate if I should kill this boy, but where should I put his body?

"Woah, don't get angry and dump water on me again," He jokes which I never found funny.

I wait for him to move out of my way so I could walk to the gym, but unfortunately, he wasn't moving.

I walk around Keaton before speaking. "Didn't me dumping water on you show you enough to tell you to leave me alone?"

I hear him sigh aggravatedly with his footsteps behind me. "I'm sorry, I'm sorry that I over done it. I just wanted to get to know you better."

"Well, I don't, please leave me alone," I plead, turning around facing him.

He holds his hands up. "Why do you hate me so much? What did I ever do to you? Why are you so keen on not letting me get to know you?"

"Because I don't like you, it's that simple, Keaton. I don't want nothing to do with you."

He doesn't say anything and I take that as my cue to leave, I walk outside while looking at the time on my phone, an hour had already passed since I last talked with my dad, I seen him running around giving orders, and as he sees me, he smiles.

I walk to where he stands and he puts his hands on his hips.

"Almost game time huh?" I tell him and he nods.

"I thought you were going to wait with Mrs. Hyde?

I shrug. "I figured you could use some help."

"We're almost done and it's five forty now," He states, looking at his watch. "You can go sit at the booth and wait on people and take their money until Mrs. Hyde takes your place."

I nod. "Okay, sounds good."

I make my way towards the little black booth that had a grey metal case for money to be filled in, I sit down in the single chair waiting for people to arrive. Not even five minutes later students from the school and elders paid me to get in and took their seats in the bleachers as I put their money safely in the grey case.

I feel a tap on my shoulder and I look up seeing Mrs. Hyde giving me a smile.

"I can take your place now, go have fun and enjoy yourself," She states and I nod getting up from the seat. "Oh, and find a boyfriend while you're at it."

I turn around rolling my eyes as Mrs. Hyde laughs at my retreating back. I look around to see any familiar faces and none to my dismay I knew or even talked to. Until I saw the redhead that was destined to talk to me was waving her hands trying to get my attention.

Oh, she got my attention alright.

I step on the step beside the bleachers to get to Winnie who was watching me all the way until I got to her.

"How'd you get in, I never saw you get your ticket?" I asked confused.

"I got in for free," She state, shrugging.

I raise an eyebrow. "How?"

"I stay after school in the boy's locker room with Landon until it was time to leave and just exited the back door of the gym and came here," She explains her well planned out plan.

I'm not even going to ask what they do in there during that time.

"I'm impressed," I nod my head at her and in return she shrugs, flipping her hair.

Looking at the time, I see it read, six thirty-nine, the game was about to start any minute now. I crossed my arms as I hear the loud music booming on the speakers and everyone screams as the football players run through the posters that the cheerleaders made and out onto the field.

I hold my ears as Winnie screams out Landon's name and I shake my head. The other school we were competing against did the same as our school did and not even a few minutes later the game had begun.

After twenty minutes later into the game, I get hungry and bored so I take my money in my back pocket and tap Winnie.

"I'm getting something to eat, you want anything?" I ask her, and she looks at the game before looking at me.

"Just a water, thanks!" I nod before rushing down the steps to get in line at the food stand.

I never thought that this game would be packed until I came off the bleachers and actually looked back up at it, it amazed me at how some of the people were really into this game and some were just trying to get noticed.

I stand in line waiting forever until it was my turn, I order popcorn and two waters for me and Winnie before heading back up the steps with my arms filled.

Winnie takes her water in a hurry as I get to our spot and I munch on my popcorn not really into the game.

Heck, I didn't even know who was winning.

I watch my dad on the sidelines hollering at the boys before chewing at his nails watching the game impatiently, I smile knowing that if mom were here, she would be so proud of him. I noticed my foot got stuck to the bleachers and as I look down gum was stuck to the bottom of my converse.

I cursed myself in my brain for thinking maybe this would be a great boring night, but no, it wasn't. I wasn't even going to try to pull it off and decided that when I get home, I'd save myself from getting another disease and wash my shoes.

After long hours of waiting for the game, it had finally come to an end, which I was so stoked to get home and climb into my warm bed. I walk down the steps carefully, trying not to bump into some stranger and finally made it off the high steps, I threw my trash away with Winnie behind me following my steps.

I had no idea who had won, so I turn around to ask Winnie.

"Who won?"

Winnie snorts. "Us, duh."

"Right..." I trail off as my eyes catch onto Keaton and his dad arguing by themselves on the field.

Keaton had his helmet in his hand while his other was tugging at his sweaty hair, his face was beat red and as he gets yelled at, he shakes his head disgustingly up at his dad before throwing his helmet down off the ground and walking off angrily and into the school.

My dad witnesses the whole thing as he walks up to Keaton's dad and his dad hands Keaton's helmet to my dad. They say a few words before Keaton's dad walks off angrily just like Keaton had done.

Winnie squeals from behind me and I turn around seeing Landon picking her up from the ground kissing her deeply. I smile at the two before turning around looking at the door Keaton had just gone in and looking around to see if anyone would see me.

I quickly walk into the school with me being my nosey self, trying to look for the angry golden boy. I walk past the cafeteria seeing no sign of Keaton, I finally reach a corner hearing low grunts and cries from what sounded like a boy.

I take slow steps near the boy that was punching the lockers inside the school, I hear his sniffles letting me know he was crying. After another punch on the locker, he meets my eyes, his eyes were bloodshot red and his cheeks were a tint of pink.

"What? Are you here to tell me to not even look at you?" His quivering voice asks in sarcasm and I shake my head.

I play with my hands nervously. "No, I'm here to see if you were alright."

"I'm great as you can see," His sarcasm causes me to roll my eyes.

"I saw what happened with your dad."

"No shit," He glares at me before sliding down the lockers and sitting on the ground.

"Okay, I'm leaving," I state, turning around getting ready to walk away from the sadden boy.

"*Don't.*"

I smile and turn around walking towards him and sit beside him on the floor.

"You don't know what it's like with my parents," He starts and I listen in closely. "You don't know what it's like to be perfect all the time."

I don't say anything again, I stay silent.

"My dad got onto me because I didn't make a touchdown tonight and Landon did, he was so angry at me, and my mom looked disappointed, they are always on my ass about everything," He explains, leaning his head back on the lockers.

"Mhh, I wonder where I relate to that," I joke referring to when he wouldn't leave me alone and I earn a glare from him.

"Your dad should be proud of you, you are like the star of the school and watch you get into some prick school next year," I tell him sincerely.

Keaton cracks a smile. "Is Tae Lambert giving me a compliment?"

I shove his shoulder. "Don't get used to it."

He laughs out before his face goes serious again and he looks off in the distance.

"It'll get better with your dad, I might not know what goes on at your house, but I do know that this will get better," I try to cheer him up, which felt good.

It was the least I could do after the argument we had.

He doesn't say a word and I roll my eyes; I bite my lip wanting to tell him but more like ask him, I was debating it, but I didn't want to look stupid.

"Would it make you feel better if you took me to my doctor's appointment?" I raise an eyebrow.

He turns his head swiftly at me looking deep into my eyes. "Doctor's appointment? Are you okay?"

"I'm fine, I just have to go to the doctor every once in a while, to get checked up on," I explain and he nods understanding.

I bite my lip. "So?"

"You want me to drive you there?"

"If my dad lets me," I state, and he nods.

"Okay, cool. Sounds like a plan," His face seemed to change some, but I was happy that I got him to cheer up somewhat.

"Maybe after we could get some ice cream-" I cut him off short.

I hold my finger up. "Baby steps, Keaton."

He laughs but nods in understanding, I give him a smile before we both have to leave before my dad comes and hunts me down out of worry.

"Okay so, my doctor's appointment is at four tomorrow, don't be late," I give Keaton a pointed look as he stops by his Jeep.

He nods while slinging his gym bag over his shoulder. "I'll be there."

"You better," I turn to see my dad waiting on me in the truck.

"You better go before your dad gets your ass," He scolds.

I nod. "True."

"See you tomorrow," He tells me.

I salute him before saying. "Bye jock."

Chapter Twelve

Tae's Pov.

"I thought you didn't like Davis?" I hear my dad ask as I stick my head through the cabinets in the kitchen, looking for pancake mix.

"I don't. He was just stressed about the game last night and the game coming soon, I thought I was being too harsh on him and thought maybe he could come with us to my doctor's appointment," I shrug it off like it was nothing as I threw the mix on the counter in front of my dad.

He looks up from the newspaper he was reading with a smile. "I thought you wanted this all a secret?"

"He found out when I passed out on the field and he had to take me to the nurse," I explain. "All thanks to you, he haunts me every day."

"He's not mean to you, is he?" He raises an eyebrow.

I *wish*. Only if he was it would be so much easier to hate him.

"More like opposite. He's not what I thought he would be," I give in, but hold my finger up as I see my dad about to speak. "And that doesn't mean he won't switch up on me."

My dad sighs. "I don't see the problem in being friends with him."

I ignore him as I pour the mix into a bowl and pour some milk in with it, the phone cuts me off from cooking, stopping me in the middle of pouring the milk and sliding down toward the house phone that was hung up on the wall.

I quickly answer. "Hello?"

I had a smile on my face hoping that Georgie's voice was heard from the other side but to my dismay, it wasn't. It was just a recording of a women talking about a cruise, I hang up the phone back to the wall while hanging my head low.

"Tae, he'll call soon. I promise, he's probably busy with classes and work," I hear my dad make excuses for Georgie for not calling and all I did was nod.

My feet take quick steps towards the stairs forgetting about the pancake mix on the counter that I didn't have the energy for suddenly.

"Tae," My dad sighs out, but I ignore him.

Entering my room, I slam my door shut with a bang. I know I was acting like a brat, but every time I had a phone call from someone, I would always think it was my brother. I hate him being so far away, but soon I'll be with him in another year, hopefully.

Today is going to be the first day Georgie didn't attend my doctor's appointment, my mind seemed blank as I get ready with an empty stomach. I slide on my high-top converse over my skinny jeans as I hear a light knock on the door.

I look up seeing my dad's head pop in and then his whole figure was standing tall in my room.

"How about you call him after we get out of the doctors?"

I give him a blank stare. "He's most likely not going to answer."

"You'll never know if you don't try, but I came up here to tell you Davis is here," He states and my eyes go wide.

Oh shit, I'm not ready.

I stand up in a hurry causing my dad to smirk before leaving my room while closing the door behind him, I pull my hair up into a quick and easy ponytail while grabbing a pair of leggings with a t-shirt.

I obviously didn't care how I looked; I was just surprised that time went by quickly. Going into the bathroom, turning on the sink and splashing water on my toothbrush that had toothpaste on it, I hurriedly brush my teeth.

I make my way out of my room and down the stairs to where golden boy was sitting at the counter across from my dad. They were laughing about God knows what and I give them a confused look as I stick my head into the fridge.

"Hey Lambert," Keaton's voice was in a teasing tone and I turn around in my spot with the orange juice bottle in my hand with a raised eyebrow.

"We're going by last names now?" I ask him while I pour myself a glass as he watches me closely.

I watch him shrug in the corner of my eye. "You call me jock, so it's only fair."

I roll my eyes before placing the orange juice bottle back in the fridge.

I hear my dad hum as he goes into the living room and I quirk my eyebrow at him beginning to get suspicious.

"I got a lot of paperwork to do, so I might have you guys go together by yourselves," I almost choke on the juice and spew it out on the counter but I cover my mouth when Keaton's head turns toward mine quickly.

What paperwork? He's a football coach.

"Um no..." I exclaimed.

"I mean if you really have to then I could take her to get it off your hands," Keaton shrugs.

I could've sworn I just seen that boy smirk.

"But you might have to be there because you don't want to miss something important," I try to get out of the situation because there's no way I'm getting back in the car with Keaton alone.

Tell me why I asked him to come with us again?

Oh right, because I'm a nice person that feels bad for others.

Great.

"True, plus this is your first appointment after summer..." My dad trails and I so badly wanted to jump up and down in excitement.

I nod. "Yes, and this is the first appointment without Georgie and I don't know how to feel about it."

"Don't worry, Keaton's here to take his place," My dad jokes but I found nothing funny.

I watch him walk upstairs to get ready and I turn toward to face Keaton with a glare.

He raises an eyebrow. "What?"

"Nothing," I roll my eyes, shaking my head at the thoughts on how I should murder this boy.

"I forget Georgie was your brother," He calls out as I to sir my pancake mix that had been sitting there since I went upstairs.

I decide not to make pancakes and just to throw the pancake mix away, Keaton's eyes watched me as I walked back and forth throughout the kitchen to find something to eat. I decide to go with cereal.

"You want some?" I asked him finally looking up at him.

He shakes his head. "Nah, thanks though. I ate before I came."

I nod before putting the box of cereal and the jug of milk back in the fridge to keep cool.

"So, what would you have done if you hadn't come with me today?" I ask him, munching on my food.

He leans forward on the counter, shrugging. "Probably just stay at home or practice some more for the next game."

"Or party," I add.

"I don't go to parties," He states, tapping on the counter with his finger lightly.

I could tell I was getting into a touchy subject.

"And why not?" I ask him ignoring the fact that he was getting nervous. "You're the golden boy of the school you should be out partying and making friends."

"Says the girl that doesn't have any," He retorts and I shrug.

"Touché, Keaton, touché."

"The reason why I don't party is because-" As he goes to explain to me why he doesn't go to parties, my dad walks in giving us a cheery smile.

"Alright, you guys ready?" He asks and I nod before placing my bowl and spoon in the sink.

As my dad grabbed his keys Keaton turns around and tells me. "I'll tell you later."

I nod at him and we head out the door.

"I call shotgun!" I yell and before I could run to get in the front seat, my dad pulls me back.

"Keaton's our guest, he should sit up front," My dad states and I look up at him in shock.

My dad rounds the truck, getting in, while I stand there not believing he's letting Keaton sit up front and not me. Keaton comes in my view with a smirk and I see his mouth moving.

"Looks like I get shotgun," He winks at me before hopping in the truck beside my dad and I carry my feet toward the back.

This is going to be a long ride.

****

Seeing the hospital for the first time since summer really hit the spot, I didn't want to be back here. Memories fade my mind and I couldn't help but want to jump right back in the truck and drive off.

Bad thoughts invaded my mind as I look up at the ginormous hospital that I spent my whole years fighting for my life at. I hope this wasn't bad, I hope I didn't have to take chemo, I wish I was cleared from this disease and go on being a normal teenager, but that was all in my dreams.

A hand lands on my shoulder breaking me from my thoughts as I look over seeing Keaton giving me an encouraging smile.

"You, okay?" He asks and I would be lying if I said that didn't feel good for someone to ask me how I was.

I smile. "Just a little nervous."

"You're not a fan of hospitals either?" His smile grows wider as he asks me.

"Nope, you would think I'm used to it since I've been going here since forever, but I'm not," I shrug.

"I hate when I had to go with my dad to take my mom here."

The sliding doors of the hospital opens for us, we walk in with the Nurse up front greeting us, I sit down in one of the chairs in the waiting room as my dad speaks with the Nurse, Keaton looks around at the hospital, before sitting down beside me.

My dad finally finishes his conversation with the Nurse and makes his way to sit with us.

"She said it won't take long for them to let you go back," My dad speaks and I let out a breath of nervousness and I watch Keaton's leg bob up and down.

Looks like I'm not the only one scared of hospitals.

The white door that the patients go through opens up to an exciting Nurse Rita, I smile as she wiggles her eyebrows at me.

"Tae, it's so good to see you," She exclaimed, walking quickly toward me as I stand getting tackled by her hug.

I smile, hugging her back. "You're the only person I missed here."

"Except for Doctor Simmons, of course," I add.

She laughs. "He's been on his toes waiting for you to turn up here."

"I bet," I comment, rolling my eyes.

Rita looks at my dad and says her greetings before seeking Keaton, a smirk forms on her plump face and I roll my eyes.

"And who is this?" Rita asks and I smile awkwardly.

Keaton smiles. "Hey, I'm Keaton."

"Keaton, mhm," Rita looks him up and down before giving me a look.

"Let's go," I state, grabbing Rita's hand pulling her toward the white door I was dreading to go in.

Once we enter the long hall Rita looks back at Keaton and turns back around at me.

"He's cute," She whispers with her hand over her mouth.

I ignore her statement and kept walking to God knows where.

"So, we'll be going into this room right here and wait for Doctor Simmons to arrive," Rita states in her Nurse tone voice, pointing toward the blue room I always go in when I'm here.

I enter the room first then Keaton, my dad, and Rita follow in behind. It was like a regular patient room; fish were drawn on all over the wall and hand prints from little kids were painted on it as well. I hopped on the hard bed type table waiting for Rita to continue talking.

"So, I'm going to ask you a few questions so I can give Doctor Simmons some feedback," Rita Starts.

I nod, sighing loudly.

"How's your breathing?" She asks me.

I shrug. "It's how it always is."

"Okay, so, as your dad told us, that you and him have been exercising, how is it then?"

"I can't run, but if I walk a far distance then yeah my breathings bad, but everything else seems to be normal," I explain and she nods writing a few things down on her notepad.

"Taking your medicine on a regular?" She asks again.

I nod and more question kept coming following after, she leaves after and I so badly wanted to leave already.

"Hopefully Doctor Simmons comes in and checks on you and everything is alright," My dad comments and I nod.

I noticed Keaton was quiet, I'm guessing letting us have our space just in case something was wrong, but this was the first time I've seen him quiet. His face was something I couldn't read, He watched the floor with his hands put together, leaning over.

My dad sits up straight as we hear a knock on the door, entering the room was Doctor Simmons, who we were expecting.

"Welcome back," Doctor Simmons states with a giddy tone.

"Not like I have a choice," I comment back causing my dad to give me a pointed look.

Doctor Simmons chuckles. "Not happy to be here, are we?"

"Nope," I tell him.

"Well then you're not going to be any happier when I tell you this," He gives me a smile.

I sigh out. "What?"

"I have to give you a CT scan..." He trails, and I groan.

The thing about CT scans were that you had to lay on a table type bed and it moves you inside this circle type that x-rays you, which wasn't that bad but you have to be still at all times or they'll have to take the x-ray again.

"Let's get this over with," I hopped off the bed and as I do, Rita walks into the room handing me a gown.

I already knew this routine, I walk into the bathroom to change into a hospital gown and walk back out with the clothes in my hand, I hand my clothes to my dad before we all get up moving to the CT scan room.

My dad and Keaton stay behind the glass window looking through at me, I lay down keeping my eyes on my dad, he gives me a thumbs up and I smile. My sights land on Keaton who was staring back at me with an anxious look, he had his fingers in his mouth, biting his nails.

I try not to laugh as Rita moves my hands above my head before giving me an encouraging smile. The small plastic bed moves in and my x-rays begin.

A while later, I get back dressed as Doctor Simmons and Rita look over my x-rays, they both take my dad back to speak with him, and Keaton blows out a breath.

"That just brought back so many memories," He goes to tell me.

"I'm glad your mom is better," I get surprised that I'm being nice to him, but I can tell this was bringing back old memories of when his mom had to do the same thing and he had to watch it all.

He smiles. "Yeah, me too. Soon you will be too."

I freeze in my seat; he has to be joking. His mom was very lucky that she got cured but me? That's a real joke of someone thinking I could get freed from cancer.

"Wanna do something after this?" He asks and I look over at him.

"Like what?"

"Like we could get ice cream or something," He shrugs and I sit up at the sound of ice cream.

He laughs noticing me getting excited. "Ice cream it is then."

My dad walks in the room, closing the door he turns around wearing a smile on his face.

"Did they say I was fine?" I ask him.

"They said it was the same as last time, nothing has changed," He gives me a sad smile, but something in me didn't want to believe him.

I shake off the feeling before we all leave the hospital with a new appointment; Keaton lets me sit up front with my dad in which I take it quickly before my dad could tell me not to.

Once we get to my house, I had forgotten that Keaton was supposed to take me to get ice cream until Keaton brought it up to my dad.

"Do you mind if I take Tae off your hands for a while? I'm taking her out for ice cream," Keaton asks my dad who turns around smirking at me.

I roll my eyes hearing my dad speak. "Where will this be taking place at?"

"Greenhouse Diner," Keaton replies causing my dad to nod.

"Sounds good to me, only if it's alright with Tae of course," My dad states, pointing his head toward me.

I scoff. "Heck yeah, who would turn down ice cream?"

"Alright, we won't be away for too long," Keaton promises my dad.

"I trust you with my daughter, Keaton, don't make me regret it," My dad gives him a pointed look but you could tell my dad was joking.

Keaton nods and I wave bye to my dad before hopping into Keaton's Jeep, I know I said I didn't want to be alone with Keaton in his car again, but this is ice cream we're talking about.

"So, we're going back to that Diner again huh?" I joked earning an eye roll from Keaton.

"This time, don't run off," He begs, cranking up the car and pulling out of the driveway.

I laugh out. "That would mean me running away from ice cream and what kind of idiot would I look like doing that?"

"An idiot?" Keaton's face held confusion which made me get confused at what I said.

End the end we both laugh it off, this was weird. But the good kind of weird, me being nice to Keaton was new, I never knew that he would be this chill of a person, but I did judge a book by its cover though, so it was my fault really.

Keaton parks his Jeep in the Diner's parking lot; we both hop out of his Jeep and enter the Cafe. Smiles from the workers came our way as we find a seat to sit in over at the ice cream bar.

Tommy, the guy I met from last time walks to us leaning against the counter in front of him.

Giving us a smile, he says. "Back again I see."

"Still annoying I see," Keaton jokes earning a glare from Tommy.

"I see how it is, what do you want?"

"Ice cream. What does it look like I want?" I lay my head on my hand watching the two go back and forth.

A hand rubs my shoulder catching my attention, I turn around in my seat seeing the sight of Ally.

"I'm happy to see you're back," Her country accent was strong and was meant to be heard.

I couldn't lie that Ally was indeed beautiful, her short brown hair fell upon her shoulders and her sweet southern smile could be seen a mile away. She wore an apron over her outfit with a Coffee pot in her right hand.

I give her a smile since I didn't know what else to say.

"Don't be shy, let me put this back in its place and I'll show you our best ice cream," She states and I nod.

I watch her do as she says, I turned around towards Keaton as he just begins to stare back at me.

"I can see why you love this place so much..." I trail, nodding my head toward Ally.

He lifts up his head in question. "Why?"

"They're so welcoming, which I know that's what you're supposed to do at restaurants, but they treat you like family," I shrug while explaining, earning a smile from him.

"I also like the food too," Keaton comments and I shove him playfully.

Ally makes her way back toward me with a white cup filled with ice cream in it, Tommy hands Keaton one as well which ours weren't the same, but I took the cup in gratefulness.

"What flavor is this?" I hear myself ask.

Her eyes go big. "You're not allergic to nuts, are you?"

"Oh no, I was just asking because it looked familiar," I laughed out which made her smile.

"It's homemade peanut butter pecan," She tells me and my heart warms.

My mom's favorite.

I take a bite, enjoying the tasty flavor that it brought into my mouth. Now I know why this was my mom's favorite.

"This is really good," I tell her truthfully.

"This best right?" Keaton nudges me in which I nod and smile at Ally.

"Thank you both," She winked at us before leaving us to get back to work.

"It's on us, by the way," Tommy cuts in, looking between Keaton and I.

Keaton shakes his head. "Tom, this isn't that much, I can pay."

"No man, I got you..." Tommy trails as I take another bite. "Especially when you're with your girl."

I almost spat my ice cream back in the cup, not from it being so cold, but the comment Tommy made. Before

I could correct him, he had already walked away leaving both Keaton and I in an awkward situation.

"So, when's your next game?" I ask, trying to make the awkwardness goes away.

He swallows his ice cream. "In a few weeks, why? Are you coming?"

I didn't miss that smirk of his, so I reply. "Wasn't planning on it."

"Why? Scared you're going to catch me crying again and feel bad so you ask me to do some shit like this?" I look up to see him smiling while placing his spoon into his now empty cup.

"No, the games are boring," I tell him honestly.

He ticks his tongue with his teeth. "Not if you had friends."

I give him a glare before he laughs and waves me off.

"No but seriously, I had a fun time going to the Doctors which is a weird thing to say and doing this," He never once looked away from my eyes while telling me this.

I smile. "Me too."

What was that? Did I actually agree with Keaton for having fun with him?

Chapter Thirteen

Tae's Pov.

"That's the last cone," I tell my dad who had just finished practice with the boys.

"Thanks, go get your stuff and I'll meet you at my truck," He instructs, in which I salute him before turning around, making my way towards the exit door we always walk out of.

I walk in the gym which was loud when bunch of the guys were done getting showered and dressed and were waiting for whatever their reason was. Seeing Keaton walk out of the locker rooms hit me different, we had spent time yesterday, yes, but didn't mean we were friends.

I wish I could lie to myself and say that hanging out with Keaton wasn't fun.

I hear a whistle which echoes throughout the gym, looking up I see Keaton staring at me who was smiling. Landon and Reece who were walking beside him turn their heads to see who he was smiling at.

I give Keaton a small wave before grabbing my bag off the gym bleachers, the doors of the gym open revealing the crazy redhead that always wants to talk to me comes running in completely ignoring Landon who gives her a confused look.

I get a face load of Winnie who smiles brightly at me.

"I need a favor..." She trails.

I give her an awkward smile. "What?"

"Since you like to read and to go to libraries, my mom needs help around the library today and I tried to think of who the right person could be and thought of you."

"Oh, lucky me," I reply sarcastically.

She sighs. "I know we don't know each other that well, but if we keep hanging out, I'm sure we could be great friends."

This girl was honestly too good for this world.

"Sure," I couldn't help myself to say.

"Okay, good, come with me."

As she goes to grab my hand, I stop her.

"I have to ask my dad," I state in a 'duh' tone voice.

She nods following in behind me as I head out toward the field where my dad was.

I catch him checking things off a clipboard and I cough, catching his attention.

"Hey blondie, all set to go?" He asks, but immediately sees Winnie once he looks behind me.

"Dad, this is Winnie, Winnie meet my dad," I introduce them together.

Winnie waves. "You probably don't know me, but I know you quite well."

"I'm sure you do since I'm the Coach," My dad states, nodding.

"Right..." I trail.

"Winnie's mom needs help in her library and needs my help," I add.

My dad nods. "Okay, just be careful."

"I *always* am," I wave bye to him earning a smile.

"I'm so glad he's letting you come," Winnie states, placing a piece of her hair behind her ear.

I cross my arms. "My dad wants me to go out and hang with other kids."

"Why don't you?" She asks and I freeze. "I mean, I've noticed you're always by yourself and closed off."

"I'm just anti-social," I shrug.

"Well, I can help with that," She laughs.

We keep walking through the parking lot.

"You have your restricted?" I ask her and she nods.

"Yep, but I'll be turning seventeen soon," She explains and I nod.

She stops at a bug looking car which makes me awe at the sight, the car looked perfect for Winnie and it fit her personality.

"This is it," She opens her arms up to the car.

"Adams, you better not leave without saying goodbye!" I hear the familiar sound of Landon's yell out.

I turned around seeing the three stooges all in one walking toward Winnie and I, I awkwardly stand near Winnie as Keaton's eyes land on me. His face turned into a surprised one which I would be too if I saw me with Winnie.

"Oh god Winnie, you're going to ruin her," Reece teases Winnie, who didn't find his joke funny.

"Do you want your dick snapped off?" She smiles up at him as he covers his private area.

I could help but chuckle at the two, Keaton nods at me.

"Since when do you two hang out?"

"Since today," I reply, shrugging.

"She's going to talk your head off," Reece tells me, causing Winnie to jump forward and Reece jumps back to avoid a hit from Winnie.

"Landon, control you're pig of a friend," Winnie snarls out.

"Reece, cut it out," Landon's dad voice comes out.

Reece rolls his eyes and Keaton shakes his head in annoyance.

"Where are you two heading off to?" Keaton asks, fixing the strap of his book bag on his back.

"None of your business what we're going to do, we don't need you guys snooping around," Winnie gives Keaton a pointed look.

"Alright, miss bossy pants, jeez I was just asking," Keaton defends which I couldn't help but snort, earning a playful glare from him.

"Now if you'll excuse us, we have some girly things to do," Winnie said, kissing Landon's cheek and heading over to her side of the car.

"Bye," I said quietly before entering Winnie's tiny car.

The three guys watch us as we pull out of school and on to the road with bored expressions, Winnie turns up the radio which turns on a smooth jazz music.

"What kind of music do you listen to?"

I shrug. "Old timey music I guess."

She nods before turning up the radio more and switching the station to old music, she rolls her windows down before sticking her hand out and yelling. I laugh at her while staring at her like she's crazy.

We make it to her mom's library in a total of ten minutes and we both head out of the car and into the little book palace.

"Mom?" Winnie calls out as she enters.

"I'm up here dear!" A sweet tone calls out from above.

I look up seeing Winnie's mom on a ladder placing books on a book shelf.

"This is Tae, she's my friend from school that will be helping us," Winnie introduces me.

I smile and give her mom a little wave.

"Oh, how rude of me!" Her mom exclaims, climbing down the ladder.

"Hi, I'm Bonnie, Winnie's mom," She adds, handing her hand out for me to shake.

I smile in politeness. "Hi, it's really nice to meet you. You have a wonderful library."

"Thank you, my husband built this place when we were younger," Bonnie explains exactly what Winnie told me last time.

"He did a well-done job," I tell her, causing her to smile brightly.

She looks over at Winnie. "I like this girl."

****

Keaton's Pov.

I go to unlock the door of my house but before I can stick my key into the lock, the door opens and shows my mom. Her face had a frown plastered on it and I knew she was upset about something.

Always something.

"Keaton, your father wants to speak to you," She states, and I nod.

"He *always* wants to speak with me."

I dropped my backpack on the ground before heading into my dad's office, I knock three times before entering seeing that my dad was standing in front of his window with scotch in his hand looking out at the view of the big backyard.

"You said you wanted to speak with me..." I trail.

He turns a little letting me see the side of his face, which he was not happy.

"I've heard you've been hanging out with some girl," He explains causing me to roll my eyes. "I have eyes everywhere and which I know you've been taking her to that little Diner of Ally's."

"Okay and?"

He turns around fully. "Turns out she's the Coach's daughter."

"Yeah, I know," I nod, crossing my arms.

"Don't tell me you're seeing her."

"No, I'm not, she's a friend, even if I was why would it concern you?" I raise an eyebrow.

"It concerns your grades, your future, your everything," He starts his shit again.

I roll my eyes. "Dad, not this again."

"No, don't dad me. I have worked too hard for you to just flush this down the drain," My dad yells and I tug at my hair.

"What are you even talking about?! I've worked my ass off just to get here and you're still treating me like shit?" I fuss back.

"Yes, and obviously you're not working your ass off because I found these in your trash," He throws the letters from Ohio state on his desk that I had thrown away.

I slap my hand on my thigh. "I wasn't really going to throw them away."

"All we've talked about was you going to Ohio, and now you're suddenly wanting to change your mind just like now? At times like this?" He asks and all I do is groan. "I thought you wanted to go to Ohio?"

"I do, or at least I did. I don't know, I guess I was having second thoughts," I shrug my shoulders as I speak to him.

He shakes his head. "It's that girl, I know it."

"Bring up Tae one more time, she has nothing to do with this, I swear."

"Best hope so, I don't want to see something like this happen again," He points at me.

I hold my hands up in surrender. "You won't."

"You're going to Ohio and that's *final*."

Chapter Fourteen

Tae's Pov.

I slowly enter the kitchen with light steps trying to hear what my dad was saying over the phone, he was being awfully quiet to my liking which made the situation more suspicious. I curse at the hardwood floor that creaks slipping my dad's attention away from the phone.

He turns around with the phone in his hand.

"Okay, thank you for letting me know. I'll speak with you soon," My dad says through the phone then proceeds to hang up.

I lean on the counter. "Who was that?"

"Just a dad that called and said their kid is sick today and told me that they couldn't make it to practice," He shrugs as he explains to me.

I nod before stealing a banana from the fruit bowl. "Okay, I'm ready, let's go."

"Meet me outside, I got to run upstairs really quick," I nod at his instruction and we both split apart as I walk outside near my dad's pickup truck.

A few minutes later, my dad's head pops out of the house and we both hop into his truck for another drive to school.

"You still haven't spoken to Georgie?" I watch as my dad takes a shortcut to get to school.

I watch him shake his head in the corner of my eye.

"No, which I find strange because he'll usually send us a text saying he's busy or something," My dad was right, it was strange that Georgie hasn't spoken to us in ages.

"He's just living the college life, dad, you knew this was coming."

"Yeah, but I didn't think it was going to be soon, He better not come home over winter break with a pregnant girl," He mumbled the last part which causes me to chuckle.

I rub his shoulder. "Georgie might be a little crazy, but he's not crazy enough to get a girl pregnant."

"Let's hope so," He shakes his head as he stops the truck to let me out in the front.

I give him my goodbyes and begin to head into the school, the first thing I do is go to my locker to put my book bag in it, then to grab my first period booklet and work.

As I get the last of my things, I hear swearing and stomps coming from the left side of me, I raise an eyebrow while watching the scene in front of me. The crazy redhead and Lydia and her puppet Mandy were fussing in the corner where a few watchers were.

Winnie was backed up against the wall with a scowl written on her face while Lydia was glaring at the red head. I walk a little closer to know what the drama was all about.

"If we weren't in school right now, I'd beat your ass," Winnie snarls out, leaning forward.

I then hear Lydia laugh. "Go head, bitch."

"What's stopping you?" Lydia adds.

My eyes go wide as Winnie's face turn beat red almost as red as her hair but I don't think nothing can beat that hair. Winnie pushes Lydia out of the way so she could have room to hit her I'm guessing and goes to smack her, but my feet get the best of me and I run to Winnie and stop her from smacking the snobby girl.

"Tae?!" Winnie questions and I nod.

You might be wondering why I helped her, and the answer is *I don't know*. I just didn't want her getting in trouble then crying about it to me, I guess.

"Who are you?" Lydia cuts in and I give her a look.

"That's Tae Lambert, the coach's daughter," I hear Mandy whisper in Lydia's ear.

Lydia's eyes grew massive and she stands up straight. "Oh."

That was she all said to me before walking away with her puppet right behind her, both Winnie and I give each other a confused look.

"What were you thinking when you were about to hit Lydia?" I drop Winnie's hand making it plop on her thigh.

"I was going to give her a taste of this," She holds up her fist while replying to me.

I roll my eyes. "She's not worth it."

"I'll be damned if she isn't, she was the one that told me to do it," She points back to where Lydia walked away.

"Yeah, but don't get down to her level, you're better than that," I tell her and she crosses her arms.

"I would've done had her on the ground..." Winnie trails and I so badly wish I didn't stop Winnie from hitting her now.

That would've been a show stopping sight to see.

"Why do you hate her so much?" I ask. "I know you guys were friends but I didn't know y'all were enemies now."

"I'll have to tell you later, the bells about to ring," Right as she said that the bell rung in which I nod.

We walk together for our first period class, it felt weird knowing Winnie was beside me walking with me. I never had somebody to do this with, and why did it feel good? I hope I wasn't changing; I made a promise to myself that I wasn't going to let anyone close to me and look at me breaking that promise.

"Good morning Ms. Adams and Ms. Lambert," Mr. Pine gives us a pointed look as we take our seats.

Winnie sighs before dumping her books onto the table in front of her. "Good morning, Mr. Pine."

Mr. Pine nods with a smile in triumph before writing on his white board, Winnie rolls her eyes and I could tell she was aggravated, I could understand though, Mr. Pine has been taunting Winnie ever since school started.

Students file into the class and that was Mr. Pine's cue to give us an hour lesson. After first period, I head to my second period class still wondering what really happened with Winnie and Lydia. They used to be so close, yet now they're enemies.

Later on in the day, I was still on my toes about the talk Winnie was supposed to give me, until I realized I haven't seen Keaton around today nor his weird friends. Why was I thinking about him? Did I want him to bug me? That's nonsense.

I make my way into the Nurse's office to see Nurse Pattie at her computer and her face looked to be in concentration. I knock twice gaining her attention.

"Hey Tae, I'm sorry I didn't see you," She greets me.

I smile. "Don't worry, I see you got your hands full," I point towards the computer which had wedding arrangements.

She laughs before clicking off the site. "'I was bored, plus I was killing time before students start rolling in."

"That's adorable," I mumble, sitting down the table like desk.

"So.." She trails nervously.

I nod for her to continue.

"I was wondering if you wanted to be one of my bridesmaids, and I know that sounds silly, but we've grown close over the four years you've went to this school and I want you there for my wedding," I watch her fumbling around the office, carrying medicines and shots and neither of them was for me.

"Pattie, I'd be honored to..." I smile. "But, is this okay with Chris?"

She nods. "Yes, you know Chris loves you, your dad and brother is invited as well."

My heart squeezes. "When is the wedding?"

"Next year," She states, applying her gloves on her hands.

"Wow, I can't believe you're getting married in a year," I said in shock.

She nods at my statement, Pattie has always wanted to get married, she had trouble in the past with guys. They thought since Pattie was so sweet and caring they could break her and hit on her, she met Chris in the hospital, when Pattie tried to get away from her last boyfriend, he decided he was going to follow her in his car and cause her to have a wreck.

His plan succeeded, it was a miracle that Pattie is alive right now, but with the help of Chris she was able to make it out alive. Then Chris found out about the situation and decided to help Pattie, but what he didn't know that four years later they were going to be married.

"And in a few years, you will be too," She winks before handing me my medicine and a cup of water.

I give her a crazy look before swallowing the pills and water in one go. "Not happening."

"Just watch and see."

After our little talk Pattie and I had, I decided it was time for me to go back to my locker to put my books inside my locker and head towards Mrs. Hyde's room for lunch.

I did just that and made my destination to Mrs. Hyde's room, then after lunch I spent my day like any other, in a classroom with a bunch of snobby kids. By the end of the day, I went to the agriculture class where Winnie was already seated.

"Hey," I greet her, which was a weird thing since she always greets me first then ends with me ignoring her.

She smiles. "Hey, after class we'll walk together outside and I'll tell you everything about Lydia."

I nod and we begin talking amongst ourselves, a few minutes later I finally see the golden boy, Keaton walking in with Reece and Landon. Landon comes to Winnie and I's desk and kisses the top of Winnie's head; he sends me a nod before sitting at the table beside us.

"What's up, Lambert," Keaton's voice rings in my ears.

I look up to see him standing next to my side of the desk. "Hey, Keaton."

"Haven't seen you all day, where you've been?" He questions me.

"I could say the same about you," I retort, crossing my arms.

He chuckles. "So, you were looking for me?"

"No," I quickly recall. "You're usually up my butt all the time"

"Does that bother you? That I wasn't up your ass?" His cocky response made me want to punch him.

I turn my head forward, ignoring the laughing boy who sits down right beside Landon. This hour was going to be hell.

****

An hour later.

"Okay, class dismissed," Mr. Hollis states to the class who all gets up in a hurry to go home.

I pack my things and look up to see Keaton and his friends have gone to go to practice, I'm guessing Winnie was waiting for me to get done. As we enter the hall she sighs out.

"Where do I start?" She has her finger on her mouth and a concentration look on her face.

"Maybe, how you and Lydia became friends," I shrug and she nods.

"Lydia wasn't always a bitch believe or not," She rolls her eyes at the thought.

"She was my best friend, when people tell you high school changes you, you should listen to them. In freshman year, Lydia became a cheerleader and of course I did too. We did everything together, I was friends with Keaton at this time and Lydia had always had a crush on him, throughout those two years of high school together, Lydia was trying to get head cheerleader, but I got it," Winnie adds.

"Didn't Keaton and Lydia date?" I hear myself ask.

"I'll get to that..." She trails, opening the exit door of the school. "Lydia then started dating Keaton, I wasn't mad because I thought Lydia was good for him at that time. But when Lydia cheated on Keaton it broke Keaton, I was mad. While those times I was helping Keaton get over his break up, Lydia was plotting to put drugs in my gym locker, and she did. I got kicked off the team and Lydia took my spot, ever since then I hated that bitch for hurting my best-friend and stealing my spot."

We sit down on the bench at football practice and I sit there in shock, so all of this was for being head cheerleader?

"Did you not want to prove that it wasn't your drugs?" I ask her.

She shakes her head. "It would be useless, and what I hate her most for was, was that during that time my dad had died so I felt betrayed by my own best friend and I had to fake a smile on for Keaton."

She points her head towards Keaton who was too busy to even notice us, what really caught my attention was, the person beside him while talking to my dad.

"Is that Keaton's dad?" Winnie asked what I was about to ask.

I squint my eyes to see further. "I think so."

We both look at each other with confused looks before looking back at the scene.

What was Keaton's dad doing here?

Chapter Fifteen

Keaton's Pov.

I slam my backpack on the ground with my hands bawled in a fist, blood was pumping through me and I could tell my face was red. The door shuts behind my dad and I as I try hard not to rare back and hit him.

I turn around quickly. "Why the hell did you show up?"

"I can't watch my son practice?" My dad sarcastically states.

"No, it's unnecessary, you never watch, but why now?" I knew he was doing, this because of Tae.

He huffs. "I don't have to explain myself to you, Keaton, just know that I'll be showing up to your practices every day from now on."

"Like hell you are," I retort, slamming my fist down on my mom's coffee table.

"I just want your head on straight, I don't want you going down the road that you once were down before," The tone in my dad's voice clearly stated that he didn't care.

It was all for his image.

"I'm tired of you controlling me," I state, trying to control my temper.

My dad steps forward. "I'm not controlling you; I'm helping you."

"No, you're controlling me. Ever since I made the mistake of drinking and going wild you have had this obsession on me, football this, football that."

"I'm sick of it," I add.

"How would that look on my reputation? What about yours? Your moms?"

I tug at my hair. "What if I don't want to do football anymore?"

"What did you just say?" His tone was in a more aggressive tone and he takes slow steps toward me.

He was daring me to say it again.

"You know what, I don't want you here right now..." He trails.

Did I say something wrong?

Why the hell is he acting like this?

"Fine, I'll go up to my room," I waved him off before heading up the stairs.

"No Keaton, I mean I don't want you in this house tonight," His demand stops me in my tracks.

I turn around slowly. "What? You're over exaggerating, are you seriously kicking me out?"

"For tonight I am, yes," He states, nodding. "Since you obviously miss living in the wild life, then go head, go."

I stood there confused until he opens the front door.

"I don't want you here tonight, go do whatever I don't care, but when tomorrow comes you better be at school on time and you better come home tomorrow."

"You're making no sense, I'm not leaving," I tell him.

"Yes, you are, or I'll make you leave," He threatens and I stood there in shock.

My mom walks in the house with a confused face. "Close the door, honey, you'll let bugs in."

"No, Keaton's about to leave," Dad tells her.

I clench my jaw and look away as my mom turns her head to look at me.

"What's going on?" She asks.

"Your son wants to go out and party and get high, while he lays down with a girl, so I'm letting him do that tonight, I just don't want him here," Dad explains to her and she shakes her head.

"My son isn't leaving, are you crazy? He's just seventeen and you're going to let him out late at night?!" Mom exclaims, pushing at dad's chest.

"He did it behind our backs before," I roll my eyes before walking out of the house with my mom calling out for me.

I then hear nothing as I watch my dad close the door, I get into my Jeep but my dad walks outside.

"Give me the keys son."

"Where am I supposed to go?" I ask him in barely a whisper.

It hurt me for my dad to kick me out of the house without any thinking.

"Go to the bar," He smirks, snatching my keys from my hands and locking the Jeep as he walks inside the house.

I stare at the house I grew up in still in shock, he was just going to leave me on the streets alone.

I take out my phone deciding on who I should call, this was embarrassing to tell whoever I was going to call and tell them about my dad kicking me out for no reason. I couldn't call Landon because he already has his hands full with his parents' newborn baby and two other little ones, that'll just add more stress on them and then Reece is in an orphanage so of course I could ask to stay with him.

The only one I could call was somebody that was close, that I knew would pick up as soon as I called.

I dial the seven numbers I knew by heart and wait for the second ring; a silent hello reaches my ears causing my hands to shake.

"I need a favor."

****

Tae's Pov.

Pushing my glasses up on my face, I quickly type my essay listening to Whitney Houston, the front door slams open and I hear two people talking. I press pause on my radio and open my bedroom door trying to listen in on who was here.

I hear my dad talking then he yells out. "Tae, get down here!"

I jump at the sound, but I comply on what my dad demands, I quickly walk downstairs and enter the kitchen where my dad and Keaton stood.

I stood there frozen in the kitchen with my pjs on giving eye contact with the most popular boy in school, could this be more embarrassing? *No.*

"What are you doing here?" I ask him, giving Keaton and my dad a suspicious look.

Keaton looks away from me and my dad leans on the kitchen counter. "Something has happened at home so Keaton is going to stay the night with us."

I cross my arms. "Okay, where's he going to stay?"

"In Georgie's room."

I had to blink before realizing what he said, did he just say-

"What?!" I exclaim, with wide eyes.

"If it's a problem, I can always leave," Keaton laughs slightly.

"No, you're fine, Keaton. Tae will show you the room," My dad gives me a pointed look in which I turn around with a fuming face.

I'm so going to murder my dad in the middle of the night.

Walking up the stairs I could tell Keaton was afraid to talk to me. He should be afraid, because if it were up to me, he would be sleeping on the couch not my brother's room.

I stop at the door with hesitation to open it, I look at Keaton who was watching every move I made, and I open the room letting the cold air fall upon our skin. I walk in flipping the light switch on and turn around to see Keaton looking around the room, observing the area.

"Don't touch anything," I demand, crossing my arms.

He nods. "Promise."

"I really don't like the idea of this..." I trail, sitting down on the soft bed.

"You seem like you miss him," Keaton observes, looking at the picture frame of Georgie and I.

I nod. "Yeah, very much."

He hums before taking a seat next to me. "My dad kicked me out of the house for the night."

"What? Why?" I turn my body towards me as I ask him.

He shrugs. "I told him that maybe I didn't want to do football and he went crazy on me."

"But you love football," I tell him, and he nods.

"I do, but my dad just makes me hate it."

"It's that bad huh?"

He nods. "Nobody knows what it's like with him, he pressured me into doing football, he's pressuring me into going to Ohio. He's controlling my life."

"Do you want to go to Ohio state?" I question, biting my lip.

"It's a great school from what I have seen, and it'll get me as far away as possible from my dad," He laughs out causing me to crack a smile.

"If you don't want to do football then don't, but go to Ohio and do something else, you'll be eighteen soon and he can't do anything or tell you anything," I shrug. "I personally think he shouldn't make you do anything now, you're your own person, Keaton, you decide what you want your future to be."

"So, she does have a heart," Keaton jokes in which I glare at him.

"Not funny, I'm being serious. I've seen you work so hard and your dad still isn't happy, that's not fair."

"What's not fair is that you still won't tell me why you have this wall up between us, you won't tell me why you won't let anyone in and why you keep pushing everyone away," Keaton turns it around on me.

"It's getting late, I should get to bed for school tomorrow," I lie, it was only seven, it was too early for bed right now.

I go to get up, but Keaton grabs my arm stopping me from moving.

"Just tell me, I'm not gonna judge. I have told you a lot and you still haven't told me shit about you," His tone was soft as he lets go of my arm.

"Keaton," I start, but with a shake of his head I knew he was being serious.

I sigh out, getting comfortable on the bed again. "When my mom died, it took a toll on all three of us, my dad had to go on depression medicine and Georgie acted out on it, I was in shock the whole time and I've never been the same, a few years later, I was diagnosed with the same disease that killed my mom."

Keaton listened in, slowly nodding as I looked at him while explaining why I was so caged in.

"Everyone that my mom knew was devastated when she left, so, I promised myself that I wouldn't let anyone close to me, I stopped believing in faith when my mom died and I'll never have it, because I know when I'm gone my brother and dad is going to break, I stop people from having a broken heart, that's why I didn't want to get close to you or Winnie, but looks like your plans butted in with mine," I then add.

I stare at the door of my brother's room as Keaton and I were both silent, we both didn't know what to say. One thing good about this situation though was that it was good to finally let it out in front of someone who was an actual person and not my pillow.

"You're a teenager, Tae. High School is supposed to be the best and worst time of your life, you're supposed to go out with friends, go to prom, go to parties, do things with friends, you keep yourself in this tiny bubble that nobody can get themselves into because you're guarding it, if you do live, and you will, you're going to regret this decision of not making friends and not going out, being a kid," Keaton explains or at least tries to.

I shake my head. "See, even you don't understand."

"I do, I do get it, you think that if you don't let anyone close to you then nobody else will have to suffer and be in pain while you're gone," He states. "That just proves that you're a good person and that you're looking out for people, but you can't live in fear for people."

"They get to choose, they're going to remember how much of a beautiful person you are, inside and out. They're going to remember the best moments with you and cherish them, don't stop doing something just because fear is getting in between," Keaton adds.

Tears well up in my eyes and I curse myself and tell myself that I won't cry in front of him, especially him. I was cracking, he had found the key to this cage and broke it setting me free and exposing my truth. Stupid jock.

I laugh out of nowhere; Keaton looks at me in surprise.

"Thanks," I tell him honestly, grabbing a hold of his hand in a friendly way.

He puts his hand on top of mine and sends a charming smile.

Chapter Sixteen

"Party at mine!" Winnie's voice yells through the halls of Westside High.

Keaton sends me a look. "On Halloween?"

I shrug, and we both walk towards the redhead who was handing out flyers to students of the school. Winnie's face lights up at the sight of Keaton and I, and she hands both of us a flyer.

"Party at mine tonight, wear costumes," Winnie tells us, giving out more flyers.

I stare at the flyer that had 'WINNIE'S BIG SPOOKY BASH' at the top, I laugh at the thought of Winnie making this because of so much glitter at the bottom of the paper. I crumble the paper up and throwing it in the trash can.

Keaton nods his head toward the trash can. "You aren't going?"

"I don't go to parties," I state the obvious.

"Come on, it'll be fun," Keaton nudges me.

I fix my book bag on my shoulder. "You aren't allowed to go to parties either."

"Yeah, but Winnie's parties are always the best so I go to those and I don't drink, so that's a plus!" He thought he made the idea of going to the party better if he said he didn't drink, but how was that any better?

"I don't know..." I trail, thinking it's a bad idea.

"Come on, Tae. This will finally be something you could do to get yourself out of your comfort zone," He begs.

I roll my eyes. "Fine."

"Great! I'll be over at your house to get ready with you," Winnie cuts in, causing me to frown.

"What?"

"This is going to be your first party, isn't it? So, we can twin together at the party so you won't be uncomfortable," She explains to me and I nod.

Keaton shakes his head. "No, Winnie, don't make her wear something revealing."

"Or what? You're gonna go into a jealous rage? Stop complaining, I know she's not used to this so I'll go easy on her, but next year I'm turning you into a sexy-" As she goes to finish her sentence, Keaton's hand blocks her mouth from speaking by his hand.

"I wasn't talking about that, you know what I meant," Keaton tells her.

I watch the two fight, and that meant for me to slip away for some quiet time and go to my locker to put my things away, I grab my books for first period and once I shut my locker, Keaton and Winnie are right in front of me.

"We're done now," Winnie comments, and I nod slowly.

"Do I have to dress up at this party?" I whine but ask.

Winnie nods. "You have to dress up no buts about it."

I groan which earned a laugh from Keaton, the bell rings letting everyone know to get to class. Winnie and I split from Keaton, and we both make our way to our first period.

****

The last bell rings, I lift my head up from taking a nap. I pack my things and Winnie waits on me as usual.

"So, I was thinking that we should dress as the devil and angel," I give her a wide-eyed look as she comes up with ideas for costumes.

"Can I guess which one you'll be," Reece cuts in with a sarcastic reply, causing Winnie to glare.

I shake my head at the two, squeezing my way through the two as they argue, Keaton waits for me at the classroom door and laughs at my facial expression.

"Not funny," I growled playfully, walking in front of him as he follows behind me.

"What's something you like? Maybe I can help," He laughs out, and I pause looking him up and down at his clothes before continue walking.

"What was that?" He quickly adds.

I turn around a little. "What was what?"

"That look you gave me, you're acting like I can't dress," He complains and I bite my lip stopping me from laughing.

"Hey!" He accuses me.

"What are you dressing up as?" I question him, unlocking my locker.

Keaton leans against the lockers beside mine. "You'll just have to see tonight."

"Do you guys have practice today?" I ignore his statement, and ask him a different question.

He shakes his head. "No, it's Halloween, Coach is letting us off for the day."

"You must be happy about that," I observe at his posture. "But what are you going to do about your dad?"

"I'm just going to piss him off even more," He shrugs, and I wave my hand for him to continue.

"He's not going to be home when I go home, so he'll only see me home late tonight."

"Smart," I state sarcastically, nodding.

"Well, I should go, but I'll see you tonight and if you need me, you have my number and-" I cut him off from blabbering.

"I got it, I'll see you tonight," I give him a slight smile before watching him exit the building.

"Damn, you guys walk fast," Winnie gasps out, bending over.

I laugh out. "I'm going to text my dad really quick and let him know I'm riding with you to the house."

"Okay," She nods and I take out my phone texting my dad if it was alright if Winnie comes over and we are going to her party.

A few minutes later, I get a text back saying 'yes, but be careful and don't get back home late', I smile at the text and turning around to Winnie.

"Come on," I wave her out of the school.

She raises an eyebrow. "He said yes?"

"Mhm," I nod.

"Thank god."

"Let's get to work," She adds.

When we get to my house, we go straight to my room, Winnie looks around at my eighty's style room and she nods in impressment.

"So, I take it you really like old time things," She observes and I chuckle but nod.

"I do," I tell her, sitting down on my bed.

"Why don't you dress like an eighty's girl?" She asks me and I think about it for a moment.

Maybe that wouldn't be so bad.

"Sure," I then say.

"Great, do you have any leggings?" She asks and I nod.

"What for?" I question.

She smirks. "You're going to be in a sexy eighty's workout outfit."

My eyes widen and I knew this was only going to cause trouble.

An hour later, I was in a colorful work out outfit, I looked like I came straight from an eighty's movie. My dirty blonde hair was pulled back in a high bun and was teased to make it puffy. What looked to be a one-piece bathing suit over some tights and some tennis shoes.

Winnie applied eyeshadow on my eyelids which was a pop color, I looked in the mirror at myself feeling a different person. I turn around at Winnie.

"Are you not dressing up?"

She nods. "I will once I get to my house, but you look amazing, Tae."

"It was all you," I state, smiling.

"Yeah, but with your looks makes this outfit so much better."

I give her a smile before looking at the time.

"Okay, let's head to mine so I can get ready," Winnie cuts me in my thoughts.

I raise an eyebrow. "Who's getting your house ready?"

"My mom, I would never have her make her decorate, I'd do it all myself, but she insists," She shrugs and I shrug after her.

We leave my house and head for Winnie's, if I knew I was going to feel poor around Winnie, I would've been prepared. The gates to Winnie's house open slowly, letting her huge house come in view.

I stare at her house in awe as she parks in the thick driveway.

She stares at me in confusion. "What?"

"Your house-" I start.

"It's too little isn't it?" She freaks outs, rushing out of the car taking a look at the huge mansion like house.

"No, not even close," I close the car door behind me, staring up at the beautiful house.

She sighs. "Okay."

I watch Winnie walk towards her house and think, maybe Lydia is jealous of Winnie, maybe she was just being Winnie's friend because Winnie is rich.

Winnie never once acted like a rich snob, she was and is always polite to me, I don't think there's one mean hair on her body.

Except when it comes to Lydia.

"Come on," I hear Winnie who was already at her door with it open.

"Sorry," I shake my head, heading inside of the house.

Walking inside the house almost made me pass out, seeing Winnie's mom, Bonnie, standing with a guy that was decorating the ceiling sees us and greets us.

"I'm so glad you guys are here, Tae, wow, your costume is so awesome," Bonnie compliments me.

I blush. "Thank you, Mrs. Adams, your house is lovely."

"What did I say about calling me Mrs. Adams? Call me Bonnie," She demands in a playful tone.

I nod before Winnie pulls me upstairs by my arm and takes me to her room, which was anyone's dream room, her bedroom looked like a big cloud.

"I love your room, " I commented, and she smiles.

"Thanks, but I love yours better," She states, looking through her closet.

"What do you think about dressing up as?" I ask her, sitting down on her fluffy bed.

"I don't know if I want to go as a sexy vampire, or sexy biker," She contemplates.

"Still sexy though right?"

"Very," She looks back at me with a wink.

****

Winnie decides to go with sexy biker and leave sexy vampire for next year, I on the other hand as she was getting ready was playing games on my phone while making myself comfortable on her bed. By the time she got done getting ready, it was already time for the party to start, the doorbell rings letting us know that people were here.

"Where is your mom when this is all going to happen?" I ask Winnie who was sliding her boots on.

"Out with some friends," She shrugs, sliding on her glasses. "You ready?"

I nod, feeling the nervous bubbles form inside me.

"If it gets too much for you tell me and I'll stop the party," She tries to make me feel better.

"Or I could just leave and let you continue the party?" I laugh out awkwardly and she waves me off.

"That too..." She trails, opening her bedroom door and running down the steps to open the front door.

As I see people walking in, I run towards the bathroom to give myself a breathing check and then I could head out. I hear the music start playing and I lean my hands against the sink.

"You got this," I whisper to myself.

I look at myself one more time before opening the door of the bathroom and walking out and running into someone. Wow, what a great start to tonight.

"Shit, sorry!" I apologize quickly, before looking up to see what surprised me.

Keaton whistles before checking me out. "If I knew you were going to be this hot, I would've brought a mat for us."

I give him a blank stare. "This is a workout outfit, not a yoga outfit."

"Same thing," He fights back.

True.

"Still... not funny," I cross my arms, walking down the stairs.

"It wasn't supposed to," He says, mocking me by crossing his arms while following in behind me.

I roll my eyes. "Was it supposed to turn me on?"

"No..." He trails, looking out in the crowd that was dancing.

He might be good at football but he sure is a sucky liar.

"But you do look good," He compliments me, getting too close to my ear.

Which wasn't the weird thing, the weird thing was that I liked it.

"Thanks, you too, and I don't even know what you are," I laugh out at the end.

"So do I, all I did was found some glow in the dark paint and applied it on it me and boom," He points to his face at where the glow in the dark paint was.

"What's the leather jacket for?" I ask him, and he shrugs in reply.

"Thought it looked cool," He explains.

"I like your jersey jacket better on you," I tell him truthfully, which the leather jacket didn't look bad on him, I don't think anything would look bad on him, but his jersey jacket was what fit him.

It was made for him.

"And I think no clothes looks better on you," He chuckles as he bites his lip.

I push at his chest which only makes him laugh, and then his next step was what made everything change.

He grabs my arm when I pushed at his chest, pulling me closer to him. It felt like a yank more than a pull, my chest was against his, Keaton's face that was once a smiling goof was now a serious jock.

I pull away quickly, my heart racing to the max. My cheeks turned red as a tomato, I stood there in shock as he stares at me with the same expression. I turn around quickly and with fast steps I walk away from him with him calling out behind me.

A boy with a leather jacket that looked the same as Keaton's but his hair was slicked back blocks me from entering the kitchen.

"Hey, I'm Quentin," He holds out his hand for me to hold, but I don't bother touching it.

As I go to walk around him, he grabs my waist, pulling me toward him so that my backside would meet his front side and his hand slipped down my stomach then to my private area.

"Stop! It's not funny," I yell at him, trying to pull myself away from Quentin.

He cups my private area through my tights which causes me to go in panic mode, I see Keaton coming towards me from where I'm standing but it gets blurred as I watch Quentin get pulled away from me and is on the ground.

"What the fuck was that? Huh?!" Keaton screams into Quentin's scared face.

Landon and Reece were right beside Keaton the whole time, was this a guy thing? Did guys normally do this when they're in a fight?

I look to my right to see Winnie beside me holding my hand and I jump in fear, but my heart said another thing. Keaton was taking up for me, that boy had touched me in a place he shouldn't have and Keaton is now hurting him for it.

I place my shaky hands on Keaton's shoulders. "Keaton, it's okay."

"Why the hell are you touching her for?" Keaton screams again and ignoring what I said.

Quentin shakes his head. "I'm sorry dude, I didn't know she was taken."

"Don't mess with any girl like that unless they want you too, and clearly she didn't," Keaton slings the him off to the floor in front of all his friends.

Landon and Reece stood behind Keaton to make sure that all the other guy's friends knew he wasn't alone. Winnie's hands were on my shoulders squeezing them in reassurance.

"I best not see any of you bitches at any of the parties I go to, because I won't hesitate to snap each one of your heads off," Keaton snarls out, pointing at them.

My head felt queasy and all I wanted to do was go home, I didn't want to be here anymore and I sure didn't want to be around an angry Keaton. As I could see from where I was standing, Keaton's bottom lip was bleeding from where Quentin hit him.

"I think I'm going to be sick," I tell Winnie who nods, running me upstairs to the bathroom.

She lets me have space as she waits outside, or at least I think she is. I dump the remaining food that I ate today in the toilet while letting tears from my eyes fall down on my face. Music played in the background letting me know the party was still on.

I check the time on my phone, seeing that it was nine, I wipe my eyes, I wanted to call my dad and tell him to pick me up, but I didn't want to make him worry.

I hear a soft knock on the door already knowing that it was Winnie.

"Tae, Keaton wants to speak with you," Her soft tone voice spoke through the door and I sigh out.

"I don't want to see him right now," My voice came out a quiver and I hear hard knocks on the door.

"Tae, let me in, I wanna see if you're alright," Keaton now says through the door.

"I'm fine, Keaton," I yelled out in frustration.

I hear another hit to the door. "I gotta see for myself."

I don't say anything else because I was too busy throwing up, seeing that blood and an angry Keaton just didn't mix well to my stomach. I then hear a click of the bathroom door opening and then it shuts, I hold my hand out to try to stop him walking towards me, but he wasn't listening.

He takes a hold of my hand that was up in the air and brings it down toward him as I leaned against the toilet. He holds a piece of my hair just in case I have to throw up against.

"This is embarrassing," I comment, wiping under my eyes to see no sign of crying so that was a good sign.

One rule is to never cry in front of a boy because that could lead them thinking that you're weak, and that's how they can control you.

"I don't care, I wanted to see if you're okay," He replies, and I wipe my mouth for any throw up I had on it.

"Why couldn't Winnie come in?" I ask him.

"She's not a fan of puke, plus I demanded to see you first," His soft tone was music to my ears, I stare at the cut on his lip which caused him to bite his bottom lip keeping me from seeing it.

"I'm sorry you had to see that," He apologizes.

I shake my head. "You helped me, thank you."

"I'll always be here for you, I care about you, Tae," My eyes widen at his choice of words and I was waiting on him to correct himself but he never did.

He stands up before reaching out for me. "Let me take you home."

"Okay," I nod, letting him do what he wanted because I was in his hands now.

Chapter Seventeen

Tae's Pov.

Yesterday was a mess, I knew when we got to school that everyone was going to be talking about the party and how Keaton punched a guy for the Coach's daughter. I just hope my dad didn't see. Everyone today had their phones out and was staring at me as I pass by them.

I knew going to that party was going to be a bad idea.

Ever since I met Keaton and started hanging around him and Winnie everything has changed, some good and some bad, it's not like that I don't like hanging around them because I do, I just don't want drama going around. I walk the halls of Westside High with my head held low, this morning was worse than this, I couldn't count how many phones Mr. Pine had to take from students that were looking at the video that was going viral all-around school.

But we all knew that Keaton was the king of this school and anything that he did everyone would know.

Stacking folders in my locker, I shut it after I get done and I wished I had not. Keaton stood there in his almighty self.

"You're famous, who knew," My sarcasm never went dull talking with him.

He rolled his eyes playfully. "It'll go away soon."

"I just don't want my dad to see it," I look around to see oncoming lookers which makes me feel uncomfortable.

"Don't worry about it, if he does then he'll know nothing happened because I stopped the guy."

"True..." I trail, then hearing the sound of the bell ringing.

"I'll see you at lunch," Keaton states. "And you're joining me and my friends for lunch."

"Aye aye captain," I salute him, before heading towards my class.

"Tae, wait up!" I hear the most unwanted person I wanted to hear.

Lydia Brock, struts up toward me. "Have fun at the Halloween party last night?"

"Yeah, lots," I try to move around her to get to class because I don't have time for her lecture.

Her hand grabs my arm and I stare at it in disgust. "I bet you were so happy that Keaton swooped in and saved you from Quentin."

"Yes..." I trail, trying to get away again, but her grip tightened on me.

"I want you to know, Keaton's mine. I don't care what you think or how you think it, he's mine, if I see you hanging around him, I'll make your life a living hell and I'll mess up your reputation just like I did with Winnie's," She lectures me which I was wanting to get away from.

"Too bad I don't have a reputation to keep up like you," I give her a sarcastic smile.

She smiles right back; the sarcasm was clear in sight. "I will find something on you, Tae Lambert, I *always* do."

"Stay on my good side," She adds before strutting off.

I shake my head kicking myself in reality, before rushing to class.

In between classes, I couldn't help but think about what Lydia said, she always found a way to get me in trouble, what if she does the same thing to me that she done to Winnie? What if she somehow finds out that I'm sick? I couldn't let that happen, I didn't need the humiliation, I didn't need the pity, I didn't need the fake lies, and I really didn't need the drama.

Was it best if I stay away from Keaton? *No.*

Was I going to try to stay away from him? *Yes.*

****

Lunch came around and that was the least of my worries, I knew if I didn't go sit with Keaton he would come after me, so I could only do the simplest thing. Sit in the girl's restroom. I know I was acting dumb and I shouldn't be scared of Lydia, but I couldn't chance it.

It was fun while it lasted, at least I got to know someone, which didn't last long.

It wasn't going to work anyways; Winnie needed a friend that was loyal and that was always going to be here. Keaton, God, I don't know what's happening between us.

I take out my sketch book to kill out time, the door of the bathroom opens and I freeze. Slow steps walk toward my stall, and a soft knock on the stall was heard.

"Tae, why aren't you at lunch?" Winnie's voice echoes through the bathroom.

I sigh out. "I-I-"

I didn't know what to say, I didn't really have an excuse.

"Are you on your period? Did you bleed through?" She asks me and I try hard not to laugh at how she asked me.

The bathroom door opens loud and Winnie sighs in frustration.

"We are having a conversation, that is so rude, Keaton," Winnie screeches. "And you're not supposed to be in the girl's bathroom."

"You're not supposed to go in the guy's locker room and bathroom but you still do to get dick, so please, don't come at me," Keaton sarcastically taunts.

"You better thank your mama for giving you good looks because I would punch you right now," Winnie replies.

The door of the bathroom opens again and I sigh out wondering who was this.

"So, we're going to start hanging out in the bathroom now?" Reece asks, then I hear a hit.

"Tae started her period, shut up," I facepalmed myself, and I hear Keaton sigh.

"I'm out," I hear Reece say before leaving the bathroom.

I roll my eyes before unlocking the bathroom stall and exiting it, Winnie turns around and Keaton connects eyes with me.

"I didn't start my period," I state, flinging my book bag over my shoulder.

Winnie walks closer to me to where we were almost touching lips. "Are you pregnant?"

"What?!" Keaton and I both exclaimed.

"Is that why you've been acting weird? And that's why you threw up at the party last night? Who's the baby daddy?" Winnie questions kept coming one after another.

I shake my head in confusion. "What? No-"

"It's okay, a lot of girls get pregnant at sixteen and I'll be there through every step of the way, did your baby daddy leave you? Keaton can be your new one," She points back at Keaton who was raising his eyebrow.

"I'm not pregnant, Winnie," I facepalm myself.

Her face goes confused. "You're not?"

"No, she's not, how would she be pregnant when she doesn't talk to anyone?" Keaton states the obvious.

I nod in agreement with Keaton. "I've never even kissed a guy."

Winnie's face then goes shocked with a shocked Keaton as well.

I groan out as I realized I said that out loud. "Just pretend I never said that."

"Hell no, I can't believe you've never had your first kiss," Keaton laughs out.

I cross my arms, giving him a glare. "I'm sorry that I don't go around kissing a lot of guys and letting them get into my pants."

Keaton chokes on his laugh and I walk around the red head and the stupid jock, not feeling like getting made fun of today.

"I was just joking, Tae," Keaton defends himself.

I turn around with my arms still crossed. "Really?"

"No, I'm sorry," He laughed out, and I smile at him in sarcasm.

And this is why everything is going back to the way it was before, no more Keaton, no more Winnie, won't have to deal with Lydia nor her puppet.

Chapter Eighteen

Tae's Pov.

Pulling back the curtains in my room letting the sun seep through my balcony doors, I take a deep breath in and close my eyes. How much I missed my mom would always cross my mind, I missed her to death and I can still hear her laugh in my ears when I picture her.

I wanted to go up in the attic to find the self-tapes mom always used to do, to remind us of how much Georgie and I have grown. *Georgie.* I missed him as well, even though he wasn't gone, he was gone from this house and that was what it took for me to break.

"Knock, Knock," I hear my dad knocking on my door before entering in.

I turn around greeting in my dad. "How are you so chirpy in the mornings?"

"Three cups of coffee will do the right trick," He replies, and I shake my head at the thought.

"There goes your butt hole for today..." I trail, chuckling.

"Coffee doesn't make me poop though," He says in confusion.

I scrunch my nose. "I was joking, god, dad."

"Sorry," He holds his hands up in surrender.

"By the way, I meant to ask, what happened to our morning jogs?" I hear myself ask as I zip up my backpack and sling it around my shoulder.

As I turned around to look at my dad, I happen to see his facial expression in which was a frown.

"I thought you hated the morning jogs?" He raises his eyebrow.

"I do, but that doesn't mean I'm not curious as to why we don't do it anymore..." I trail off, crossing my arms.

"Well, I've been doing them every morning without you because I thought you should get some rest," He shrugs and I gape at him in shock.

"You never cared about me resting! Are you running with someone else instead of me?!" I accused, causing my dad to shake his head.

"Of course, not..." I see him hesitate.

I shake my head in disgust. "You cheater, don't talk to me."

I put my hand in his face before walking off and out of my room, freshly fit for the day and head outside waiting on my dad to walk out to get in the truck.

How dare he go running by himself or with someone else?! Is this his way of telling me I was too slow? Or that he was tired of jogging? Okay, maybe I'm over exaggerating a bit.

I hear my dad's truck unlock letting me know my dad was about to come out of the house, so I hop in getting buckled.

As my dad gets in, I ask him. "Still haven't spoken to Georgie?"

"No..." He states, reaching for his seat belt.

"We haven't seen or spoken to him in forever and you're acting like it's normal?!" I exclaimed, slouching in the seat as we roll off toward the high school.

I see my dad shrug in the corner of my eye. "The kids busy, Tae, He is in college. And when he's ready to call us, we'll answer."

"How-" I begin to say but a boy and his dad running catches my eye.

What in the world was Keaton and Mr. Davis doing late running when it's almost time for school? Keaton was never late to school; I wonder what's going on at his house.

"Dad..." I trail, biting my lip.

"Yeah?"

"You know what's going on with Keaton at home?"

He looks at me before looking back at the road being in a confused state. "Yes, why? Do you?"

"I heard it's not pretty good," I comment, playing with my fingers.

"Yeah, but that's not our business, it's theirs," He scolds causing me to nod.

My dad pulls into the school, dropping me off at the entrance and driving away to park in the back. I open the school doors letting that stinky smell of rotten high school.

As I try to reach my locker Lydia pops up in front of me, my shoulders fall and my face forms into a frown.

She hands me a paper with a big football on it and some writing. "Football game is this Friday, hope to see you there."

She sends me a fake smile, under that fake smile was a dark, evil soul lying, just waiting to be revealed. I couldn't stand the girl. Of course, don't forget her puppet Mandy following her around.

I crumble the piece of paper before attempting to throw the paper away in the trash but failing miserably and make it to the floor.

"Nice aim," I heard a voice call out, I turned around to see that it was none other than Reece.

I ignore his fake nice gesture and continue unlocking my locker and stuffing my things inside.

"So, I get it that you're not a people person," Reece was closer this time, he was right next to me.

I smile sarcastically. "You think?"

"Woah, spit in fire. I'm being nice," The buff boy holds his hands up.

I roll my eyes. "Since when are you nice?"

"Every day," He leans in while telling me.

"Mhm, and this is me telling you nicely to leave me alone," I nod at him, slinging my book bag over my shoulder before slamming my locker shut and not wasting any time into walking around the guy that just wanted to get laid and head to my first class.

Entering Mr. Pine's class, I had one priority to do. And that was to not sit beside Winnie, I knew I was going to hurt her feelings by not speaking to her or sitting next to her, but I don't think this friendship or whatever you called Winnie and I would work.

I needed to focus on getting better rather than messing with the popular kids, all they were going to do was them end up getting hurt from me being gone. Students file into class and I knew the red head was going to be here soon, I just had to wait a few more minutes. One minute after another Winnie's figure pops in the class and she gives me a confused look as to why I was sitting next to the gothic kid that nobody sat nearby.

She tried to mouth something to me, but I look away and just in time Mr. Pine walks in a hurry, fixing his tie and yelling out to the class to take their seats. I sigh in relief but also regret, this was going to be one long day.

****

After the first period, I had run out of class just before Winnie could catch up with me. Second period I avoided everyone as usual and the rest of the classes I did the same. I knew lunch was going to be hard, but I was going to Mrs. Hyde's room this time.

No more hiding.

"Hey come in, Tae," Mrs. Hyde orders me in which I comply.

I sit down in front of her desk and she leans forward in her seat. "How come I didn't see you yesterday?"

"Decided to spend my lunch in the bathroom," I tell the truth, because honestly lying wasn't going to get me anywhere.

She raises an eyebrow. "The bathroom? That's gross, why the bathroom?"

"Wanted to get away from all the craziness," I shrug and she nods.

"I noticed that you've been hanging around Keaton a lot," She states and I nod.

I sigh. "Yeah, not anymore though."

"Why? He's a good kid," She exclaims.

"You know how I feel about the friend thing," I cross my arms, looking away from her pointed look.

I hear her sigh. "Is this really how you want your high school to be like?"

I shrug not saying a word.

"Please don't keep doing this to yourself, Tae, you need to enjoy your high school times," She scolds and I keep quiet.

Mrs. Hyde finally gives up on the friend talk with me and eats lunch with me in her office as we talk about her life and of course me complaining about Georgie not calling. It felt good going back to the way things were.

But did I somewhat miss Winnie and Keaton? *Yes.*

Was I making a mistake. *Sure was.*

Chapter Nineteen

Tae's Pov.

"Good morning?" I jump at the sound of my dad's voice.

Turning around, I find my dad giving me a confused look, I slide his everyday morning coffee to him that I freshly made and give him a smile.

"Good morning" I hum out to him, placing a piece of food in my mouth.

"Why are you up so early?" He asks, giving me a skeptical look.

I raise an eyebrow at him. "Can't I give my lovely father some coffee and live in peace?"

"Cut the act, what's up-no wait, what do you want?" He gives me a pointed look.

"Nothing," I shrug, putting my dirty plate in the sink.

He gives me the same look and I held my hands up in surrender.

"Seriously, I don't want anything," I defend myself.

He nods. "Okay fine, I believe you."

"I'm going to Winnie's mom's library," I explain, earning a weird look from my dad.

"Will Keaton be there?" He questions and I shake my head.

"I don't think so, but I have to see Winnie and apologize to her."

He crosses his arms. "What'd you do?"

Everything. I knew I was going to regret avoiding her. Wow, one day and I can't even get passed avoiding her and I feel bad.

"I ignored her the whole day yesterday which I feel really bad for, she tried talking to me but I ghosted her completely," I get confused at myself for feeling bad for being rude to Winnie.

"Tae, you've got to stop cutting people out of your life, Winnie's a good girl, she may not have the best reputation, but she seems sweet to me," I roll my eyes at the statement my dad made.

Winnie reputation? Was he talking about the drug incident?

I didn't want to tell my dad about something Winnie told me, what she told me was meant to be a secret. Or at least I think it is.

"Well, can you drive me to Bonnie's library? Winnie will probably give me a ride unless she doesn't want to talk to me," I ask him, overthinking the talk that I was about to have with Winnie.

He nods. "Yeah, sure. But if you need me, be sure to call me."

"Yes sir," I salute him, before we both head out of the front door with my backpack in hand and hopping in the pickup truck.

After a few minutes of driving down the little roads of our town, my dad pulls up in front of the tiny library, Winnie's mom has tried so hard to keep it up from it being so old. I wave to my dad and he leaves in a roar.

"I don't know if I want to paint this light pink or dark brown? What do you think, Winnie?" I hear Bonnie ask Winnie as I walk into Bonnie's library.

Stepping foot in here again felt weird but also good, I loved reading, but I never did once check out a book from here.

"I like the light pink," Winnie replies back to her mom.

Bonnie looks toward me which shocks me that she knew I was here. "What do you think, Tae?"

"Uh..." I trail as Winnie turns around smiling softly.

"I like the light pink," I add.

"Great, I'll put that down," Bonnie says, before leaving the room to go write something down like she said.

Winnie raises her eyebrow at me. "What are you doing here?"

"I wanted to apologize for how I treated you yesterday," I begin. "I should've never ignored you without explaining myself."

"What was wrong yesterday?" She questions, crossing her arms.

"Lydia came up to me the other day and said some things, I overthink and that's why I ignored you. I'm new to this whole friendship thing and-" I go to finish what I was about to say, but I get interrupted when Winnie gives me a bone crushing hug.

You would think I was lying when I say that her hair smells like cherries.

"Whatever Lydia says is a lie, she's full of shit, she even eats it for breakfast," Winnie jokes causing me to giggle.

We both pull away from the hug.

"If you ever get confused or if she says anything to you, come to me. I'll roundhouse her ass," She then adds, and I cover my mouth to stop me from laughing.

And I thought I was dead set on ignoring this girl.

I look at the time on my phone to see it was almost time to get to school. "Can you give me a ride to school?"

"Yeah, let me tell my mom bye and we'll head out," She states and I nod.

As Winnie goes to the back to say bye to her mom, Bonnie steps out of the backroom.

"I gotta go, mom, but I'll come back after school," Winnie tells her mom who looks back at me with a smile.

"Okay, you girls be safe while driving in that car," Bonnie instruct us to do. "Oh! And tell Keaton I said Hey."

I raise an eyebrow at her as she stares in my direction while telling us, she winks at me and Winnie comes to my rescue when she pats my back instructing me to leave the building. Winnie and I leave her mother's library and make it towards the school.

Winnie walks beside me while I head towards my locker to gather my things, she crosses her arms and looks off in the hall at the students passing.

She sighs. "You know what I miss?"

"What?" I look up at her as she looks the other way.

"Cheer..." She trails, nodding at what's in front of her.

I raise an eyebrow and look behind me to exactly what she's looking at, Lydia with the cheer team, strutting down the hall acting like they owned the place, I roll my eyes at the sight and look back at Winnie.

"So, you can't try out at all this year?" I ask her, thinking of how there could be some way she could get out of this.

"Even if I did, Lydia would try to make my life a living hell," She frowns at me.

"Hello teacher's pet and hello drug head," Lydia greets us and I have to bite my tongue from saying anything smart to her.

Winnie moves forward and before she could lay a hand on Lydia, I pull her back, I give her a warning look and in return she retreats and looks away. Lydia looks Winnie up and down with a 'humph', and walks off with a smirk plastered on her face.

"I want to rip her to shreds," Winnie growls lowly and I frown.

"Don't stoop down to her level, she's not worth getting expelled."

"Woah, what happened to you?! Look, your face matches your hair now," Reece's tries to jokes but no one around laughed.

Landon gives Winnie a concerned look. "What's up?"

Winnie grumbles looking off and away from us and Landon turns his head toward me and gives me the same questioning look.

I shrug. "Lydia."

"I should've known," He sighs but laughs in between. "I was wondering if you've seen Keaton?"

I furrow my eyebrows in confusion. Why would he be asking me this? Wasn't he best friends with Keaton and knew where he was at all times?

"Not since yesterday, why?" I answer, raising an eyebrow.

"He hasn't replied to any of my calls and I didn't see him in the parking lot where we usually meet," He replies and I shrug in response.

"Maybe he woke up late?" I tell him in question and he shrugs after.

I kept getting weird looks from Reece, but from which I ignore because I don't pay ignorant people attention.

"Yeah, but that's not like Keaton to get to school late, if he ever was his dad would kill him," Winnie comments, looking concerned.

"Anything could've happened, I mean, Keaton doesn't need to be perfect all the time," I tell her, then hearing Reece scoff.

I was confused, did Reece have a problem with me?

"If he doesn't show up today then one of us can go check up on him at home," Landon nods at all of us.

"He's probably fine guys, I think you're overreacting a bit. He's probably at the school right now in some class to get there early," Reece butts in and I nod agreeing.

"Okay..." Winnie trails off, worry was clear in her voice.

We all split away from each other to get to our classes when the bell rings, we spend the whole day learning and getting lectured about stuff we needed and stuff we would never even use in our jobs in the future, the last bell rings for the end of the day and Keaton still didn't show up.

I wasn't too worried about it, but Winnie currently was on edge about the situation.

I sling my backpack over my shoulders and heading towards my locker.

"Can you ask your dad if you can come with me to Keaton's?" Winnie's voice enters my ears causing me to jump and close my locker.

"Will Keaton's parents be there?" I ask, not wanting to meet anymore parents right now.

She shrugs. "Most likely."

"Yeah, nope," I deny her request for me to go with her.

No way was I meeting Keaton's parents.

Winnie follows me down the halls begging me to go with her, until we're outside the building.

"Oh, come on, Tae, don't you wanna know what's happening with him?"

I shake my head. "Not really, no."

"Oh please," She scoffs, crossing her arms.

"Oh, please nothing, he's probably sick or something. Besides you can go by yourself, you do it almost every day," I explain, leaning against the railing waiting for my dad.

"Yeah, but I don't want to go alone if his dad is being rough on him," She comments and I raised an eyebrow.

"What do you mean by being rough on him?"

"Like screaming and stuff..." She trails, playing with her bracelets on her wrist.

Liar.

"I'll go, but we better not stay for long," I warned and she smiles.

"Promise," She nods.

My dad soon exits the school with his binder in one hand and his gym bag in the other, giving me a smile.

"How was today?" My dad asks and I shrug.

"Like every other day," I reply. "Winnie wants me to go to Keaton's house to check up on him and I was going-"

"Go," My dad cuts me off short.

I furrow my eyebrows growing confused that he let me go so quickly, is he running a fever?

"Okay, I won't be back home late," I promise him and he nods before kissing my forehead.

"Just be careful, blondie," He warns and I salute him.

"Thanks, Mr. Lambert," Winnie calls out as we walk closer to her car.

He waves goodbye to us and soon we head off toward Keaton's home, or should I say mansion.

Did Winnie nor Keaton tell me that they were rich? Because I think they left that part out.

Well of course Keaton's rich, that's why they call him the golden boy.

Winnie parks her car in the driveway before cranking it off and turns toward me.

"Before we go in there, I should warn you that his parents are very intimidating," Winnie states and I look back up to the house.

"I feel really poor right now," I tug at my clothes and Winnie laughs.

We get out and I shut her car door with shaky hands, nervousness bubbles within me as Winnie knocks on the two big doors of the house. A woman with long blonde hair with a smile on her face answers the door.

"Winnie, hi! Nice to see you again," The women says to Winnie in which they both hug.

"Julie, this is my friend, Tae," Winnie greets me to who I'm guessing is Julie who is probably Keaton's mom.

Julie smiles at me. "Oh, so this is Tae."

I smiled awkwardly, but confused that she knew who I was.

"Keaton talks a lot about you," Julie tells me and I blush.

"Speaking of Keaton, where is he?" Winnie asks and Julie points up to the stairs.

"In his room, him and his father had a disagreement and things got ugly," Julie replies.

I frown and so does Winnie.

Julie lets us come inside the house and I'm mind blown at how big it was, chandeliers hung from the ceiling at which I awed at.

"Tae, you should go up first and then I'll come in after you," Winnie states and I nod.

Why does it have to be me?

"His room is the first door on the left," Julie explains and I thank her quietly before walking up the steps taking my time.

I stop at the door, Julie told me where Keaton's room was, inside I was hoping that he wasn't in the room but a little part of me was hoping he was. I knock once, then twice getting no answer, I furrow my eyebrows before looking around and shrugging before grabbing a hold of the doorknob.

"Keaton?" I call out, cracking his door open slightly, too scared I might see a naked Keaton. "Can I come in?"

I get no answer so I enter the room anyways not caring if I was going to see something, I close the door behind me and I lean on it as I find Keaton sitting on his bed shirtless with his head in his hands keeping him up on his knees.

As I get a closer look, I see bruises on his shoulders and all up his arm. I get a full view of his room which looked just like how I imagined it was, but it was all messed up and cluttered, his bookshelf was on the ground and books scattered on the floor. Clothes were also scatter across the floor with his shoes.

I look back to Keaton to see him staring back at me, I give him a worried look and walk slowly toward the bruised and broken boy.

"What happened?" I ask him, looking around the room once more.

"My dad and I had a fight..." He trails, staring down at the floor.

"Like an argument? Because this looks like a fist fight to me," I point to his body before pointing at his messy room.

"It looks that bad?" He asks, choking on his own words.

I shake my head clearly lying and he looks at me like he doesn't believe me.

"So, this is why you weren't at school?" I ask.

With a shake of his head, I knew it was more than that.

"I didn't go to school to make my dad pissed and he went psycho on me," Keaton explains, licking his lips.

He had no expression on his face, I was clearly surprised that his dad would go this far to hitting him. This was uncalled for.

"I'm so sorry, Keaton," I slightly touch his arm making sure I wouldn't cause him any pain. "I can't believe he hit you."

"I can," He retorts, laughing slightly.

"Does your mom know about this?" I ask referring at how calm his mom was.

He shakes his head. "What can my mom do? My dad owns her, if she tried to leave, she couldn't take me because he's the one with the money."

I shake my head. "There has to be a way out of this, you're staying at mine tonight and no buts, just tell your dad that you're sleeping over at Landon's or something."

"You're so caring, Tae. Why do you try to hide it?" He smirks, leaning in close.

I awkwardly back up and stared into his eyes seeing that they were bloodshot red, I was wondering if he was drunk or high.

"Are you drunk?" I hear myself ask, giving him a confused stare.

He shrugs. "I might be a little buzzed."

"Oh, well-" He interrupts me when he slips a piece of my hair behind my ear earning butterflies to spread all over my stomach.

He moves a little closer and I watch his eyes switch to my eyes then my lips.

I push his chest a little. "Keaton..."

"Don't push me away, please," He pleads with me as he tries to move closer but I wasn't having it.

He was trying to kiss me, and I didn't know how to act so I do what everyone would've done in that situation, I pushed him with all my might away from me. I get up from the bed with panic filling within me, I shake my hands off like they were wet, trying to fan myself.

Is it hot in here or is it just me?

"What the hell, Tae?" Keaton stands up from the bed.

I turned around to look at him. "No! I should be what the helling at you, why would you try to kiss me when I specifically wanted to be your friend?"

"I'm sorry, I can't be friends with you, I've-" As he goes to say what I know he's about to say I stop him.

I shake my head. "Don't. We're friends, Keaton."

He goes silent and I go to leave his room before hearing his voice.

"Tae, don't leave, please. I'm sorry-" The door slamming shut, shut out his voice and I race down the stairs.

Winnie sits talking with Keaton's mom and I give her a pleading look of 'let's get the hell out of here' her eyes go wide before she says something to his mom and stands up.

I put on a fake smile as I greet Keaton's mom again. "Thanks again for letting me talk with Keaton, your house is lovely, but I have to get home before my dad freaks."

"Thank you for coming, Tae. I'm so glad I got to finally meet you, Keaton talks a lot about you, he just adores you," Mrs. Davis tells me causing me to blush.

"And Winnie, it was so good to see you again. You both come see me again, yeah?" She adds and I nod.

As Winnie and I both head out the door, I hear a faint yell out for me, I knew it was Keaton who was calling for me, I shake my head at Winnie who was going to turn around to talk to him but seen my face.

"What happened?" She asks as we hurriedly get into her car.

I shake the feeling off before explaining. "He tried to kiss me that's what happened."

"What?!" She yelled, with wide eyes.

"Can we go?" I plead with my eyes and she nods before backing out of Keaton's driveway.

"What'd you do when he tried to kiss you?" I hear her question me.

I sigh. "Pushed him away."

"Oh my god," She sounded surprised, but the only one who needs to be surprised is me.

The most important thing that happened was what he was about to tell me, and why my heart felt the same.

Chapter Twenty

Tae's Pov.

Winnie places her books in front of me as I sit in the school's library, she sighs before placing her book bag on the ground beside her and sits down in front of me.

"Guess who got an A on Mr. Pine's test?" Winnie gushes and I smile.

"You?" I laugh out.

She squeals. "Me."

"I'm proud, now Mr. Pine won't irritate you anymore about your grade," I tell her and she nods.

"He's a bitch," Her choice of words made the librarian look up and stare.

"Who's a bitch?" Landon's voice cuts in and Winnie's posture lightens and her cheeks flare red.

"Mr. Pine," Winnie answers.

Landon nods then looks over at me. "Someone's been looking for you."

I roll my eyes at the thought.

"Who? Keaton?" Winnie asks and Landon nods, reaching his arms around her shoulders.

"I'm easy to find," I shrug, bouncing my leg up and down nervously.

Landon hums before saying. "Yeah right, says the person who's been invisible for years now and just pops up when Keaton finally sees you."

Was that supposed to be offensive because I can't bother to agree.

"You can't hide from him just because he tried to kiss you," Winnie tells me.

I give her a look to be quiet but as I look at Landon's unbothered face, I knew that he knew in the beginning.

"I knew Keaton liked you from the start, he's been watching you ever since you walked into school on the first day," Landon leans forward while stating. "And here comes pretty boy now."

I freeze in my seat as Winnie and Landon look up staring at Keaton.

"Hey guys," I then hear Keaton's voice which was right beside me.

The chair beside mine scraped against the floor as Keaton plops down in it, his busted lip was looking better today, but that didn't change the fact that he tried to kiss me.

I look down at my book with my hands connected together on the table and Winnie hums while playing with her curls as Landon awkwardly sits back. I feel Keaton's eyes on me which made me feel hot, but that also could be the rain jacket I was wearing.

"So how about that game tomorrow night?" Winnie makes conversation and I smiled softly at her.

"We're totally going to win tomorrow, am I right Landon?" Keaton states, chuckling.

"Yeah," Landon says. "Will you be there Tae?"

I could tell Landon was wearing a smirk on his face at the tone of his voice, my eye twitched but I ignored his cockiness and answered.

"Probably," I answered, playing with my ponytail.

"Good, but don't be quiet this time," Winnie comments, crossing her arms.

"That was only because I didn't know you last time that good," I explain, but also because I didn't like her.

Winnie smiles. "Well now you do."

I nod, noticing Landon getting up from his seat, he has his binder in hand and grabs a hold of Winnie's hand.

"We'll see you guys later, we aren't going to the janitors closet to make out," Landon gives Keaton and I a pointed look and I beg Winnie with my eyes to not leave me alone with Keaton.

"Alright, I'll stay with Tae for a while," Keaton tells him and Winnie and Landon both head out the library leaving a silent awkward pause between the golden boy and me.

I go to pack my things until Keaton grabs my bag causing me to make eye contact with him.

"Can we talk?"

I give him a bored look. "If it's about you trying to kiss me yesterday then no."

"But we need to talk about it, talk about what happened and why it happened," Keaton pleads with me, but I shake my head.

"It's pretty simple to me, you tried kissing me, I rejected you, you got upset and yeah..." I trailed, reaching for my bag but he pulls it away fast enough.

He shakes his head. "I know that, but I didn't get to tell you why I did it, I have-"

"You don't need to tell me, please don't make it weird between us," I snatch my bag from his hand before standing up and walking quickly out of the library and into the hall with him right on my tail.

"I'm not making it weird, it's all in your head. I know you feel it too just-" He tries telling me but I cut him off short again.

"Maybe this was a mistake, maybe this whole friendship thing has gotten way too far between us," I tell him, shaking my head at the thought.

"What?! Are you being serious right now?" He asked out of disbelief.

"I'm being dead serious, stay away from me, that's what you should have done in the first place, that day that you took me to the Nurse you should've left immediately, you and I are total opposites and shouldn't be seen together," Once I get finished with what I was saying I was out of breath.

I begin to feel nauseated, and once I turn around, I find Lydia staring back at us with a frown. I roll my eyes at her not even bothering to look back and I bump shoulders against hers. I was so heated but sick feeling at the same time that I didn't even know what I was doing.

I dialed my dad's number on my phone calling to tell him that I didn't feel good, I should've known he would've told me to go to the Nurse's office, I knock on Nurse Pattie's door with a frown and as she opens the door, I let all my emotions come down.

A tear slips down my face then comes another; Nurse Pattie comes in view when the door opens and her smile turns into a frown once she sees me.

"Oh baby, what's wrong?"

She lets me in her office with open arms.

"I just feel so confused and I don't feel good and I'm crying like a baby," I wipe my eyes, explaining not that good as to why I'm crying.

"What are you confused about?" She hugs me tighter.

I sniffle. "Just stuff that's happening, new friends and drama, it's really hard and I don't know if I can take it."

"You're going to find drama anywhere, whatever you're going through right now it will all be okay because you're strong," Nurse Pattie tells me.

I smile sadly. I wish that were true.

Chapter Twenty-One

Tae's Pov.

"Do I really have to be there at the game?" I whined to my dad who was driving towards Westside High.

"Yes, Tae. you need to get out and do things," He says as he watches the road.

I cross my arm, frowning. "You never cared in the beginning."

"Yeah, but that was before..." He trails not saying anything after.

"Before..." I wave for him to continue and he sighed in return.

"I noticed how happy you looked when Winnie is around and Keaton, I know they make you happy and I don't want you to push them away," He explains and I look away from him and out of the window.

Keaton did make me happy, but until he tried to kiss me, I couldn't let us be anything but friends and obviously that's not working for him. Friends was enough, I couldn't start a relationship with someone, it was crossing the line, when you're in a relationship you care so much more to that person and if something happened to me, it breaks someone.

It'd break him.

But the other half of me was saying another thing, I hated the way my heart felt for that boy, it's funny how much I hated him in the beginning without knowing a single detail about him. Deep down I always knew Keaton had a good heart because of the way people talked about him, even his one-night stands said he'd take care of them but always instruct that it wasn't going to be anything more than that.

Word goes around quick, and if you don't know me by now, I get the juicy stuff by just sitting there listening in on someone's conversation.

My dad pulls into the packed parking lot, my face was not amused nor happy to see this place, I had a gut feeling something was going to happen tonight, good or bad, I don't care I wanted out.

I step out of my dad's truck with a frown fixing my hoodie, I look down at the outfit I was wearing already knowing that as soon as I step onto the bleachers different types of girls would be showing skins whilst there's me with a big sized hoodie on with some leggings and black converse.

I feel hands attach my shoulders; I look up to see my dad. "Something tells me you're gonna have fun tonight."

Yeah, okay.

I scoff quietly as my dad walks in front of me clearly excited for the game, crossing my arms, we get to a little table like last time with Mrs. Hyde sitting down in a chair taking money from kids who were just waiting to see the game.

Mrs. Hyde lets both My dad and I in for free since he is the coach, she waves at me and I take a seat beside her as my dad walks toward the field to get ready for the big game.

"Wow, Tae, I love this school spirit," Mrs. Hyde sarcastically states and I smile softly.

I look around as people pay for popcorn and snacks at the food stand. "I didn't want to come."

"Obviously," She observes, handing a kid a ticket and letting them into the gate.

"Go have fun, I'm sure there's someone waiting for you," She also adds.

I sigh. "I'm supposed to be meeting Winnie, I'll see you, because if I don't hunt Winnie down now, she'll hunt me."

She chuckles and nods. "Alright, I'll see you."

I stand up from the chair and make my way towards the bleachers looking for the redhead. It wasn't that hard to find really, all I'm looking for was a loud redhead cheering for Landon who was at the bottom of the bleachers staring at me.

Found her.

"I didn't think you were coming," Winnie yells over the loud music.

I look out towards the field seeing that the football players were running out and hear everyone scream. "I was trying to find a way to not come."

"Looks like your plans backfired," She laughs out and I nod.

"I could be at home right now, studying or reading a book with my little lamp slightly dim, but instead I have to be at this loud game where I can't even tell who's winning."

Winnie pats my shoulder. "And you're here with me, who could beat that?"

I give her a smile and as I do, a loud voice enters everyone's ears as the speaker calls out the school's number and their names. As I hear Keaton's number 'twelve' I pretend to yawn as he runs on the field with his gear and tell Winnie I needed to use the restroom.

As I make my way to the bathrooms, I couldn't help but turn around feeling guilty that I left for some reason, why was I feeling this way? I walk back towards Winnie and I finally notice her outfit, she had Landon's jersey shirt on with his numbers on the back and front and his last name written on the back.

Lines of burgundy and white were written on her face representing the school's colors and I laugh out at her blushing face as Landon sends a wave her way.

I wonder what it felt like to be in love with someone.

Winnie turns to me. "Do you want some?"

I was confused at first until she points to her face with the paint and I shake my head.

"Oh, come on, get in the school spirit. This is our last year and then we're seniors, we probably won't even go to the games anymore because Keaton, Landon, and Reece will be off to college," She whines while explaining and I sigh out.

"I can be in the school spirit and not have paint on my face..." I trail, crossing my arms.

"Yeah, but Keaton loves this," Her comment didn't go unnoticed to me as she turns me around giving me a warning look as I start to object, she lifts the paints toward my face applying two lines on each side of my face.

Once she's done, she looks at me with a smile and I give her a frown.

"Beautiful," She compliments. "Let's take a picture!"

I groan but comply because that's the only thing I could do, Winnie takes her phone out holding it up in the air and puckers her lips in the photo as I smile, she clicks a few before putting her phone in her pocket.

"Now isn't this fun?" She asks and I smile sarcastically.

"Best time of my life," I answer, looking at the scoreboard and couldn't read it.

She humphs and looks at the same spot as me. "Looks like we're winning."

"Go rams!" Winnie yells causing me to jump as Landon makes a touchdown.

Okay, I'm not that stupid, I at least know what a touchdown is.

Hours passed and by the end of the game I was dead tired, of course at the end of it, we won as usual and I could clearly see a smile on my dad's face as he congratulates the boys for their lucky win tonight. I smile at him as he turns around to look at me and give me a thumbs up, I was proud of the man my dad had become ever since my mom died, it literally destroyed him into pieces and he decided to start coaching to distract himself.

I hear a squeal as the football players walk through the gates that separated the field and the bleachers, Winnie like no other jumps into Landon's arms squeezing him tight in a bone crushing hug.

"I'm so proud, second win this year, how does it feel pretty boy?" She flirts with Landon as she playfully touches his chest.

He smiles, showing his pearly whites. "It feels good."

"Tae came like she said she would," Winnie says back to him pointing toward me.

His eyes shifted toward me and he gives me a smile. "Damn, I thought you were lying, but Keaton might sweep you off your feet."

My smile turns into a frown, my head whips around looking for the stupid jock, I had no idea why I was looking, maybe for reassurance that his dad isn't hurting him or screaming in his face, but my face goes sour as I watch the scene fall in front of me.

Lydia Brock doing the thing she always does, always up some boy's ass.

She flirted her heart away, but the thing that really did make my heart squeeze was when Keaton gently pushed her away, walking towards me, or maybe Landon, Winnie, and I. My eyes held my amusement when his steps got quicker till, he was jogging towards us.

Not wanting to speak to him, I tell Winnie that I was gonna head to my dad's truck and wait for him there and tell Landon congrats on the team winning, they both give me a disapproving look which I knew if they spoke, they would've said it was a bad idea running away from my problems.

I check my phone to see the time, the bright light pops, shining on my face as I walk off the grass of the school, I hear faint calls from Keaton's muscular voice and I knew he had noticed what my intentions were.

"Tae, wait! Please," Keaton pleads as my steps were quicker by each call that was seeming to get closer.

I noticed that I had forgotten where my dad had parked his pickup truck and I was walking a different way, trying to get away from the pleading boy behind me.

"Tae!" This time his call got louder but I continued to ignore him.

"Tae, wait!" Keaton calls out again, earning looks from others. "Fucking stop."

Even though I knew he was mad by the tone of his voice I still didn't stop walking away, until he had caught up with me and pulled me by my arm.

"Did you not hear me?!" His breathing was harsh and his hair was soaked with sweat from the helmet he had to wear during the game.

I nod. "I just didn't want to."

"You are unbelievable, I've put my all into trying to get to know you, I literally tried everything but you still push me away," He states, and I look away from his cold stare.

"Can we not do this here?" I whisper to him, looking around at the people who were walking past us giving us the eye.

He shakes his head. "I don't care what people say, they can talk shit all they want, but you- you need to shut up for once."

I gasp out loudly in exaggeration. "You will not talk to me with that kind of tone."

He pinches the bridge of his nose and sighs loudly.

"I like you, Tae. Hell, I really like you and you're too oblivious to know it," The three words I was dreading for him to say came out of his mouth.

My heart thudded in my chest and I could feel my cheeks burn red.

"No, you don't," I laugh out in sarcasm, lying to myself.

He licks his lips slowly nodding. "You don't get to do this; you don't get to push people away like this."

"No, what you don't get to do is tell me these things when you really don't mean them or tell me these things when I'm sick, how could you possibly think that this was a good idea?"

He steps closer to me but I step back. "I've liked you ever since I saw you on the first day of school and when I found out that you were sick, that changed nothing, I still liked you."

"I'm not doing this," I tell him, shaking my head. "Stay away from me, please."

"Stop pushing people away that want to be with you," Keaton lashes out causing me to shake my head.

I cross my arms. "I'm not pushing you; I'm telling you to stay away from me."

"Damn it Tae, you're so stubborn. You know there's actually people that want to be with you or just wants to be your friend, but it's your own fault you have no-one in your life."

"I'm doing you a favor! When I die-" He cuts me off short.

Stepping close to me, my heart starts to beat like I was going to have a heart attack, with each step he takes, I could feel my face getting redder by the minute and my whole body felt like it was on fire.

"Then do me this favor... be with me." His face was so close to mine, I could feel his heavy breathes from yelling over my lips.

I wanted to take a step back so bad, but I couldn't. My eyes found their way to his lips, licking mine in the process. One tiny step would make us fall in each other's arm and connect lips.

"Be with me, Tae."

His eyes were on mine and I couldn't help but to look around at the stares we were getting, I look back at Keaton whose eyes never left me.

"Keaton, can we please not do this?" I plead with him, feeling him come closer.

"If we don't do this now, when will we? Because every time you keep pushing me away, I'll just keep pulling you back because I'm not giving up."

My heart flutters as I hear him pour out his heart to me, it's like I had a barrier that caged me in until he came and broke it down. It's so weird that I hated him in the beginning and now I'm a mess with all these feelings flowing through me.

I feel Keaton's arm slide around my waist like a snake slowly pushing me against him, my hands were on his jersey feeling the soft material, my eyes wander down to his lips again and I nod.

It was time that I break down this barrier that was between Keaton and I, it was time for me to *forget* that I was sick, to *forget* all the negative thoughts, it was time for me to stop trying to ignore these feelings I had for Keaton, you only live once, right?

"Okay."

As soon as that one word left my lips, a smile appeared on his face and he connects his lips with mine. My hands found their way around his neck trying to pull him close as possible. His arms unwrapped themselves around me and his hands found their way to my face trying to kiss me harder.

My first kiss was now long gone and it was by the stupid jock I once hated so much. I was so confused on what to do so I went Keaton's pace.

His lips were soft, but yet smooth, tingles went through my body, first fingers, then my toes. As we let go, I was surprised and in shock from what happened, Keaton's face was in pure seriousness as he lays his forehead against mine.

I close my eyes, inhaling the scent of sweat but also mixed with his cologne, I hadn't noticed how tall Keaton was until I had looked up at him from this distance. There was no doubt that Keaton was handsome, the way his eyes swirled brown, but with a little green made my heart flutter, the way his veins pop out of his hands and arms made my knees weak, but also the way he smiled would kill me.

"I'm gonna pretend you weren't just kissing and head to my truck, once you're done Tae, I'll be in the truck waiting," My dad cuts in causing me to jump slightly and step back away from Keaton a little.

Keaton chuckles slightly staring back at my dad who was awkwardly walking to his truck, he looks back at me and I go speechless from there.

"I-I" I stutter, trying to find the words but nothing came out.

Keaton smirks. "I forgot that you haven't had your first kiss yet."

"Well now you have..." He adds.

"So, what does this mean?" I ask him, growing confused.

"It means y'all getting together or not?" Landon butts in and I blush.

Winnie wiggles her eyebrows at me before I hear Keaton. "We'll talk more about it tomorrow; Tae has to get home."

Landon takes a hold of Winnie's hand. "We'll see y'all tomorrow,"

I nod waving bye to Winnie and Keaton does the guy hand shake with Landon before the couple leaves, leaving Keaton and I silent.

"What's going to happen tomorrow?" I ask, raising an eyebrow.

Keaton sighs. "I have something planned for the both of us, but for now get in the truck before your dad steps out of it and whoops my ass."

I push his shoulder playfully causing him to chuckle but, in the midst, grabs my arm and kissing the top of my hand.

"I'll see you tomorrow, Lambert," Keaton tells me, kissing my hand once more.

I smile. "See you tomorrow, Davis."

We pull apart from each other and I step in my dad's truck feeling an awkward tension, my dad's eyes watched every move Keaton makes as he steps into his Jeep and drives off.

"I'm going to watch that boy," He makes a comment in which I roll my eyes at him.

I feel my pockets buzz, I feel for my phone succeeding to get it and take a look at the message someone sent.

Stupid Jock.

'Sleep tight, Lambert. I've got big things planned tomorrow and ones that are gonna make you pissed.'

I reply back with a smile.

To: Stupid Jock.

'No touchy feely, okay?'

Stupid Jock.

'Can't promise to keep my hands off you'

I don't reply and in a matter of seconds I get a message from him again, but instead of reading it I leave him on read, teasing him a bit.

Chapter Twenty-Two

Tae's Pov.

Monday morning class was a blur, Mr. Pine had given us a thirty-page essay to write and also a unit test next Monday morning. I sit in my second period with my head in my hand drawing circles all over my paper as the teacher lectures us. My eyes scan over the class seeing that nobody was paying attention, a girl with bubble gum in her mouth and around her finger was listening along but that was about it.

A boy with a plaid shirt on and a tattoo on the right side of his neck caught my eye as he leans back in his seat clearly not paying attention with a bore look plastered on his muscular face, suddenly his eyes caught mine and I look forward hoping he wouldn't say anything after class.

I wish Winnie was here, she would've made this more fun.

Keaton found me by my lockers this morning and what wasn't a surprise he had a smile on his face, but it looked to be a happier smile, if that makes any sense. I smile down at my paper just thinking of him, I catch movement at the classroom door, I take a closer look in which made my stomach go in a swirl of butterflies. Keaton stands at the door waving for me to go to him, I shake my head and mouth 'no' to him and in reply he pouts, poking out his bottom lip and giving me puppy dog eyes.

I huff before raising my hand in a quick move, Keaton's pout now turned into an achieving smile.

"Yes, Ms. Lambert?" Ms. Willow points toward me with a question look.

I put my hand down and ask. "May I use the restroom please?"

"Be quick," She states and I nod.

I close the reading book quietly and stand up in a hurry to get to the door, I open and shut the door as I come out. Keaton leans against the wall of the school and I glare.

"What's so important that I have to miss class?" I ask him, crossing my arms.

He bites his bottom lip. "Let's skip class."

"What?!" I exclaim in question. He couldn't be serious, the golden boy skipping school? Now, that's a sight I'd like to see.

But Keaton was the person who had a big reputation of skipping school and being the most stereotype thing, 'the bad boy'.

As I could tell his face was serious, I shake my head. "I'll get in so much trouble, Keaton."

"Just this once and I'm pretty sure no-one is gonna notice you're gone for an hour," He tries to make skipping school sound better, but I was hesitant.

He points toward the classroom I came out of and I roll my eyes.

"I told Ms. Willow that I was gonna use the restroom..." I can't believe I was actually thinking of skipping school with this boy.

"Man, I should've just walked in and told her that Mr. Myers needed you," He states and I grab his hand and pulled him away from the classroom so no one could see us.

I raise an eyebrow at him. "Are you okay? I mean, you haven't skipped school since your bad boy days."

"My bad boy days?" He chuckles out as he asks me.

"You know what I mean..."

"So, you've watched me through those years I was going through that phase?" He asks while smirking.

I smile sarcastically. "Well, when you're walking down the halls being noticeable and having Lydia over your shoulder, it's not that hard to notice you."

"Just admit it, you liked me," He falsely accuses and I scoff.

"More like hate," I walk passed him getting closer towards the doors of the school and turn around and expect to see him smiling, but gave me a questioning look.

"You coming, golden boy?" I smirk, as he runs toward me in full bull mode and I quickly open the doors running out and down the thousands of steps.

As I get down the steps my breathing becomes harsh and I bend over to get my breathing back right, I suddenly felt a hand on my back that rubs up and down and Keaton's presence stands next to me.

"You alright?" Panic was clear in his voice as he bends down the same level as me.

I look to him and smile. "Yeah, just lost my breath for a moment."

"Are you sure? You don't need me to carry you or anything like that do you?" We both stand up but Keaton still had his hand on my back giving me a caution look.

I grab his arm in reassurance. "I'm fine, I get this way when I run."

"No more running," He says in a demanding tone, but somewhere in there I knew he meant me pushing him away.

"Where'd you park your Jeep?" I ask him as we walk in the parking lot.

He points to his black Jeep that wasn't so far away. "Did you get your book bag from class?"

"I don't bring my backpack to English class, we're not allowed. Something about a fire hazard," I laugh out at Ms. Willow's paranoid Skeem.

Keaton chuckles, but nods as he presses his key button to unlock the car doors, I hop in his Jeep as he gets at the same time I do.

"Where are we going?" I make conversation, buckling up.

"Going to see our favorite..." Keaton jokes as he pulls out of the school.

I look back in nervousness since this was the first time, my dad would so kill me and I knew he would find out at some point.

"Who?" I ask him, furrowing my eyebrows.

"Ally and Tommy," He says in a 'duh' tone, I roll my eyes at him and smile.

As I look out at the window, I had thoughts running through my brain, Keaton really did love Ally and Tommy, which made me want to learn more about the couple and who they were. Obviously, I knew their names and that they are married and own a Diner together, but I wanted to know why Keaton looked up to them so much. I wanted to know their story.

"You must go to their Diner every day," I observe at how close they were when every time I was with Keaton when he visited them, they would treat Keaton like their son.

"Most of the time I do, if I'm not hanging out with Landon, Winnie, and Reece."

I nod and we fall into a comfortable silence, until we pull in the Cafe's parking lot with not so many cars a few minutes later.

I step out of the Jeep shutting the car door behind me softly, Keaton comes around his car with his key that were held up with a lanyard that said in big bold letters 'Ohio', Keaton holds out for me to take and I take it with a smile, feeling a blush forming on my cheeks.

Keaton places his keys in his pocket leaving the lanyard to stick out that lands on the sides of his jeans. He opens the Diner door for me in which I smile at him gratefully, entering the Diner, my eyes caught onto Tommy who was sweeping the floors until his eyes latch onto us.

"Keaton! My man!" Tommy greets Keaton and Keaton sends him a smile showing his perfect teeth.

"What's up, Tae? I'm glad to see my boy has finally settled down with a pretty looking girl," Tommy compliments me and I blush.

"Tom, stop, you're embarrassing the girl," Ally cuts in, shoving her husband's chest lightly before bear hugging me causing me to let go of Keaton's hand.

"How are you two?" She asks, looking between the both of us.

"Good," I state quietly, looking over at Keaton who was staring back at me.

"The real question is why aren't you guys in school?" Tommy raises an eyebrow at us.

Ally scoffs as Keaton goes to explain. "Don't act like you've never skipped school Tom, let the kids be kids. Come, I'll show you to your table so you can get away from retired badass."

"That was just wrong," Tommy replies before leaving us to follow Ally to our table.

Ally seats us in a booth and gives us menus, she leaves us for a while and I look across from me at Keaton.

"They're cute," I comment, referring to the couple that was play fighting a minute ago.

Keaton's pearly whites show as a smile begins to show. "Yeah, everyone that comes here always wonders how they're so young and owns a Diner and on top of that married."

"How old are they?"

"Tommy is twenty-seven and Ally is twenty-four," I nod as Keaton explains.

"So, why'd you take me here out of all the places we could've gone, you took me to a Diner?" I asked, raising an eyebrow.

"Let's call it a date," He shrugs, leaning against the table. "You don't like this place?"

"No, I love it, it's old timey and I dig that," I defend myself. "Plus, Ally and Tommy are the sweetest."

"Is that why you were wore an eighty's workout outfit at Winnie's Halloween party?" He raises an eyebrow; he couldn't help but smirk.

I nod as I reply and he smiles. "So, tell me more about Ally and Tommy."

"Okay, what about them?" He seems to get interested that I asked about them and I knew Keaton loved them just by watching him interact with the married couple.

I shrug, placing my hand under my chin that was leaning on the table. "Tell me about their story and how you got to know them."

He sighs before leaning back in the booth. "Well, Tommy and Ally met way back in the days, he wasn't in the right crowd and Ally was living with her dad who owned a little cafe just like this, I don't know what Tommy was into, but I do know that he was messing with dangerous people."

I nodded for him to continue and he gets quiet as Ally walks towards our table with drinks that we never asked for, but somehow, she knew what I was going to order which was sweet tea.

She smiles at us. "What would you guys like to eat?"

"Tommy's burgers are to die for, you have to try them," Keaton says, and I nod.

"Okay, Two greenhouse burgers with fries?" She asks and we both nod. "Okay, it'll be out shortly."

I look back at Keaton. "Okay, continue."

"Tom came to Ally's dad's Cafe one day, and of course Ally was his waitress that night and he liked her, he once told me that when he saw her, she was the most beautiful woman he'd ever laid eyes on, so he tried to take her out and spend time with her, but she knew his reputation and stayed as far away from him as possible."

I sip on my tea as I watch Keaton tell the lovely couple's story. "He never gave up, he told me if you find something worth fighting for then chase after it, not ever give up. That's what he did, he came to that exact place every Friday to check up on her and see how she was doing, she had finally grown into him until one day those bad people seen where he was going and seen Ally with him."

"She was an instant target and they wanted her dead, so Tommy got the message to not ever cross them, one day, before Tommy could even reach the Cafe. Those bad people blew up the cafe with Ally and her father in it," As he explained I couldn't help but cover my mouth keeping me from gasping, I look at Ally to see her walking around with a bright smile on her face asking customers for refills.

"When you say bad people, what does that mean?" I hear myself ask Keaton who licked his lips slowly.

"I don't know, Tommy was in a bad place and he messed with a lot of bad people," His face held confusion, the same as me.

There was no doubt in my mind when I first walked in here and saw Tommy the first time, if someone had told me he was bad news I'd believe it by his looks. Why am I always judging a book by its cover?

I shake my head to get out of my thoughts. "Finish the story."

He smiles at my frustration on wanting to know the ending. "Tommy was absolutely furious when he saw the Cafe in flames, but he went to find her. Ally's father died during the explosion leaving Ally in critical condition, but after she was healed, she broke things off with Tom and built up her walls again leaving him angry."

"Why did she break up with him?"

"She blamed Tom for the explosion and said that it wouldn't have happened if he would've left her alone, for the time being Ally had to move in with her mom and step dad back in New York and left without a trace in sight for Tom to figure out, he was heartbroken and angry at the same time. He told me that it was the worst pain he had ever felt and it just broke him."

"That's so sad, but they must've rekindled since they're married now," He nods at my statement.

"Years later, Ally came back to town and was wanting to open a Cafe just like her dads to fulfill his dream. When she was signing the papers for the same land that her dad had once owned, she came across Tom who had just got his life together and working at a land company. Tom told me that when he saw her after all those years, he thought in his head that maybe this was his second chance, and if she took him back, he was for sure gonna marry her."

"And that's what he did, he got her back and married her," Keaton ended the story just how I wanted it to be and I smiled.

"And then he built me this amazing Diner where I get to see couples like you two come in all lovey dovey and have fun," The sweet voice of Ally cuts in causing our heads to turn.

Our plates of food were in both of her hands and she sets them down on the table with a cheeky smile.

I send a smile her way before she leaves letting us have our privacy.

"Why are you so close with them and not your own parents?" I ask, popping a fry in my mouth.

"Because my parents push me away just like you did..." He trails, a smile forming onto his face as he bites into his burger.

I roll my eyes. "I had a good reason."

"And I took that reason away, and here we are on a date," He says cheekily.

"This is not a date," I laugh out denying.

"Then what would you call it?" He tilts his head just a little causing me to smile at how gorgeous he was.

This boy could never have a bad hair day or anything for that matter, he was perfect.

"Just two people having lunch together," I shrug before taking a bite of my burger and moaning.

He laughs at my reaction. "Told you, and this is a date."

"Don't you think we're going a little too fast with this?" I question, pointing towards him and I.

He scoffs. "Fast is my middle name."

"Speaking of that, what is your middle name?" I furrow my eyebrows at the thought of me not knowing his middle name.

"What's yours?" He bites back, raising an eyebrow with a smirk plastered on his face.

I roll my eyes at his childishness. "Renee, now what's yours?"

"Samuel," He looks down at his plate as the ends of my mouth raises up into a smile.

I laugh. "Oh my god, really?"

"Moving on..." He trails, wanting to get off the topic.

"What if I start calling you Samuel?" I wiggle my eyebrow and he shakes his head.

"Better not," He threatens, pointing at me.

I lean forward giving him a challenging look. "We'll see."

The so-called date went smooth and after, we had to get back to school before our next class started, sitting in Westside's parking lot waiting for time to run out, Keaton and I stay in his Jeep in a comfortable silence.

I lean my head against my arm which was leaning on the car door.

"Tae?" I hummed as a reply as he calls my name.

"I had a really great time today," He starts, "Just talking and spending time with you."

I smile at him as I turn my head towards the boy who was staring right back at me.

"I had fun too," I murmur quietly.

I sit up from the seat with my heart beating out of my chest, Keaton leans forward towards me as I do, my throat began to close up and as I inch closer towards Keaton I saw his eyes flicker down towards my lips, my eyes mimic his and close as his plump pink lips attach to mine in a savory kiss.

I smile into the kiss and begin to laugh, hearing Keaton chuckle as his hand grabs the back of my neck. I take my hand and cup the side of his face deepening the kiss and suddenly jump as the school's bell rings.

We pull away leaving me in a trance state with a blush appearing on my face and Keaton still staring at me with those beautiful brown eyes with a hint of green in them.

"We gotta go," I break the silence and he nods.

"Wait," I call out as he begins to open the car door with his backpack over his shoulder.

His head swiftly turns to me and his eyes scan me, I blush. This had been on my mind the whole day, but I didn't know how to ask him.

"What are we?" I feel my face grow hot and I knew my face was a deeper red.

Keaton smirks before grabbing my hand kissing the top of it. "We're dating."

Heart attack in three ...two...one.

"Is that okay?" His eyes scan mine for a hesitation or worry and I nod.

"I like the sound of that, Samuel," I reply, earning a groan from him as we exited his vehicle.

"I shouldn't have told her..." He says to himself causing me to giggle, gripping onto his arm as we enter the crowded halls of the school.

I can't believe I was saying it.

Never in a million years would I think this or would have ever let this boy get to me.

Keaton is my boyfriend.

Chapter Twenty-Three

Tae's Pov.

"Why in the world would you skip school Tae?!" My dad exclaimed as he speeds to school.

I roll my eyes for the hundredth time, tired of hearing his lectures since yesterday.

"I said I'm sorry, all Keaton and I did was go to the Greenhouse Diner," I defend him and I, but my dad was clearly not happy either way.

"I don't care where you went, you were supposed to be in school getting an education instead of going to some restaurant."

"This is not like you, I don't know what's gotten into you, but it needs to end now," He adds before pulling into the school.

"You said be a kid, kids skip school," I tell him, pulling the hair out of my face.

"I know what I said, but unfortunately Tae doesn't skip school," He bites back referring me to third person.

I look down at my lap in silence, I knew what I did was wrong and it wasn't like me, but I wanted to change things up a little and start living life before you know...*Death.*

I hear my dad sigh. "Look, I know with your mom gone and Georgie leaving for college has been hard on you, it's been hard on me too, but we have each other-"

"I didn't skip school because of Georgie or mom if that's what you're thinking," I cut him off, shaking my head.

"Then what made you?"

"Keaton..." I trial quietly.

"Keaton," He repeats looking out of the window. "Are you guys dating now or what?"

"Yes," I admit and he hums in reply.

"I don't care if you date him, just be careful. Don't do something or let a guy persuade you into doing something you don't want to do," He instructs and I smile.

"I know, dad," I tell him, nodding.

"Good," He nods. "So, you and Keaton have detention huh?"

"Yeah," I huff out.

"Tell him to drop you off at the house when it's over, okay?" He says, I give him a surprised look in which he shrugs and exits his truck.

Wasn't he just mad at me for skipping school with Keaton? And he turns around and lets him bring me home.

"What?" I whisper to myself as I watch the back of my dad walking away from the truck.

I hurry and grab my things before jumping out of the truck, I watch him enter the school and I roll my eyes at how much faster he was then me. Walking into the school with heavy shoulders, I walk towards my locker and unlocking it, placing my things inside.

"So, I have a theory..." Winnie trails scaring me in the process as she leans against the locker beside mine.

I raise an eyebrow. "What?"

"Keaton's suddenly happy but it's not a normal happy and then I see a picture of him and this girl in his Jeep kissing which looks a lot like you," She explains earning a wide-eyed look from me.

"What picture?!" I was panicking on the inside and I could feel my heart beat racing as Winnie pulls out her phone showing me a picture of Keaton and I kissing.

This was yesterday just before we went back to school.

How-

"It's you, aren't it?" Winnie clears my thoughts, my shoulders slump and I nod, giving her the answer, she was itching for.

"I fucking knew it," She whispers while giggling. "This is just too cute."

"Do you know who took the photo?" I ask her, furrowing my eyebrows.

She shakes her head. "Nope, but the person who took it sent it to everyone."

I almost facepalmed myself, this wasn't how I wanted Keaton and I's relationship to be out.

I frown looking around seeing that everyone or should I say every girl was staring at me either with a shocked expression or an angry glare.

Winnie pats my shoulder. "They'll get over it, news like this doesn't stay for long."

"Wow, for a minute there I thought you'd listen to me, but looks like Ms. teacher's pet doesn't know how to," I could hear her voice from a mile away, I groan and turn around and groan once more.

"Shut the hell up, Lydia and take your dog with you," Winnie crosses her arms giving Lydia a glare.

"Get out of my business and go sniff up some cocaine cause that's all your good for," Lydia bites back earning a gasp from Mandy.

Winnie steps forward, but my hand reaches out to stop her. "Winnie, no."

"You bitch, I swear one of these days I'm gonna drop kick you," Winnie ignores my demand.

Lydia rolls her eyes before looking at me. "So, you're Keaton's little new girlfriend huh?"

I stay quiet and she laughs. "Just *remember* what I told you."

With that she leaves with Mandy hot on her tail, I watch Lydia's figure disappear as she enters a classroom. God, I hate that girl.

"What's her problem?" I wondered, turning my head towards a fuming Winnie.

"I don't know, but one thing is for sure, I promise I will hit her and you can't stop me," She promises and I hold my hands up in surrender.

The bell rings causing me to get in gear and walk to my first class of the day, Winnie and I walk silently and as we enter the classroom it's mostly full of kids that didn't want to come.

I take my seat in my regular seat as Winnie does the same, Mr. Pine starts his lesson off and all I could think of was my worries of what Lydia had planned in the future.

****

"She did what now?" Keaton asks as we stand in the lunch line with our trays.

I roll my eyes. "I'm not repeating myself."

"Tae, you don't have to worry. Lydia is all talk," He tries to calm me down, but I knew he was just as skeptical as I was.

"The drug incident with Winnie was all talk?" I asked in sarcasm, giving the lunch lady some money.

I stand on the side waiting on Keaton who was paying for his lunch, he carries his tray with one hand while the other he was holding his book bag.

"Okay, you have a point," Keaton gives in, but points at me. "But what can she do? All the teachers and staff know you, so you're good."

He looks around before whispering. "And they all know you're sick."

I laugh at how ridiculous he looked while doing that, his smile never gets old.

Keaton and I take a seat at the table his friends and him always sit at, Winnie types on her phone as Landon keeps an eye on who she was texting.

"Also, I'm never skipping school with you ever again," I declare causing Keaton to scoff.

"Why not?"

"Because I'm in trouble with my dad and we got detention, and I'll have you know that I've never gotten detention in my life."

He then rolls his eyes. "It was fun, wasn't it?"

"Yes, but we can have fun other than sneaking around and skipping school," I explain, popping a grape in my mouth.

"Are you guys actually a thing now?" Reece's voice booms in our ears as the chair he grabs scrapes against the floor and sits beside me.

"Yeah," Keaton beats me to it.

Reece nods before taking a bite of his pizza, I stare at Winnie hoping she would look up, but she was too interested on her phone.

"What are you doing?" Reece asks Winnie who looks up and glares.

"I'm searching up best places to hide a dead body," She answers and I laugh.

Landon rolls his eyes while fixing his hair. "Don't let her get to you, babe. She's just wanting a reaction out of you."

"She literally put drugs in my locker and set me up to get me kicked off the team, Landon. God, you can be so selfish," I raise an eyebrow in confusion at Winnie who stands up with her tray and dumps it in the trash before leaving the cafeteria.

"What's got her panties in a twist?" Reece comments.

"Shut it, Reece," Keaton snaps, wrapping his arm around my shoulders.

This all felt new to me, I didn't even know how to feel about it.

"She's going through stuff right now," Landon says, sighing.

"Yeah, her monthly," Reece bites back, who earns a head slap from Landon.

I begin to stand up with my tray in hand, Keaton grabs my thigh earning goosebumps to form across my arms and my neck, he gives me a confused look.

"I gotta go to the Nurse," I tell him quietly as I can and he nods beginning to get up.

"I'll go with you."

He turns around at the guys. "I'll see you guys in class."

"Alright," Landon replies, nodding.

Reece doesn't say anything except stuff his face with food, Keaton and I throw our trash away before exiting the cafeteria. The halls were quiet and empty, I could hear my own footsteps and breathing.

A few minutes after walking along the halls, we finally reach the Nurse's office. Nurse Pattie sits at her desk waiting for me as usual, she turns around in her rolly chair surprised that I had Keaton with me.

"Keaton, hi," She gives me an awkward look before staring at Keaton.

"Hey, Ms. Grogan," Keaton greets her, nodding.

Pattie looks at me and frowns. "Does he know?"

"Yes," I laugh out.

"Okay," She said, handing me a cup with my medicine and another cup filled with water.

"You look good, when's your next doctor's appointment?" She adds, observing me as I down the medicine and water.

"Tomorrow," I state, and she nods writing something down on her notepad.

"Okay, just tell me how it goes and we'll go from there."

"Still planning wedding ideas?" I point towards her computer which had locations for best wedding ceremonies.

She nods. "Who knew planning out a wedding could be so hard."

"You're getting married?" Keaton asked out of surprise.

Pattie nods smiling down at the rock on her finger. "Next year I am."

"How come I didn't know this?" He asks, shocked.

"You never asked."

I shrug. "Plus, you're not as close as Pattie and I are."

Keaton playfully glares at me for teasing him in which I smile.

"The least you could do is invite me, I feel so hurt that you never once said anything about you getting married," Keaton acts like he's sad, crossing his arms.

Pattie laughs and shakes her head. "Keaton, do you want to come to my-"

"No, I have things to do," Keaton pouts as he cuts her off earning a loud laugh from Pattie.

I roll my eyes. "Come on, we gotta go to class."

I drag Keaton out of Pattie's office until he pops his head back inside. "Tell Chris I'll be there, and he better let me be one of his best men."

"Alright," Pattie laughs out.

"Let's go, Keaton," I tell him, who closes the door to Pattie's office and we begin to make our way to my locker.

"You never told me that your doctor's appointment was tomorrow," He states in a serious tone.

I shrug, opening my locker. "I didn't think it was important."

"Tae, you're my girlfriend. Of course, I'd wanna know when your doctor's appointments are, I have to keep up with you," He frowns as he tells me, and my heart races as he said 'girlfriend'.

"You know now," I state the obvious, and he rolls his eyes.

"Let me take you tomorrow," He pleads and I sigh.

"If I say yes, will you shut up?"

He nods. "Only if you kiss me though."

I want to punch him, but I comply and peck his lips before heading off to my class.

"I'll see you in detention, Lambert!" Keaton yells out, and I roll my eyes but smile.

Turning around, I say. "Later, golden boy!"

Chapter Twenty-Four

Tae's Pov.

"I can't believe you're letting me go with Keaton after what happened," I state, shaking my head as I stir my cereal around my bowl.

"All you have to know is that if you come back with hickeys around your neck then I'm kicking Keaton's ass and kicking him off the team," My dad explains cheekily.

I give him a disapproving look. "That's not fair, but I wouldn't even let him do that."

"You say that now, just wait until you're alone with him and he talks all soft to you and good looking and you'll say yeah because he's got you under a spell."

I raise an eyebrow. "You just said Keaton was good looking, and second of all I know how boys work. What you need to be worrying about is getting Georgie on that phone hoping he didn't get some girl pregnant."

"Oh, whatever," He says in defeat and I smile.

A knock at the door catches my attention and I go to answer but my dad beats me to it, Keaton greets our eyes and his smile never fades as he speaks with my dad. Keaton wears a short sleeve shirt with some blue jeans pants with a hat that fits just right on the top of his head.

I hadn't noticed that I was staring too long until I snapped myself out of it and placed my cereal bowl in the sink to be washed, I walk towards the front door that my dad still had open and Keaton outside with a blush on his face.

"What are you doing?" I ask my dad who looks at Keaton once more then gives me his attention.

"Just chatting with Keaty boy," My dad replies cheekily, I roll my eyes.

"Well chatty time is over because I have to go," I tell him as I kiss his cheek.

My dad frowns before giving me a pointed look. "Be careful, and when you come back, tell me how it went."

"Aye aye captain," I salute him before heading out the door.

"Oh, and Keaton?" My dad calls out causing Keaton to turn around. "I have a baseball bat and a pistol ready for you if something happens to her."

"Yes sir," Keaton nods, turning around towards me laughing.

We both get into his Jeep with me groaning. "He's so embarrassing."

"Nah, I'd act like that too if my daughter was going out with some boy," He says, cranking up his Jeep.

"Yeah, okay," I laugh out, putting my seatbelt on.

"I'm being for real, honestly, I probably wouldn't even let her go," I roll my eyes at his statement.

"If you have kids, what are you gonna name them?" He asks looking at me before looking back towards the road.

I shrug. "I don't know, what about you?"

"Greyson for the boy..." He trails and I smile.

"Greyson..." I nod. "I like that."

"And I don't know for the girl, I just like the name Greyson," He states.

"I like the name Anastasia," I tell him as he looks at me while stopping at a red light.

He nods. "Me too."

"So, when you get out of high school what do you want to be?" He asks and I sigh.

"What's with all the questions?" I asked, raising an eyebrow but couldn't help but smile.

He shrugs. "I just wanna know what your future is gonna be like."

"If I even live to see one," I mumble quietly so he wouldn't hear.

We stay silent for the whole ride until we get to the hospital where all types of people who have diseases come to.

"Are you nervous?" Keaton asks as I play with my bracelet around my wrist.

I nod. "Kinda, it's always nerve wracking to find out if something's wrong or if you're better or it's worse."

"I don't know how many times I was up here as a kid watching my mom getting needles put in her and getting x-rays and worst of all, chemo, I always wondered why my mom lost her hair until I realized it was the treatments she was taking, I hated to see her so weak, but in the end, she was the strong one," Keaton explains as he looks up at the enormous hospital.

"And one day, you're gonna hear someone say you're cured, because I know you can beat this, Tae," Keaton adds, taking a hold of my hand and pressing his lips onto the back of my hand.

I smile. "Hopefully."

Did I believe that I was going to get cured? *No.*

Keaton and I walk into the hospital, hand in hand, with shaky hands, I signed myself in and sit down in the waiting area with Keaton beside me. I couldn't help but shake my leg with anticipation, earning a look from Keaton.

"You good?" He raises an eyebrow.

"Mhm," I hum out, ignoring his worried eyes.

A door opens revealing Nurse Rita, she smiles at me. "You don't know how happy I am to see you."

"Me too," I answer back, standing up with my hand still in Keaton's.

Her eyes attach on our conjoined hands and eyes Keaton, giving him a smile.

"Do I sense a relationship?" She points between the two of us and I nod.

"And you told me y'all were just friends," She laughs at the last time I was here when I told her Keaton and I were just friends. "What a funny joke."

I roll my eyes at her teasing me and she waves us to follow her, Keaton held the door open for Nurse Rita and I and she awes at it.

"And a gentleman I see," She observes causing me to facepalm myself.

"What? I gotta to see if he's a good guy," She defends herself, before turning around.

I feel a hand slide against my waist and wraps around me, I turn my head at the culprit who smirks at me then looking back in front of us as Nurse Rita stops at a room.

"Dr. Simmons will be here shortly," Rita tells us, staring at Keaton's hand on my waist before closing the door behind her.

Keaton sighs taking his hand off my waist to run it through his hair, I take a seat on the bed like table and shrug my jacket off.

"Was your mom nervous going here?" I start off the conversation.

He puts his hands in his pockets while he stares at the pictures on the wall. "If she was, she never showed it, but I think the idea of my dad there made her feel safe."

I smile at him as he swiftly turns his head to look at me. "Are you nervous?"

"Of course, I am, I'm worried about what they're going to say," I answer with a nervous tone.

"You're gonna be fine," He walks towards me slowly and I look down at my lap.

"I hope so," I murmur quietly, feeling Keaton's hand cup my chin raising my head to let my eyes meet his.

His eyes held something I couldn't describe, but what I do can explain is that he made me feel some type of way.

"No, you don't hope, you know you're gonna be fine," He tells me in a demanding tone.

I nod looking up at him with a soft smile, his eyes droop down to my lips as mine does the same, we both leaned forward painfully slow until our lips collide, Keaton smiles through the kiss as his tongue slide through my lips that are slightly parted.

A knock on the door interrupts us, causing me to push Keaton away from me with a slight squeal and wipe my lips staring back at Keaton who has a smug smile plastered on his face with his hands on his hips looking at Dr. Simmons that walks in not knowing what had happened a few minutes ago.

"Good morning, Tae, how are you?" Dr. Simmons asks, giving me a small smile.

I blush as Keaton sends me a look and quickly looks at Dr Simmons who waits for me to answer his question.

"I'm doing great, how are you?" I ask back politely.

Dr Simmons looks behind him to see Keaton and his smile grows bigger. "Is this the boy from your last appointment?"

"Yeah, this is Keaton..." I introduce while biting my bottom lip.

Keaton holds out his hand for Dr. Simmons. "Her boyfriend."

I give Keaton a pointed look but, Dr. Simmons shakes his hand. "When did this happen?"

"I thought you didn't want a boyfriend? Or your last words were; I don't need or want a boyfriend," Dr. Simmons adds as he looks back at me.

I shrug. "Things change, I guess."

"Well, I'm happy for you, I know how your situation is at school and how you put stuff in your head to where you don't socialize."

"It wasn't that easy when he wouldn't leave me alone and kept following me around everywhere," I state, pointing toward Keaton who rolls his eyes playfully.

Dr. Simmons laughs. "Someone had to do it, but you seem happier."

"Happier?" I question.

"Your posture and your face have a glow to it," Dr. Simmons observed and I nod slowly understanding.

"The school's Nurse, Nurse Pattie, gave me feedback on how you've been doing at school and it looks normal, but we need to up your medicine and give you your first dose here to see how you react," Dr Simmons explains and my hands slowly start to get sweaty and nervous bubbles fluttering in my stomach.

Keaton's eyes connect with mine and it was like he talked through them, his eyes were soft as they stayed on me, his posture looked hard and he had his arms crossed causing his muscles to flex and his shoulders to tense.

Nurse Rita walks in with a tray of needles and a bottle of the medicine I was getting prescription to, she sends me a warm smile as she notices my nervous eyes attached on the needle. I feel arms wrap around my waist and their fingertips fish under my shirt to barely touch my side, I turn my head giving Keaton a smile out of thanks.

Rita slips on her gloves as Dr. Simmons observes with his clipboard writing a few things down as we go along. Rita wraps gauze around my arm and tightens it to get a vein, she sucks the medicine in the sharp needle in which she squirts a little to see if it works well, Dr. Simmons lays his clipboard down to take an alcohol wipe and wipe it on my arm where Rita's going to poke me.

"You alright?" Keaton whispers in my ear causing me to give him a hurried nod.

He whispers soothing words in my ear as Rita pokes the needle in my arm causing me to close my eyes as the burning sensation of the medicine goes into my system and goes through my bloodstream. As I opened my eyes, I see Rita taking out the needle from my arm and Dr. Simmons gives me a smile.

"How do you feel?" Rita asks, eyeing me as Keaton holds onto me.

I nod. "Normal."

"Take a few minutes and if nothing happens, then we're done and you'll be off, but if something happens that's normal too because you're new to the medicine," I nod as Dr. Simmons explains to me that I had to stay there under there watch until I'm good.

A few minutes later nothing had happened so we were off and with a new appointment in hand.

"I love you and I'll see you later!" Nurse Rita's cheery voice gives me her goodbyes as Keaton opens the door for me to exit the building.

"Love you too, I'll see you," I tell her before walking out with Keaton beside me.

"So, where to now?" I hear Keaton asked as he opens the passenger door for me and I hop in.

I shake my head. "It doesn't matter."

He gives me a look as he enters the Jeep and I laugh out already knowing where he wanted to go.

"Let's go see Ally and Tommy," I state, earning a smile from Keaton and he hurriedly cranks the vehicle up and pulls out.

As we make our way to the Diner, I couldn't help but wonder one thing, why did they change up my medicine?

"What are you thinking?" Keaton asks as he reaches his hand over to lay on my thigh.

Was I overthinking this too much? I was fine with my last medicine.

"Why would they change up my medicine? Why would I need a higher dose?"

Keaton looks at me before looking back at the road. "They did that all the time with my mom."

"How bad did your mom get?" I ask him, not meaning to bring the past back up.

"Pretty bad, it got to the point where she was seeing death," I put a hand over my face while sighing as I listen to Keaton.

His hand squeezes my thigh. "You're fine."

As he parks the Jeep at the Diner, I was quietly thinking about the stuff that could happen to me, Keaton's mom was lucky to be alive and that's a chance of a lifetime.

I feel Keaton's hand leave my thigh to grab the sides of my face and he leans forward.

"Don't worry about it baby, you're going to be fine and you're going to fight through this and I'll be here to help along the way, I *always* will be, I promise," He tells me, pecking my lips, but my mind was on the fact that he called me baby.

I smile cheekily causing him to raise an eyebrow. "What did you just call me?"

The edges of Keaton's lips raise up into a smile and he leans in close almost touching my lips.

"Let's go inside," He says, quickly pecking my lips and opens the side of his door.

I kept smiling like an idiot as I exit the Jeep, I watch as Keaton waits for me, he leans his head back as I walk up to him, I wrap my arm around his neck leaving my other to lay on his arm while he wraps his one arm around my waist while the other holds on his lanyard that holds his keys.

"I think it's cute that you called me baby," I gush, causing him to roll his eyes as I tease him.

"No, what you're doing is making fun of me," He fake pouts and I shake my head.

"I like it," I tell him, kissing his cheek.

We pull apart as we get to the doors of the Diner and enter with our hands in each other's.

Chapter Twenty-Five

Tae's Pov.

"Hey Tae, wait up!" I hear the oddly familiar voice of Winnie as she calls for me behind me.

I turn around greeting her in the process as she makes her way in front of me.

"What's up?" We walk down the almost empty hallway as students' files out of the school getting ready for the football game tonight.

Winnie slings her red hair over her shoulder before throwing me a look. "You going to the game tonight?"

"Yep," I nod, opening the doors of the school and entering the chilly outdoors.

"Well, after do you wanna go watch a movie or something?" She asks and I smile giving her a nod.

"Great! But ask your dad first," She orders and I salute her.

"So, how are things with you and Keaton?" She questions earning a blush from me.

I look down as we walk down the steps and hold onto the railing. "Good actually, I'm surprised we haven't gone a day without ripping each other's hair out."

"That would be you," Winnie states, nodding.

I laugh. "Yeah."

"Where did you and Keaton go yesterday? He told me he was hanging with you, but never told me where," She asks and my shoulders tense.

Don't you dare lie, Tae.

"We went out to dinner at the Greenhouse diner," I answer her question earning a nod from her.

Alright, I know I didn't tell her the whole truth, but at least I told her what we did after.

"Keaton loves that place. Have you met Ally and Tommy?" She excitedly asks and I nod.

"They are wonderful people."

"Yeah, they are..." She trails, looking off at the field causing me to look as well.

Keaton and Landon stand on the field as they throw a football at one another, Landon looks back at Winnie, waving her over towards him.

She turns around to look at me. "Come on."

She holds onto my hand as I hold onto my books while Winnie drags me across the field to meet the eyes of Landon and Keaton.

"Hey beautiful, you coming tonight?" Landon asks Winnie as he hugs her from the side and she cringes away from him.

She playfully pushes him off her. "You're sweaty, but how could I miss watching my boy play on the field?"

Landon stares at her with love in his eyes and I smile at the two, I walk over towards Keaton who waits for me to get out of my daze and speak to him.

"Hi Mr. Quarterback," I bite my lip as I greet him.

He smiles. "How's it going, Lambert?"

"Nothing much, just got dragged down here to see you guys," I tell him, shrugging.

"You didn't want to see me?" He playfully pouts and acts like he's hurt.

"I thought you guys were busy practicing," I explain, pressing my books up against my chest.

"You better come tonight," He demands, playfully glaring at me.

I nod. "I will."

He nods before setting the ball down on the ground and grabs my hand. "Come with me."

My eyebrows furrow. "Where are you taking me?"

"The locker room," He states and I try to yank my hand from his.

"Keaton no, I don't wanna see guys half naked walking around, plus if-" He cuts me off.

"First of all, I wouldn't dare let you around some other guy almost naked and second, the guys are outside helping out your dad and chilling, so you're good," He explains, tightening his hold on me.

"Oh, so you want us to be alone so you can take out your hanky pank on me," I retort, glaring at him from the side as he opens the door of the locker room for me.

I walk in to smell the mixture of axe and sweat with clothes and shoes all scattered, I hear Keaton laugh behind me as he closes the door.

"What the hell is a hanky pank?" He asks, walking past me to God knows where.

I awkwardly point down at his pants as he opens his locker while staring at me waiting for his question to be answered.

"You know..." I trial, waving my hand.

"My dick?" He raises an eyebrow and I nod.

He laughs again and reaches in his locker and grabs a jersey and closes his locker back.

"I'm not that type of guy, I wouldn't do something you wouldn't want me to do, I know you're not that type of girl," He explains, walking closer to me and handed me his jersey, but doesn't let go as I reach for it.

His eyes stare at me with this intense gaze, I couldn't describe how it made me feel, but I do know that it made my legs weak.

"Good," I mumble, tugging the jersey away from him, but he doesn't let go. "What is this for?"

"I want you to wear this tonight," He states.

3...2...1... heart explode.

I smile down at the jersey and then look back up to Keaton to find him still staring at me with that intense stare.

"Quit looking at me like that," I hit his chest causing him to smile and let go of the jersey and letting me get a look of it.

"Other guys around you stare at you, but you don't seem to notice it," He gets closer as he whispers in my ear causing shivers to shake my body and goosebumps appear on my arms.

"Okay," I snort, folding the jersey and laying it on top of my books in my hand. "How could they when I don't talk to anybody and hardly anyone knows me?"

"People know you, guys don't make it obvious that they're staring and I catch them looking at you," He states, pulling a piece of my hair behind my ear. "You really are beautiful, Tae."

"Thank you," I whisper as I watch Keaton lean in while his eyes stare at my lips then looks back up to my eyes.

Keaton gently slides his hand around my waist and quickly wraps his hand around the back of my neck and smashed his lips against mine, I drop my books along with Keaton's jersey on the floor as he backs me up against the lockers.

I wrap my arms around his neck and drag my fingers through his hair as Keaton's tongue glides across my bottom lip causing me to open on instinct and I hear the door of the locker rooms open, I push Keaton's chest causing him to rip away from me.

My dad enters the locker room and his face is surprising to me as he watches me pick up my books and the jersey.

"What the-" He goes to say, but I let out a tiny squeal watching him smirk as his thoughts come together.

I quickly walked to Keaton and kiss his cheek; he had his hand on his mouth acting like he was scratching his chin as they were red.

"I'll see you tonight," I whisper to him and he nods.

Walking past my dad awkwardly, I rush out while wiping my lips. Winnie and Landon were on the bleachers talking amongst themselves and I hurriedly run up them and sit down next to them.

Winnie turns to me. "Don't think I didn't see you getting caught by your dad in the locker room alone with Keaton."

"We weren't doing anything bad," I state, shrugging.

Landon laughs as he leans forward to look at me. "Your cheeks are flushed and your lips are red, I'd say y'all were making out."

"Mhm," Winnie agrees with her boyfriend.

"Y'all are mean for teaming up on me, let's go Winnie," I order, standing up to walk down the bleachers.

"Where are we going?" Her and Landon follow my moves.

I shrug. "Either going to my house to get ready for the game or yours."

"Ouuu let's go to yours since I haven't been there," She says, giving Landon a side hug as a goodbye.

"Okay, let me go tell my dad, you go ahead and wait for me in the car," I instruct and she salutes me, copying my actions.

I roll my eyes at her playfully, I head towards my dad who was already giving me the dad look, Keaton was on the field practicing and I see Landon run past me and get in on the field with the others.

"Tae," My dad said in a warning tone.

I nod. "I know, I know. I shouldn't have gone in the locker room, boys' privacy, I'm sorry."

"If it wasn't me that caught you then it would've been somebody that would've snitched and got you in trouble. You need to watch your actions young lady," He points the finger at me.

I nod. "I know, I'm sorry. Keaton just wanted to give me his jersey to wear to support him tonight."

He looks at the jersey in my hand and looks back to me. "Okay, I'll let this slide, but if I catch you in the locker rooms again or he's in the girls, y'all are in big trouble."

"Okay," I nod.

"Winnie and I were wanting to get ready at the house for tonight," I add, looking back at Winnie's little bug car as she sits and waits for me.

"I guess, but be careful and don't get here late," He demands and I nod, kissing his cheek and leaving him to start practice on the boys.

****

"I like your house..." Winnie comments as I unlock the door of my home.

I smile back at her. "Thanks, it's nowhere near as nice as yours."

"I'd rather have a small cozy home then have a big lonely house," She states, shrugging while looking around at the place. "Ever since my dad died my mom wanted to move, but she wouldn't cause of the memories she had."

"I get why she's doing it," I tell her, thinking of my mom.

"So, where's your room?" She asks excitedly and I point towards the stairs and we both head to our destination.

Entering my room, Winnie and I were silent as we could be, she looks around my room staring at my old record player that was just for looks and the Beatles posters hanging on the wall.

"So, I take it that you like the old times stuff," Winnie makes conversation and I nod.

"Yep, I don't like the crap that's on today," I state honestly.

She smiles. "I've never met someone like you before..."

"Is that a good thing or a bad thing?" I raise an eyebrow, sitting on my bed.

"It's good, you're so much different than the kids at Westside."

"I can't stand the people at Westside," I said, rolling my eyes.

"Me neither," She laughs out, taking out the face paint in her bag.

She turns around staring at me with a smirk. "Let's get to it!"

****

"Stop staring at yourself in the mirror, you look great, Tae," Winnie demands playfully.

I groan. "I'm sorry, it's just ever since Keaton and I-"

"Ever since you and Keaton started dating you can't help but want to look good, I get it, I used to do it all the time with Landon. Just wait until a year or so you won't care anymore," She explains and I nod.

I was nervous about the game today, not just the game, but me going to it and everyone seeing Keaton's jersey on me, pretty much everyone knew Keaton and I are together but some don't and will know once I step out of Winnie's car.

I look down at my outfit to see that Winnie did a good job picking it out, I was wearing a long white sleeve shirt under the jersey Keaton made me wear, his jersey was white and burgundy so Winnie put lines of burgundy and white face paint on my face.

My jeans were high top waisted jeans with rips in the thigh parts and for the shoes I was wearing white converse. My hair was wavy due to me braiding it and straightening on top of it then letting out the braids.

My thoughts disappear from my mind as soon as Winnie pulls into the school parking lot, the chilly night football game was packed filled with kids and parents and the stadium was lit up so bright some girls had sun glasses on.

I grab my five dollars out of the back of my jeans and wait in line for Winnie and I's turn to give Mrs. Hyde our money.

As it was our turn Mrs. Hyde smiles at us, grabbing the five dollars I hand her. "How are you girls?"

"Good," Winnie and I both said at the same time making us look at one another.

"That's good, enjoy the game!" She says, handing us our tickets and we make our way inside.

Winnie takes my hand in hers looking back at me as we walk up the steps. "Let's sit in the front."

"Okay," I yell out from everyone being so loud.

It wasn't hard to find seats since everyone loves to be at the top, Winnie and I had a good view of the boys playing football and my dad screaming at them. The game had already started before Winnie and I got there, but we were only a few minutes late.

I look at my surroundings and see that it was pretty normal for our high school games, but what caught my eye was Keaton's dad in the bleachers with his mom, I guess Winnie was wondering where I was staring so she found out herself and shook me.

I look at her as she speaks. "Oh no, trouble."

I give her a small smile in return and look at the game, suddenly everyone stands up cheering and so does Winnie, I stand up really quick not wanting to look stupid and clap my hands.

I give Winnie a questioning look and she points at Keaton who had the ball in his hands.

"Keaton made a touchdown," She states in obvious and my mouth forms into an 'O'.

My mouth felt dry so I tap Winnie and tell her I'm gonna go get a water and she nods; I walk down the bleachers and to the food stands and order a water in which I get in minutes.

I turn around opening my water in the process and look up to see the witch itself.

"You look good Tae," Lydia's fake compliment didn't put a smile on my face as she crosses her arms with her pom poms around her wrists.

"Don't you have a game to be cheering for?" I roll my eyes as I ask her in sarcasm.

She fake smiles but as soon as her eyes meet the number on the jersey, I was wearing her face turned blood red and her smile dropped. "So, I see you're wearing Keaton's jersey."

"Yep," I fake a smile just to annoy her.

"Lucky you," Her voice cracks as she looks down again and I almost feel sorry for her, but then I realize she cheated on Keaton and that pity was long gone.

I laugh. "I know right."

I leave her in her sad form as I step up on the steps, but I hear my name being called, I turned around seeing Lydia.

"Yes?" I raise an eyebrow.

"Just know I wore the same jersey when Keaton and I were dating and when he gave it to you did, he take you in the guy's locker room? Because that's where he took me and fucked me against the lockers, apparently did that with all the girls," She sighs out, looking out in the field at Keaton.

After she said those two words my brain went into mush and I was blinded by anger.

I knew she was doing this to see my reaction and I was gonna react, but not like you think I was, but how did she know he took me to the locker room?

I smile at her fakely and open my half-filled water bottle; I take a sip before splashing the water all over her which hit her face and wet her hair. I knew it wasn't much but I didn't care.

Lydia gasps. "You bitch!"

"Oops sorry," I gave her a fake apology and throw the empty bottle in the trash before heading up the bleachers.

I get back in my seat and Winnie looks at me. "What took you so long and where's your water?"

"Long line and they were out," She hums at my response.

"So, what did I miss?" I ask her who steady looks at the game.

"If Landon throws the ball to Keaton and Keaton makes a touchdown we'll win for sure and that'll, be it," Winnie explains and I sigh out.

"Thank god," I said, because I was tired of being here.

After thirty minutes of waiting, Landon finally catches the balls then runs almost getting tackled in the process, until he throws the ball towards Keaton and him almost missing but catches and runs to God knows where and everyone goes wild, I throw my hands up excited to go home, but also because we won.

"There's Landon," Winnie squeals pointing toward the sweaty blonde boy who runs through the field after getting tackled by his team and passes the gate to get to Winnie.

Winnie walks down the bleachers side by side with me and jumps off the bottom steps to tackle Landon in a hug.

"You did so great baby," Winnie pushes back Landon's hair as she speaks to him and he smiles.

"I kinda wish it wasn't over though..." He trails, letting Winnie down and smiles at me.

Winnie raises an eyebrow. "Why?"

"I just like the rush of what football does to me," He says, running his hands through his hair.

I smile at the two who kiss in which I look away for their privacy, I feel a tap on my shoulder and turned around to see a sweaty huffing Keaton, in one hurried quick step I wrap my arms around the neck as he wraps his arms around my waist.

"I'm so proud," I tell him, looking up at him.

He smiles, showing his pearly whites. "I was thinking about you the whole time."

"Mhm sure," I roll my eyes playfully and pat his shoulder to let me go.

"Well done son, see, this is what I was talking about!" Hearing his dad's voice suddenly scares me and I flinch keeping an arm around Keaton's waist as he does the same.

Keaton goes stiff and I rub his back for comfort.

"So, who is this?" His dad asks pointing toward me.

I smile at him and go to tell him, but Keaton beats me to it. "This is Tae, my girlfriend."

"You have a girlfriend?" His dad gave him a stern look and I shrink down feeling awkward.

I feel Keaton's arm go stiff and Keaton's mom comes to the rescue as she was watching us from afar while she was speaking to another parent.

"Hello Tae, nice to see you again," Julie states, side hugging me.

"Nice seeing you again too," I reply, making her smile.

She looks at her husband who stares at me with an uncertain look, she grabs her husband's shoulder and smiles at me again.

"Randy, this is Tae, Coach Lambert's daughter," She introduces me in which I smile at Randy.

"Can you wait for me with Winnie and Landon please, I need to speak with my dad," Keaton politely asks and I smile at him.

"Yeah, sure," I nod before walking away and putting my hands on my forehead.

"Hey, what's up?" Winnie asks as I get to them.

I cringe at the thoughts. "I had an awkward moment with Keaton's dad."

"His dad is not very likable," She replies.

Landon nods. "I agree on that one."

"I don't think he likes me," I comment, looking back to see Keaton and his dad fussing.

"He never likes anyone when he first meets them, hell, he didn't like me until a year of being friends with Keaton," Landon says back, shaking his head.

"I don't think he wants me and Keaton dating," I mumble.

Winnie scoffs. "If he let Keaton date slutty Lydia then he'll for sure let you date Keaton."

I nod, looking back to see Keaton making his way towards us, he gives us a smile as he reaches us.

"Hey guys," He greets us, looking at me.

Winnie crosses her arms. "What was that about?"

"What was what about?" Keaton raises an eyebrow at her.

"Don't play stupid. The conversation with your dad," Winnie snaps at him making Keaton frown.

"Just about the game and college, just the usual," I look away from Keaton's stare knowing he was lying so I wouldn't get upset, but I knew they were talking about me so why lie?

"Well, how about we go celebrate to a movie and then after we go to the Greenhouse Diner?" Landon cuts in trying to change the subject.

We all nod and I asked my dad if I could go in which he says yes of course and just not to be late at home.

I ride with Keaton of course and he changes before we leave and he tries making conversation with me, but I stayed silent with the thoughts running wild in my head.

"Just know I wore the same jersey when Keaton and I were dating, and when he gave it to you did, he takes you in the guy's locker room? Because that's where he took me and fucked me against the lockers, apparently did that with all the girls."

Chapter Twenty-Six

Tae's Pov.

"Are you okay?" Winnie asks, scraping her shoulder with mine to get my attention.

I smile and nod in return as we take a seat in the theatre, I sit in the middle of Winnie and Keaton and Landon sits on the other side of Winnie. I had no clue what we were about to watch because all I could think about was Keaton, his dad, Lydia, and what she said.

I know I shouldn't let it bother me but it did.

Keaton tries touching my hand and placing his hand on my thigh, but I instantly move away signaling that I don't want to, I knew he knew something was wrong because Keaton could sense something wrong with me from a mile away.

"I'm going to the bathroom," I comment, pulling my hand away from Keaton who tries to touch mine again.

Without looking back, I walk out of the theatre and make my way to the bathroom. I sigh out and look under the stalls to see if I was the only one in here and just my luck I was. I rest my hands against the sink and stared at my reflection in the mirror.

The bathroom door slammed open, causing me to jump from my spot and look to see who came in and of course it was the creep who came into the girl's bathrooms because he doesn't care.

"What the hell is up?" Keaton asks, holding his hands out.

I point towards the door. "You better leave before someone walks in and sees you."

He rolls his eyes before walking back towards the door and flips the lock, my mouth stays wide open as he walks back close to me and leaned against the sink.

"What's going on with you?" He asks in a more demanding tone.

"You're so extra-" I go to change the subject, but he wasn't having it.

"Oh, come on, Tae. Just tell me what's bothering you, clearly something is up because ever since the game you haven't even looked my way or let me touch you," He explains and I sigh looking down at my feet.

"If it's about my dad-" He goes to say, but I cut him off by shaking my head.

"Lydia," Is all I say and he gives me a confused look.

"Did she say something to you? Why would you believe anything she said?"

I shrug my shoulders. "I don't know, maybe because she knew how you gave me your jersey."

He gave me a look saying 'okay and?'

"I know you guys had a past, but I didn't know you were going to do the same stuff that you did with her," I push the hair that fell in front of my eyes as Keaton watches my every move.

"I'm not-" I cut him off.

"It's like you're using me to get over her, and I'm not the type of girl-" I try to go on but Keaton stops me mid-sentence.

"Why would you even say that? Why would I work so hard to be with you just to use you?" He raises an eyebrow and I shrug.

"I don't know, guys work that way I guess," I state, rolling my eyes.

"I would never hurt you, Tae. *Ever.* I'm not that type of guy, I care about you too much to let you go and I'm going to say this now and don't let it scare you, but I'm not going anywhere, you're not getting rid of me, I'm here to stay," He stands up from the sink as he grabs me by the waist and pulls me in close.

"And yeah, she might've been the first girl I brought in the locker room with me, but you're the last and that's a promise," He says before kissing my forehead.

I nod, giving him a smile.

"If you're ever confused or if you find out something about me that you don't like, don't hide it, talk to me. We're not going to be like those other couples that fight before they even talk about things," He explains and I nod.

"Okay, so talk then fight," I patted his chest, giving him a smirk before walking around him and unlocking the bathroom door, looking back to see a smiling Keaton.

I walk slowly so Keaton could catch up with me, I feel a pair of arms wrap around my shoulders and front of Keaton's chest touches my back.

"You thought that was funny huh?" Keaton's voice whispers in my ear and the feel of his lips touch the corner of my ear.

I smile leaning my head to the side as Keaton kisses my neck slightly. "Yes."

"Tae Renee Lambert, you are something," I smile at the thought of him remembering my middle name.

****

"So, how was the movie?" Winnie asks as she throws her straw paper at me.

After the movies we all decided to go to the Greenhouse Diner, which was no surprise there.

"If you weren't busy tonguing Landon down then maybe you would know," Keaton sarcastically states, throwing his straw paper at her.

Landon chuckles and Winnie gasps. "You can't tell me shit, Keaton. You haven't even dicked down Tae yet."

My cheeks instantly go red, and I start to get hot as I feel Keaton's eyes on me, I give him a quick look to see him smiling and look away.

"Babe, look what you did to her," Landon calls out, pointing at my cheeks.

Winnie gives me an apologetic look and a smile before changing the subject. "Are we going to order because I'm starving."

I feel my back pocket buzz and I quickly fish for my phone, I see that my dad is ringing me and I grab Keaton's attention.

"My dad's calling me, I'm gonna go outside since it's so loud in here," I explained to him and he nods letting me out of the booth.

"What do you want to eat?" Keaton calls out.

I turn around shrugging. "Just order something."

He shrugs, letting me answer the phone call and I swing the Diner's little door open.

"Hey dad," I let out, looking inside the Diner to see the group laughing at each other.

I smile at the sight of Keaton being happy.

"Hey, where are you?" I then hear my dad's voice ask.

"Greenhouse Diner, after I'll be heading home," I tell him and he hums in reply.

"Guess who I just got off the phone with?" He states and my heart speeds up.

"Georgie?" I excitedly ask.

"Yeah, he called to check on us."

"That's great, but I wish he would've called me..." I trail, frowning down at the ground.

Dad sighs. "I know, he told me he wanted to call you but if he did, he'd probably come back in a flash because he misses you so much."

"Yeah, well a phone call would be nice."

"I'm sure he'll call back soon and next time it'll be your phone," He tries to cheer me up.

I sigh. "I guess... Anyways, I have to go my food is ready, but I'll be home in a few."

"Okay, love you!" He speaks.

I smile. "Love you too, dad."

I hang up the phone before entering the loud, crowded Diner. As soon as Keaton spots me, he stands up letting me slide in the booth before sitting back down.

"What he say?" Keaton asks, eating on his fries.

"Georgie called my dad... " I trailed, looking at my plate to see chicken fingers.

Keaton raises his eyebrows. "Really? How is he?"

"I don't know, he was just asking how me and my dad were," I tell him, shrugging.

"He'll call you, Tae," Keaton rubs my back slowly and I smile at him in gratitude.

"Who's Georgie? A boyfriend?" Winnie wiggles her eyebrows at Keaton trying to get him started.

I shake my head. "My brother."

"You have a brother?" She exclaims, looking at Landon who shrugs.

"Is he hot?" She adds causing Landon to choke on his drink and give her a warning look.

I laugh. "He went to our school last year."

She furrowed her eyebrows and Landon looks up with wide eyes.

"Your brother is Georgie Lambert?!" He exclaims and Winnie raises an eyebrow.

She repeats Georgie's name in silence trying to figure out who he was, I nod at Landon causing his mouth to open.

"How the hell did I not get this?" Landon asks Keaton who shrugs and eats his food.

I take a bite of my food watching Landon look at me then look back Keaton, Winnie gasps looking up.

"The black curly haired kid, who was the quarterback?" She asks with a smile, leaning against the table.

"Yeah," I said, taking another bite of my food.

"I had the biggest crush on him, how did I not know he had a sister?" She asks.

Landon gives her a look. "You had a crush on him when we were dating?"

"You can look but not touch," She states, crossing her arms.

"So, If I checked out another girl you wouldn't get mad or if I had a crush on someone else..." He trails.

"I'd rip off your nut sack," She finishes with a glare.

"Damn," Keaton comments, laughing.

"I wouldn't be laughing, because if you did that, you'd be wishing I'd rip yours off," I give Keaton a sarcastic smile and he gives me one back.

He leans in close so only the two of us could hear what he was about to say, and I wish the lord prepared me for what he was about to say.

"And you know that dicked down comment Winnie made?" Keaton whispers, and my head moves on its own and nods.

"By the time I got done with you, you'd be wishing you never said that," He continues and shivers went down my spine and arms.

To be honest with you, I had gotten a second heartbeat, which was a new feeling to me.

Chapter Twenty-seven

Tae's Pov.

"Yo, what the hell happened to you man?" Keaton calls out to Reece looked high as a kite with his hair flying all over the place.

Reece looks at all of us and his eyes stay on me for a little longer.

"While you guys were going on a double date, Reece here got high with a few friends and I think I hooked up with someone," Reece answers, his eyes leaving me and going toward Keaton.

Keaton chuckles. "You could've gone with us."

"Oh, hell no, I don't want this sulky bastard coming with us on double dates," Winnie butts in, slinging her book bag around her shoulders, pushing Reece out of the way.

Reece glares at the back of her head. "Yeah, well, I don't want to see that ashy looking thing that's between your legs."

"Tae, hold my bag," Winnie launches her bag at me causing me to let out an oomph sound.

"What does she got in here?" I ask, furrowing my eyebrows.

"Probably tons of bricks so she can throw them at Reece," Keaton laughs out, looking down at the bag in my hands.

Reece playfully glares at Keaton before taking off towards the school doors with Winnie tagging along behind him, Landon rolls his eyes at the two.

"I should probably go stop her from beating Reece into a pulp but then again I kinda want to see it," Landon comments and Keaton laughs.

"Go get her before she gets in trouble," Keaton says while chuckling a bit.

Landon nods, giving me a smile in a way of saying bye, Keaton watches Landon walk into the school and turns to me.

"What are you doing this afternoon?" He asks, taking Winnie's heavy bag into his hands.

I shrug. "Probably do some homework and spend time with my dad."

"Want me to come by later?" He asks and I nod excitedly making him laugh.

The bell rings interrupting our thoughts and I pat Keaton's chest.

"I'll see you at lunch," I tell him, pecking his lips and grabbing Winnie's bag to give it to her in first period.

I go to leave, but his hands stop me and brings me back to his arms.

"Keaton," I groan. "I have to get to class."

"I know, I just don't want you to go," He groans with me and I smile.

"I'll see you at lunch," I pecked his lips again and this time he lets me walk off to get to my class.

Walking into first period, Mr. Pine is writing on the board of the assignment we were going to work on today, Winnie's smile never once left her face when her eyes landed on me walking in, which put a start in my day.

"What are you doing after school?" She suddenly asks and I raise an eyebrow.

"Keaton's coming," I shrug while answering her.

"No, you both are attending my party tonight," She demands and I groan.

"Winnie..." I trail, snatching my books out of my bag and laying it on the desk.

"No buts, this time the party is going to be small so it'll be more fun for you," She explains, which didn't make me feel any better.

I scrunch my nose up at the thought. "Do you not remember last time?"

"Yes, but you're always going to have creeps at a party and plus I'll make sure he's not allowed to come," She states. "On second thought, I don't even know who that guy was, I don't think he goes here."

"Besides you got hunky quarterback Keaton always up your ass so he'll be around," She wiggles her eyebrows making me blush.

I roll my eyes and before class start, she made a statement. "I'm making you and Keaton go."

There was no arguing with Winnie so I left it at that, I had a bad feeling about this party Winnie was having and usually you need to always listen to your gut, but just like last time I didn't.

After the first period, I went straight to my locker to get my books for second period. Hands wrapped around my waist and I smile out of instinct, a pair of lips touch my temple and I quickly turn around to Keaton.

"What are you smiling for?" I ask him as I watch his smile grow even wider.

He chuckles. "Winnie always talks you into doing shit."

"So, you must know about the party?" I ask him earning a nod.

"I told her I didn't want to go," I add.

"Yeah, Winnie doesn't take no for an answer," He states, earning a nod from me.

"Do you think it's a good idea?" I ask him and he says nothing.

I slap his chest playfully. "You think it's a good idea?"

He shrugs while smirking giving me a look over and I roll my eyes.

"I don't think it's a bad idea, Winnie said it was going to be small and she was going to pay some guys for some high security shit," He explains himself, but I still wasn't happy.

I gave him a frown and he laughs before pecking my lips. "Tae, you're sixteen, you're supposed to live life to the fullest and stop worrying about things that might not even happen."

"You're forgetting that I have leukemia and people who have that don't party, they stay home and try to get better," I remind him which only made him roll his eyes.

"And must I remind you that you used to have a bad reputation in partying and if your dad found out he would flip his shit," I add and he starts smiling.

I raise an eyebrow and he smiles even more. "And that's why I want to go so I can piss him off."

I slam my locker shut and turn back around to look Keaton in the eye.

"I'm not going," I state, walking the other way to get to my second class of the day.

A tug on my arm stops me in my tracks.

"First you forgot our goodbye kiss and second I'll change your mind in a little bit," Keaton says, going to kiss me but I push at his chest.

"And how will you change my mind because I've already made it up," I cross my arms causing him to smirk.

"Lambert, I'm pretty good at persuading people," He replies, pecking my lips before heading off to his class.

I watch his figure disappear as he enters a classroom and I turn around slowly, still not processing what just happened and why did my legs feel like jelly when he said it like that, I head to my class and sit in my seat for another hour of another lecture.

****

"Lambert!" I hear a voice yell at me as I walk down the field to wait on another day at football practice.

I turn around already knowing it was Keaton, I turned around too fast apparently and bump into his chest, just as I'm about to fall backwards Keaton grabs me just in time.

My hands were on his arms while his were on my waist, he smirks looking down at the position we were in.

"Wow, you're already falling for me," I slap his chest as he makes a smart remark.

I let go of his arms as we get up right, I finally get to see him fully and my jaw almost dropped to the floor. He wore sports leggings with Nike shorts on top and a black tank top to fit in with the look. A piece of his hair dangled down on his forehead and my heart was about to explode just by looking at him.

"What did you want?" I ask him, trying to not make it noticeable that I was blushing.

"I wanted to see you before practice starts," He replies and I grow confused.

"But you would be seeing me at practice?" I said in confusion, and his eyes said something else.

He looked behind me and I mimic his actions seeing that Winnie stood there with her bags in hand.

"What are you doing here?" I ask her and she smiles.

"Keaton told me you said yeah to come to my house to get ready for the party tonight," She states and I slowly turned around to give Keaton a death stare.

"Why would you tell her that?" I whisper out and he shrugs.

"Because you need some fun in your life plus your dad's totally in for it," He explains.

"My dad said yes to me going to a party?" I laugh out, pointing at myself.

Keaton nods. "You went to that Halloween party and your dad didn't care."

"Because it was a Halloween party," I said, crossing my arms.

"Same thing, but this party is going to be smaller."

"Don't worry, Tae. Keaton and I went to your dad in advisor and he said he didn't care as long as Keaton kept an eye out on you," Winnie explains, rubbing my arm.

"This is the last party I'm going to and I mean it," I tell them both and Keaton nods while Winnie smiles.

When does she not ever smile?

Winnie runs to her car and grabs my bag to put them in the trunk, I turn around before leaving to kiss Keaton, but as soon as I go to back up, he leans in for one more and this time he grabs a hold of my face and deepens the kiss.

I laugh throughout because I couldn't pull away, I grab Keaton's hands and he finally pulls apart.

"If you weren't so good looking, I'd punch you," I said to him, and he smiles showing his pearly whites.

"And if we weren't in public right now, I'd do something to you that you're probably not ready for," He retorts and I smack his shoulder playfully.

"I'll see you at the party," I tell him and he nods.

I turn around and walk towards Winnie's car, she lips sings something which I couldn't hear until I open the door which was a rap song.

She turns it down as I sit down the seat and turns to me.

"You and Keaton are looking like y'all are pretty serious," She says, backing up from her parking space.

I shrug as she looks at me.

"You should see how Keaton looks at you," She comments.

"What?" I furrow my eyebrows.

"He just gives you this look," She tries to explain but couldn't.

We head on to Winnie's house and as we get there, I receive a text from my dad saying to have fun and be careful and that he loves me, I send him a text saying that I love him too.

"I'm thinking maybe you could wear a red dress, oh no, black! Yes, that'd be so hot," Winnie says, turning off her car.

"Why can't I wear this?" I point down to the blue jeans and yellow shirt I was wearing.

"You don't like dressing up?" She asks and I shake my head.

"Well, you don't have to but I just thought that one of my black dresses would've looked good on you," She replies as she opens her door.

I follow her steps and she takes out her stuff and mine from the trunk.

"I look fat in dresses," I tell her and she gives me a bored look.

"Tae, girls would die for your body, your body is the definition of perfect," I smile at her comment, but on the inside, I was saying 'if you only knew what was killing my body'.

"Thanks, but I think it should be the other way around where I'm saying your body is to die for," I said and Winnie laughs.

"You hungry?" She asks and I nod.

"Very," I answer.

"Come on, I'll whip us up a meal right quick then we can get ready," She tells me and I nod following her in her humongous home.

We reach the kitchen and I was in awe from there, I don't think I'll ever get tired of seeing her house.

"You should stay over one night," Winnie comments, taking out a pot from a cabinet.

I take a seat on a stool near the bar watching Winnie pour water into the bowl.

"Yeah, that'd be fun," I nodded my head.

"Yeah, it would, just us, none of the stupid boys," She laughs out.

"Sounds like paradise," I sarcastically remark.

"But I don't think Keaton could go one day without you," She says, rolling her eyes playfully.

"What do you mean?"

"Keaton spends so much time with you, I hardly have time to spend with you," She playfully pouted as she explains to me.

"We could always have a girl's day out and stuff," I shrug.

"Ouuu yes," She excitedly says.

After we had eaten which was pasta, we went up to Winnie's room which wasn't a room really, to get ready for the party. I thought of Keaton as I watch Winnie brush out her beautiful luscious red hair.

He was excited for this party, the only reason why I was even going was because of Keaton, and Winnie of course because I couldn't bear to see her upset with me. Keaton spent so much time on trying to get to know me and be with me, I needed to do something for him.

I wanted to be a part of his world, which meant parties.

Plus, this was Keaton's last year of high school and I want to make him smile because I know when he wears that cap and gown and walk across that stage to get his diploma his dad will be even more intense with him about college.

Who knows if Keaton and I will be together when he leaves for college, and if we aren't he will *always* have something to look back on to *remember* me. That I attended parties with him and that I listened and was there for him through thick and thin.

"Winnie," I hear myself say.

Winnie turns around with a curling iron in her hair. "Mhm?"

"Show me the dress."

****

Around night time we got finished getting ready and Winnie ended up putting me in the black dress she wanted me to wear in the first place and some black heels that aren't too high for me but wasn't my type.

If this is what will make Keaton happy then I would wear heels every day. Kidding, or am I?

Winnie's 'security' had arrived and her mom had left to go out on a date, Winnie brought out the liquor that her mom stashes and sodas out on the tables. I helped Winnie around by grabbing the cups and going into her room to get her Bluetooth speaker.

When I was about to leave, a picture caught my eye. It was of Winnie and her dad when she was little, she was wearing his baseball hat while on his shoulder with the same big smile she always wears every day.

"Tae, the boys are here-" Winnie stops mid-sentence once she enters the room and spots me staring at the photo.

I look away and stare into her eyes which held no sadness. "I'm sorry-"

"Don't, I'm not afraid to talk about him," She cuts me off with a smile.

I stay silent as she picks up the frame with her and her father.

"I miss him every day, but I *always* keep a smile because that's what he would've wanted me to do," She lets out, before putting the picture down.

"Don't be afraid to talk about your mom to me, and if you're not ready, that's okay because I'll be here waiting patiently."

"Thanks," I give her a smile.

"And if you have any questions, come to me," She adds and I nod.

"Boo!" Reece jumps out in the room causing me and Winnie to jump.

"What the hell did I say about scaring me," Winnie screams, hitting Reece in the chest.

"You said not to, but it only makes me wanna do it more," He remarks, smiling.

Landon walks in wearing a blue jean jacket with some converse which made him look like a school boy.

"I heard you guys from downstairs," Landon cuts in, kissing Winnie's forehead.

"Yeah, probably because of Winnie's big ass mouth," Reece states, jabbing his thumb towards Winnie who stays glaring.

Reece looks back at me and gives me a look over.

"You look nice," He comments and I was surprised that he even looked my way.

"Thanks," I reply, smiling.

He smiles back before looking down at my legs that were full on display, Landon hits him on the shoulder grabbing his attention.

"What?" Reece asks.

"Dude, if Keaton saw you just now you wouldn't be able to play the next game," Landon warns him, and Winnie looks back at me before walking towards her closet.

She grabs a blue jean jacket and hands it to me.

"Keaton will kill me if he saw you in that with nothing covering your arms," She explains and I take it with a smile.

I put on the jacket which seemed to fit nicely around me, I was wondering where Keaton was in the first place.

"Where is Keaton?" I ask, crossing my arms.

"He's outside on the phone with his dad," Landon says, fixing his hair.

I nod before heading out of the room and down the stairs to go find him, I open the front door and spot Keaton's black Jeep but no Keaton, I walk further out of the house to see more cars coming down the road and into the long driveway of Winnie's.

"I don't care, Lydia," I hear Keaton's masculine voice, but the name I heard coming out of his mouth made my heart stop.

Lydia.

She was here.

Of course, she was, because everywhere Keaton is she is going to be there.

I follow the sound of his voice and go around to the back of his Jeep to see him leaning against it with Lydia in front of him in a dress with no support for her boobs so they were just out there.

Typical Lydia.

"Listen Keaton-" She starts but her eyes meet mine as I stand there watching with my arms crossed.

"Great," She mumbles, hitting the ground with the heel of her shoe.

Keaton turns his head so fast he could've caught whiplash, his eyes stayed on me and he stands up slowly.

I can finally see him and what he was wearing which was some black jeans and a black button up jacket.

"This is why Winnie told me to wear black, typical," He says, putting his hands in his pockets.

He forgets about Lydia and just ignores her and walks towards me until he's in front of me, even with heels I had to look up from him being so tall.

He looked down at me and stares at me with so much passion in his eyes, he wasn't even touching me and I was shivering to the core.

"You look beautiful," He compliments, licking his lips.

I smile. "Thank you."

"What was that about?" I ask, watching Lydia staring at us from behind him.

He sighs. "She is a shit faced liar, that's all I gotta say."

He grabs my waist and walks me towards the house, I look back at Lydia giving me a frown with her arms crossed. The music had started once we walked in and more people started entering from behind us, not a few seconds later, Lydia walked in with Mandy by her side.

"Who the hell invited her?!" Winnie yells through the music to me.

I shrug my shoulders. "I don't know."

"I'm gonna get security to escort her out," She says, before walking towards one of the security guys.

I turn around to face Keaton and watch him stare at Lydia with his jaw clenched, she meets his eyes and smirks before disappearing in the kitchen.

I had a weird gut feeling about this, Winnie came back and grabbed me by my wrists and took me out where everyone was dancing.

She swung my arms and danced around me while I smiled trying to get Keaton out of my mind. I swayed to the music with Winnie, but my eyes stayed on him, my heart dropped when I saw him walking into the kitchen.

What the hell was going on?

"I'll be right back," I tell Winnie who nods.

I quickly walked into the kitchen to see Keaton jugging down a beer with Lydia by his side speaking to him, he leaned his upper body over the counter and Lydia sits down on one of the bar stools.

A hand touches my shoulder and I turn my head to see a fuming Winnie.

"What the hell," Winnie mumbles watching her best friend talking to Lydia.

I stay quiet with a frown on my face.

"What the hell is this?" Winnie shouts, grabbing my arm gently.

"We were just talking," Lydia states, smirking at me.

"No, you were, I was just hearing you pout," Keaton glares at Lydia which causes her to frown.

"Are you serious? Tae is literally the best girl for you and you decide it would be a great idea to talk to Lydia who broke your heart," Winnie says, laughing sarcastically.

Keaton shakes his head. "I wasn't doing anything; I just came in here for a beer."

I didn't want to be that jealous girlfriend or that type of girl to accuse their boyfriend of doing something, but it seemed like he came here for a reason and he watched her come in here.

Keaton looks at me. "I swear Tae, I told her to stay out of my life."

"You know what, I'm so tired of watching you two try to be the perfect couple, I thought you weren't going to last because obviously Tae's not Keaton's type. Keaton, you're controlled by your 'daddy' and Tae, you're just living in the shadows of us and the only reason why you're known is because Keaton here saw you as a toy or something like that," Lydia blurts out, before drinking her beer.

She smiles before standing up and walks towards me, she gets in my face before whispering. "He might like you now, but you're not what he needs or wants, what he wants is something that'll put out more."

After that she bumps her shoulder against mine and walks out of the kitchen.

"Let me go get Landon so he can help me hide her body once I get done murdering her," Winnie mumbles, hurriedly exciting the kitchen.

"What did she say?" Keaton hurriedly asks, setting his beer bottle down.

I look down at myself and wonder why I was wearing this in the first place, but then I remember it was for Keaton.

"I knew this was a bad idea," I mumble, crossing my arms.

I move my feet around trying to ache them from there tiredness.

"Tae, what did she say?" " Keaton walks closer to me and I push a piece of my hair behind my ear.

"I want to go home," I tell him, before walking away and out the door of Winnie's house.

A few people were outside either smoking a cigarette or puking their guts out.

"What the hell did she say, Tae?" Keaton grabs me and turns me around to look at him.

"I know you had a past and I said I would talk to you about everything because we're not like other couples, but it does bother me that she had you first and she keeps rubbing it in my face about the times you two had, I'll never be like her just know, I'll never be the hot and sexy you crave like her," I pour out my heart that's been eating at me to say.

He stays quiet, giving me a confused look.

"I don't even know why I'm wearing this; I hate heels, my boobs are so small to look good in this dress, I don't even wear makeup, and god, my mascara is running down my face. But the point is you deserve so much more, Keaton, I care about you so much I don't fit to be in this role."

"I'm sorry," I quickly add in a quiet whisper, tears falling down my face like a waterfall.

Looking down at the heels in my hands and sigh out, I quickly look up to see Keaton inches away from my face and his lips were on mine in seconds, as we pull apart his hands were clasped around my face and he looked deep into my eyes.

"You are more than enough Tae Lambert, I picked you because you are the strongest person I know, you don't need to change because of me, you're perfect just the way you are. What me and Lydia had is different from what we have, we have so much more. Lydia and I was built up by lust and yeah, I did love her and yeah, she did break my heart, but I got over it, me and you are in too deep now, you can't leave me because I won't let you first of all and second is I don't think I can get over this one. I like you too much to let you go, I deserve you just as much as you deserve me," He says, captivating me with his eyes.

I remove his hands gently from my face and wipe under my eyes.

"Just take me home," I demand quietly, looking over his shoulder at Winnie who was giving me a worried look.

"I couldn't find her..." She trails, with a baseball bat in her hand.

Keaton turns around to Winnie. "I'm gonna take Tae home."

"Okay, let me get my hug first," Winnie said, walking over towards me giving me a bear warming hug.

"Are you okay?" She asks, giving me a worried look.

I nod. "Yeah."

"Alright, text me when you get home."

"Okay," I tell her.

I knew the car ride with Keaton was either going to be awkward or either him begging me to talk to him, but I knew I had to face it.

Keaton and I enter the Jeep and he cranks up it before reversing out into the road, he tries reaching out for my hand during the ride home, but I jerked my hand away. I don't understand what took over me.

Was it jealousy?

Thirty minutes later we're at my house with no talking, it was awkward and too painful.

"Talk to me, Tae," Keaton begs, reaching over to me after he cranks his car off.

"I'll see you tomorrow," My comment was short and stiff.

I hurriedly opened the passenger door and shut it behind me, I walk up the steps to my house when I hear his Jeep door open and slam shut.

"Don't be like this," Keaton says, trying to catch up with me.

I go to turn around but the porch light turns on and the front door open revealing my dad.

"What's going on?" My dad asks with tired eyes.

"Nothing, Keaton was just leaving," I tell him, looking at Keaton who was giving me a begging look and I open the front door and slam it closed.

I hear my dad and Keaton's voice talk, but the door was muffling them, I walk upstairs to go take a long hot shower.

This night turned into a disaster and I wasn't too sure how we were going to turn this one around.

Chapter Twenty-Eight

Tae's Pov.

"Good afternoon students, I join you guys today for this assembly to share with you the information on when we come back from winter break in two weeks," Principals Myers spoke through the microphone.

I sit in the bleachers listening in, Winnie sits beside me typing on her phone. I felt eyes on me during the whole assembly and knew who it was, he had been trying to talk to me all day and luckily, we didn't have seventh period because the assembly was going to take up the time.

I finally let my eyes land on Keaton who had been staring at me throughout the hour, he was leaning back against the bleachers with his hands connected, he was wearing a black hoodie with some sweatpants which looked too good on him.

He pointed to his phone and mouthed the words. 'Text me'.

I snatch my phone from my back pocket and read the text he had sent.

Keaton
'You look beautiful today'

I look up giving him a bored look, but seeing his smirk made it so hard not to smile.

"Merry Christmas everyone and a happy new year!" Principal Myers ends the assembly and everyone leaves to get their things to leave the school.

Loud screams filled the halls and papers filled the floors, everyone bumped into everyone and Winnie and I stayed close together.

"Damn, can people calm down, they'll get home sooner or later," Winnie says, throwing her gum in the trash as we passed one.

Landon slips into Winnie's arms and I just knew Keaton was close by, a hand on my waist was conformation for me.

I turn my head to see Keaton smiling down at me.

"Keaton," I greet, with no tone in my voice.

"Lambert," He mimics my actions and I roll my eyes.

"Are you still mad at me?" He asks, letting go of my waist as we get to my locker.

"Hell yeah," Winnie answers for me causing Keaton to glare.

I roll my eyes at the two.

"Did you think that text was cute? That I would fall back to your arms and drop my panties?" I ask him, raising my eyebrow.

"I wouldn't complain," He holds his hands up in surrender.

"Disgusting," I mumble, grabbing my backpack from my locker.

"Did you think what you pulled on me last night was cute?" He retorts back, holding onto the locker door.

"Yes, actually I did," I sarcastically said, causing him to playfully glare.

"Well, I guess you'll think your dad inviting me over for dinner tonight is cute too," He replies back, giving me a sarcastic smile.

I pause, slamming my locker door shut. "What?"

"Yeah, he said it would be good to talk things out because I explained to him that you were upset with me," He explains, licking his lips.

"I'm going to kill him," I mumble, causing Keaton to smile.

My dad walks the almost empty halls and I push Keaton out the way so I could have a chat with him.

I grab his arm. "Why did you invite Keaton to dinner tonight?"

"Because you were mad at him and he wanted to talk but you were being stubborn," My dad explains, shrugging.

I roll my eyes. "Next time when you want to invite someone over for dinner let me know before."

"Yes ma'am," He salutes me, looking beside me.

I turn my head towards the person who grabbed my dad's attention, Keaton stands beside me with his book bag on his shoulder with a cheeky smile on his face.

I squint my eyes at him, glaring so hard that maybe my eyes could shoot lasers out of them.

"Keaton?" I batted my eyelashes as I call out his name.

"Yeah?" His eyes stare right into mine as I give him the fakest smile possible.

"Why do you do these things to annoy me?"

He chuckles. "It's my job, I started day one and I'm not stopping now."

"You will stop once I shove my knee up your-" He cuts me off by covering my mouth with his hand.

"Tae," My dad warns me causing me to sigh.

"I'm going to the truck," I state, pointing towards the door.

My dad nods. "Head on out there while I'll chat with Keaton."

I nod my head before heading out of the school and make my way to my dad's old pick-up truck, I wonder what he's telling him right now? Probably an idea to annoy me.

I unlock the driver door and hit the unlock button and swing around the truck to get in on the passenger side, it doesn't take long until I see my dad and Keaton walk out of the school wearing smiles on their faces.

I unhook my bag from my shoulders and lean more into the seat as I watch Keaton and my dad walk towards the truck. Keaton comes around my side of the truck and points downward meaning to roll down the window.

My dad joins me in the truck and I grab the petal to roll down the window and I can now see Keaton clearly; his bright smile never fades from there.

"I'll see you tonight at six," He says, leaning in to kiss my cheek.

Him and I both knew if my dad wasn't sitting there, he would've kissed me on the lips, but being respectful was one of the main keys for Keaton Davis. *Sometimes.*

"Okay," I tell him, giving him a real smile this time.

His face brightens up once he sees my smile and he nods before backing up to let us out, my dad heads off in a hurry to get dinner started because he only had three hours and when my dad's cooking, he takes up the whole day.

"Keaton seems to like you a lot, Tae," My dad interferes as I look out of the window. "More than I thought he did."

"Winnie keeps saying that too," I said, rolling my eyes.

"He'll probably take you to prom," He insists, shrugging his shoulders while keeping his eyes on the road.

I scoff. "You know how I feel about prom."

"Tell me one of your other excuses now," He sarcastically remarks, rolling his eyes.

"Okay," I shrug. "You spend way too much money for only one night and sometimes your night turns into crap, why would you go to some lame prom when you could stay at home and watch movies all night?"

"Because it's supposed to be one of your high school memories, once you get older you look back on that and say well at least I went," He states, looking at me before looking back at the road.

"Can we stop talking about this?" I plead, crossing my arms.

"Yes, but only because you know I'm right," He points his finger at me.

I laugh. "Yeah, right."

We get to the house and I couldn't be happier seeing the little tiny home I grew up in, I couldn't believe I only had one more year of high school left and then I was off to college. I wasn't going to go to a college so far away like Georgie did, yeah maybe that was his dream school, but I could never leave dad alone.

Speaking of Georgie...

How was he?

"Have you spoken to Georgie?" I hear myself ask my dad as we exit the truck.

He shakes his head. "Nope, last time I heard from him he was talking about how busy he was."

"Yeah, busy catching stds," I joke, causing dad to chuckle.

My dad unlocks the front door and we enter the smell of cinnamon and pumpkin scented candles we left out earlier.

"I'll get the food out," My dad calls out, setting his keys down on the counter.

"I'll get the pots and pans," I say back, sighing.

For the next two hours, my dad and I worked on cooking and baking a cake which took so much patience and hand coordination, but end the end the meal looked too good to be true.

I clasped my hands together. "Well, we did it."

"Yes, we did," My dad says, holding up his hand for a high five.

I slapped his hand and just then the doorbell rings, my eyes go wide and I snatch my phone out of my pocket to see texts from Keaton saying that he was on his way and then he was here.

"He's here!" I exclaim, taking my apron off.

"Keaton?" My dad asks, watching hurriedly run up the stairs.

"Yes!" I holler back, wiping the powder off my face.

I quickly change my top and put on the Beatles t shirt with some black leggings, I put my hair into a messy ponytail and my heart races as I hear talking down stairs.

"Shit," I cursed, falling as I try to put on a sock.

As I fall, I try to reach for my closet door which wasn't a good idea and it slams back into the wall creating a loud noise. I stay quiet hoping that nobody walks up the stairs to check up on me.

I slip on my socks and reach up for my shoes, but as soon as I look up, I find Keaton staring down at me.

"You alright?" He asks, trying not to laugh.

I glare. "Don't laugh."

"Here," He holds out his hands for me to take to stand up and I gratefully do as just that.

"Thanks," I mumble, before snatching my shoes off the floor and slipping them on.

"What are you doing here an hour early?" I add.

He shrugs. "Just wanted to make a good impression for your dad."

"I'm sure he already likes you since you're his Quarterback," I retort, sitting on my bed.

"It's all about how you play, Tae," He says, following my actions sitting right next to me.

"Yeah, but when I fainted that day on the field, he trusted you to take me to the Nurse's."

"True," He nods his head slowly.

I look down at my hands while sighing out quickly, I felt bad about last night, jealousy took over my body and I wasn't thinking clearly, plus I felt like Lydia was trying to play games and I knew she would've won if I said start.

"I'm sorry," I tell him quietly, making his head turn towards me.

"About what?" He raises an eyebrow and I finally look up to his beautiful brown eyes.

"Last night, I acted out of hand, I was jealous when Lydia started talking to you and I felt self-conscious because she looked like every guys dream and I was looking like a stick with no boobs," I can't believe I actually said 'no boobs', why the heck would I say that?

But I couldn't help but stare at him with my big brown eyes full of guilt from last night as he stares at me with so much mystery I was about to explode, soon his frown turned into a grin.

"Tae, you have nothing to be jealous about, Lydia might be nice looking on the outside, but she sure is nothing like that on the inside. You, are something that every guy needs to have, you are so much more than any of the girls at Westside high and I could tell you that every single day for the rest of my life because you're worth it Lambert," He pours out his heart to me as I sit there taking it in staring deeply into his eyes.

He takes ahold of my hand and kisses the top of it causing shivers to run down my spine, it was so hard not to resist this boy and I don't know when I'll be able to hold on.

"Stop downing yourself, because you're beautiful. Every inch. I want you for you not what everybody wants you to be," He finishes, wiping a stray tear from under my eyes.

I groan. "It's like you're not even real, you say the right words at the right times and you always make the situation better. You're like the prince in every fairytale book I used to read."

"What can I say, I got smooth words," He jokes, shrugging while sarcastically flipping his hair in the wind.

I laugh out as he smiles, but suddenly his face forms into a serious one.

" I'm serious about the whole we're not like other couples where we run away from our problems, you come to me if you feel insecure and unsure of things and I'll do the same," His voice came out sharp and I couldn't help but smile even more.

I nod. "Okay."

"Promise?" He holds out his pinky waiting for mine to connect with his.

I raise an eyebrow suddenly surprised that he knew about that kind of stuff but went along with it.

"Promise," I connect my pinky with his as I finish.

"Okay twirl your hand with mine now," He says, twirling his hand around to where his hand was in front of my face and mine was near his.

"And..." He trails, slowly kissed my hand which felt too good while staring into my eyes.

I do the same with a smile and we both unhook our hands from each other.

"You're one weirdo, Keaton," I tell him, giggling softly.

"I might be one, but I still made you smile," He says.

I take ahold of his face with both of my hands and press my lips upon his.

As I pull back, I tell him. "You *always* do."

Chapter Twenty-Nine

Tae's Pov.

"This is the first time I've seen your room when it isn't messy," I say proudly, looking around at the spotless room.

Keaton shrugs as I turn around to give him a cheeky smirk. "My dad had some business to attend and is not here for a while so no fights have been going on."

"I hate that you and your dad can't get along," I tell him, sadly laying my book bag down on the ground. "He's so rough on you when you try your hardest and it's not fair that he tries to decide your future for you."

As I explain to him how unfair he was being treated I hear Keaton's door being shut and locked causing me to swiftly turn my head toward Keaton who was leaning against his bookshelf with a smug smile.

"Why are you smiling at me?" I couldn't help but smile and the blood rushes up to my cheeks.

"Because I love how you worry so much about others, especially over me. I don't deserve it, I really don't, I didn't deserve a second chance when I went a wall during my mom's sickness and I could've lost my spot on the football team," he finally spits out, frowning a bit.

I walk slowly toward the buffed-up boy who watches me passionately. "Everyone deserves a second chance, we make mistakes and a lot at that, you don't need to be perfect and especially for your dad, or anyone for that matter."

As he leans against the bookshelf, I wrap my arms around his waist and flutter my eyelashes at him.

"You're a good person, Keaton. You have the kindest heart someone could ever have," I state, truthfully.

Keaton unwraps his arms from himself and lays both of his hands on each side of my arms with a smile plastered on his face.

"You're amazing, you know that?" He says, rubbing my arms slightly.

I shrug. "I don't mean to brag, but I kinda am."

"I like you a lot, Lambert," He admits, sighing out.

My heart pounds out of my chest.

"I like you a lot too, Davis," I cheekily say back, causing a smile to rupture onto his face.

He begins to bend down to place his lips on mine gently and I begin to stand on my tippy toes to connect mine with his, I smile into the kiss as I feel Keaton's hands find their way to my neck and my cheek.

Ever so slightly I felt Keaton's tongue slide against mine causing me to shiver in delight, my hands went from his waist to his chest in minutes and I brushed them against his abs feeling him shiver, I smile even more into the kiss.

Keaton chuckles causing me to pull away and I patted his chest lightly.

"Let's get started on what we're actually here for," I state, giving him a smirk making him groan.

"Why can't we just chill? We're not even in the same classes, what do we need to be studying together for anyway?"

I take out my math notebook from my book bag. "Well, instead of us not hanging out because of studying all day, we can study together while hanging out, plus we have agriculture together and we have a test in a few days."

He nods while slowly licking his lips.

The both of us finally take a seat on his bed, but eventually that ended with us laying on each other while I study for the agriculture test and Keaton runs his fingers through my hair. Which I'm not complaining.

An hour later, Keaton groans out.

"Tae please, can we do something else," He pleads out, taking the book out of my hands.

I raise up looking down at the tired looking boy. "I was reading that!"

"Stop being a sourpuss and have some fun," He complains, setting my book down on his nightstand.

"I have done fun stuff, like going to parties which did not end up well, I skipped school which got us in detention, so please let me have my book back so I can finish studying so I won't get a bad grade," I explain to him, reaching for my book, but his hands caught mine.

I laugh out of annoyance. "Keaton, stop."

"You've been studying for an hour; don't you think it's time to stop and have a break?" He asked, raising an eyebrow.

"And in that hour, I couldn't focus because you kept on touching me and you were distracting me," I tell him who smirks.

"All I did was put my hand on your leg," He shrugs.

"Yeah, and it was distracting," I blush as I admit to him that he was a distraction when it came to him touching me.

He smirks and I quickly snatch the book out of his hand when he wasn't looking, he playfully glares at me and I smiled in triumph before laying against the headboard and open the notebook.

I feel Keaton move around the bed and all of a sudden, he's above me giving me a look like he's wanting to eat me.

That came out wrong.

My eyes were locked with his and it was like I was in a trance, his finger gently pushes the top of my book and pushes it down, my chest feels heavy and I felt hot suddenly, in a quick flash, he grabs the book out of my hands and tosses it across the room.

My mouth opens a little and my palms get sweaty.

"I-I need to get home because it's getting a little late," I stuttered a bit, as I watch him lean forward.

He licks his lips before smirking. "Uh huh."

"I had fun though," I state, before tossing him off me quickly with a pattering heart.

He stands up from his bed with a confused look and I snatch the book from the ground.

"You good?" He asks, seeing me in my blushing sweaty state.

I nod. "Yeah."

"Okay," He says, bending over to grab my book bag.

I couldn't help but stare at his perfectly shaped butt, football players must do squats because this boy sure did have some cake on him.

Before I could even think straight, my hand comes across his butt letting out a loud slap, I realized what I had done when Keaton quickly stands up straight, I cover my mouth from laughing when his head slowly turns to my direction and his eyes squint as he playfully glares at me.

"I'm sorry," I giggle out, holding my hand out as I see him drop my book bag down on the floor and slowly starts to trail towards me.

"You're just asking for it now," He states, sarcastically laughs.

I back up as he gets close to me, he tries grabbing for me but I squeal and throw the book out of my hands, I run towards his window not even realizing that it was a bad idea. He blocks me but I hurriedly swoop under his arms before running towards his bed and crawl over it.

"I said I was sorry," I point at him, but he shakes his head and laughs.

"You think you're slick," He says, pointing at me mimicking what I did.

He runs across his bed in a flash and I curse him for doing football at this moment, I go to turn around to run but I had nowhere to run to, a pair of arms wrap around my waist, and yanked me down on his bed in a swift move.

My back was against the bed as I look up at Keaton with big doe eyes.

"How come I can't touch you like that but you can do that to me?" He asked, raising an eyebrow.

"I only did that one time," I admit, giving him a bored look.

He raises his hand and brushes the hair out of my face, I smile up at him as he mimics my actions.

"You're so damn beautiful," He confesses, looking at me with a pure look.

"Thank you," I blushed, feeling his hand caressed my cheek.

He hums before pecking my lips. "I'm gonna make you fall in love with me."

My heart drops and my face flushes even more, he gives me an intense look and I couldn't help but stare at him in surprise.

Now that's a challenge.

But on the inside, I knew he was up for it and maybe he could actually make me do it. This boy was powerful.

Chapter Thirty

Tae's Pov.

"Woah Tae!" My dad exclaims as I back out of the driveway.

"What?" I huff, looking over at him with annoyance written on my face.

"Don't go so fast," He states, looking at me with wide eyes.

I turn around in the car to see we were still in the driveway and didn't even move an inch from the spot we were parked in.

"Dad, we literally haven't made it out of the driveway yet," I point out, giving him a bored look.

He looks back in relief. "Oh."

"Do you wanna do this another time?" I ask, pointing at his sweaty forehead.

"No, I'm fine, just a little nervous," He assures, but I wasn't believing a word he said. "We can go."

"Okay..." I trail, beginning to back up a little and watching my dad at the corner of my eye.

I stop just in time because of the familiar black Jeep pulling on the side of the sidewalk in front of my house, a smile reaches my face and my dad exhales a breath of air.

"Maybe Keaton will help you," My dad says, hurriedly rushing out of the car.

I huff out of breath before putting the truck in park, I step out with the truck still running just in case Keaton says yeah.

Keaton steps out of his Jeep with a bald cap on his head but backwards, my knees grow weak at the sight of him and he gives my dad a smile along with a handshake.

"Keaton! How are you doing man?" My dad greets him.

Keaton smiles. "Doing great, wanted to stop by to see Tae."

"Well, you're just in time, she's practicing how to drive before her big test and we were just about to leave, you wanna join?"

"Are you a good driver?" Keaton asks, a smirk now plastered on his face.

"Yes," I state, crossing my arms.

"Yeah, I bet," He said sarcastically.

"Instead of me just me dying I'll have you with me too," My dad jokes, causing me to playfully glare at him.

"Yeah, I'm in."

"Great, let's get this over with," My dad informs.

"Do not wreck my truck," He adds, turning around towards me.

I hold my hands up in surrender and nod, Keaton laughs.

Keaton walks towards me as my dad goes for the passenger in the truck, Keaton kissed my cheek before giving me a little hug.

"You better not kill us," He murmurs, placing his hand at the bottom of my back as we walk towards the truck.

"I won't because I'm a good driver," I assure, getting into the driver's seat as Keaton gets in the back.

"Okay, Tae. Back up slowly," My dad instructs and I sigh out before backing up.

I back out of the driveway without my dad yelling for me to stop and I thank the lord that he didn't because I would've probably run out of the truck. I put the car in drive after and press on the gas, my dad holds onto the seat.

"Woah," He quietly says, earning a laugh from Keaton.

"We're fine see," I tell the both of them, stopping at a stop sign.

"I guess..." My dad trails, carefully looking out for cars.

I turn my blinker on before making a left seeing that no cars were coming.

"She seems like a pretty good driver to me," Keaton comments.

I smile. "I told you."

****

Two hours later we were back home and safe, my dad quickly got out of the car and dramatically tried to kiss the ground, Keaton slips out of the back seat chuckling at my dad while I roll my eyes.

I hand the truck keys to my dad who stands up and walks towards the house and unlock the front door, heading inside.

I put my hands in my back pocket and turn around to Keaton.

"What do you want to do now?"

"It's Christmas break, we can do anything," He reminds me, crossing his muscular arms.

"Mhh," I mumble, thinking.

"The Diner?" I ask, shrugging.

"I'm *always* down for it, let's go tell your dad then we'll leave," He says, and I nod.

We head into the house to find my dad in the kitchen on his laptop.

"Hey dad, Keaton and I are going to Greenhouse Diner," I tell him and he gives us a thumbs up.

"You want to go?" I add.

"No, you guys go ahead," He states, waving us off.

I kiss him on the cheek before heading out of the house.

Keaton wraps his arm around my shoulders before kissing my temple.

"You wanna spend the day with me tomorrow?" He asks, slowly licking his lips.

I nod. "Of course."

"My mom's throwing me a little party tomorrow," He states, opening the passenger for me.

"Why?" I raise an eyebrow.

"Birthday," He rolls his eyes, and I froze in my spot.

I turn around not even bothering to get in the Jeep.

"Your birthday is tomorrow?" I raise an eyebrow.

He nods. "Yeah, but it's not a big deal."

"Not a big deal?" I slap his chest playfully. "You're turning eighteen, of course it's a big deal."

"It's just another reason for my dad to get stricter on me," He says, shrugging.

"You could literally move out Keaton, which I'm not telling you to, but you're an adult and he can't tell you what to do anymore after tomorrow," I remind him, laying my hand on his arm.

"Maybe you're right," He shrugs.

I kiss his lips. "I know I am."

He smiles when I turn around and hop in, he shuts the door before walking to his side and gets in.

"You ready?" He asks and I nod.

Keaton turns up the heat and blows in his hands waiting for the Jeep to heat up, I wrap my arms around myself shivering from the cold.

Keaton reaches in the back and holds out a hoodie for me to take.

"That jacket looks so thin," He points out at the grey thin jacket I was wearing.

I take his hoodie. "Thank you."

"You're just wanting to go to the Diner so you can see Ally," He laughs out.

I nod. "Also, Tommy cause he's good looking."

I smirk at him as I teased him, he slowly turns his head towards me as he stops the Jeep at the stop sign.

He playfully glares. "What did you just say?"

"Nothing," I squeak out, biting my bottom lip.

"Mhm," He mumbles, putting the Jeep in park.

He quickly jumps at me causing me to jump and hold my hands out as he reaches his hands out to tickle my sides.

"Keaton, stop. What if someone pulls up behind us," I giggle out, trying to be serious.

"Well then they'll have to either wait or pull around," He states, putting both of my hands in one of his hands leaving the other to tickle me.

"Keaton, stop!" I laugh out, trying to push him off.

"Who's good looking?" He asks, stopping his attacks and cupping his ear.

I lean my head back breathlessly looking up at him.

"You," I breathed out, smiling.

He grins. "Thank you."

He bends over to touch his lips with mine and I quickly pecked his lips before pushing him off me to get in his seat and leave before someone comes up behind us.

During that time his hat fell off into his seat and he grabs it and puts it on his dashboard, I couldn't help but stare at the mouthwatering boy, watching him fix his hair was so satisfying.

How in the world did I hate this boy at one point?

Chapter Thirty-One

Tae's Pov.

Looking around my room for some tape was harder than expected, how can someone lose tape in under thirty seconds? I check under my covers to see if it accidentally fell on them.

"Dad!" I yell out.

"Yes?" He yells back.

"Do we have anymore tape?"

"Uh I'll check," He says.

I hear him walking around the house downstairs, I huff out trying to get everything perfect for Keaton today, I open the box with Keaton's birthday present inside, nervous bubbles start to form within me and I close the top quickly and breathe out.

I was scared that he won't like the gift, it came to the heart and also, I didn't know what to get him. I've never really had a boyfriend and I didn't know how this stuff worked, it was so much easier getting a woman a gift than a man and I didn't know why.

Probably because I'm a woman.

"I found some," My dad calls out, leaning against my bedroom door frame.

I felt something hard from under me as I plop down on my bed, I furrow my eyebrows and grab what was poking me, I sigh out in frustration as my hand holds the tape, I was looking for the whole time.

"You're stressing for no reason," My dad says, entering my room with the new tape in hand.

I place the tape in my hands on the bed. "I'm not, I just want today to be perfect for Keaton."

"Keaton's always made every day perfect for me so I need today to be perfect for him, I hope he likes my gift," I then add.

"He will," He assures, sitting down on my bed.

I look down at my hands. "I wish Georgie knew about Keaton."

"Next time he calls you can tell him all about it."

Next time he calls...

That could've made me laugh, but it didn't.

I missed Georgie so much, I didn't notice that he missed so much of what happened in my life and what's changed, and I also probably missed big changes in his life. What if he cut off his big bushy hair? What if he got taller? What if he got a girlfriend?

The girlfriend thing.... Nah.

Georgie never once had a girlfriend in his life, so if he brought home a girl it'd be a shock to all of us, but I couldn't talk because I never had a boyfriend until Keaton came around.

"If he ever calls me," I retort, huffing a bit.

My dad checks his watch and he coughs before saying. "We should probably head towards Keaton's."

I nod before grabbing the box and placing it in the bag with Keaton's other gifts, my dad and I head out of the house and into his pick-up truck, it didn't take long for us to get to Keaton's home, cars filled the yard and driveway and I just wanted to turn back around seeing that the driveway was filled the party would be worse.

I held my head up as I hop out of the truck and see Winnie's head pop out of her red dune buggy.

I laughed in my head as my eyes traveled down her body to see what she was wearing, no doubt about it that Winnie was beautiful, not only her face was, but her body had all the right curves. She wore a red fitted tied up shirt with laces going down in the middle and dark blue jeans with heels.

No wonder Lydia was so jealous and why Winnie is so popular.

Winnie turns her head hearing my dad slam his door and a smile reaches her face and she waves before trying to run towards me in her heels, her curly hair bounces against her shoulders and her bright white teeth were on full display.

"I'm so glad you're here! Keaton is gonna be so happy," She states, wrapping her arm around mine.

My dad walks behind us as we walk down the long driveway.

"I wouldn't miss it, but why are there so many people here?" I ask, looking around once more.

She waves it off. "Keaton's parents go over the top when it comes to his birthdays, he's always wanted it just to be him and his friends hanging out, but look what happens."

"Oh wow, does Keaton even know these people?"

"Half of them, no. Some of them, yes."

I nod. "Wow."

Winnie rings the doorbell and in just a few seconds the door opens and in all of his glory, Keaton appears behind it.

He breathes out a breath. "Thank god you guys came, I can't take enough of my mom's friends squeezing my cheeks."

Winnie walks in giving Keaton a hug and telling him a happy birthday.

"Where do I put these?" She holds up four birthday gift bags.

"Find my mom and she'll tell you," He rolls his eyes as she grins before leaving.

He turns back to me as I hold his gifts in my hand. "Lambert, I was starting to worry you wouldn't show."

"I could never miss your special day," I tell him, spreading my arms open for a hug and he copies my actions.

"Thanks for coming Mr. Lambert," Keaton kisses the top of my head as he speaks to my dad.

"Happy Birthday, Keaton," My dad says, patting his back before heading off to find Keaton's dad.

Keaton shuts the door before turning back towards me with a smirk.

"I really didn't want a big party like this..." He trails, looking around at everyone.

"I wouldn't either, but at least it makes your mom happy," I point out at Mrs. Davis who was smiling from ear to ear at the present table.

Speaking of presents...

I hold up the bag in my hand. "I want you to open this last and not in front of anyone."

"Okay, let's put it in my room before my mom sees it and snatches it," He jokes, but I wasn't too sure with his tone.

I follow him upstairs and into his room and he closes the door before locking it.

I raise an eyebrow. "Why'd you lock the-"

I was cut off short by the feeling of Keaton's soft lips on mine, I lightly dropped the bag on his carpet floor before holding onto his arms so my legs wouldn't cause me to fall from the feeling of jelly in them.

I gave him a little push before giggling. "What was that?"

"Just to show you that I missed you," He shrugs.

I gave him a soft smile before handing him his gift, the door was already locked and we were here alone so he should just go ahead and open it.

"Happy birthday," I whisper out, blushing as he slowly retrieves the bag.

He shakes his head. "You didn't have to get me anything, I have you and that's the best gift I could receive."

"You're so cheesy," I tell him, taking a seat on his bed.

He follows my actions while looking into the bag, he takes out the grey Calvin Klein shirt I bought him, he eyes held a sparkle in them as he grabs the other gift, I had gotten him.

"Tae, are you serious?!" He exclaims, holding up the tiny box with the chain necklace in it.

I nod, smiling brightly.

"How much was this?" He asks, giving me a serious look.

"Don't worry about it, it's yours," I said, watching as he grabs the last thing, I had bought him.

His eyes lit up once he saw the blanket with his football jersey printed with his number on it.

"Tae, this is so fucking cool," He tells me, with a bright smile.

He bites his bottom lip as he looks back at it.

"I was afraid you weren't going to like it; I didn't know what to get you so I decided to just go with that," I explain, shrugging.

He shakes his head. "No, I love it. But you shouldn't have spent that much money on me, especially the chain."

"Did your dad buy this?" He asks.

"No, I spent all my money that I had saved up from birthdays and Christmas," I state, feeling proud of myself.

"Thank you, really. This is more than enough," He says, folding the blanket back up and placing it on the bed.

"I hope to see you wear that chain every day," I joke, pointing my finger at him.

"I'll put it on now and never take it off," He jokes, but clips it on around his neck.

I don't know if a flash of wind hit me in the face or punched me, but when Keaton slipped that necklace around his neck a feeling ran through me and I shiver.

The chain fit perfectly which I was afraid that it would be too dangly, it fell above his chest and it went well with his outfit that he had on.

He places a hand on my thigh. "Thank you, seriously."

"You're welcome," I smile.

"Keaton, come down here you have to open your presents!" Keaton's mom, Julie screams out.

He rolls his eyes. "What am I? Four years old?"

I laugh out and he pecks my lips before we head back downstairs, Winnie comes to my side and Landon grabs both of Keaton's shoulders shaking him a little and laughing amongst each other as they both sit beside each other talking.

"Here's some punch," Winnie announces, handing the red juice substance and I take it gratefully.

"Thanks," I smile at her in which she does the same.

I lean against the staircase, smiling gently as I watch the boy that had changed my ways and the way I thought as he opens his gifts like a little kid. Keaton's eyes connect with mine a few times and he couldn't help but smirk at me as I take a sip of punch.

I felt eyes watching me from the side of me and I wanted to look but something told me not to, but I did anyways, my breath got caught in my throat as I made eye contact with Randy, Keaton's dad.

He gives me a disapproving look causing me to gulp and he walks away suddenly as he takes a sip of his punch.

"Keaton is something else, isn't he?" Winnie catches me in my daze.

I nod giving her a fake smile as my eyes look back over to where Keaton's dad was, I look back up to Keaton who had a fake smile plastered on his face as he stands near his dad who grabs both of his shoulders and smiles.

Landon rubs the back of his neck nervously and Randy hollers out. "Thank you all for coming tonight, it was a pleasure seeing all of you. I can't believe my boy is eighteen today, next he'll be off to college."

Keaton begins to frown when he knows what his dad is about to do.

"Why don't you introduce your new girlfriend? I'm sure your family that hasn't seen you in a while wants to meet the special lady," Randy speaks out.

Half of Keaton's family looks around and some nods their heads.

"She doesn't like big crowds," Keaton awkwardly laughs out, keeping eye contact with me.

Randy's smile grows. "We won't bite, I'm sure she wants to meet the big family as well."

"Dad," Keaton warns, but smiles at the crowd that he calls family.

"Tae! Come on up here and show Keaton's family what you look like," Randy instructs, connecting eyes with me.

Winnie rubs my arm before nodding towards me. "It'll be okay, maybe he won't make a fuss."

I walk slowly up to where Keaton and Randy stand and awkwardly smile at the crowd, where was my dad when I needed him?

"Everyone this is Tae Lambert, Keaton's girlfriend," Randy introduces me while he wraps his arms around my shoulders and I hear Keaton intake a breath.

I smile as everyone tells me how cute I was and saying I look fit to be with Keaton.

"Does she know you're going to Ohio?" Randy asks, smirking at Keaton.

"Randy that's enough! Thank you all for coming everyone, have a safe trip back home and we love you," Julie states, and everyone goes to leave.

Julie looks back at her husband with an emotion that I couldn't describe.

"How could you? You should've seen their faces, they were as awkward as Tae was standing up here," Julie calls him out.

"You really sure know how to ruin someone's day, you knew Ohio is a touchy subject for me and you're going to talk about it in front of the family like that and some of the people I don't even know," Keaton tells him, yanking his father's hand off from around my shoulders.

I look behind me to see Winnie with a worried expression and my dad trying to hide any expression with the cup near his mouth watching us closely.

"The family wanted to know your decision and I let them know really quick where you're going," Randy spits out to his son.

That's when Keaton snaps.

"I never even made a decision on where I was going, are you crazy? You're fucking unbelievable and on top of that you made Tae half ass meet my family in the shittiest way possible," Keaton blurts out.

"I wanted to know if you were serious with her, I wanted to see if you were going to stop me because you didn't know if y'all were going to last, I don't want you to have any distractions."

"I'm sorry Randy, my daughter is a distraction?" I hear my dad's angry voice blurt out asking.

I feel hands grab my arm backing me away so if anyone goes to punching, I wouldn't get hit, I look back and gave Winnie a smile knowing her warm touch.

"It's *always* something huh?" She asks, shaking her head.

I nod.

"Of course not, Bo. I just don't want my son to be distracted from his future," Randy comments back.

Keaton shakes his head and mumbles something under his breath.

"So, you're definitely saying my daughter is a distraction," My dad says.

"Don't you want your daughter to have the same success that I'm trying to get my son to have?"

My dad sarcastically laughs out. "I'm done talking with you, me and my distraction are going to leave now because obviously she's not wanted here."

Keaton quickly flashes his head towards me giving me a pleading look not to leave.

"You are wanted here Mr. Davis, I'm so sorry my husband is acting this way, he's been drinking too much of his booze lately," Julie tries to make amends.

"Clearly," My dad states, looking back at Randy with disgust.

My dad grabs my hand and Winnie whispers that she's sorry and I look back at her with a soft smile.

"Mr. Davis, please don't leave because if you do, you'll get to thinking and you won't let me see Tae again," Keaton walks after us, but my dad ignores him as he walks with heavy breath towards the door.

"Maybe that will be a good thing, if your daughter will keep her legs closed then maybe Keaton will stop chasing after her," I gasp out as we stop in our tracks.

I knew Randy said that to get my dad riled up, I thought they liked each other?

I couldn't help what happened next in a flash, hearing Winnie's yelps and Julie's screams, I tried pushing me away from the scene. I had my dad in place so he couldn't get to Randy, but I couldn't stop Keaton from turning around and in a flash, he was on his dad beating his face in.

"You ruin everything!" Keaton screams out.

"You're the one ruining everything," Randy says as he gets hit again.

"Dad, stop," I tell him, calming him down.

"You can scream at me, hit me, tear my room apart, lock me out of the house, but you won't speak about Tae like that *ever* again," Keaton warns looking scary as he hovers over his bleeding dad. "You hear me?"

"Yeah," His dad says stubbornly, looking away from his eyes.

Landon grabs Keaton off of his dad and Julie helps Randy up, Winnie stands in the room quiet as a mouse with a pale face.

"You should've let me at him, he wouldn't be able to talk," My dad states, as I let him go.

I pat his arm. "Both of y'all would've killed him if I didn't stop one of y'all."

"Tae, I'm so sorry," Julie calls out, with tears hovering over her eyes.

I shake my head. "It's fine."

"No, it's not, you and your dad should always feel welcome in my home, you guys can come anytime and you stay with my son," She says, grabbing a hold of my hands.

"Okay," I tell her and she smiles before leaving to pick up her husband and help him to the kitchen while fussing at him for the mess he caused.

"I'll meet you in the truck to cool off some more because if I don't, I don't think you could stop me the second time from running into that kitchen and beating the shit out of him," My dad tells me and I nod.

Winnie walks to me with her heels clicking the floor. "I'm sorry I didn't help you stop your dad; I just froze when all that happened."

"It's fine, all I had to tell him was calm down for mom and he did," I shrug and she gives me a sad smile.

"Keaton won't stop staring at you, you better go to him before he goes crazy and think you're gonna end things with him over this or something crazier," She jokes but I wasn't too sure with Keaton.

I walk towards Keaton and Landon who was talking while keeping eye contact with Keaton, Landon smiles at me before walking past to Winnie.

I smile softly at Keaton earning a smile from him back.

My smile turned into a frown and I hit his chest causing him to raise an eyebrow.

"Are you stupid? Why would you hit your dad when you know he would have hurt you?" My voice cracks at the end.

"Because he had it coming, he ruined tonight and he knew he shouldn't have talked about you like that," He explains, shrugging.

"I know it was wrong of him to say that, but you shouldn't choose violence over talking over things," I point out.

He nods. "I'm sorry."

I wrap my arms around his neck and his arms wrap around my waist, I lay my head on his shoulder before sighing.

"I'm glad this is all over," I let out.

"Me too, I was thinking one of us was going to the hospital," He jokes but I never laughed.

"What does your dad think?" He asks.

"Probably that your dad is a dick."

He nods. "Happy birthday to me, right?"

Sarcasm was laced with his words and I awkwardly smile as he does the same, this night turned into a disaster and I knew it would knowing who Keaton's dad was, but him and I were okay and that's all that mattered.

Chapter Thirty-Two

Tae's Pov.

"Damnit Tae, that shit hurts!" Keaton exclaims, hissing as I wipe a wash rag against his bloodied knuckles.

I stare down at the bleeding boy seeing the bags under his eyes from staying up all night, Keaton came by the house at one in the morning texting me to 'open my window'. I almost screeched out when I had seen his appearance, but closed my mouth because of my sleeping dad in the next room.

He sits on the toilet as I stand in between us legs while his other hand lays against my nude leg.

I huffed. "Well, if you didn't go out late last night and sneak into a bar and fight some random guy then we wouldn't have this problem."

"I know..." He trails, looking down at his hand. "I'm sorry, I just got so mad at my dad, I couldn't be at the house."

"You could've come here and stayed the night rather than go fighting random people because you're mad, you can't take your anger out on people," I accuse, pointing my finger at him.

"Look at you being bossy," A grin spreads upon his face as he jokes but not once did, I laugh or crack a grin.

I slap his chest getting his attention. "I'm serious Keaton, you tell me to come to you about my problems, but you don't do the same with me, maybe at first you did, but now you don't speak a word."

"I should be the one who you run to talk about your dad, not to the bars and get drunk, that's not you, it's the old you."

"I know, I'm sorry. My dad pushed it way too far yesterday and I snapped, I still wasn't over it, I would've come to you trust me, but I didn't want me to do something I'd regret," He explains, shaking his head.

He facepalms himself. "Shit, I didn't mean it like that, I'd never hurt you-"

"No, it's fine. I didn't take it like that, I understand, but you could've run it off or something," I cut him off short, taking a hold of his hand.

He nods before proceeding to lick his lips. "And next time I will, no more fighting and no more drinking, I promise."

"Pinky promise?" I hold up my pinky finger in front of his face causing him to silently chuckle.

"Pinky promise," He says back, kissing my hand as I kiss his sealing the promise.

"Oh! And no more making your dad angry, I know how you like to push him to get angry," I tell him, pushing the piece of hair out of my face.

He nods. "Okay."

"Okay, you can sleep here for tonight, but you have to leave in about six hours cause my dad will be up then," I instruct causing him to nod.

I knew my dad wouldn't care if Keaton slept here but he wouldn't care if Keaton slept in my bed.

He stands up from the toilet and I put the peroxide and bandages back in the cabinet, I turn back to Keaton to see him looking down at his black hoodie with dried blood on it, I reach up to hug him afraid that if he let go, he'd be gone in a second.

"Don't ever scare me like that, you literally almost gave me a heart attack when you messaged me," I warned, looking up at him with my arms wrapped around his neck.

"I'm sorry I didn't mean to, I just needed you to open your window fast," He chuckles out a bit.

His eyes sparkled and I couldn't help myself by rubbing my thumb across his cheek.

"Tae, I think I lov-" My heart pounds in my ears as I thought I almost heard him say something I was scared of him saying.

Before I could hear anything, he said I hurriedly cut him off. "I'm really tired, aren't you?"

His face held an emotion in them I couldn't describe, he nodded and I took his hands in mine and led him out of the bathroom and into my bedroom. I let go of his hand before going around the bed on my side, leaving him on the other side.

I point at his hoodie with shaky hands. "You can take that off if you want."

I'm sure he didn't want to sleep in a hoodie with dried up blood on it, and I'm sure I didn't want it on my bed.

He nodded before grabbing the bottom and sliding it off his body, I tried so hard not to stare at his abs, but it looked too good to be true, his body was a work of art and if I touched it, I was scared it'd disappear.

I blush as we catch eye contact.

I slid in my still warmed bed and Keaton slid in beside me, we faced each other and I was glad the room was dark except for the little lamp was on beside me.

"Don't you sleep with your pants off too?" I ask quietly, putting my hands under my head as I lay on my side.

He nods. "Yeah, but I think the shirt off is getting too much for you since your red as a tomato."

"Oh..." I mumble, biting my lip.

Keaton raises up resting his palm against his head as he stares down at me.

"Thanks for taking care of me tonight," He whispers, leaning down towards me.

I smile. "Of course."

Keaton stops just above my lips so his lips hover over mine, I inhale a breath as his eyes keep trailing down to my lips then back up to my eyes until I finally grab his head and push him down on me.

I don't know what came over me when my lips claimed his, butterflies filled my stomach as I feel him smile throughout and his hand lays on my arm then travels down towards my back. My toes curled as he hovered over me slowly and my hands slowly reached down his neck.

I never felt this way before, it was new, I was scared but it felt too good to stop.

We pulled apart and I was left breathless as his lips connected to my neck, I looked over his back to see it flexing and my eyes couldn't help but to roll back as he kissed a spot that felt like I was on cloud nine.

My hands go straight towards Keaton's hair and I rub through it causing him to groan.

Keaton's lips stop moving and pull away from my hot neck, he connects eye contact with me and I watch his hair fall down just above his eyes.

"Bet you've never experienced that before," Keaton whispers, biting his lip.

I shake my head.

"If you thought that felt good just wait until my tongue is down there," As he whispers closely against my ear, he rubs his hand gently, but hurriedly so I couldn't stop him.

And I wouldn't.

When he swipes his hand down on my area, I inhaled a breath before letting it out once he falls back in place where he once was.

I was left shocked but with a weird feeling, I bit my lip before looking over at him as he stares at me with the same look, I was giving him.

Hunger.

But we both knew I wasn't ready for that big step, and I knew he wasn't going to rush anything, he was just going to let me have little tastes of what it's like.

And I was ready.

"Merry Christmas, Lambert," Keaton gently says, but with a grin.

I bite my lip before laying on my side. "Merry Christmas, Keaton."

****

"He did what?!" Winnie exclaims, plopping down on my bed.

I shush her from being so loud. "I have no idea what came over me, but I had this feeling and when he stopped it's like I wanted to kick him in his teeth."

"He got you horny, Tae," She laughs out quietly.

"So, that's what it feels like?!" I exclaim, tightly closing my legs.

She nods. "Just you wait, but didn't you learn this in health class?"

"They only taught us the basics not how you'd feel."

"Well, y'all only made out and he was making you feel good by kissing your neck, just wait till he fucks-" I cut her off short.

"God, Winnie, no!" I said, covering my ears.

She laughs and I uncover them. "You'll be fine."

"Can we stop talking about this now?" I ask and she shrugs.

"You brought it up first," She accuses, holding her hands up in surrender.

"I needed someone to tell because I was about to bust because I couldn't tell anyone," I said, huffing.

"About what time did he leave this morning?" She asks, grabbing a book from my desk.

I hum, thinking. "Around six or seven."

"You rebel! You didn't even tell your dad he was here."

"Well duh! How did you think he was in my bed, my dad would've never let him," I state the obvious.

I felt my phone vibrating and I decided if I should answer it or not, but I decided to go with answering it because I would've felt bad in the end. My eyes almost pop out of my head when I read the name across my phone.

I click the answer before screaming. "Georgie!"

Winnie's eyes get huge but goes to mind her own business by reading the book in her hands.

"Was-sup, I missed hearing your voice," Hearing his voice brought tears to my eyes but I shoved them down.

I cough as Winnie smiles at me knowing I started to cry. "I missed hearing your voice too, why haven't you called in so long?"

"I'm sorry Tae, I had test after test after test up my ass and I didn't have the chance to call, but man, college is so fucking fun," He explains, laughing at the end.

"I'm glad you're having fun," I state, smiling sadly.

"I already called dad to tell him Merry Christmas, but Merry Christmas Tae, I love you and miss you so damn much," He says, with voices in the back hollering.

"Merry Christmas and I love you too, I hope to see you soon," I hope he would give me a date when he was off and could fly home.

But to my dismay, he didn't.

"I know right, I can't wait to see you and dad, but hey! I have to go I'll give you a call soon alright?"

I sigh out. "Okay."

I click end and plop my phone on the bed, waited so long for that call and not even five minutes had passed and his voice is gone. Neither did he ask how it was going with school or if I had gained friends or even how I was dealing with cancer.

"You, okay?" Winnie's voice popped in my ears and I turned my head towards her.

I smile. "Yeah."

"I tried not to be noisy, but I couldn't help but overhear him and he sounded like he was happy," She states and I look down at my phone.

He did sound happy that was for sure, that was the happiest I heard Georgie been in a long time since mom had died, I put on a fake smile and nod.

"I'm happy that he's happy, he deserves it," I was honest with my words.

Georgie deserved to be happy with all that he went through.

"Well, Keaton, Landon, and Reece might be here so we should head downstairs," She says, nodding her head towards the door.

I nod before following her downstairs hearing guys laughter, all three of the guys stood by the door with their hands in their pockets, Keaton never surprised me with what he was wearing, he never failed to amaze me with his looks.

He was wearing he black hoodie with a blue jean jacket over it, with some jeans on and tennis shoes.

"Damn, took you girls long enough," Reece mumbles earning a slap from Winnie on the side of his head.

I was wearing a cheetah print turtleneck with some black jeans and black boots; Winnie had curled my hair and Winnie was wearing a plain dark green long sleeve shirt with a brown skirt to go with her fit.

Landon wanted all of us to go out for dinner at the Greenhouse Diner, which didn't surprise me when it was probably Keaton's idea.

"You look beautiful," Keaton admires, wrapping his arms around my waist giving me a loving stare.

I smile. "Thank you."

He smiles before pecking my lips.

"I hope you know it's snowing and you have a skirt on," Reece laughs out, staring at Winnie's legs.

Landon hits Reece's chest causing me to laugh and Winnie glares at him.

"She can wear what she wants," Landon defends Winnie, and she gives him a smile.

"Y'all ready to head out?" Landon asks and we all nod.

"Please be careful and Keaton take care of my daughter for me, okay?" My dad cuts in and Keaton nods.

"*Always* will," Keaton replies.

I give my dad a kiss on the cheek before hugging him. "I love you and I'll be back soon."

"Alright, have fun," He waves to us bye and we head towards the cars.

Reece rides with Winnie and Landon while Keaton and I ride together in his Jeep. The car ride was silent as Keaton swipes his thumb across my hand while holding it.

I was nervous from this morning's actions and I didn't know how to start a conversation.

We get to Greenhouse Diner in silence, but with the low music in the background from the radio, Keaton unbuckles himself then looks at me.

"Was last night too much for you?" He asks, giving me a worried look.

I shook my head. "No, it was great, more than great actually."

"I just don't want to be pushing it..." He trails, looking at the Diner before looking back at me.

"Trust me, you're not," I grab his thigh.

He nods before we head out of the Jeep with Winnie, Reece, and Landon getting out of Landon's truck at the same time.

"Damn, it's freezing out here," Reece mumbles, chattering his teeth together.

"I know," Winnie agrees.

"Let's go inside," Landon tells us.

Keaton gently moves his arm behind my back as I walk with everyone.

As we walk in, familiar faces stand at the front and a smile appears on my face when Ally runs towards me.

"Oh my god! You guys made it!" She exclaims, taking a hold of my hands.

She hugs me before going to Keaton and doing the same.

"Couldn't miss spending Christmas with you and Tommy," Keaton replies.

"Aww your too sweet, come and sit! You guys look like you're freezing," She observes, taking us to a booth.

"We are," Reece grunts, but smiles at Ally.

She smiles back at him. "I'll make Tommy turn up the heat."

"Where is he by the way?" Keaton asks, raising an eyebrow.

"In the back cooking," She states, pointing her finger towards the back.

Keaton nods and she gives us menus. "Y'all figure out what you guys want and I'll be right back."

"Thank you," Landon says, smiling.

I feel Keaton's hand cover my thigh and I turn my head towards him and smile which he does the same. I felt eyes on me and I turned my head to see Reece looking over his menu staring at me.

I felt weird vibes coming from him but I shook them off.

Maybe I had something on my face? *Or not.*

Chapter Thirty-Three

Tae's Pov.

"How'd you do?" My dad asks me as soon as I step foot into the house.

I look down at the paper in my hand and smile brightly. "I passed!"

"That's great!"

I left my dad an hour ago to take my driving test, to say I was nervous wouldn't be the right word I was feeling. I knew I had it in the bag but I still had the nervous jitters.

"I know, I'm just so glad that I got it over," I sigh out, sitting at the kitchen counter in front of him.

"My little girl is growing up..." He mumbles, giving me a sad smile. "Soon you'll be graduating then going off to college and then getting married and starting a life."

I smile not letting the negative thoughts get in the way this time, maybe planning the future wouldn't be a bad idea. I mean of course I knew what I was going to college for, but I never thought I was going to make it there.

I feel my phone buzzing in my back pocket, I take it out seeing that I was receiving a group FaceTime from Winnie and Keaton.

"I'll be right back," I tell my dad, holding up my dad signaling that I had a phone call to take.

He nods before turning towards the fridge opening it, I make my way upstairs hurriedly so the phone call wouldn't go away.

I hit answer as soon as I stepped foot in my room and closed my door, Keaton and Winnie's face pops up on the screen as mine pops up in the third square.

"Did you pass?!" Winnie excitedly asks, getting close to the camera.

I laugh. "Yeah."

"Alright!" Keaton calls out, chuckling.

"We should celebrate!" Winnie calls out, setting up her phone so she shows her whole body.

"It's really not that important to celebrate," I tell her awkwardly, taking a seat on my bed.

She dramatically gasps. "Yes, it is, also we should celebrate Keaton turning eighteen since the party didn't turn out too great."

Keaton groans. "I'll pass."

"Stop being fun kill you two, you guys are always down to go somewhere where it's just you two, but when we all want to hang out one of y'all bitches don't want to cooperate."

"Did you not think that's how I thought when I wasn't invited to do stuff with you and Landon?" Keaton raises an eyebrow.

"Well... no..." She trails, looking down.

"Exactly," He says, smirking.

"Please, and I know the perfect place," She begs, poking out her bottom lip.

"Where is it?" I ask, sighing.

A smile appears on her face. "My dad used to take me on a snow trip every Christmas break and you go skiing and rent a cabin and it's fun."

"Doesn't sound too bad," I shrug.

"Thank you," Winnie smiles.

"Eh," Keaton hesitates.

"You'd usually be the first one down to do this, besides what else is there to do in this town?" I state, and he shrugs but nods.

"Fine, but your dad would never let you go without a parent," He says, shaking his head.

"That's where my mom comes in," Winnie cuts in, holding her finger up.

Keaton sighs. "Okay, when should we do this?"

"Tomorrow," Winnie demands, and my eyes go wide.

"Tomorrow? No, why? I still have to ask my dad and pack," I exclaim, standing up from my bed in panic.

She giggles. "Well, you better get to asking and get to packing cause we're going, I'll call you guys later to tell Landon and Reece the news."

"Winnie-" Keaton start, but gets cut off by Winnie leaving the group FaceTime.

"Are you actually wanting to go?" Keaton asks, raising an eyebrow at me as he lays in bed shirtless.

I nod. "Yes, I think it would be fun."

"Okay, if you want to go then I want to go," He agrees, staring at me deeply into the camera.

"Well good," I smile at him.

"Keaton!" I hear in the background Keaton's dad calling.

"I have to go, but text me and I'll call you tonight and see you tomorrow if you can go," He tells me.

"What about you?" I raise an eyebrow.

"My dad trusts Winnie's mom," He shrugs it off.

I then shrug. "Okay."

"Bye Lambert," A cheeky smirk slides its way onto Keaton's face causing me to smile.

"Bye," I mumble, hitting the end button.

I drop my phone down on my bed before standing up to go downstairs to tell my dad about Winnie's plan.

"What are you making?" I ask him as I watch into the kitchen smelling the goodness of the mystery food.

"Chicken Alfredo," He states, turning around with his famous apron that says 'kiss the cook'.

Mom loved that apron...

"Sounds good," I tell him, sitting down that the same spot I was in when I first came in.

"It probably won't be as good as your mom makes it but let's hope that it's eatable," He jokes, rolling his eyes at the pot on the stove.

"It smells good," I try making him feel better about the way he cooks.

Dad was never the cook around here, mom always was, but when she passed, he had to step up and cook, of course I would've, but he never let me touch mom's favorite pots and pans.

"So, Winnie wanted Keaton and I to hang out with her Landon and Reece..." I trail, not even getting to the part that we will be on a snow trip.

He shrugs. "Okay, that sounds fine to me."

"But I missed one little detail," I play with my hands nervously.

"Okay..." I finally got his attention as he presses his hands against the counter and leans against it.

"She wants to go on a snow trip with all of us and she said her mom will be there," I explain, finally looking in his eyes for any hesitation.

"Where will you guys stay?" His question was calm but too calm.

"A cabin..." I trail, biting my bottom lip.

"Mhhh," He hums, looking down. "I don't know, Tae. I mean it's not that I don't trust Winnie's mom and that I love that you're finally wanting to go out and do stuff, but Bonnie can easily look away for one second and Keaton can be in your pants."

"Plus, I don't think I'm ready for you to leave, you've always been in my eye sight and you know you can't go rough because you're sick, and I'm sorry that I'm bringing it up, but-" I smile cutting him off.

"No, it's okay, I know you're being cautious and worried about me. I'm sure Bonnie will make sure that Winnie and I and her will share a cabin together and the boys will take another," I explain, shrugging.

He stares at me in debate and I hold my hands up together as they are connected giving him puppy dog eyes.

"Tell Keaton that no getting in the cookie jar, if he tries slipping the top of the jar open, I will rip his slim Jim off his body and tie it around his neck," He warns causing me to sigh out in relief.

"And please make sure if you feel weird or anything, please call me or tell Keaton so he can call me," He sighs out.

I nod. "I will."

"Good, then you can go. I'll give you some money in the morning when you head out," He tells me before I head back upstairs to tell Winnie.

I quickly send a text to Winnie and Keaton both telling them that I can go and within minutes they reply that they are happy because they can go too. I huff out a breath before turning to get to my closet to find my bag.

Packing was going to be a lot harder than expected because I never know what to pack and where to start.

Chapter Thirty-Four

Tae's Pov.

Hugging my dad goodbye was a hard thing to do, I haven't left the house without him in a long time, and this wasn't some little drive around with Keaton for a few hours this was a three-day snow trip with these guys.

"I miss you already," My dad dramatically tells me, sadness laced in his voice.

I poke my bottom lip out. "Same."

"Don't worry, Bo. Tae's in good hands," Bonnie cuts in, shutting the car door behind her.

I watch as Winnie sits up front in the passenger seat smiling at me, she rolls her window down letting me know to come to her.

"Are you ready for this?" She asks, biting her bottom lip.

I nod. "Yeah, it's gonna be fun."

"You look a little nervous which is fine because I know how close you are with your dad."

"Yeah, I hate to leave him alone," I look back at the man that has raised me since I was a little girl.

"He could've come with us and he still can," She states, shrugging.

"He wants to stay here," I shrug back at her, frowning.

"Well, this will give you good practice to be away from him because soon you'll be off to college and won't see him much because you'll be living with me in dorms," She clicks her tongue finishing her sentence.

I raise an eyebrow. "How are you so sure that you and I will be in the same dorms."

"It's a Winnie feeling," She shrugs before looking behind me.

I turned around to see that my dad was standing close by.

"Call me if you need anything and make sure you call tonight, and no boys in the rooms," He warns me, swaying his finger in my face.

"You know I would never let a boy in my room, dad," The lie sliced through my teeth as I told him.

Winnie coughs causing me to turn around, giving her a quick glare before turning back around at my dad, he gives us a skeptical look before shrugging.

"Good, have fun and I love you," He kisses the top of my head.

"Love you too," I smile, hugging him.

"We have to go pick up Keaton and then Reece and hurry on the road before it gets dark," Bonnie quickly states, hurriedly getting into the van while staring at the watch on her wrist.

"Alright, be safe you guys," My dad calls out to us.

I open the van seeing that Landon was sitting in the back with his headphones in bobbing his head with his eyes closed.

My eyebrows furrow, I had no idea he was even in here.

Winnie looks back and laughs. "We picked him up before we came and got you because he lives down the street from my house."

"Gotcha," I murmur, plopping myself in a seat before closing the door.

We all head down towards Keaton's home and we slide through the gated doors and stare at his beautiful home as we wait for the star Quarterback to enter the van, just our luck Keaton walks out of his house with his bag in hand and goes to the back to put his things in the trunk and walks around the other side of the car and opens the side door before getting in.

"Hi Keaton," Bonnie says, looking back at him in the rear-view mirror.

Keaton smiles. "Hey."

Winnie smiles at Keaton before turning back to her mom making conversation, I smile at the two being so close and I couldn't imagine what Bonnie and Winnie were going through with their husband and dad passing.

"You didn't text me back last night," Keaton accuses, staring straight at the side of my head.

I turn my head giving him a confused look. "What did you say?"

"I said 'goodnight I'll see you tomorrow'," He replies.

"Oh, I'm sorry I fell asleep," I tell him, frowning.

He shakes his head. "No, it's fine, you just had me worried."

"Aww, I promise I won't fall asleep until I text you goodnight," I say, laying my hand down on his making him turn his head around and laces his fingers with mine causing a smile to rupture on my face.

When we arrive at Reece's home, my face drops when Reece steps out of the house, outside of the home was a sign that said 'Orphanage'.

Reece is a foster kid.

Reece enters the van and sits down beside Landon with a blank face, once he sees me staring at him too long his face turns into a frown, I quickly turn my head and Keaton squeezes my hand for reassurance and smiles at me.

This was going to be a long car ride.

****

By sunset, we make it to the cabins Winnie was talking about, we gather our things from the van and take them in the cabin. I look around at the huge cabin in awe, chandeliers hang from the ceiling, walking under them while looking up, gazing at them they would twinkle in the light.

"This is amazing," I murmur, dropping my bag at the door.

"I know," Winnie says from behind me.

"So, this is where your dad used to take you?" I ask her, making conversation.

"Yep, every Christmas," She states, smiling at me.

She waves for me to follow her. "Come on, the rooms are even better."

I followed her down the long lighted hallway with my bag in hand and she opened one room and began to open another. I was in awe from there, just looking at the king size beds made my body ache to lay down and never leave.

"Wow," I say breathless, staring at the nude white walls with blue little flowers painted gently at the bottom of them.

"You like it?" Winnie asks and I nod. "It's yours."

"Don't all the rooms look the same?" I ask, setting my bag down at the door.

"Yeah," She giggles out causing me to let out a snort.

"Winnie! Tae! Come down here and eat the boys will be here any minute and there won't be any left," Bonnie yells for us to come down to the kitchen.

"Okay," Winnie yells back and waves for me to follow.

She looks back at me while walking down the stairs. "What do you wanna do after dinner?"

"We can't really do much, maybe watch a movie? And we can do something fun tomorrow," I tell her, shrugging.

"Okay, sounds good," She smiles.

We enter the kitchen and in matter of seconds, the boys hustle in the cabin being loud and noisy stirring up the house as Keaton and Reece wrestle. Landon walks over to Winnie kissing her cheek before grabbing a plate and putting food on it, Winnie rolls her eyes as she looks at me and I laugh.

"I totally won," Reece exclaims, pointing at Keaton.

Keaton scoffs. "Who was the one that put you in the choke whole? Oh right, me!"

Reece playfully rolls his eyes and Winnie and I hold our plates up as we head towards the rooms trying to avoid the loud boys who were eating like pigs.

"You aren't going to eat with me?" Keaton grabs my elbow gently as I take a sip of the tea in my cup.

I look at Winnie who shrugs her shoulders before making her way to the couch to sit near Landon, I smile at Keaton. "Sure."

I sit down with Keaton, right beside me Winnie stands up bringing us a blanket to cover over our legs and I thank her kindly in which she nods before going back to stuffing her face.

Keaton finishes his food in a hurry and I stare at him in shock from the quickness of him swallowing his food, he lays his hand on my thigh under the blanket and I finish my food and lay my empty plate on top of Keaton's before leaning into his touch.

His lips touch the top of my head and I close my eyes at the feeling, this trip had a good start to it and something told me I wouldn't want it to end.

Chapter Thirty-Five

Tae's Pov.

"Tae," A little whisper in my ear made me turn over and moan out from being woken up so early.

I fall back asleep within minutes before hearing another whisper of my name, I shake the person's hand off of me before covering my head.

"Tae! Get your fine ass up," Keaton screams out, snatching the covers off of me showing my bare legs.

I raise up glaring at the now chuckling boy.

"Nice shorts," He points out, staring at the ducks on my shorts.

I glare. "Do you know what time it is?"

"Time for you to get up, we're going skiing," He states, throwing the blanket on the floor before grabbing ahold of my hands pulling me to get up.

I lay my head back as I slide on the bed. "Why this early?"

"Because we don't want it to be packed, then we'll never be able to ski," He explains, grabbing my face in his warm hands gently and squeezing them lightly making my face puff up.

I whine. "Please let me stay in and sleep."

"You wanted to come here, so no whining," He demands, pushing my hair out of my face.

He brought butterflies into my stomach when he gave me this look in his eyes, it held so much pureness and adoration.

I poke my bottom lip out. "Fine."

"Don't pout, we'll have fun I promise," He states, kissing my lips.

I stand up from the bed and go to stomp towards the bathroom, a slap on my butt woke me from my thoughts and I turn around to glare at the culprit who laid a hand on me.

He grins cheekily at me and I stick my tongue at him before proceeding my destination to make a leak in the toilet.

I hear his light footsteps exit my room and new one's approach, I quickly wash my hands and exit the bathroom seeing Winnie dressed appropriate for skiing.

"You look good," I comment, pointing towards her outfit.

She smiles. "Thanks."

She was wearing a bright blue puffy jacket with some leggings with Ugg's.

"Did Keaton wake you?" She asks and I roll my eyes while nodding.

"He told me he was, but I thought he would cave if you gave him those puppy dog eyes of yours," She states, causing me to laugh.

"He's too smart for those," I retort, rolling my eyes at the straight A student.

"True, want me to help you get ready?" She asks. "I have nothing else to do."

I shrug. "Sure, if you want."

"Okay, good," She claps out in excitement.

After thirty minutes I get done with my French braids and I stare at myself in the mirror and nod.

"I look alright, I guess," I said out loud to Winnie.

She scoffs. "You look great."

I wore a light brown puffy jacket with some black leggings just like Winnie, I wore a brown beanie to match my jacket and to go over my braids, I wore some Ugg's of mine to go with the look and I was set to go.

A knock on the door causes us to turn around and wait for the person to come in.

Reece's head pops out. "They're ready!"

"Why the hell would you open the door before they could tell you to open the door, what if they were naked?!," I hear Keaton's voice call out behind the door before he opens the door fully, revealing himself giving me a look over.

Reece scoffs. "I wouldn't be seeing much, Tae barely has any chest and Winnie's chest looks like old granny's, no offense."

"None taken," I wave him off already knowing I had no boobs.

Keaton glares at Reece. "Watch it."

"Sorry," Reece holds his head down.

Keaton turns his head back to me and smiles. "You look beautiful."

"Thank you," I say in awe.

Winnie gasps. "What about me?!"

"You look good too," Keaton nods at her.

She flips her hair. "Thank you, but I don't need a boy to tell me I'm gorgeous."

After that she leaves in a dramatic exit and I giggle.

Keaton turns to me and raises an eyebrow. "Didn't she want a compliment?"

"Don't ever question Winnie," I laugh out, holding my hand up.

"Women," Reece scoffs, exiting the room and closing it behind him.

I look over at Keaton's outfit and he's wearing a black puffy jacket just like mine and Winnie's with some blue jeans and a white beanie on which looked too cute on him.

"Was your dad nervous to let you go?" He asks, sliding his arms around my slim waist.

I nod. "Yeah, but I guess he knew someday he'll have to let me go."

"Yeah, my dad didn't want me going because he thought I wouldn't come back," He explains, rolling his eyes.

"Wow..." I trail, nodding slowly.

"What did he say on the phone last night?"

"To not let you in my room when I'm here," I reply with a smile, because we weren't following the rules right now.

He chuckles. "Well, looks like I'm getting my ass kicked when I get back."

"He doesn't have to know," I laugh out, but my smile soon turns into a blank expression as soon as I see his serious one.

I cough awkwardly. "You good?"

"You're just so beautiful," He calmly states, cupping the side of my face with his huge hand.

I smile. "You're sweet."

He smiles back at me before pecking my lips, he backs away slowly still staring at my lips, my eyes look down at his before claiming them. His lips fit on mine like they were made for touching, he slowly slides his tongue in my mouth like a snake trying to catch his prey and he caught my tongue with his.

He takes both of his hands and now has them on both sides of my face as my hands reach behind his neck to bring him closer.

We pull back a few minutes later breathing heavily with both of us staring at each other with hunger.

"I love-" Keaton gets cut off by someone busting through the door.

Which happened to be Reece. "We're heading out guys."

Keaton sighs out frustratedly and runs his fingers through his hair. "Alright."

Reece looks between us two and I awkwardly leave the room with my heart pounding out of my chest.

I knew he was about to confess that he loved me, but I was so glad Reece busted through the door when he was about to do it, not that I'm not happy that Keaton loved me, but I didn't know if I was ready to say that back to him.

I enter the van getting in the back with Winnie, she gives me a confused look as to why my lips are swollen.

"I'll tell you about it later," I say, waving it off as the boy's head into the van.

She nods before putting a smile on as Keaton looks back to make sure I was okay.

When we get to the skiing place, my stomach turns at the tall mountain. Winnie gives me a ski-board and a helmet before giving out the same thing to everyone else.

"Have you ever done this before?" Keaton asks, placing his helmet over his beanie.

I shake my head. "Nope."

"Damn," He mumbles.

"Okay, you guys walk up the stairs to get to the mountain and ski down it as much as you want," Bonnie calls out, pointing towards the start of the stairs.

I hold onto the helmet and boards while walking beside Keaton.

"Are you scared?" He asks, looking at me then looking back at the steps making sure he doesn't slip.

"Oh yeah, are you?"

"No, I've been down this mountain a hundred times," He replies, shrugging it off.

My hands start to shake as we get to the top and my breathing gets heavy as I look down.

"I brought this just in case since this is your first time," Winnie states, holding onto a long snowboard to where three people can sit on.

"I brought one for me and Landon too," She adds and I nod feeling better.

Keaton touches my back. "See now you have nothing to worry about."

"I'll be right behind you," He adds, giving me a reassuring look.

Reece completely ignores the four of us and gets on the board by himself and skis down. Landon shrugs before sitting down on the red board opening his legs for Winnie to sit in between him.

Keaton sets the blue board down and takes a seat copying Landon's actions. I blow out a nervous breath before sitting in between Keaton's legs.

"I'm here," Keaton whispers in my ear assuring me.

He gently takes ahold of my hands rubbing my palms and I sigh out leaning back into him.

"Okay ready?" Winnie screams out excitedly.

"Hell yeah," Keaton says back, laughing.

"One...two....three...go!" Landon calls out, holding onto the straps to control the board.

Keaton pushes us off and we slide down the mountain with ease, my heart was racing through my chest, I've never felt more alive.

A smile lingers on my face as we finish, I hurriedly stand up almost tripping, laughter fills my ears as Winnie and Landon make it down the mountain and I watch as Keaton goes to get up from the board. I collect snow in my hands before balling it up and throwing it at Keaton making it go all over his jacket and he jumps from the action.

"Ouuu damn," Reece mumbles, laughing while taking his goggles off.

I giggle while covering my mouth with my hand and Keaton gives me a glare, he sarcastically laughs before clicking his tongue.

"Funny," Keaton comments, bending over gathering as much snow he can hold in his huge hands.

My eyes go wide and I make a run for it, a pile of snow hits the back of my head and I freeze with my mouth open wide and turn around staring at the grinning boy.

"Oh, you're on," I exclaim, bending over to grab some more snow and watch him make a run for it.

"Snow fight!" Reece yells, grabbing snow in his hands and throwing it at Winnie's face.

She gasps. "You bastard."

"Oops," Reece shrugs before running from Landon who tries to throw one but misses terribly.

I run after Keaton with a smirk and he falls over a snowman and I laugh out before throwing the snowball at his face and hitting him right in the spot.

He chuckles evilly and I start to jog away giving him time to get up, but in a flash, he picks me up and swings me around in his arms causing me to let out the biggest ugly laugh I've ever let out.

"Okay, okay, I'm sorry," I laugh out, as he puts me on his shoulders causing my braids to fly in front of my face.

"Landon you better not!" Winnie screams out.

I hear her gasp before grunting, I get confused as to where Keaton was taking me, but that ended quickly when he drops me in a pile of snow on my back and I gasp out from the coldness.

"You son of a-" I get quickly cut off by Keaton manly chuckle and his lips attack mine.

I smile in between and wrap my arms around his shoulders pulling him into me causing him to slip and fall on me, we both laugh and pull away.

"I had fun today," He comments, licking his lips slowly as he locks eyes with me.

I run my hand through his hair and smile. "Me too."

"Tae, I really do-" As he's about to finish his sentence it's ruined by Reece shoving snow in Keaton's face causing him to spit out cuss words and playfully glare at Reece.

"Let me catch this bastard," Keaton says, pecking my lips before helping me get up and leaving to find Reece who ran off after the stunt he pulled.

A smile reaches my face, but as soon as it does it turns into a frown when I feel heavy breathing start to form in my lungs, my chest heaves up and down and I start to worry because I wasn't running.

A hand attaches to my back and I turn to see Landon giving me a worried look.

"You, okay?" Worried was laced with his words and I gave him a fake smile.

"Yeah," I tell him, waving it off.

He nods before watching Keaton shove snow in Reece's face and laughing.

Was I really, okay?

Chapter Thirty-Six

Tae's Pov.

I tie the belt around the robe I was wearing before heading out of the room I was staying in; I stop in my tracks as I bounce off a chest. I look up to see Keaton looking down at me before staring back up to my eyes.

"Where are you going?" He asks, raising an eyebrow as he gawks at the open entrance of my robe.

I closed the robe so he couldn't see my nude self before saying. "Hot tub with Winnie."

"I thought we could hang out today..." He trails, poking out his bottom lip.

"We always hang out, I need to hang out with Winnie for a change," I explain, grabbing his hand because I felt bad.

He playfully glares at me. "Fine, but we're hanging out tomorrow."

"Yes sir," I tell him, saluting him.

He kisses my cheek before letting me go, but as I'm leaving a hand slap down on my butt. I turn around and give him a death stare.

"I won't be accused for my actions when you're in the hot tub and I watch you," He holds up his hands up in surrender.

"You better not!" I warn, pointing my finger at him.

He shrugs. "We'll see."

I roll my eyes before storming off into the hot tub room, smoke filled the room as I walk through, I see Winnie's red hair lay against the floor as she leans her head back sighing, already in the hot tub.

"You got in without me," I pointed out, causing her to open her eyes and lifting her head.

Her eyes light up and she smiles up at me. "Come on in! The water feels so good."

I nod my head before slowly untying my robe, Winnie looks away giving me privacy and I'm thankful that she did because I was starting to feel insecure. I finally take my whole robe off and step in the water and sit on the side of the hot tub, the water touches above my breasts making them disappear in it.

"This is our first time being alone in a while," Winnie states, floating her hands around the water.

I nod. "I know, it feels nice to hang out with a girl for once."

"I'm surprised Keaton even let you out of his sight."

"I told him I needed to spend time with you," I tell her, shrugging.

She scoffs. "Bet you five bucks he's behind that door watching you right now."

"Don't get me thinking that," I giggle out nervously, staring at the door before looking back at Winnie.

As I get done laughing my breathing starts acting funny again, my smile forms into a frown and I hold onto my chest as it speeds up.

Winnie frowns. "Are you alright?"

"Yeah..." I mumble, closing my eyes.

"You don't look alright," She states, furrowing her eyebrows.

"I'm fine," I assure, uncovering my chest and opening my eyes.

Worry filled my mind and that was what I could think of, Winnie starts talking and I don't hear her until she snaps her fingers in my face.

"Tae!" She exclaims.

I shake my head out of my thoughts. "What?"

"You just spaced out, you completely ignored my question," She explains, giving me a worried look.

"What was your question?" I ask.

"Never mind...." She trails, waving it off.

She looks down before looking back up to me. "My dad used to space out like that."

"Oh wow," I state.

"Yeah, you scared me when you went out like that. Sometimes my dad would space out for a few minutes and then other times he would space out for an hour or two and you couldn't speak a word because he wouldn't listen."

"I'm sorry about your dad passing, you seemed like you were very close with him," I felt so bad that her dad died when Winnie was still a child.

Winnie and I were both missing one thing in our life.

A parent.

"I was, when he passed, I didn't speak to anyone for a month, I couldn't talk about it without crying and sometimes I couldn't talk about it at all, I pushed everyone away except for Keaton. He wouldn't let me, he was there for me when I needed someone the most," She explains, tearing up.

I take a hold of her hand and give her a sad smile.

"I know it hurts you talking about your mom, because I was the same way, Keaton made me talk about my dad a lot to him to make me feel this way now."

I sigh out. "My mom died from leukemia."

Her face falls and she covers her mouth to stop her sobs. "Oh my god."

"She was my best friend and everything above all else, and when she left it felt like a part of me died with her. I finally just closed up everything in me and shut everyone out," I let out, feeling tears form in my eyes.

"Is that why you hung out with the teachers all the time?" She asks, a smile never once came upon her face.

I nod. "Yeah."

There was also another reason for that, but I don't think I could tell her this secret.

"Makes sense."

"I'm just glad that Keaton opened you up and your friends with us now," She adds, side hugging me.

I smile as I wipe under my eyes. "Me too."

"What are we crying about?" Landon screams out, entering the room with Keaton behind him.

Winnie and I roll our eyes before covering our chest as the boys walk closer.

"Leave you idiots!" Winnie exclaims, pointing towards the door. "We're having a girl's night."

"We know, but we just couldn't stay away," Keaton says, walking around Landon, giving me a smirk.

"Fucking freak..." Winnie mumbles under her breath.

I giggle at her facial expression and she cracks a smile as she stares at me.

I jump feeling a hand lay on my shoulder, I turn my head to see Keaton bending down.

"Nope! No touching us when we're naked," Winnie demands, smacking Keaton's hand off of me.

"Landon has seen you naked plenty of times," Keaton sarcastically states, chuckling.

Winnie gasps. "I know and that's why I'm protecting Tae from your horny ass."

"She knows I would never touch her where she didn't want to be touched," Keaton replies, bending down even more to kiss my cheek and I smile.

"Be careful Tae, once a guy gives you this weird look and makes you feel some type of way boom, your pants are off and his face is in between your legs," Winnie tells me, giving Keaton a glare.

My mouth hangs open and she nods, I give Keaton a look and he shakes his head like Winnie's lying. I grab the robe I laid down and quickly wrap it around me making sure no one was looking.

Keaton wipes my cheek before checking my eyes. "You've been crying?"

"Winnie and I were having a girl talk," I explain, sniffling.

"About?"

"Her dad and my mom," I state, and he nods letting go of the conversation.

"One day we're gonna have to go somewhere where the boys can't find out where we are so we can actually have a girl's day," Winnie says, holding onto Landon's arm.

"Yeah," I nod, laughing.

Winnie unclamps herself from Landon before walking out of the room, and Landon turns to us.

"Watch, I'm gonna talk sweet to her in the room and I'll be in between her legs," He states, chuckling a bit before rushing behind Winnie.

"Mhhh, maybe we should do that," Keaton says, shrugging.

I gasp before grabbing his arm and push at his chest causing him to fall in the hot tub.

I laugh. "Say some more slick stuff like that, I've got a lot more of that coming for you."

He playfully glares at me before hurriedly standing up trying to reach for me, but I quickly run before he could.

"You're getting it now."

Chapter Thirty-Seven

Tae's Pov.

"Rise and shine," Keaton's voice mumbles next to my ear.

My eyes crack seeing a little sunlight seeping through and when I finally open my eyes Keaton faces appears and I finally remember we're in the car.

"We're home," He says lightly, brushing a few strands out of my face.

I groan. "What time is it?"

"About twelve in the afternoon," He states.

"Oh..." I mumble, staring off in space for a bit.

Keaton chuckles. "Come on, let me walk you in."

I nod making myself exit the van with sleepy eyes, Keaton lays his hand on the small part of my back as he carries my bag in one hand and I drag my feet against the sidewalk.

I knew I looked like a screaming mess and was I going to look in the mirror at all today?
No sir.

The front door opens showing my dad's glowing happy face and a smile spreads on my face.

"I'm so glad your home, I missed you so much," He exclaims, holding out his arms for me to hug him.

I wrap my arms around his waist with no hesitation and breathe in his scent that I missed so much, we were both acting like we hadn't seen each other in a month, but three days were too long without my dad.

"Is Keaton going to stay a while?"

I shrug before turning around giving Keaton a questioning look.

"If you want me too," Keaton shrugs.

"Of course, I want you too," I retort, playfully hitting his arm.

"Then I'm staying," He states, nodding a little.

I smile at him and my dad lets us in the warm cozy home I grew up in.

"So, tell me about your trip," My dad states, grabbing my bag from Keaton and placing it near the staircase.

"We went snowboarding but it ended up being a snow fight, the cabins had a hot tub which Winnie and I couldn't resist sitting in," I explained, sitting on the stool at the kitchen counter as my dad gives me the biggest smile in front of me.

I guess he was just soaking in at the fact that I was truly happy for once.

"And Tae here only hung out with me when we went snowboarding and then completely forgot about me the rest of the time," Keaton accuses, sitting next to me.

I shrug. "Winnie wanted to spend some time alone."

Keaton rolls his eyes and I poke out my tongue at him to tease him, my dad chuckles.

"I'm glad to know you guys enjoyed yourselves, but I can't say the same for me the house was lonely and empty without you, I couldn't even read my favorite novel without looking up the stairs for three seconds," He begins to explain and I sigh out.

"I know, I could hardly go to sleep because I'm *always* used to hearing 'goodnight, Tae love you' before I hit the hay," I poke out my bottom lip giving my dad the puppy dog eyes.

I hear the Quarterback laugh beside me. "Hit the hay?"

"What? It's an old saying," I defend myself.

"Yeah, let it stay in the past," He says, covering his mouth when I give him a glare.

"I don't make fun of you when you say stuff so hush!" I tell him, poking my finger at his temple making his head turn a little.

My dad rolls his eyes at us. "I'm making dinner, so you two run along I want this to be a surprise."

"M'kay," I mumble, grabbing Keaton's hand and dragging him upstairs.

"Make sure you leave the door open!" My dad yells through the house.

"Okay!"

I leave the door open and as Keaton looks around my room with his hands in his pockets, I couldn't help but walk to him the quickest I could and muster up all the negative thoughts and push them away as I cup his face with my hands and plant my lips right against his.

Keaton silently chuckles and tugs his hands out of his pockets before cupping my face with his large hands.

He pulls us apart. "What's gotten into you? You've never made the first move."

"Yes, I have," I gasp out.

"Maybe there's been a few times, but it's never like this."

I shrug. "I don't know, I just wanted to kiss you."

"You can do it again if you want," He chuckles out, tugging my bottom lip with his thumb.

I smile before leaning up against before claiming his lips with mine.

"I don't hear any talking!" My dad interrupts our moment by yelling at us and we instantly break apart, rubbing our lips.

"Wanna go for a walk?" I quickly ask, trying to not make anything awkward.

"Yeah," He nods.

We both begin to make our way downstairs and when we pass the kitchen both of our heads went straight and I tell my dad that we're walking down the neighborhood and will be right back.

Keaton grabs my hand as we make our way onto the street, a few cars pass by slowly trying to pass our figures. His fingers laces with mine and we swing our hands lightly.

"I'm dreading school next week," He states, sighing as he looks out in front of him.

"Same," I roll my eyes at the thought.

"Exams, more exams, and finals are coming up then college," He mumbles quietly.

"You forgot about summer," I try to make the conversation funny, but a smile didn't crack on his face.

Ouch.

"Summer is usually when my dad is the toughest on me because he wants me to stay in shape and always work out, be healthy, practice football with him," He explains, looking at me.

I look down at my feet as we walk. "You're eighteen, Keaton. He can't make you do things now."

"It's harder than what you think," He states, his jaw tightening at the thought.

"Then tell me, are you scared that your dad is gonna disown you?"

"Tell me what you really want to do in the future Keaton, not what your dad wants you to do," I then add.

"I wanna go pro in football," He lets out truthfully.

There was a pain in his eyes, Keaton loves football and he *always* will, but his dad went too far with it and makes Keaton slip away from it.

"Now tell me what you wanna do, 'miss I think I can tell Keaton what to do and he does it in just a snap of a finger'," He jokes around, pushing his shoulder against mine.

"I never really thought about it..." I trail. "I never thought I was gonna be here this long, so I didn't plan out a future for me."

"But now you can, you're stronger than what you think you are. So, what do you wanna do with your life after high school?"

"Go to college that's for sure," I nod.

"Oh yeah, you've got the brains," He says, nodding along with me.

"A nurse maybe? I wanna help people I know that..." I trail in question, furrowing my eyebrows.

"You'd look sexy in a nursing outfit," He smugly remarks.

I playfully gag. "Nurse is out of the picture now."

"Oh, come on-" He begins to say but gets cut off by the sound of his phone ringing.

Keaton pulls out his phone from his back pocket and furrows his eyebrows at the caller id, he slides his thumb against the glass screen and holds the phone up to his ear.

"Hey mom, what's up?" He says, his face growing hard by the minute as he listens in on the other side.

What was going on?

"He what?!" He exclaims, giving me a side look before looking forward.

"Alright, stop crying. I'm on my way," He demands before hanging up.

I furrow my eyebrows. "What's wrong?"

God, I'm so nosey.

"My mom and dad are at it again and he's slamming stuff," He says in a hurry, dragging me towards my house.

"Can your dad give me a ride to my house?" He asks, his eyes filled with worry.

I nod quickly before heading inside. "Dad?"

"In the kitchen!" He states.

"Hey dad, Keaton-" I stop in my tracks as my dad holds up a spoon with a red substance on it with his hand under it.

"Come try this and tell me if this is good," He tells me, nodding me over.

I awkwardly look at Keaton before staring back at my dad. "Keaton needs you to drop him off at his house."

"Okay, is everything alright? I thought you were staying for dinner?"

Keaton shakes his head. "I would love to stay, but I have some family issues at home and I need to get home asap."

My dad quickly nods and pulls off his apron and flips the off switch on the oven before grabbing his keys and I lock the door on our way out.

As my dad drives down the street in a hurry, he must know what's happening by the way the vein of his forehead is looking, I hold onto Keaton's hand feeling him tense, but soon lose his tension and let go.

"I hope she's okay," He mumbles quietly to me.

I nod. "She is."

My dad gets to Keaton's house within minutes and Keaton kisses my cheek and tells my dad goodbye before hopping out of the car, my dad begins to back up, but I stop him.

"Don't you think we should stay here until we know everything's okay?" I ask him and he shakes his head proceeding to back up.

"It's not our business..." He trails.

I nod. It's not our business.

Keaton, you better be alright the next time I see you. If not, I'll kill you.

Chapter Thirty-Eight

Tae's Pov.

I yawn as I pull my hair into French pigtail braids, sliding the rubber band across the ends of my hair three times and finally get up from my spot on the floor in front of my mirror and grab my backpack.

I read the text that Keaton sent me, *'I'm here'*.

I found it weird that Keaton didn't come in, but maybe he wanted to get to school quickly.

Closing the door behind me, I make my way downstairs, I find my dad leaning against the kitchen counter reading the newspaper.

"Good morning," I hum out, smiling at him as his head turns toward me.

He smiles. "Good morning blondie."

"Keaton's here, I'll see you on the field this afternoon," I tell him, jabbing my finger towards the door.

"Okay, be careful. I love you," he says, kissing the top of my head.

"Love you too," I mumble, hurriedly walking to the door.

Keaton's black jeep sits in my driveway, I see him looking down not even noticing I was out here. I cross my arms trying to get warm but the coldness cuts through my hoodie and lands on my skin causing chills to shiver down me.

I open the passenger door getting Keaton's attention, he raises his head giving me a quick smile before looking ahead.

"Hi," I say quickly, buckling myself up.

"Hey," His voice was short and quick as he backs up the Jeep out of the driveway.

I furrow my eyebrows in confusion but don't say a word about his tone.

After ten minutes into the drive, I stare at Keaton wondering why he wasn't talkative, he wasn't like this ever. I take a good look at him and twist my body further up on the dash to look at the other side of his face, he turns towards me with a questioning look, finally letting me see what he was hiding.

A black eye.

My heart drops down to my butthole and I gasp.

"Keaton!" I exclaim, covering my mouth with my hand.

"What?" He shrugs, looking at me before looking at the road.

I point at his eye. "So, this is why you've been so distant, it's because you didn't want me to figure out you got a black eye."

"Leave it alone," He demands, his jaw tightening.

I glare at him. "How am I supposed to leave this alone?! Did your dad hit you?! Of course, he did what am I saying, how could he do this to you?"

He pulls into the school's parking lot as he pulls into his parking spot, I grab his chin making him look me in the eye, his eyes were hard and his jaw was locked.

"Talk to me," I beg.

He grabs ahold of my wrist and snatches my hand off his face and it lands on my lap.

"Don't worry about it."

I shook my head at him, looking away and couldn't believe he was shutting me out. Wasn't he the one not letting me shut him out and now he's doing what I was doing?

"Fine," I give in with an attitude, opening his car door grabbing my book bag.

"Where are you going?" He asks, annoyed.

I glare at him. "I'm going to school; don't worry I'm not worried about it."

"Stop," He grabs my upper arm stopping me from exiting his Jeep. "Shut the door."

I huff before shutting the door giving into him because I knew he was going to tell me what happened.

"Tell me what happened," I demand, setting my book bag on the floorboard.

I stared at the steering wheel for a few seconds before hearing let out. "After you guys took me home, I went inside and saw my mom on the floor crying and rocking herself with her phone cuddling up to her."

"My dad and mom had gotten into a pretty bad fight, which ended up shit breaking in the house and my mom's shirt was ripped and she had a handprint on her cheek from where he slapped her, by that time I seen everything all I seen was red, I yelled at my dad and him and I were back and forth and he pushed me a little and I said shit then he said shit which leant him to punching me," He adds, slowly rising his head and staring at me.

His eyes were filled with sadness and I couldn't help but feel heartbroken for the boy in front of me.

"Why didn't you do anything?!" I asked, with wide eyes.

"Because I promised you no more fighting," He states, gently grabbing my hand kissing my palm.

My heart drops.

"Keaton..." I mumble, feeling some type of guilt for the reason why he took the beating.

"I'm alright," He promised, nodding his head. "After he punched me, it was like he went back to himself and didn't realize what he had done and when he did, he told me how sorry he was, but I knew it was all bullshit."

"You shouldn't have to live in that house anymore, your mom either."

"I'm gonna be out soon," He reminds me.

College. A dorm.

"But still, I can't bear the idea you're getting hit while I'm sitting at home knowing that you are and I can't do anything about it," I tell him, watching his thumb rubbing against the top of my hand.

"I really really like you, Tae," He chuckles out, biting his bottom lip.

I smile. "I really really like you too, Keaton."

He leans in closely so our cupid bows were touching, I closed my eyes waiting for our lips to clash together.

Keaton's hand touches the side of my face, removing the fly aways out my face, then our lips collide and throughout I couldn't help but smile.

No matter the time of day or night, I'll never get off the fact that I've kissed Keaton Davis.

I lay my thumb lightly across his eye that was covered with a bruise, a frown plasters on my face and Keaton plants his lips against mine to distract me.

"For some reason I couldn't stop thinking about you last night," He mumbles against my lips.

"Mhm really?" I smile, feeling a giggle arouse in my throat.

"Really," His sexy deep voice comes out.

"Tell me more," I said, biting my lip as we pulled away.

"Your thighs," He smirks throughout explaining, his hands carry themselves down to my thighs.

I laugh out, covering my mouth letting him continue, I feel his lips touch my neck bringing goosebumps to lay across my skin.

"That sexy laugh of yours," He states, chuckling.

"Those lips of course," He adds and I nod. "Did I already say your thighs?"

"Yes," I giggle out as I feel him squeeze both my thighs feeling a spark source through me.

I bit my lip as I feel a heartbeat down there growing stronger by the minute, I couldn't stop myself from my actions when I looked in the back of his Jeep seeing his seats were laid back and it was nothing but trunk in the back.

"Let's go back here," I instruct, crawling in the back and sitting down looking at his surprised eyes and his lips were glossy.

He nods quickly giving me an innocent look and he hurriedly crawls in the back copying my actions, but instead he crawls on top of me as I lay back.

My heart was about to explode out of my chest and I was hoping he didn't hear my heavy breathing.

"What do you want?" He asks, slowly licking his lips.

I was thanking the lord above that the Jeep windows were tinted and no one could see through and see the action we were about to do.

My shaky hands slowly reach down to the button of my pants and I slide my zipper down first, Keaton grabs my wrists gently and brings them up around his neck.

"I got you," He mumbles, kissing my lips softly.

He knew I was nervous so the kiss was basically a distraction for when he unbuttons my pants, I was so nervous that I grab a hold of Keaton's hair and pull it gently trying to distract myself as his hands crawl inside my pants and into my panties.

My breath gets caught in my throat and I gasp out as I feel his cold fingers rub against me, my mouth opens wide causing Keaton to smile staring down at me. When he pops in a finger in me, my head throws itself back and I groan out from it being so tight and wince at the same time.

"You've never touched yourself?" He asks, raising an eyebrow.

I shake my head and he nods.

He leans in and kisses my cheek before leaning closely into my ear.

"You don't ever have to be shy in front of me especially when I do stuff like this," He whispers and I let out a moan as he quickens the pace of his finger.

"Do you trust me?" He asks, licking his lips.

Before I could tell him anything he pops a second finger in causing me to squeeze his shoulders and I rock my hips along with his hand out of instinct, I guess.

Wow, sex ed and a lot of research really did help with this kind of stuff.

"Yes," I gasp out, feeling a funny sensation at the bottom of my stomach wanting some sort of release.

"Shit," I curse, feeling a fuzzy feeling in my head and a wet feeling leak out of me which normally meant that I had an orgasm.

"Good," He smiles, releasing his fingers from inside of me and licking them.

My eyes almost bulge out of my head and I smack his chest before buttoning my pants.

"What?" He laughs out, hovering over me.

"Don't do that," I cringe.

"Why? It's hot," He says, slowly kissing my lips and I smile at him.

"Whatever," I tell him, playfully rolling my eyes.

I can't believe I did this.

No- I can't believe I did that with Keaton Davis.

Where did all that confidence come from?

Now I'm all shy? How-

"I think we need to go in," I say, staring at the time on my phone.

He nods. "Yeah."

I nod and he opens the back of the Jeeps door helping me get out and closes it. I open the passenger door getting my stuff and shutting it, hearing a click sound meaning Keaton locked the doors.

"Aye Keaton! Ready for the last game tomorrow?" A guy hanging around a group of cheerleaders yells out.

"You bet!" Keaton yells out back.

"You best get that touchdown," The guys demands playfully, pointing at him.

Keaton grabs my hand and our fingers collide together.

"Or daddy gonna whoop that ass," Reece comes up behind us grabbing Keaton's shoulders shaking them a little.

Reece's smile begins to fade when he catches eye sight with Keaton's bruise around his eye.

"What the hell man? Your dad at you again?" He asks, with a concerned look in his eyes.

"Yeah," Keaton nods, his big shoulders slagging.

"Damn, listen, I know the perfect thing to get your mind off it," Reece states, letting his pointer finger jab onto Keaton's chest.

Keaton rolls his eyes playfully. "I don't want no weed, Reece."

"It's not weed, it's Xanax," Reece says, mumbling the last part looking around to make sure no one heard.

"No thanks," Keaton chuckles, bumping arms with him.

"Ahh, you suck," Reece waves him off. "What about you, Tae? You need something to make you chill?"

"No Reece," Keaton cuts in, shaking his head.

Reece holds his hands up in surrender. "Alright, fine. You know where I am if you need me."

"Alright, bro. See you," Keaton and Reece do their handshake thing whatever they want to call it and Reece walks off talking to a stoner kid.

"You never really talk about Reece much," I point out, looking up at him as we walked.

"I didn't think you wanted me to cause you don't like him," He answers, shrugging.

"Still, he's your friend," I retort, entering the school as Keaton opens the door for me.

"Well, as you know Reece is in an orphanage, but once he turns eighteen, he'll be on the streets, he's a stoner kid really, but he's Hella smart, he doesn't have a job if you count being a drug dealer one then okay," He explains, making it out like a joke but he was dead serious.

"Is he going to college?" I ask, earning a shake of the head from Keaton.

"He might be a dick and all, but he really means no harm."

"Wow..." I mumble, not knowing what to say.

As Keaton talks, I zone out as my eyes catch onto the familiar ones I seen a while back, the black-haired boy with a tattoo written across his neck and with light blue eyes gives me a deep stare as he walks the halls with no-one around him.

I shake my head out of my thoughts and turn my attention back on Keaton.

"Huh? Sorry, what was that?" I ask, leaning against the lockers.

Keaton shakes his head. "Nothing, I'll see you after class and here comes Winnie, so let me go so she won't chew my head off about not meeting them up before school."

He hurriedly pecks my lips before running off, patting a guy's back that said Hey to him and walking into a classroom.

"Damn it, Keaton," Winnie mumbles, out of breath.

I smile at her and she shows me her pearly whites. "Just the gal I was looking for."

"Oh, were you now?" I raise an eyebrow.

"Yes, you look different? Is it your hair? No- wait you had sex!" She exclaims, but whispers out.

I shake my head. "What? No."

"You sneaky little bitch, Keaton either fucked you, sucked you, or touched you, which one?" Winnie wraps her arm around mine as we walk towards first period and she giggles.

How did she know?

"I'll tell you later, just not in school where everybody can hear," I tell her whispering and she excitedly nods.

What was I going to do with this one?

Chapter Thirty-Nine

Tae's Pov.

"How's it going? Since you literally forgot about me," Mrs. Hyde asks, laying her hands on her hips.

I take a seat soaking in the familiar smell of pumpkin spice. "I'm actually doing good. I'm happy for once."

"And who is the cause of that?" She raises an eyebrow, teasing me.

Of course, it was Keaton.

"You were right, so was my dad. Friends really do change everything, especially getting into a relationship," I explain to her, finally giving in that she was right all along.

She smirks, sitting down at her desk in front of me. "Mhm, maybe just say it again so I can soak it in really good."

"Not happening."

"I know I was right, you're one stubborn girl," She tells me, pointing her finger at me.

"Tell me about it," I roll my eyes, agreeing with her for once.

"I really can see a difference in you, at the beginning of this year you were this saddened girl with nothing to live for and now you're this upbeat girl with everything she's ever wanted," Mrs. Hyde comments, sitting back in her rolly chair with a smile plastered on her face.

"I never thought I could feel like this again..." I mumble, playing with my fingers nervously.

"It was okay that you felt the way you felt Tae, everyone goes through trauma in a different way and you just so happen to shut everyone out," She explains and I nod.

"If it wasn't for Keaton that opened me up, I'd still be the same person," I say, sighing.

"Look at you being in love," She awes and my eyes go wide.

I shake my head quickly in denial. "I'm not in love."

"Tae, I can see the way you two look at each other, you two are in love."

"Okay... I'm leaving," I state, standing up from the chair I was sitting in and heads towards her office door.

She laughs. "Tae no, I'm serious."

"And I'm serious as well," I tell her, looking back at her. "Bye, I'll see you when you're done thinking I'm in love."

"Whatever," She rolls her eyes playfully as I exit her office.

I am not in love with Keaton Davis.

There's no way I was.

Do I act like it?

I go about my day thinking about what Mrs. Hyde was telling me about, I walk into my seventh period which is Agriculture and take a seat beside Winnie who has her head held down with her arms covering her.

"Is saying you're in love with someone cringe?" I ask her even though I have no clue if she's awake.

Winnie quickly brings her head up letting me see her honey eyes. "No?"

"I feel like it is..." I trail, biting my lip.

"What's going on?" She raises an eyebrow.

"Nothing, I just wanted to know what it's like. Are you in love with Landon?"

"I mean..." She shrugs. "Yeah, probably."

"How do you know?"

She sighs. "It's hard to explain really, but it's like you don't want to lose them-"

"No cringe stuff Winnie, please," I whine, holding my hand out stopping her mid-sentence.

"Fine," She huffs.

"He's like your number one best friend, you could tell anything to him and you'd trust him just like that," She adds, snapping her fingers.

I nod for her to continue.

"You'd do anything for that other person, and if they're gone just for a second you feel like the whole world is about to collapse."

"Every breath you take you're constantly thinking about him and ugh don't get me started on the feelings," She moans out, closing her legs together and I scrunch my nose up.

"I think I got it," I tell her, nodding.

Who knew Winnie could be so gross?

"Just saying. Why did you ask? Are you wondering if Keaton is in love with you or something?" She asks, pushing a lock of her red hair out of her face.

I shake my head, lying. "No, of course not."

"You can tell that boy is dead deep in love," She sighs out like she's in a daze as she watches the class door as it opens.

I sigh out, thinking too over my head and the boys rush in before the bell rings along the whole school. Mr. Hollis stares at everyone before coughing and writing something down on the white board.

"You can have free time because I have some grades, I have to put in the grade book and grade your tests from last time which will take up the remainder of class, please do not be loud and do not be tonguing your peers," He orders us, giving us a death glare at the end.

Surprisingly, everyone got up quietly and walked around the class to get to where they were headed, except for the boys, Landon, Keaton, and Reece slid their chairs causing it to make a loud sound and racing to Winnie and I's seat.

I roll my eyes at the immaturity, but sit up as Keaton pulls a seat beside me.

"Damn it's cold outside," Reece mumbles, putting the hood from his hoodie over his head.

Keaton nods. "It was so cold that the doors of my Jeep wouldn't open and I had to run inside to get hot water and pour it over my car."

"Right, my truck took forever to warm up," Landon exclaims, shaking his head.

Winnie gives me a disgusting look referring to the boys and I roll my eyes.

"Do you want to spend the night tomorrow night?" Winnie asks, earning the guy's attention.

I nod. "Sure, I'll ask my dad in a bit."

"Great, I've been waiting on this day since we met," She states, clapping her hands.

"I thought we were going to spend the day together," Keaton says, feeling offended.

I grab ahold of his hand. "We always hang out."

"Yeah, but still..." He trails, swirling circles with his thumb on my hand.

"You guys hang out so much that you never let me have time with her," Winnie argues, pointing her finger at him.

He shrugs. "She's my girlfriend."

"And I could be her best friend, but you won't let me get the chance."

"You guys do hang out a lot," Reece cuts in, nodding.

"Did I ask for your opinion?" Keaton sarcastically asks, raising an eyebrow.

Reece shakes his head. "No, I just felt like I was being too quiet."

"Jesus Christ help me," Landon mumbles up to the ceiling.

Winnie grabs Landon's shoulder and shakes him before saying. "Baby, can you please knock some sense into Keaton before I actually hurt him."

"Cut the boy some slack, he's in love, if he wants to be with his girlfriend twenty-four seven then let him do it," Landon shrugs and Keaton smirks at Reece and Winnie.

My body freezes at the words Landon says and I try to *forget* it, but each time my mind brings me back to it.

'He's in love'

"Can we talk about something else?" I hurriedly ask, giving Keaton a side look.

They all nod and we end up talking about the game, the five of us actually had a great time and it didn't end up with Winnie trying to choke Reece and Keaton trying to tackle Reece down for saying something slick.

"Ready for our last high school game?" Reece comes up with elbowing Keaton causing him to chuckle.

"I'm kinda sad though, to be honest, cause college football games are more crowded and more important," Landon reminds, tsking his tongue.

Keaton's smile soon turns into a small smile and then a frown, I knew Keaton was having a hard time picking a college or even knowing what he was going to do in the future, his dad was on his tail twenty-four seven about his future when Keaton just wanted to live his life and be a normal high school kid.

An hour later with long talks about football and Winnie gossiping about how she needed a manicure, the school bell rings indicating that everyone could leave.

Mr. Hollis tells us his goodbyes and everyone swamps through the door and out of the school.

Keaton swings his arm around my shoulders as we walk through the halls.

He raises an eyebrow at me. "What are you thinking about wearing to the game? My jersey?"

"Of course, I got to support my boyfriend," I hit his chest with the back of my hand.

He puts his hand over his mouth being dramatic. "I'm really enjoying that title right now."

"God, can you be anymore cringe Keaton?" Winnie scrunches her nose in disgust.

"You're just jealous because your boyfriend is giving fat ass more attention than he is you," Keaton says, pointing out to Landon and Reece talking.

Winnie's face blooms red and she fists her books in her hand. "Why do I hang out with boys so much? I really need to start looking for girlfriends."

"You've got me," I pointed out, smiling cheekily.

"Keaton steals you away every time I wanna hang out," She pouts, giving Keaton a glare.

"Whatever," Keaton mumbles, rolling his eyes.

I shake my head at Keaton before looking back Winnie with sympathy. "I'm asking my dad to spend the night with you tomorrow, and there he is now so I'll go ask."

"You do that, say hi for me will you?" She excitedly states.

I nod. "I will."

"I'll see you at the game?" Keaton asks, raising an eyebrow.

I couldn't help but smile at the hopeful look spread across his face, I nod and kiss him on the cheek.

"I wouldn't miss it for the world," I state, giving him, reassurance and he nods pecking my lips before I split apart from the gang.

It didn't take much walking to get to my dad when he was walking towards me as well.

"Hello father," I sarcastically greet him, hanging onto his arm.

"Hello daughter," He says back in the same tone.

I sigh out in hope. "How was your day?"

"Cut to the chase, Tae. I know you want something," He rolls his eyes, smiling down at me.

"Well...." I trail off. "Winnie and I want to hang out tomorrow and hang out I mean me spending the night with her."

"I don't care as long as it's okay with her mom," He shrugs, giving me a warning look.

"Of course, are you excited for the last game of the season?" I ask, seeing a little glimpse in his eye.

"Honestly....no," He sighs out.

I stop in mid tracks. "What? Why?"

"Because all of my good guys on the team are leaving this year and next year, I won't know who to put as Quarterback," He explains, looking down at his clipboard.

"That's next year, you've plenty of time to choose," I laugh out.

"Yeah, but I don't know..." He trails, scratching his head.

"You'll pick some good guys to fill in the spots for the ones who's gonna leave and I'll even help you when try outs come," I try making the situation better and him giving me a smile draw hope in my heart.

"Are you staying behind with me to help me get ready or are you going with Winnie to get ready?"

I shrug. "I'll probably talk her into getting ready here in the school's bathroom so I can help you out some."

"Great! Take this..." He hands me his notebook. "And run outside and fetch the guy's names so it'll let me know who's all here."

"Yes sir," I salute him before completing my mission and heading outside finding the boys prepping up for practice before the big game.

"Tae Lambert," Keaton whistles out, with his hands on his hips.

I lay my bag down on the cold grass before giving him a smile. "Hey."

"I thought Winnie would've snatched you up by now and you guys get ready at her house," He states, smirking down at me as I take a seat on the bench.

"No, I'll just get ready here, I wanna help my dad out and prep you guys up for the game," I explain, shaking my head.

"I'm glad you're here," He sits down beside me.

"Me too," I give him a soft smile.

****

I look out at the boys who were running out on the field in their uniforms and I look back up at the crowd and smile, the game had just started twenty minutes ago and my dad was already on his toes.

Lydia and Mandy and the rest of the cheerleading squad was already cheering out to the crowd and Lydia gives me a look of disgust in which I ignored trying to not let her get under my skin.

As some of the boys would rush off the field to sit out, I'd give them water or Gatorade to fill their thirst.

Did I get a lot of sweat on me? *Yes, yes, I did.*

But it was Hella worth it seeing the huge smile on my dad's face and watching Keaton from afar enjoying the sport he loves. My eyes catch on seeing that Keaton's mom and dad were standing at the crowd, I frown as I watched Keaton's dad, Randy, watch the game with judgmental eyes, he kept his eyesight on his son and nothing but him.

"Tae!" I hear Winnie's voice call from afar.

I turn around seeing her hold up two water bottles jogging towards me with Landon's jersey on.

"Thank you," I thank her, taking the water bottle from her hands.

"I wouldn't want you to get mouth fungus from drinking out of the jug," She points at the jug that stood three inches from us.

"Oh yeah," I laugh out, taking a sip.

I jump hearing the man on the microphone telling everyone that it was break time, all the footballs players went on their sides and I saw my boy taking off his helmet looking down at the one glove he had on before ripping it off.

His smile grows huge as he takes sight of me and he runs towards me and just like that in slow motion, I was picked up off the ground and twirled around before getting a kiss slapped on my lips.

"I'm literally one lucky guy," He states, biting his lip.

I wipe his sweaty hair out of his face and smile. "I should be saying that, not you."

"I don't care, I'm saying it anyways," His raspy voice speaks out and butterflies erupt in my stomach.

I hear the buzzer meaning that break time was over, I pout, poking my bottom lip out and Keaton lets me down.

"I'll see you after the game," He states, backing up and pointing at me. "And by the way, you look gorgeous."

"Thank you," I giggle out causing his smile to grow.

"Get em' tiger, I love you," Winnie tells Landon before smacking his butt.

He smirks. "*Always* baby, love you back."

Landon runs off behind Keaton and the game starts just as quickly as the break started.

"Landon makes you happy, doesn't he?"

She nods. "For sure."

"Keaton makes you happy I can tell," She adds, winking.

"The happiest," I mumble, watching him catch the ball in one go and the crowd goes wild.

I felt eyes on me so I looked up in the crowd seeing that it was Randy staring hard and angry at me, my eyes quickly left his and the whole night I couldn't stop thinking about what he must be thinking.

By the end of the game, the boys didn't end up winning but it was a fair game and the boys weren't too mad at it, but my dad sure was.

"I can't believe it," My dad mumbles to himself looking up at the sky.

I laugh as Keaton holds my hand with his helmet in his other, I watch my dad walk off to talk to Mrs. Hyde and Keaton's nose touched my temple and his lips were close to my ear.

"Since I didn't win the game tonight maybe I could win something of yours," He whispers, backing up from my ear at the end giving me a teasing smirk.

"Down boy," I pushed at his chest, but it only made Keaton's hand grab for mine and bring me into his chest.

He gave me this loving long stare that my stomach couldn't bare but to do front flips and I bite my lip before kissing his lips.

Was I falling hard for Keaton Davis? *Yes, yes, I was.*

Chapter Forty

Tae's Pov.

Slamming my locker shut with my school bag on my back and my night bag in my hand, Winnie decided that she wanted me to spend the night today instead of yesterday because she wanted "girl time". I couldn't be happier to spend time with her because every time we tried to hang out our little talk gets interrupted by the boys.

I feel a figure beside me as students pass by me to leave the school, I glance to my side to see Keaton leaning against the locker beside mine with arms crossed and a smirk plastered on his face.

"What are you happy about?" I raise an eyebrow as I hear myself ask him.

"I'm happy to see you and Winnie getting close," He truthfully lets out.

I nod. "Me too, I'm glad you have at least one girl in the group so I won't have to blow my brains out every time one of y'all talk."

He chuckles lifting himself off the lockers before him and I head towards the doors of the school.

"So, what are you going to be up to while I'm at Winnie's?"

He shrugs. "Probably hang out with the guys."

"Hmm, not gonna get into trouble, are you?" I ask, half away smiling because some of it was a joke.

Half of it was not.

"Can't promise I won't," He smirks, teasing me.

I roll my eyes as the foolish boy and open the door seeing the sunlight glare in my eyes.

"Nah, I won't. We'll probably work out or go to see Ally and Tommy," He adds, letting my worries flutter away.

"Okay, good," I smile at him.

Seeing Winnie's bright red dune buggy pull in front of the stairs at the school was a sight to see, she parks before opening her door and her red hair and herself pops out of the vehicle.

"What's up bitches!" She squeals, with her hands in the air.

Keaton slightly waves before connecting eyesight with me.

"I'll miss you..." He mumbles sadly, poking out his bottom lip.

"Keaton, it'll only be for a day, you go have fun with Reece and Landon," I demand him, poking his chest.

He nods slightly. "Okay, text me?"

"Of course," I say before pecking his lips.

I rush down the stairs being greeted by an excited Winnie, Keaton hollers out at Winnie to make sure we behave, but Winnie ignores him and gets into her car.

"That boy is something else..." She trails, looking up at him as he watches us from afar.

I laugh out as he waves. "I know."

She drives off and blasts the music until our ears bleed.

"So, what's your favorite color?" Her odd question surprises me and I glance at her.

"What?" She adds.

I shake my head. "Way to start the conversation."

"It's a good question, come on, what's your favorite color?" She defends herself, keeping her eyes remaining on the road ahead.

"Probably grey, what about you?" I give out, sighing.

"Hmm, red," She giggles out, causing me to laugh.

I roll my eyes playfully. "Why did I even ask? Obviously, it is because you see it everywhere."

"What? Red is a pretty color," She gasps out, giving me a wide-eyed look like I had said something wrong.

I hold my hands up in surrender. "Okay..."

****

We reach Winnie's house and enter her home with tiredness in our bodies, Winnie falls face first on her bed.

She then turns around. "What do you wanna do?"

"It doesn't matter," I shrug.

"Oh, come on, we have the rest of today and tonight to do stuff and you don't know what to do?" She asks, giving me a weird look.

I shake my head answering her question, I drop my bag on her floor before taking a seat beside her on her bed.

"Do you like to paint your nails?" She asks.

"I haven't painted them in a while, last time I painted them was when my mom was alive," I tell her, staring down at my fingernails.

She gives me a saddened look. "Well, do you wanna do each other's for the time being and then watch a movie?"

"Sure," I agreed, shrugging.

She claps her hands before standing up and taking out a bucket from under her desk top, a pink bucket filled with fingernail polish, fingernail polish remover, fingernail clippers.

"What color would you like?" She asks, taking out a few colors.

I point out at the light blue she laid out before she picked out another. "I love that one."

"Oh, me too! Want me to do it that color?"

"Yeah," I say, nodding.

She nods, taking my hand and navigates me to sit on the floor in front of her.

"I never really had a true girl best friend," She starts the conversation. "Truth be known, I can only trust boys."

"Well now you can say you have one," I let out, smiling.

She looks up and smiles. "You never talk about your family with me."

I furrow my eyebrows in confusion and she adds. "You've told me that Georgie is your brother, but nothing juicy."

"There's really nothing to it, it's just me and my dad at home waiting for Georgie to call one day," I opened up to her.

"Where does he go to college?" She hums out.

"Harvard," I answer, watching closely as she paints the light blue substance on my fingernails.

She smiles. "He must be smart."

"Oh, he is, he got a football scholarship as well."

"That's so cool," She seemed so amazed about my family when she spoke none of hers.

"Do you have any siblings?" I ask.

"Nope, just me, my parents tried for another, but my mom couldn't carry anymore," She states, before trying to dry my hand after she gets done painting.

"I feel so bad for your mom," I sigh out.

I feel so bad for any women that couldn't go through with pregnancy; I'm surprised my mom even could get pregnant with her disease.

"Speaking of your mom... Where is she?"

"She's working, that woman constantly keeps moving at all times," She shakes her head at the thought.

"Oh okay," I said.

She looks up at me and smiles. "My turn!"

****

Night time arrived and Winnie was downstairs fixing popcorn to watch a movie, I flip through the pages of an old magazine Winnie had laid out because she knew I was into old timey things. Sitting on the floor in my pajamas smiling to myself as I hear Winnie's footsteps rushing up the steps.

"I see you have taken a liking in my magazines," Winnie observes, setting down the bowl of popcorn with our sodas on the side.

I nod. "Oh yeah."

"You and my mom would be best friends if she knew, she's always tried telling me about how it was back then but I never seem to listen," She laughs out, handing me a soda.

I thank her before popping the top. "I just don't find our century fun."

"There's a lot of things you can do," She shrugs, throwing a piece of popcorn in her mouth.

"Yeah, there is, but it's expensive. Back then you only had to pay five cents for a t-shirt and now you have to pay thirty," I explain, and she shrugs.

"True..." She trails, turning on the tv.

"What would you like to watch?" She adds, looking over at me.

"Something scary?" I ask, feeling the need to jump.

Her eyes light up. "I was hoping you'd say that."

I giggle, feeling my phone vibrate from under me, I take out my phone seeing that Keaton sent me a text.

'I miss you.'

I smile down at the message before gliding my thumb over the letters sending a text back.

'I miss you more.'

"Tae?" Winnie speaks out with fear mixed in her voice.

I look up alarmed. "What?"

"Do you hear that?" She whispers but asks.

I shake my head, being quiet so I could hear, I waited a few minutes and all I heard was silence.

Then, I heard it.

Slight taps on Winnie's bedroom window bring fear to my core, I quickly caught Winnie's eyes and she mouths 'stand up' and I did just that.

We both jump up with fear in our veins, she quickly tip toes to the closet and I stand there not knowing what to do, the window slightly opens and my eyes go wide.

"Winnie," I whisper.

She pops her head out of the closet and finally comes out bringing a baseball bat, she stands in front of me ready to swing at the intruder, I didn't know what to hold or do but I wanted to help, so I grab one of Winnie's pillows on her bed holding it near my chest as the window slams opens and in comes three boys with hoods over their heads wearing all black.

Tears form in my eyes and sweat appears under my pits, I close my eyes already knowing Winnie couldn't hit all three of them at once so the both of us were wishing for a death wish.

"You dumbasses," Winnie exclaims, and I hear the boy's chuckle.

I open my eyes and my eyes catch onto Keaton, Landon, and Reece.

I stood there flabbergasted with my mouth open, the light turned on making my eyes close for a few seconds.

"Why the hell would you do that? You could've gotten hurt," Winnie states, pointing at the boys.

"I'm sorry, but you should've seen your face," Landon says, laughing.

"And who's idea was this?" She asks, crossing her arms.

Keaton and Landon point towards Reece and he glares at the two.

"Wow, thanks for kicking me under the bus," He rolls his eyes.

"Of course, it was the freaks idea," Winnie rolls her eyes.

I lay the pillow down and Keaton stares at me from across the room and chuckles.

He points down at the pillow I laid down. "The hell were you going to do with that pillow?"

"Just in case if someone did come in, I'd hit him with it," I answer, shrugging.

"We need to do this more often," Keaton says, looking back at the boys and they nod.

Winnie shakes her head. "Nope, I'll make sure I lock my window good next time."

"You're a party shitter, Winnie," Reece tells her and she sticks her tongue out at him.

"All I wanted was a girl's night," Winnie whines to Landon looking up at him as she lays her chin on his chest.

Landon nods. "I'm sorry, baby."

Keaton walks to me kissing my cheek. "Are you mad at me?"

"Kinda, you know Winnie and I were trying to hang out," I tell him. "Alone."

"Come on, you can't say that wasn't fun," He defends, chuckling.

I give him a blank look. "No."

"How about I make it up to you?" He asks, raising an eyebrow.

"How?"

"Take you on a date tomorrow?" He asks, grinning from ear to ear.

"Mhhh," I say, putting my finger on my chin. "I'll think about it."

"Nooo, you're gonna say yes," He says, nodding.

I hit his chest lightly before earning another kiss on the cheek.

I wanted a good jump....

And that's what I got.

Chapter Forty-One

Tae's Pov.

"Where are you taking me?" I giggle out, closing my eyes as Keaton wraps a blindfold around my eyes.

His mouth attaches to my ear as he whispers. "You'll see."

Goosebumps appeared down my arm and I couldn't help but smile as I felt the Jeep put in park. Last night Keaton asked for me more like he demanded to go on another date and I insistently said yeah, I got ready with Winnie on FaceTime asking her for pointers and moves I could make tonight.

I really did like Keaton and I knew he wanted tonight to be perfect since he blindfolded me.

The blindfold slowly comes off letting my eyes catch on the sight in front of me, a smile plasters on my face and I bite my bottom lip as I turn my head towards Keaton.

"You shouldn't have," I mumble, turning to look at the sight.

Keaton took us to a lake and propped up a blank sheet with a projector in front of it ready to play the movie.

"I've had this date on my mind for a while now I just didn't know where to start," He says, shrugging.

He opens his console to let me see the snacks and drinks he had out.

"This is perfect, thank you," I say, smiling from ear to ear.

"I got pizza in the back..." He trails, pointing towards the pizza box in the back.

He lifted his back seats down and I couldn't help, but smile at the pile of blankets beside it.

He backs his Jeep up to where we have to lay in the back to see the movie, we both get out jumping in the back and cuddling next to each other as we dig into the pizza.

Almost as the movie is over, I couldn't help but notice Keaton staring at me throughout instead of watching the film.

I look over at him and raise an eyebrow. "What?"

"Just admiring my view," He mumbles, smirking.

"Stop with the cheesy stuff," I push at his chest.

"I'm not trying to be," He shrugs. "You really are beautiful."

"Well... Thank you," I tell him gratefully.

"I got something I wanna tell you," He says, with a nervous tone.

"Okay," I nod. "Tell me."

I turned so that my front was facing him and my eyesight was only on him.

"I love you..." He lets out, making my whole figure freeze up and he notices.

"I really do," He blow out a breath, shaking his head.

I stay silent as he pours out his heart to me.

"I'm the luckiest guy alive, any guy would kill to have you. I'm crazy for you, Tae. I knew since the day I met you that we had something there, you give me this ray of hope every day and just to see you smile is enough for me," He adds. "All I want is to protect you and to show you how much I really do love you."

I stay quiet for a few seconds until I open my mouth. "Keaton, I-"

I was scared to admit to myself and say that I loved Keaton, I sat there speechless as he cut me off.

He shakes his head. "You don't have to say it back, I know you're not ready, but I just had to tell you or I was gonna blow."

I didn't know what to say so instead, I grabbed a hold of his face and slammed my lips onto his, the feeling of his lips made me feel at home, I felt safe in his arms. His arms wrap around the sides of my face as we set in for a passionate kiss.

I cared for Keaton and a lot at that, but doubts were still running in the back of my mind, disappearing my thoughts about Keaton.

He pulls apart letting his forehead connect with mine. "Don't ever think for a second that I'm ever letting you go, Tae Lambert."

"I don't," I said quietly, pushing myself away from him.

"Wanna get in the lake?" He asks, biting

"What? No, it's winter, Keaton," I exclaim, with wide eyes as he jumps out of the back.

"So?" He says, turning around to give me a smirk and takes off his shirt and throws it back at me.

"You're gonna get sick," I yell out at his retreating form.

"Still won't stop me..." He sings out, chuckling.

He stops right at the shore to take out his pants and runs into the water after.

"Come on," He yells out, waving for me to come in.

I huff out before taking off my shirt and pants wearing nothing but my underwear and bra, I quickly walk into the water and gasp out at the coldness as the water touches my skin.

"It's not that cold," He says, rubbing his chest.

"Yes, it is," My teeth chatter as I talk.

He splashes water onto me and I gasp out glaring out at the starting Quarterback.

"You did not!" I exclaim, gasping.

"Oh, I did."

I take my hands and hit the water making it splash on him and he closes his eyes as the water falls onto his face. He playfully glares at me before taking off towards me, I squeal out trying to move in the water but didn't go far because of the pressure the water had on me.

I scream out as Keaton's big arms wrap around my small waist and rip me out of the water and spin me around.

"You started it, I only finished," I defended myself, holding onto his arms as he let me down, sitting me to face him.

The tips of his hair stuck to his forehead causing him to get ten times hotter, he was left breathless looking down at me and his chest kept coming in and out, his smile grows huge as my own does and he grabs the sides of my face as I take my hands and cover his arms as his lips attack mine with a kiss.

"Watch us both be sick," He tells me in between the kiss as he chuckles.

I shake my head. "It doesn't matter."

I didn't care if I was going to be dog sick the next day if that meant spending the next minute in this lake with Keaton Davis.

****

"Why are you guys wet?" My dad asks Keaton and I as we enter the door damp as ever.

I laugh, looking at Keaton's worried eyes before returning my eye sight on my dad.

"We were watching a movie and I decided to run in the lake," I explain, completely taking the fall that it was my idea that we went in the lake.

"No sir, it was my idea..." Keaton mumbles, keeping eye contact with my dad.

"It's not me that's gonna get sick, it's y'all two," He points at both of us.

He heads out of the kitchen calm as ever and heads up stairs.

I look back at Keaton and shrug. "He's good."

"So, we're not in trouble?" He asks, raising an eyebrow.

"Nope," I mumble, taking off my shoes.

"Good, I gotta head home, I'll see you tomorrow," He tells me and I nod.

He kisses my lips before mumbling. "Goodnight, I love you."

"Goodnight..." I trail, feeling afraid he was waiting for the 'L' word.

He smiles at me before heading out of the door and I let out a breath of air.

I head upstairs with my shoes in hand heading towards my room until I hear sniffles coming from my dad's bedroom.

I look through the crack of my dad's bedroom to see my dad leaned over the bed whispering to himself.

"I miss you so much, Carrie, why'd you have to leave me?" He asks, looking up at the ceiling. "Tae's done found her a good guy and I'd wish you were here to meet him."

My heart breaks in two and I feel tears form in the corners of my eye, I hurriedly walk towards my room not wanting my dad to find out that I found him crying out to mom.

I knew dad was upset about mom's death, he never really spoke about how he felt, all he said was he really missed her and we have to be strong but never once did he cry. I *remember* him crying at the funeral but that was it, he'd always do it behind closed doors.

My phone buzzes letting me know I have a text and I see that I have one from Keaton and another from Winnie.

Keaton
'I had fun tonight.'

Winnie
'How was your date with Keaty boy?!!

I reply back to the two with a smile on my face but a
frown soon pops up as the memory of my dad pops up
in my mind that I couldn't erase.

Chapter Forty-Two

Keaton's Pov.

As Tae explains to me about Mr. Pine bumping her grade down and she's upset, I couldn't help but admire the beauty in front of me, the way her nose crinkles when she's upset and the way her little fists ball does things to me in a way it's never done before, she leans against the lockers complaining to me as I sit on the bench in the locker room tying my shoes.

"Keaton!" She catches my attention by snapping her fingers in my face.

I shake my head clearing my thoughts. "Yes, what?"

"Did you not hear me?" She asks, laughing.

"You were talking about Mr. Pine," I nod.

She shakes her head. "No, I'm on another topic now."

"Oh well, then no," I laughed.

"I can't believe high school football is over forever..." I mumble, staring down at my jersey hanging up in my locker.

Tae sighs. "On the bright side you'll get to play football in college if that makes you feel any better."

"Not exactly the same as it is here," I tell her, laughing lightly as she gives me a frown.

Her beautiful dirty blonde hair dances as she combs out her hair with her fingers, the curls she once had this morning were gone and in came the waves.

"Graduation is getting closer and closer," I remind her.

Tae takes a seat next to me and sighs out loud.

"How do you feel about that?" She asks, with her big doe eyes staring back at mine.

"It's nerve wracking, usually people would be thrilled for this moment, but I'm really not all that excited," I let out, truthfully.

"I have to pick a college before graduation."

Her eyes went wide. "Wow."

"Growing up sucks," She mumbles, laying her head down on my shoulder while sighing out.

"Yep," I say, popping the p.

"Tae! You ready?!" I hear Coach Lambert's impatient voice yell out.

Tae takes her head off my shoulder before grabbing her bag. "Yeah, I'm coming!"

She turns her head back to me, giving me a sad smile. "FaceTime me when you get home?"

"Of course," I smile back up at her.

"Good, and don't be sad you're too good looking for that," She takes my chin in her hand and takes her other hand and lightly pats my cheek.

Before she leaves, she kisses my lips and I tell her quietly that I love her in which she freezes up but smiles covering up the fact that she totally froze and leaves the locker room.

I knew Tae wasn't ready for the 'L' word yet and I wasn't going to push it but damn, would it be something to hear her say it back.

I tie my shoelaces together and hear the locker room door open and slam shut and footsteps approach me, I turn around seeing my childhood best friend giving me a worried expression.

"Winnie..." I greet, giving her a confused look.

"Hey..." She says quietly, looking down.

"I- uh," I look at my bag in my hand before looking back at her. "What are you doing here?"

"I wanted to talk to you about something," She states, biting her lip.

"Okay..." I wave for her to continue.

She seemed nervous by the way she was moving her fingers together.

"I wanted to talk to you about Tae..." She finally comes out.

"Okay, what about her?" I asked, confusedly.

She raises an eyebrow before saying. "Does she have asthma?"

"No, why?" Why was she asking this?

"Because every time Tae does certain things her breathing gets hard," My nerves were unsettled as her lips moved and out came her sentence.

"I-" I couldn't come up with anything.

"And don't tell me some lame ass excuse, I need some answers, you two are hiding something."

How the hell does she know this?

"I'm not hiding anything," I shrug, not letting her see past my lie.

"Yes, you are Keaton, she keeps going to the nurse every day and you sometimes go with her, don't think I haven't been watching you two," She accuses, shaking her head.

Shit.

"Nothing is going on," I keep up the wall between us.

"Fine, whatever," She lets it go and turns around but then turns around again as I sigh. "My own best friend isn't telling me what's wrong with my girl best friend when I know something is wrong with her."

"Winnie..." I close my eyes, getting tired at her whining.

"What?" She asks frustratedly, throwing her hands in the air.

I trusted Winnie.

"Tae has cancer," I let out, holding onto the bridge of my nose.

I can't believe I just told her...

"What?" She huffs out. "I don't understand."

"Best believe it, you gotta promise me you won't say shit to anyone," I stand up in front of her.

"Cross my heart," She nods, looking up at me.

"Good, Tae's gonna be pissed when she finds out," I sigh out.

"I can't imagine what her and her dad is going through right now," Her voice cracks. "Why didn't she want anyone to know?"

"She didn't want people pitying her, also to think she's lying," I tell her. "She wants people to think she's a normal girl."

"Poor Tae," Winnie whispers, holding onto her chest.

"Seriously Winnie, don't tell a soul," I shake my head at her.

"I won't say anything, I promise," She says, giving me her word.

"Thank you," I finally sit back down, relaxing.

"Also, don't act weird around her now or she'll get suspicious," I add.

"Got it," She nods.

I looked down at my phone to check the time. What a day.

"I should probably get home before dad has a hissy fit," I explain, holding up my phone and she smiles softly.

"Yeah, I need to go help my mom in the library," She states.

Winnie leaves before me as I grab my shoes and leave the building, heading towards my Jeep was quiet and gave me some time to think.

I felt guilty for telling Winnie when I promised Tae, I wouldn't tell anyone, but Winnie wouldn't have left it alone if I didn't.

"Keaton?" I hear a familiar voice shout. "What are you still doing here?"

I turn around to see Reece. "I should be asking you the same thing."

"I had to stay behind to get some extra help in class, you finally got your stuff from your locker?" He asks, pointing towards my gym bag.

I nod. "Yeah, makes me actually open my eyes to see that we're growing up and graduation is just around the corner."

"Then college," He reminds, smiling.

"You going?" I asked, surprised.

Reece never talked about going to college.

"Nope, fuck college. If I can hardly make it through twelfth grade then how the hell am I gonna make it through college?"

"You could make it," I encourage him, but with the shake of his head I knew he already made up his mind.

"Plus, college is a waste of time," He exclaims, shrugging.

"Well, I would love to stay and talk but I gotta get home," I tell him and he nods.

"No worries, I'll text you in a bit," He reminds.

"Okay," I nod.

We split up and go our separate ways and I hop into my Jeep driving it out of the prison we like to call high school.

Once I get home, I try face timing Tae, but she ends up not answering and responding with 'helping dad with dinner'.

I lay on my bed with my phone between my hands looking up at the ceiling until my bedroom door opened. I lay up thinking my mom wanted something, but instead it was the devil in distress.

I roll my eyes as he shuts the door behind him and he holds up his hands in surrender.

"I'm not here to fight," He says.

"Okay, so leave because all you ever do is fight with someone when you enter the room," I accuse, huffing out.

"I just came to ask how my son was doing, is that a crime?"

I stand up from my bed taking off my shirt before slipping on a tank top.

I look back at him. "I'm doing great."

He gets quiet, putting his hands in his pockets and I sigh out.

"How's uh- how's Tae?" I stop in my tracks giving him a glare.

"Why do you care? All you ever had to say about her was horrible, so why care now?"

"Because my son is being distracted by a sick girl when we both know she's gonna be gone very soon, and you got so much to think about than some girl getting ready to die," He explains, shaking his head.

I stare at him like he's just knocked the shit out of me. "How could you say that? Your wife was on her death bed with the same thing Tae has and you say some slick shit like that?"

"I'm sorry that was harsh, Keaton, but you have to look at it my way, before you met her-" I cut him off.

"Before I met her my life was going to shit, Tae shown me something that you were supposed to show me, she is so much better than that bitch Lydia and you know it, I was heartbroken and you didn't help me, not once, you just hate the fact that I'm happy now and you want to take it away, but guess what dad, I love her, there I said it, I love Tae with every bone in my damn body and you can't say shit," I point my finger at him, tearing up a bit.

"When mom was sick you didn't fight for her, all you did was sit on your ass and sulk and I can't say the same because of what I did, but I sure as hell am going to fight with and for Tae and you can't stop me."

"What's gonna happen when Tae's on her deathbed? You're gonna go on your little ramp page?" He raises his eyebrow.

Fiery was deep within his eyes but I didn't give a shit, I wanted him to know what I was feeling.

"No," I say, shaking my head.

"All I ever wanted was for you to have a great future and marry the right girl," He whispers, letting his arms flops to his sides.

"This is your future, dad, not mine," I fight back.

"And what is your future, Keaton? Have you even thought about it?"

Yes.

I stay quiet because I was tired of fighting and I knew if I kept on, he would do the same.

"I'm leaving," He states, turning around.

"Good..." I mumble to myself.

The door slams shut as he exits my room.

"My future is *her*..." I said quietly, staring down at the carpeted floor.

Chapter Forty-Three

Unknown Pov.

Walking in the school's hallway had me thinking as I was heading to the locker room to grab my bag. My grades were shitty and I was probably not going to get that scholarship. Not like I was going to college anyway.

Great.

Opening the locker room doors, I hear voices talking amongst each other.

"Because every time Tae does certain things her breathing gets hard," I hear Winnie speak towards Keaton.

I don't think they noticed me, so I hide behind a set of lockers listening in.

"I-" Keaton tries to say.

"And don't tell me some lame ass excuse, I need some answers, you two are hiding something."

"I'm not hiding anything."

"Yes, you are, Keaton, she keeps going to the nurse every day and you sometimes go with her, don't think I haven't been watching you two," She states.

What the hell? Tae's going to the nurse?

"Nothing's going on," Keaton tells her.

"Fine, whatever," She sighs out. "My own best friend isn't telling me what's wrong with my girl best friend when I know something is wrong with her."

I roll my eyes at the over dramatic redhead.

"Winnie..." Keaton sighs.

Come on Keaton boy, tell the secret.

"What?"

"Tae has cancer," Keaton lets out.

I cover my mouth with my hand trying so hard not to laugh, wait till Lydia gets a load of this.

"What?" Winnie's shaky voice came out. "I don't understand."

"Best believe it, you gotta promise me you won't say shit to anyone," Keaton begs her.

"Cross my heart."

Sorry Keaton, I don't keep promises.

Just you wait...

Keaton Davis, I have always been second to you, I've seen you to the highest point in your life to your lowest, you were a major fuck up and to see you have a second chance was not it for me. You don't deserve Quarterback, you don't deserve that scholarship, you don't deserve to be the guy everyone wants to be, and you most definitely don't deserve Tae.

And I'm going to make sure that you don't, oh, you'll have the scholarship, popularity, the greatest spot on the team, but I'll make sure you won't have *her*.

Chapter Forty-Four

Tae's Pov.

"Are you sure you don't wanna go to lunch with us?" Keaton asks, pecking my lips once more.

"We're going to see Ally and Tommy," He sings, causing me to giggle.

I pushed at his chest as he kept pecking me. "I'm sure, I want to spend time with Mrs. Hyde."

"Okay," He sighs out, pecking me once more.

"I'll see you later, I love you," He says quickly, causing me to freeze.

Why does my body always react when he says that to me, my heart always gushes, but my body freezes.

He leaves in a hurry and Winnie pouts but waves to me and I mimic her actions before heading into Mrs. Hyde's office. She sits in her large rolly chair eating a salad.

"Nice to see you again," She comments as she finishes chewing her food.

"I know," I say back.

"So, you drop the gang to sit with me huh?"

"Yep," I smile at her.

I noticed her sitting up in her seat and she collapsed her hands together, I frown at her left hand noticing her wedding ring was gone.

"What-" She cuts me off before I can ask.

"Rick and I are splitting up," She spits out, frowning down at her hand.

I shake my head. "What? I thought you guys were great after what happened last year."

Rick and Mrs. Hyde had problems before this, they were split up and moved into different places and then just like that, they solved their problems and back in they go.

But this time was different, never had I ever seen Mrs. Hyde take off her ring.

"Yeah, we were, but things got bad again with bills so we decided to file for divorce papers," She sighs out, giving me a small smile.

"But I-" She cuts me off again.

"Tae, not everyone has happy endings, and just so happens between me and Rick, we weren't meant to be," She explains and I nod.

"I understand that," I look down at my hands. "I just thought you two worked out your problems."

"By working out you mean not talking about them and just getting back together, that just leads us to here," she says. "Anyways, let's talk about something else."

"Okay, I agree," I tell her, nodding.

"How's school?"

"Great, I've got A's and B's and I'm proud," I smile at her.

She grins from ear to ear. "I'm so proud, Tae."

"I'm sure your dad is as well," She adds.

"He is..." I mumble, smiling at the memory of me showing him my report card and his smile just melted my heart.

"So, I-" Before I could get a word in the bell rings causing me to frown.

"We'll talk some more tomorrow or whenever you want," She says.

I nod. "Okay, I'll see you later."

"Bye dear," She waves and I leave her office with a small smile.

I walk the crowded halls in thought, I open my locker grabbing my books I needed for my next class.

"Tae Lambert," The voice I didn't want to hear saying my name rung in my ears.

I turn my head at Lydia with Mandy on her side giving her a fake smile.

"Yeah?"

"I wanted to talk to you about something..." She trails, picking at her acrylic nail.

Mandy covers her mouth trying hard not to laugh and my expression on my face didn't once break to a smile.

"What?"

"Does cancer run in your family?" She asks and my heart sinks to my butthole.

"What?" My voice quivers.

She laughs. "Don't be stupid silly, does cancer run in your family?"

"I don't know what you're talking about," My face begins to get hot.

How the hell does she know?

"You know what, I'm done being nice..." She trails.

When were you ever nice?

"Who knew you had cancer, how long have you had it? Aw, are you going to the hospital soon? I'll make sure to bring you some dead flowers," She says.

I try going around her, but Mandy stops me. "Sorry, but we're not done talking to you."

"Does Keaton know? Wait- what am I talking about? Of course, Keaton knows," Lydia exaggerates.

I try going around Mandy while giving her a glare, but she stops me again and this time Lydia speaks up.

"You're just a sick little girl that will soon be dead. He'll forget all about you. I don't why you get involved with him," She tells me while Mandy tries to hold in her laughs.

I shake my head while my head spins with thoughts. My heart feels heavy and my mouth goes dry as I feel my cheeks go wet with tears.

She laughs. "Soon he'll be gone to Ohio state after this year and leave you here. He needs someone like me to be on his arm as he goes, plus long-distance relationships don't turn out well."

Everyone now was crowded up around us, making me feel suffocated. It felt like I couldn't breathe. I needed to get out of here and fast before I passed or did something.

"Oh, is the leukemia getting to you?" My heart stops.

How did she find out? I only told Keaton, no way could he possibly tell.

I trusted him. I thought we made an agreement.

"You wanted that to be a secret, didn't you? Oops sorry. Hey everyone get ready for a funeral!"

As she shouts out to everyone all I heard was laughter, my secret was out, I couldn't hide it anymore. Some people in the crowd were looking at me with sympathy but some were laughing with Lydia, only making me cry even more.

"Thank Keaton for me, why don't you? Tell him that Lydia sends her love and thanks for telling me about this whole mess," She states and with that she grabs Mandy's hand then walks off like nothing happened.

Keaton...

Keaton told...

Whispers were all I heard as I walked down the hall with my books close up to my chest, I felt upset and angry at the same time, I felt like I was about to explode with so many emotions. I ran out of the school with tears running down my face, the school police officer gave me confused looks as I rushed down the steps and away from the horrid school.

I see Keaton and his friends walking down the hill while laughing, I turn, walking along the concrete trying to breathe for air. I hear my name being called, but I couldn't bear to turn around. I felt betrayed by him, I can't wrap my head around the fact that he told the most important person I didn't want to know about my secret. I kept that secret since I was a freshman and I was looking forward to keeping it a secret because of this.

But he had to tell, things were going great. Why would he tell? How could he tell?

"Tae!" Another call from him, but I couldn't get myself to turn around instead I walked faster on the sidewalk.

I soon heard footsteps running towards me and instantly knew he caught up with me so I finally grew some balls and turned around with tears running down my face because I didn't care anymore. His smile begins to fade as he reaches me and studies my face.

"What's wrong?"

I scoff. "You want to know what's wrong? You *really* want to?"

"Yes, actually I do. What happened? Did someone hurt you-"

I cut him off. "You! You are the one who hurt me. How could you? How could you tell Lydia that I was sick?"

"What are you talking about? I didn't tell her," He states, shaking his head in denial while I wipe my face.

I point my finger at him. "I trusted you and I let you in which was a mistake."

"Don't say that! I didn't tell Lydia anything I swear," He shakes his head again while moving forward to touch me.

"I don't think this between us is going to work Keaton, I didn't want to trust you in the first place. I was so stupid letting you in I shouldn't have, just stay away from me," I tell him gripping my books in my hand tightly because if I don't, I'll probably end up hitting him.

He shakes his head rapidly. "No, I'm your boyfriend! I promised you I would never tell a soul; Tae please don't break up with me."

"It was never going to work anyways Keaton, I'm gonna die soon and I'll just leave you and you'll end up getting hurt this will be better for the both of us," I look to see behind Keaton to see his friends watching us with concerned eyes.

I sighed out. "You're the school's golden boy anyway you shouldn't be with me. After the school year ends, you'll be going off to Ohio State and I'll be here."

He grabs my hand, giving it a squeeze. "We can work this out Tae, I swear I didn't tell Lydia. Don't give up on us."

"Just stay away," I demand him while yanking my hand from his hold which hurts to witness seeing his face fall even more.

I turn around walking away from the sad boy, my vision gets blurred by the tears and I can't stop myself from crying even more. I walk home with a tear-stained face.

I realized I couldn't cry anymore because I cried so much, but not until I entered the house where my dad was cooking dinner with mom's apron on and he smiles at me, but then frowns once he sees my face.

I forgot since football season is over that meant he was off work till next season, which was next year.

"What happened?" He asks and I couldn't say anything but run into his arms.

I cry into his arms as long as I can until he releases me and makes me sit on the counter.

"What happened?" He asked again.

I sigh out while fiddling with my shirt. "I broke up with Keaton."

"What did he do? If he hurt you I-"

I cut him off by laughing. "I just thought about it and thought I don't need a boyfriend; it was too much to worry ab-"

"Liar. Keaton made you happy I could tell, I'm your dad. Something happened I know and you don't have to tell me but just know that I'm here if you need me."

I nod, beginning to feel thankful. "So, what are you cooking?"

"Well...I was looking through your mom's cookbook and decided to make spaghetti but I burned it," He explains pointing to the burning noodles sitting in the sink and I couldn't help but laugh.

"You could've just waited until I got home so I can make it."

He sighs leaning against the counter. "I know, I just wanted to surprise you."

"Well, you did now move over so I can show you how to make spaghetti," I tell him and he moves away, letting me do my magic.

I think I was trying to distract myself from the whole ending between us, I didn't tell my dad about the whole situation about Keaton telling Lydia about me being sick and she telling the whole school because I just felt like I shouldn't.

I start the stove, and grab a new clean pot out of the cabinet, putting it over the stove while water is sitting in it and taking a box of uncooked noodles out, pouring it into the boiling water that was in the pot.

My dad watches me. "You look just like your mom."

"I miss her," I tell him, smiling sadly.

"Me too."

He helps me finish with the spaghetti and we eat dinner alone together just like we *always* have. It felt good with it being just us, but sometimes it feels lonely without Georgie and mom.

My phone buzzes letting me know I have an incoming call; I take my phone out of my pocket and read that it's from Georgie.

I almost fell out of my seat but I answered. "Georgie!"

"What's up loser?" His voice sounded the same and I started missing him more than ever.

"Just eating with dad," I tell him, giving dad a smile and he gives me a wink.

Georgie laughs. "Ew that old man! Why don't you just eat with me instead?"

I furrow my eyebrows and begin to think he's going insane. "How?"

"I'm coming home," He tells me and I almost scream. "But only for a few days because I got classes that I need to come back to."

"Oh my god! That's great Georgie, when?"

"Dad was supposed to tell you, but he made me call you instead but tomorrow, y'all are picking me up from the airport."

Then I scream and stand up from my chair. "No way!"

"Yeah, I missed you guys so much I just needed to come home," He says, sounding sleepy.

"You need to stay home, that's what and transfer to Tri County," I insisted, but I knew he wasn't up for the offer.

He laughs out. "You know I can't do that Tae; I got a scholarship from here you know how many people would kill for this opportunity?"

"Yes, I know millions," I mocked him from last time.

"That's right, but hey I got to go, the flight attendant says Wi-Fi is being cut short because of the storm. I'll call you when I've landed okay?"

"Okay I love you Georgie," I say hearing the phone cut out a bit.

"Love you too loser."

I smile as he hangs up wanting to stay on the phone longer, I missed him so much I wanted to cry but I think I had enough crying today.

"Surprise!" My dad shouts and I laugh.

"I can't believe we get to see him tomorrow," I say, smiling at the thought.

He nods. "I wanted to tell you so many times but I wanted him to be the one to tell you."

"I would've been happy if you told me too," I exclaimed.

"Yeah, I know, but a phone call from him was much better, wasn't it?"

"Oh, much better," I state, helping him clean the dishes.

I couldn't wait for tomorrow; I wonder if he looked different? If he had a girlfriend? I hope so because he needs to get tied down, but then again Georgie has a girlfriend? That's impossible.

Chapter Forty-Five

Keaton's Pov.

Watching Tae walk away from me was probably one of the hardest things I had to witness, how the hell does Lydia know? It took forever for Tae to actually let me in and not let her fear control her feelings for me now, that was all down the drain.

And all because of Lydia.

My fist clench as I turn around glaring at Winnie, the only one I told.

Because I trusted her more than ever.

"What the hell did you do?" I grit out, causing her to cower away from me.

"What are you talking about Keaton?" She asks me.

"You fucking told Lydia, didn't you?" She shakes her head in denial and I grit my teeth.

"Keaton, I'd never do that to Tae-" She gets cut off.

"I told Lydia," I hear the sound of my now ex friend who was staring at me with no remorse.

"Reece!" Winnie gasps.

I grew confused. "How the hell did you find out?"

I'm so beating this kid's ass.

"I overheard you and Winnie talking, I only did it for you, for us."

What is he talking about?

"What?"

"She was messing with your head, ever since you saw her that day you've been in this trance, I was tired of seeing that freak with you," Reece grits out, pointing off to where Tae headed off.

I freeze. "What the hell did you just say?"

"I said-" As soon as I knew he was going to repeat his words, I took no time to jump on him.

"Keaton, stop! He's not worth your scholarship," Winnie screeches.

Fuck that scholarship.

I sent blows on Reece's faces with no hesitation, blood was racing through my veins and I was just waiting to hear his bone crack in his nose. Blood started to form on my knuckles, both containing mine and Reece's blood.

I feel hands grab onto my arms trying to pull me off this son of a bitch but I was glued to him.

"Keaton, calm down," Landon yells into my ear but I ignore his pleas.

"You ruined my relationship, you ruined Tae's trust for me, and now you probably ruined my scholarship," I spit out, gripping onto the collar of his t-shirt.

Reece laughs as he spits out blood. "And after Tae ran away from the golden boy, I was going to be there between her thighs giving her the best-"

"Keaton no!" Winnie screams as I send another blow to his mouth.

"You'd never get with Tae, ever. I'd be there to make sure she doesn't," I snarl out, standing up getting ready to kick him on his left side, but a group of arms pull me back.

My breath was ragged and all I could see was red, as I somewhat calmed down, my eyes caught on Winnie's pale face and Landon's worried looking face as he let go of me along with the rest of the boys that were holding me.

Everyone was quiet, everyone was in shock.

Until Winnie walks off from the fight.

"Winnie wait!" Landon calls out for her.

I felt around in my mouth noticing that it was busted, I ran after Landon who was chasing after Winnie.

She stops at her little bug of a car and turns around.

"Where the hell are you going?" Landon asks her, stopping her from opening the door of her car.

She looks back at me before saying. "I'm going to see Tae; she needs a friend right now."

I take a step forward. "No, let me go."

"No," She's quick to disagree. "You just got into a beat down."

"Yeah, you're probably going to get expelled," Landon tells me.

"No, he's not," Principal Myers says from behind me. "I heard everything, what he said about Ms. Lambert was disgusting and I'm sure her father would love to hear that."

I wanted to speak on my behalf but I went against it.

"And for you Mr. Davis, you'll need to come with me so I can talk with you," He nods for me to follow him.

I nod and follow Principal Myers lead, I was glad that I wasn't in trouble, but I wouldn't have cared if I was, for Tae I'd do *anything*.

"Now, I have to give you some type of punishment or people will start to talk, so I'm making you create posters and such with Ms. Lambert for the prom," He demands, pointing his finger at me.

"I never knew Tae was into that type of stuff," I raised an eyebrow at him.

He nods. "Oh yeah, she's always been a help around here when a prom and such comes around."

"Why are you letting me off the hook? I did throw the first punch," I ask, feeling confused.

"Because, you're a good boy, Keaton, you're the top-of-the-line student and I can tell you've taken a liking in that young girl. You've chosen the right one," Myers explains.

I stay quiet, staring down at the floor.

"Unfortunately, I'm having to let you out early because of what happened, but come tomorrow as regularly and I'll deal with Mr. Paul," He states, and I nod.

"Yes sir," I tell him, walking away from the man who saved my ass from getting into shit ton of trouble.

I swing the school doors open exiting the building and Landon runs up to me.

"Dude, that was crazy," He laughs out. "What did Myers say?"

"I'm not in trouble, but he's making me work on posters for the prom," I shrug, stepping down the stairs.

"That's not too bad," He states, chuckling.

"Yeah..." I trail, with Tae on my mind.

Where is she? Is she home? Is she safe? Did Winnie find her?

"Where are you heading off to?" He asks, noticing I was walking towards the parking lot.

"Going to see Tae," I tell him, wiping my lip again.

"Let her blow off some steam, coming from a guy that's been in a long relationship, don't go up to a raging girl, unless you wanna be hit," He warns.

"Then what am I supposed to do?" I hold my hands up in the air.

"Chill for the day, I'll skip so you won't be bored," He tells me, grabbing my shoulders while shaking me.

"I got some beer in the back of my truck, wanna go to the dock and drink?" He asks, raising an eyebrow.

With the day I had, *hell yes*.

"Let's do it," I nod.

We both race towards our cars before hopping in and zooming off towards the lake we'd always go to as kids and sit at the dock.

Once we get there, Landon brings out a four-pack case of beer and we both take a seat at the end of the dock letting our feet swing off, our shoes barely touching the dark blue sea.

"Man, I missed this," I say, cracking open a beer.

"If only Reece didn't fuck up the way he did then he'd be here," Landon says, before sipping the cool alcohol.

"I don't know why he had to go do what he did," I say, not understanding the selfishness he had caused.

"He was jealous," Landon said in a 'duh' tone.

"Why would he be jealous?"

"He's a junkie and you're the clean, neat going guy," He explains, shrugging.

"Let's stop talking about him before I reverse my Jeep back into that school and whoop the kid's ass again," I say which causes Landon to chuckle.

I chug the rest of the beer I had left in my can before throwing it behind me, my mind kept going back to the blonde that had me wrapped around her finger, I knew she was still going to be upset with me about me telling Winnie, but maybe she would consider us getting back together since I didn't tell Lydia.

What the hell was I going on about?

We weren't broken up, she was just upset and angry and she misunderstood the whole situation, once she figures out the truth she'll come back.

Or will she?

Had Lydia changed her mind for good?

"You're thinking too much..." Landon mumbles, looking out across the lake.

"Huh?"

"She'll come back, she loves you, man," He tells me, grinning at me.

"You think so?" I smirk at the thought.

"I fucking know so," He laughs out.

To say at the end of that night we stayed out there we were drunk, after the four packs we drank, Landon brought out another pack and then another. My first time getting drunk in a while which didn't feel too good when the blonde girl in my head kept giving me a disapproving look.

Tomorrow I was gonna feel like shit.

Chapter Forty-Six

Tae's Pov.

Sitting in my room, I was a mess. After dinner with my dad and the phone call with Georgie I went straight to my room to cry my eyes out in happiness and sadness. I didn't want it to be true that Keaton told Lydia that I was sick.

And you ask why I'm overreacting about this whole secret.

I didn't want anyone to know because of what had just happened a few hours ago, I felt betrayed by Keaton but I still had feelings for him.

I was stupid to let my guard down.

"Whatever he did, I'm sure he didn't mean to do it," I hear my dad say as I wipe my eyes.

I look up at him standing at the door frame.

"Do you want me to kick him off the team?" He asks, joking.

I smile through my tears. "No."

"Your mom used to tell me that you'll cross bad people in your life but you'll also meet some really good people," My dad explains and I smile at him.

Something my mom would say.

"Keaton's a good kid," He adds as he sits on the edge of my bed. "He has a good heart."

He really does.

"And he's crazy about you," He laughs out while shaking his head.

I play with my fingers as my smile never leaves my face.

A horn from a car causing me to jolt from my bed, I push my blinds open seeing Winnie's red bug parked in my driveway.

"Is that Keaton's friend?" My dad asks and I nod.

"Yeah, Winnie," I tell him.

Just as he's about to respond, the doorbell rings.

"I'll be in my room," He states, running out of my room and into the hall.

I drag my feet in the hall and down the steps as I hear my dad's door shut, the doorbell rings again and I hesitate in opening the door, but I do it anyway.

Seeing the familiar redhead giving me a small smile. "Hi."

"Hey, come in," I open the door wider for her and move myself out of the way.

She comes in but not without saying a gentle 'thank you', I close the front door and in comes the awkward silence.

"I'm so sorry about what happened Tae," She gives me a guilty look.

I nod. "It's fine."

"I just want you to know that I never once did tell, I swear," She crosses her heart, telling me that she honestly didn't do it.

I stop in my tracks. "I-"

She cuts me off. "Keaton told me, but only because I was wondering and Keaton trusts me and I'd never break that."

I nod, still feeling a bit confused.

"I-"

She cuts me off again. "Keaton didn't tell Lydia, Reece did."

My heart drops. I knew that there was something going on with that dude.

"How did he find out?" My voice quivers while asking.

She looks down. "He overheard Keaton and I."

"Oh," I said in a confused tone.

"We found out the second you left, and Reece got what he deserved," Winnie giggles while explaining.

I raise an eyebrow. "What?"

"Keaton fought Reece."

"What?!" I panic, I start to feel my heart racing.

She shakes her head while holding onto my hand. "Keaton's okay, just a busted lip."

I sigh out. "Where is he now?"

"He had to stay back at the school but he's probably gone now."

I nod, making her smile at me. "I just came to see if you were okay."

"I am now since you came," I tell her, causing her face to brighten up.

She takes a seat on the couch while I follow her moves.

"Tomorrow, Lydia and her clown Mandy are in for a ride," She states and I raised an eyebrow.

"What does that mean?"

"You'll see," Her smirk never left her face.

I was confused but a part of me was feeling I was going to love it and part of me was going to hate it, my mind wandered if Keaton was alright, did he get in trouble with the school? Was he expelled? Did he go crazy after all that happened?

Would I be able to see him tomorrow, to give him a hug or even a kiss? Would he be mad that I thought he would betray me? *Maybe...*

I was missing his touch the most right now, with Winnie beside me talking to me about how stupid Reece was, my mind was on Keaton's touch.

"Do you want to spend the night?" I ask, biting my bottom lip.

Her eyes light up. "Yes! Maybe now the boys won't interrupt us."

"Yeah," I chuckle, but my smile soon turns into a frown.

"Ahh shit, I'm sorry," Winnie curses, holding onto my hand.

"You're fine," I smile, letting her know it didn't bother me.

Was it bad that this time I wanted Keaton to run in our room and scare us and everything be alright?

Nah...

Chapter Forty-Seven

Tae's Pov.

"Morning cupcake," Winnie squeals above and I whine into my hands.

"What time is it?" I yawn, trying to open my tired eyes to look at the time.

"It's time to send bitch, come on, let's get ready and I'll take us to Dunkin," She insists and I get up in a hurry.

I walk into the bathroom and stare at myself in the mirror, Winnie beats me to the toilet and I playfully glare at her as she pees giving me an innocent look.

"Did you sleep last night?" She asks, as I look back at myself in the mirror.

"No," I state, looking at the bags under my eyes.

The dark circles were beyond ugly, but I couldn't help that I couldn't sleep. The only thing was on my mind that mattered the most at that time.

Keaton.

"Don't worry your pretty little head, mama Winnie's got you," She says as she washes her hands.

I pull my hair up into a messy ponytail and walk out of the bathroom and into my room where my closet stands in front of me. I open the door and pick out a shirt and jeans with converse.

After I get dressed, Winnie and I go downstairs and greet my dad who was as giddy and happy as he can be, I totally forgot about Georgie coming home today.

"Don't forget, we're going to the airport this afternoon," Dad calls out before I shut the door.

"Okay," I say back, earning a smile.

****

"Why in the world are you driving so fast?" I ask, biting on my straw.

She sips her coffee before answering. "Because at a certain time in the morning, Lydia and Mandy go in the bathroom with the rest of the cheer squad and they gossip and I wanna walk in there and wham all their heads in the stalls."

"Very specific," I admire jokingly.

"Mhm," She hums, pulling into her parking place.

"Are you really doing this?" I ask her as we step out of her car.

"No-one messes with family," She exclaims, throwing her empty coffee cup in the trash can.

"Okay," I whisper to myself.

My nerves were on full high as we walked into the school, eyes were spotted staring at me which only made me more anxious. We walk till we get to the entrance of the girl's bathroom and Winnie puts her ear at the door.

"They're in there," She squeals, quietly.

She takes her hand in mine and slams the door open making it slam behind us causing all the girls to go silent.

Lydia crosses her arms and smirks. "Crackhead and cancer girl, how lovely of you to join us."

"Why are you here?" Mandy asks, staring at us in the mirror as she applies her lipstick.

"Who's this bitch anyway?" Some girl says that she doesn't know who Winnie and I are.

I was surprised that they didn't know who Winnie was when she was Keaton's friend, me not so much.

"Oh, hi I'm Winnie Adams and you're about to get a can of whoop ass," Winnie's face was a sweet smile then turned into a glare.

"Don't you dare come near me," Lydia points at her, backing up as Winnie takes large steps towards her.

"Don't-" Lydia squeals and we all hear a crack as Winnie lays her fist right onto Lydia's nose.

I gasp, covering my mouth with my hand completely surprised.

"You bitch! You broke my nose!" Lydia hollers, holding onto her bloody nose.

Winnie giggles. "There will be more than bloody noses around here if any one of you makes a single threat towards Tae or any of my friends."

"You're next bitch!" Winnie says more like growls at Mandy who backs up but stops because of the wall behind her.

All the other girls go into the stall and hide as Mandy hollers out as Winnie grabs the back of Mandy's hair and slams her face into the wall.

"Okay, Winnie stop or you'll kill her," I state, waving for her to leave.

She huffs and spits into Mandy's face before fixing her curls in the mirror and hums to herself as she leaves the bathroom with the girls crying their eyes out.

"What the heck was that? I thought you were just gonna talk to her," I exclaim as we walk out of the girl's locker room.

Winnie shrugs. "She messed with you and you're my friend, no-one messes with family."

I breathe out before laughing. "And I thought you were crazy; this is beyond crazy."

She laughs out but stops walking and her face becomes serious, and she lets out an awkward cough.

I stop walking with a frown, I look ahead of me to see Keaton giving me a look over before huffing out.

Okay, now this is awkward.

Winnie was right. He was okay, except for his busted lip, I sigh out with a smile on my face before walking over to him. He opens his arms and I copy his actions and our bodies collide in a hug.

My arms were wrapped around his neck while he was wrapped around my waist, I hid my face into his neck before inhaling his scent.

"I'm so sorry," I whispered out, feeling tears reach the bottom of my eyes.

"Don't you dare say that again, I'm sorry for telling Winnie," He mumbles, his breath tickling my neck.

I raise my head to meet my eyes with his. "It doesn't matter anymore."

"I love you," He whispers, his huge hands surrounding my head collapsing his lips down on mine.

"So damn much," He adds into the kiss causing me to smile.

Winnie awkwardly coughs and Keaton and I split apart wiping our damp lips.

"Winnie is probably going to get expelled," I state, trying to stop myself from laughing.

"Do I wanna know?" Keaton sighs out.

"Yes, you do," I tell him.

"I punched Lydia in the nose and threw Mandy's head into the wall which might lead to a concussion."

I laugh out at the memory and Keaton chuckles. "You're totally getting expelled for that."

"Don't care, it was totally worth it," She says. "Finally got my moment."

"Speaking of expelled, did you?" I turn around asking the golden boy.

"Nope, Myers let me off the hook, but I have to help a certain someone on prom posters," He sings out at the end.

"Oh no, can you even draw?" I cringe at the thought.

"Yes, I most certainly can," He gasps out.

"Ms. Adams, to my office now," Principal Myers calls out over the speaker phone and Winnie's eyes closes as she turns around and walks towards his office.

"Well, now we know Landon won't have a date for prom," Keaton says, chuckling.

"And so won't you," I tell him, causing his laugh to stop.

He frowns. "What?"

"Nothing," I sing out, walking off quickly.

He chases after me causing me to laugh.

"Tell me that again?"

"I'm not going to prom," I state, shrugging.

"Why?" Just as he asks the bell rings.

I smile, patting his chest lightly. "Talk to you later, gotta go to class."

I peck his lips as he gives me a confused look, he watches me until he can't see me anymore and I'm in the classroom.

****

"Boo," I whisper in Keaton's ear pushing at his hips and he jumps but turns around with a smile on his face.

"Don't copy me," He warns playfully, wrapping his arms around my waist.

I roll my eyes but smile, the way Keaton's bottom lip enters his mouth as he bites down on it made me feel tingly inside.

"What are you doing after you leave here?" He asks, staring down at my lips.

"Going to the airport with my dad," I state, an even bigger smile creeps up on my face as the thought of seeing Georgie invades my mind.

He raises an eyebrow. "What for?"

"Georgie's coming home today," I explain. "Do you wanna come with?"

"I would love to, but I don't want to intrude on your family," He says, sighing.

"You won't, I want to show you off to Georgie, he said I would never have a boyfriend with the way I was thinking before you."

"Well...." He clicks the top of his tongue to the roof of his mouth and gives me a look.

I hit his chest playfully. "Don't even say what I know you're about to say."

"I mean he wasn't wrong..." He trails, a grin forming on his face.

"Alright, you're not coming," I rolled my eyes, unleashing myself from his hold and turning around to leave, but before I could Keaton grabs me from behind and lays his head on my shoulder.

I smile while my insides turn to mush.

"I'm coming," He demands quickly, pecking my neck before letting me go and taking my hand as we walk down the halls of the school and out the doors.

"I'll text my dad to meet us at the airport," I tell Keaton who looks off in the distance.

I watch his face turn cold and his jaw clenched, I look to see where his eyes were caught and my eyes find the suspect.

Reece.

He picks up trash off the school grounds with a green coat on his shoulders, he stopped to see us and looked away quickly to finish his task.

I touch Keaton's shoulder lightly. "Come on, he's not worth getting mad over."

"I should've kicked his head into the concrete when I had the chance," Keaton huffs out, pressing his hands on the small space on my back and leads me to his Jeep.

We both quickly get in and I get a text back from my dad saying that he'll see us in a minute, during the ride, Keaton grows quiet and I stare at him as he stares off towards the road with longing eyes.

"What's wrong?" I ask him, grabbing his hand that was fisting his wheel and he lets loose to take a hold of my hand.

"I'm sorry for telling Winnie..." He mumbles, giving me sorrowful eyes.

"Keaton, it's okay, I'm not mad anymore, people were bound to know the truth," I explain, sighing.

"I know, but I made a promise to you that I wouldn't say shit and I told Winnie, I'm sorry," He takes his hands out of mine and lays it on the inside of my thigh.

"I love you and I would never hurt you, I'm gonna make a promise to you that I'm actually going to keep," He says. "I promise you that I'll *always* protect you with everything I have."

"Okay," I bite my lip while smiling at him.

We get to the airport within thirty minutes, he puts his Jeep in park and we sit there waiting for my dad's old pickup truck to arrive.

Keaton's hand takes ahold of the side of my face making me stare right into his eyes.

"You're my world, Tae Lambert," He whispers, pushing his head forward so that our foreheads were touching.

"You mean everything to me, Keaton, you make me the happiest," I tell him truthfully.

"That's my job," His cheeky side comes out and I peck his lips quickly before looking out at the parking lot to see my dad pulling in beside us with a smile, he waves before getting out.

I open the car door. "You ready?"

"I'm seeing my first born for the first time in almost a year, hell yes I'm ready," My dad exclaims, rubbing my back as we all walk towards the airport.

We finally walked into the crowded place seeing women and men running to their loved ones whilst my dad and I were looking for the curly haired looking boy.

Keaton grabs my shoulders stopping me from shaking. "God, Tae, you're shaking."

"I'm so nervous," I state, grabbing his hand trying to stop my nerves from getting the best of me.

"I've got you," He smiles.

"Georgie!" My dad exclaims.

"Dad!" I hear Georgie's voice come out as a laugh and it begins to muffle as I'm guessing he went in for a hug with my dad.

I look up to see my tall, skinny, curly haired, crazy looking older brother, who looks back at me.

I smile before tackling him in a hug. "I've missed you so much."

"I've missed you too," He mumbles, hugging me tightly.

I close my eyes inhaling his scent scared that if I let go, he'll be gone in a second.

"Who are you?" Georgie asks, looking up from him and I's hug to look at my boyfriend who was standing behind me.

"Georgie, this is Keaton Davis," My dad introduces, patting Keaton's chest.

I let go of Georgie so he could get a good look at him.

"My boyfriend," I add, earning a wide-eyed look from my brother.

"Wait, Keaton Davis? Son of Randy Davis?" Georgie asks, furrowing his eyebrows in question.

Keaton nods. "Yeah."

"You're the one who took my place after I left Westside," Georgie accuses playfully, pointing at him.

"Guilty as charged," Keaton comments, holding his hands up in surrender.

"Keaton is my best player, hell, he's the best out of the best," My dad overreacts and I roll my eyes playfully.

"And now you're dating my sister," Georgie states, crossing his arms, humming. "How did you two meet?"

I quickly look at Keaton who gives me the same look, I giggle in my hand.

A lot happened.

"It's an interesting story," Keaton says for me, putting his hands in his sweatpants pockets. "Also, very long."

"I've got time," Georgie shrugs.

"Let's go home and Keaton and Tae will tell you all about it," Dad instructed, and we all nod, leaving the airport.

I smile to myself as I watch Georgie put his bags in the back of dad's truck and hops in beside dad.

I look at Keaton who stares at me with the most passionate eyes. "You look happy."

"It's because I am, everything feels like it's going back to normal," I tell him quietly.

Except for that mom's not here with us.

But I was happy, let's hope this happiness doesn't shatter like glass hitting a hard spot and breaking everywhere for people to walk all over.

Chapter Forty-Eight

Tae's Pov.

"So, prom is coming up," Keaton states leaning against Mrs. Hyde's desk.

I nod. "I heard.... Are you going?"

"Yeah, I always go," He tells me, shrugging while watching me draw on the school poster like I was supposed to do.

He was supposed to be helping but he decides to make his own rule and just watch me.

"Well, have fun because I heard Principal Myers has to end prom an hour earlier because people like to snoodle each other."

I hear an ear ringing laugh and look at Keaton to see he was wiping under his eyes from laughing.

"What?" I raise an eyebrow at him.

He snickers. "Snoodle each other? What the hell is that?"

"You know..." I trail off fiddling with the poster.

"You mean have sex?" He laughs again and I glare at him.

"Not funny," I say, hitting his shoulder which did nothing but make him laugh harder.

Why does he have to be so cute? If he was ugly and rude this would be a lot easier not to like him.

"Alright anyways, I want you to go with me," I freeze in my spot and look up at him to see that he's searching my eyes.

I shake my head. "You know I don't do prom."

"Oh, come on, it'll be your first and with me," He explains and I sighed out. "This is my last prom and I want to go with you."

I stay quiet in my thoughts; would it be a bad idea to go to prom? Especially with him? This is his last one forever and he said he wanted to go with me so why not? I think I'm thinking too hard about this.

"I think you are to just go with me. I won't leave your side, I'll make it the best prom you'll ever have," He explains and I blush realizing I had said that out loud.

I laugh. "It's the only prom I'll be going to."

"But what about next year? I bet you I'll make prom so fun you'll want to go next year."

"If I'm even here next year," I mumble, rolling my eyes looking down.

Keaton shakes his head. "Don't say that."

"But it's-"

He cuts me off. "I said don't say that Tae, you're not going anywhere."

"You don't know that!" I exclaimed, shaking my head at him.

I think he was trying to hide the fact that I was telling the truth but he just didn't want to admit it.

"I said don't say that!" I could see he was getting upset by the way he was fiddling with his school jacket and his top lip wobbled.

I stayed quiet watching the clock in the room tick, until Keaton stood up to leave but I held him back by grabbing the sleeve of his jacket.

"Where are you going?"

He gives me a sided look before looking straight at the door. "Leaving, what does it look like I'm doing?"

With that he left, leaving me shocked that he even spoke to me with that tone, but I knew he was upset at what I said. I couldn't blame him.

It was my fault for bringing that up, he'll come around again and everything will be fine.

I decide it's time to go home since it's already a little over five, so I pack my things in my book bag and grab the key Mrs. Hyde gave me, locking her room.

I walk down the long halls of the school and notice someone leaning against the lockers, I instantly recognize the person and smile at the thought of him not leaving.

"I thought you were leaving," I told him, mocking him of what he did earlier.

A guilty smile spreads across his face and he takes a hold of my hand. "I couldn't leave you."

My heart jumped at that and I smiled at him, we walked together down the hall and out the door of the school as Principal Myers stands there with a smile waiting on us.

"I'm trusting you with Mrs. Hyde's key Ms. Lambert," He says, giving me a pointed look.

I nod. "I'll guard it with my life, sir."

He laughs at me and pats my shoulder, Keaton and I walk towards his Jeep hand in hand, he opens the passenger door for me and I thank him silently.

He hops in on his side and cranks up the car, he pulls out of the school and starts to drive towards my house.

"I'll go to prom with you," I give in because I want to make him happy and if this would make him happy, I'd go to millions of proms for him.

His face lights up but he shakes his head. "Don't do it just to make me happy, I want you to go because you want to."

I nod. "And I want to, I'm doing this for the both of us."

"Good," He pecks my lips before looking back at the road.

"And you don't even have to wear a dress," He adds and I try not to smile at the fact of him trying to make me happy but I already was.

"What would I look like if I wore pants to prom?" I laugh out and he smiles at me before licking his lips and placing his hand on my thigh.

A call on my phone pops up and Winnie's picture pops up behind it, I slide my hand across the answer button and press it gently before taking the phone and placing it against my ear.

"Hey Winnie," I greet, before hearing a sequel.

"Guess what?" She excitedly exclaims before squealing again.

"What?" I hear myself ask.

"You're talking to the next year's cheerleader to be!"

My eyes go wide and a smile appears on my face. "Oh my god! How is this possible? I'm so happy for you."

Keaton shoots me a questioning look and I put the phone on speaker so he could hear.

"Principal Myers and me were talking yesterday and he said that if I behave he'll reconsider letting me back on the team, I told him about the false accusation about the drugs in my locker and when he got Lydia in the room it's like she got possessed or something when she confessed that she was the one who sabotaged me," She explains.

Lydia confessed? What on the earth did she snort up?

"What the hell?" Keaton laughs out in question.

"What did Principal Myers do?" I ask, furrowing my eyebrows.

"She can still go to prom which I don't know how that's possible and she's allowed to graduate, but the only problem is that she'll lose her scholarship from Ohio," Winnie says, laughing.

"What about you? Are you allowed to go to prom?" I ask, my heart full of hope.

"I told Principal Myers that if Lydia can go to prom when she fessed up then so can I and he's letting me," She explains proudly.

"Well good," I mumble, smiling.

"Wanna go dress shopping with me tomorrow?" She asks.

"Sure," I let out.

"Can I come?" Keaton butts in and I glare at him playfully.

"No," Winnie and I both exclaim.

"When you and Landon go tux shopping, we won't be with you so it's only fair," I tell him, shrugging.

"We never said you couldn't come," He retorts, shaking his head.

"Our dresses are surprises," Winnie cuts in and I nod.

Keaton playfully rolls his eyes. "Whatever."

"Good, he knows not to argue with girls," Winnie says, giggling.

"Damn straight," Keaton mumbles tiredly, looking forward to the road as he drives.

I smile at the two annoying each other.

Finally, things were looking up.

Chapter Forty - Nine

Tae's Pov.

"Thank you so much, Tae for helping me put all those books on the shelves, if it wasn't for your help that would've taken me days to finish," Bonnie, Winnie's mom thanks me for the help and I kindly smile at her.

"It was no problem," I tell her, waving it off.

"Dang, you guys are finished?" Winnie asks, walking in with a coffee in her hand.

She walks towards us before giving her mom the coffee she asked for.

"Yep, all thanks to Tae," Bonnie smiles dearly at me.

I smile back. "I'd do it any day."

"You're a blessing," Bonnie says before sipping on her coffee. "What do you girls got planned for today?"

"Dress shopping for prom," Winnie answers, putting her hands on her hips.

Bonnie's eyes lit up. "I can't wait to see."

"You wanna join us?" I ask, and Winnie nods at her mom.

"No, but thank you, you girls go on and have fun. I've got to paint this book shelf so I can put it back up,"

She explains, pointing towards a bookshelf she had let down.

"Are you sure?" Winnie raises her eyebrow.

"I'm sure, sweetie, go on now so you find the perfect dress," Bonnie says, waving us off.

"Okay, I love you mama," Winnie tells her, kissing her cheek.

"I love you too, Babygirl," Bonnie swiftly says back.

I smile at the mother and daughter being close, you could see the love Bonnie had for her daughter and the admiration that Winnie looked up to her mother. I wonder what that felt like.

Winnie turns to me and smiles. "Let's go!"

"Okay," I nod.

"We'll be back," Winnie yells out to her mom who waves goodbye to us.

"Okay, see you soon," She smiles at us.

Winnie and I leave her mom's tiny library, gossiping about which color of dress we wanted, we take Winnie's shiny red car to the dress shop and get out with excitement.

The dress shop was elegant, it was all white with chandeliers hanging down from the ceiling, I stared up at them in adoration as Winnie takes my hand to a bunch of dresses on hangers.

"I love this one," Winnie says, picking out a dark deep red dress that had a slit at the end.

I nod. "Me too, it would look perfect on you."

"You think?" She bites her bottom lip.

"Yes," I giggle.

"What about heels?"

"You should wear black heels," I state, nodding.

"What about these matte red ones?" She holds up the pair of heels she described that matched the dress she picked out perfectly.

I nod. "Perfect."

"That was way too fast, but let's pick you out a dress," Winnie begins to say, looking through the dresses and I stand on the other side of her, doing the same.

"What color are you looking for?" She asks, looking at me then back at the dresses.

I hum before answering. "I'm thinking black maybe?"

"Black looks so good with your complexion, yes," She excitedly states with big eyes.

I smile at her before looking back at all the blue and purple dresses I saw. I couldn't find a black dress anywhere until I looked at another set of dresses that were pink and black mixed together.

A black dress hung on a hanger that caught my eye, it was low cut in the front but not enough for it to be too revealing, it had spaghetti straps with gold round metal rings at the end to connect the straps to the dress.

I was all for it and Winnie grabs my shoulder and awes at it. "This is so gorgeous; you have to get it."

"You think I should?" I look back at her in question.

"Of course," She says, nodding.

I look back at the dress and smile.

****

Keaton's Pov.

"Landon, this is Georgie, Georgie, this is Landon," I greet them both together.

Landon stands up with a beer in his hand and nods his head up at Georgie.

"Georgie as in Georgie Lambert?" Landon asks me as he keeps his eyes on Georgie while he stands around with his hands in his pockets.

"Yeah," I say, nodding.

"I used to look up to you in school," Landon tells Georgie who smiles.

"Really? That's pretty chill" Georgie says back.

"You want a beer?" I call out at Georgie who nods and I grab two for us out of the cooler.

"Your dad let you turn the garage into a workout room?" Georgie asks as I give him a beer.

I nod, looking around. "Yeah, he wanted me to always stay fit."

"Damn..." Georgie mumbles.

"Wasn't there another one of you guys?" He then adds referring to Reece.

Wow, he *remembered*.

"Yeah, but shit happened between Keaton and him," Landon says for me and I nod at him as if to thank him.

I awkwardly cough as Georgie gives me a look and I take a seat on the bench to grab the weights.

"So, Georgie, how long are you here for?" Landon creates conversation after a few minutes of awkward silence.

Georgie takes a sip of his beer. "Not long, I'm here for a week or two."

Landon nods and Georgie sits down on the coach. "You guys got any girlfriends?"

"Landon over there is dating Winnie Adams, the crazy red head that walks around school," I explain, smirking at the blonde boy who glares at me.

"Oh dang, she's still cheerleading?" Georgie asks.

"Nah, she got kicked off the team for some false shit," Landon states, shaking his head.

"And I'm dating Tae, which you already knew that," I point out.

"What about you? You got a girl?" I ask him, who smiles down at the can of beer in his hand.

"I do, but don't tell Tae this because I want to be the one to tell my dad and Tae, but yeah I do," He explains and Landon's eyes go wide.

"Who?" Landon asks.

"I ain't saying shit just in case one of you fuckers snitch, and you wouldn't know her anyways," Georgie accuses, pointing his finger at us while smirking.

"I ain't saying shit," I hold my hands up in surrender.

I know I wasn't the best at keeping secrets, but I do know one thing....

I would've never told Tae about being sick, Winnie was the only one I had spoken to about it and she wouldn't jeopardize our friendship and Tae and mine's relationship.

But Reece did and all it was about was jealousy.

Chapter Fifty

The door of my room slams open and in comes my curly headed brother singing happy birthday and I giggle out looking at him through my mirror as I braid my hair.

"How does it feel to be seventeen?" He asks, hopping on my bed and laying on his stomach.

I shrug. "Not much different from sixteen."

"What? When I turned seventeen, I thought I was the shit."

"You still think you are now," I give him a bored look but smile at him as he glares.

"Shut it," He quickly exclaims, causing me to laugh.

"Anyways, dad wants you downstairs," He adds, sighing,

"For what?" I raise an eyebrow, standing up.

He shrugs getting up from my bed and leaves the room leaving me confused, I follow after him down the steps to be met by my dad and Georgie who's wearing huge smiles on their faces.

"Happy birthday," My dad mumbles, holding up a box with a big red bow on it.

"Thank you," I tell him thankfully. "What is this?"

"It's your present," He states, handing it to me.

I give him a skeptical look and he tells me to go on and open it.

I opened the top of the box to find a white book that had my mom's face on the front, in pink written letters it said 'My story'. My dad takes the box away from me as he sees I'm about to drop it from handling the book with my hands.

"This is your mom's old photo book that I never showed you," My dad explains.

I look up at him with tears of joy at the bottom of my eyes.

"How come you never showed me?" I ask him, looking back down at the book hesitatingly trying to open it.

He shrugs. "I wanted to wait till you were old enough and strong enough to look at these."

"Thank you," I tell him truthfully.

I look back down at the book and open it getting myself prepared to see my mom with a huge smile on her face because that's what she did. She smiled.

Even when she was down, angry, sad, she smiled, she never wanted people to see her down or upset.

"She was so beautiful," I mumble, dragging my finger along the side of her face in the picture.

I flipped the page and my heart skipped a beat, it was a picture of her and my dad together, she looked exactly like me, now I get why people said that I look just like my mom when she was younger then when she got older Georgie started to look more like her.

"It's like I'm looking at myself," I tell them, smiling.

Georgie smiles. "Except, she's prettier."

I could hear the teasing tone that was in Georgie's voice and I playfully glared at him but nod and smile.

"She is," I state, nodding.

"While you look through that book, Georgie and I need to pick up your cake from downtown," My dad states, grabbing his jacket and sliding it on.

I nod. "Okay, what time will you be back?"

"Around five," He explains, looking at the clock above the stove.

I stare at the time as it hits just about three o'clock, I nod at him before telling my goodbyes and they head on to get my cake. I walk upstairs and flip through some more pages and a note falls out of it as I step inside my room, my eyebrows furrow and I bend down to grab it and the envelope reads *'To my dearest Tae'*.

My heart jumps out of my skin and I go to see what was inside, but my phone buzzes before I could even have the chance.

Keaton.

I answer the phone without hesitation. "Hi."

I sit down at my desk as I take in his voice. "Open your door."

"Are you here?" I ask, heading downstairs.

"Yep," He says.

"My dad isn't here," I tell him, feeling like I'll get in trouble.

"Good," He states before hanging up.

I stare at my phone before unlocking the front door and opening it to see Keaton's face appear.

He holds a tiny box on top of a big box and I smile at him sweetly.

He walks in as I slide to the side and he kisses my lips before mumbling. "Happy birthday."

"Thank you," I blush, shutting the door.

I lock the front door before telling him to follow me to my bedroom and he does without hesitation, we finally get inside and I close my door and he turns around staring at me with so much adoration and love and it was clearly written in plain sight.

"I got you something," He says, giving me the big box first.

"You didn't have to," I tell him, smiling up at him.

"Just open it," He orders excitedly.

I open the box to see an old white vintage looking record player from the centuries, I look up at him in awe that he *remembered* that I loved old timey things.

"You *remembered*," I state, almost squealing.

"*Always*," He winks before handing me the tiny box.

I open the box with shaky hands and my heart skips a beat for the hundredth time today. By the end of today I'll be in the hospital from having so many heart attacks.

I held up what looked to be a charm bracelet that had many charms on it, I looked up at him smiling, but with a questioning look.

"It's a charm bracelet about your life," He explains, pointing to the bracelet. "The first one is of a woman and that is your mom, the second is a man with his son who is your brother and dad."

"Keaton..." I begin to say but I was breathless by the beauty of the charm bracelet.

It had a meaning, one that Keaton made for me.

"The third is a house which is your family home, the fourth, a pickup truck because your dad drives one, and the fifth, the cancer sign, showing that you're fighting through this and you will beat the living hell out of it," He then adds, staring down at me as he holds each charm with his fingers.

I bite my lip from crying from happiness and Keaton smiles down at me.

"Now the last two is books, because you love books," He laughs out and then his face goes serious. "And the number twelve because I'm in your life."

A tear drops down from my eyes as I smile up at the boy in front of me, he was gorgeous, treated me with the most passionate a guy could ever give me and that was only him, he was patient which most guys weren't.

"This is so beautiful and probably one of the most thoughtful gifts someone could ever get me," I tell him, grabbing the bracelet and sitting it down on the letter I was about to read and turn back around to kiss Keaton.

I was trying so hard not to admit to this boy and to myself that I loved him, I can't believe I even just said that.

I love Keaton...

I love Keaton Davis...

The golden boy.

Keaton takes my face into his hands and I put my hands on his arms as he backs me up to my bed so that the back of my knees hit the bed post and makes me lay down, neither of us split apart, I was in a trance and I couldn't be stopped.

The feeling in my core was electric and it wouldn't stop until I had it dealt with.

Keaton's hand moves down my stomach and to my thigh and tickles all the way down, my breath gets caught in my throat and I part from him as his finger trickle down to the inner of my thigh, I take his face in my hands and stare up at him as he stares down at me.

"I love you, Keaton Davis, you have made me fall deeply, utterly, entirely in love with you and there's no way of stopping it," I mumble, feeling my heart rise as a smile slowly creeps on his face.

"You have no idea what you caused when you said those three little words," He whispers, staring down at my lips.

"I want to go fully with you, not the little bits and pieces, I want it all," I scrunch his t-shirt in my hands and he looks at them before looking back at me.

He stares at me for a good few seconds' thinking, and then he slams his lips against mine and I gasp out as I feel his finger pop in me.

"Are you sure?" He asks, hovering over me slowly pumping his finger inside of me and I ball my fist up with his shirt in the middle, biting my lip from moaning.

"Yes," I moan out.

He pulls my pajamas shorts off me slowly and painfully, his fingers leaving my body, I don't waste time in pulling my shirt off, leaving me in my bra and panties and he looks down at me, hovering over me.

"Are you sure you want to do this with me?" He asks, staring deeply into my eyes.

I nod. "You know me Keaton, if I wasn't sure I wouldn't go through with it, I'd be constantly over thinking it and right now I'm not, because I want you."

"I just don't want to hurt you since you know, you're a virgin," He tells me, rubbing his finger on my cheek.

"I don't care, as long as I'm with you," I smile at him.

He nods before carrying on, his lips touch mine but only for a second and then he leaves me and starts trailing his lips on the side of my neck and down to my chest and stomach, he finally gets to my covered core and I with shaky hands lift my head up to see him staring up at me with hunger and desire.

He takes my underwear in his hands and slowly pulls them down my legs and off onto the floor, he doesn't take much time into kissing down my thighs and getting straight to where his mission was, I almost scream out at the pleasure he caused when his tongue went straight to my opening.

This felt like a dream...

"Keaton," I moan out, grabbing my covers and tugging on them.

Before the sensation could take over me, Keaton stops and hovers over me giving me a smirk.

"I told you I'd make you feel good," He says to me, but I ignore him and the heartbeat feeling takes over my body and I close my eyes.

"I love you, Lambert," He whispers and I hear his clothes being taken off.

I opened my eyes to see Keaton fully unclothed, I tried not to let my eyes go below his waist but I couldn't help my nosey self.

And damn.

I lay up and unclip my bra and Keaton's dark eyes follow every movement I made, my hand throws my bra on the other side of the room and I lay my head on the pillow letting him stare me down.

For some reason every time Keaton stares at me like he's doing now, I don't want to cower away. I feel like the most beautiful girl in the world.

I wrap my arms around his shoulders and tug him in for a kiss, his hand lands on my leg and he makes them wrap around his waist, I knew what was about to come, but I didn't care, not one bit, I wanted Keaton and he wanted me.

That's all that mattered.

"Don't go slow cause that'll only make it hurt worse," I say quickly, as he positions himself at me.

He raises his head up and chuckles. "Did you do research or something?"

"Maybe..." I mumble, shrugging.

"I'm not gonna say I will try to make it not hurt because I can't do that," He explains, shaking his head. "But if it hurts too bad and you want me to stop, all you gotta do is say stop."

"Okay," I nod, earning another kiss.

"You ready?" His tip stays at my entrance.

"Yes," I breathe out.

After that, he slowly enters me and I gasp out the pinching feeling, the knot in my stomach felt unbearable and the pain entered as he gets in me fully, he slowly moves out of me and the pain feels too hard to handle, but I squeeze his shoulders and watch Keaton bite his lip in pleasure made me almost smile.

The pain soon began to feel better and soon after that I couldn't feel pain anymore, instead I was tightening my legs around his waist wanting more and desiring him like I was before.

"Does it feel good?" He asks in my ear and I nod closing my eyes feeling a sensation take over me.

I throw my head back letting out a little moan as Keaton kisses down my neck, I pull a little at his hair causing him to go a little faster than before and I smile.

"I love you," He whispers, breathlessly.

"I love you."

Chapter Fifty-One

Tae's Pov.

"Thanks for the chocolate," I thank Winnie who gives me a thumbs up.

We sit at the lunch table together alone, it felt good to be finally alone together with Winnie because every time we tried to hang out, it always ended up Keaton and Landon right by our side.

I clench my teeth and let out a breath as I move my legs in the chair, sore would be too soft for the way I was feeling, every time I walked it felt like a hammer was jabbing my inner thighs.

We have Keaton to thank for that.

"You good?" Winnie raises an eyebrow.

I bite into the chocolate bar. "Yep."

"Mhm..." She trails out, giving me a suspicious look.

"What?" I shrug.

"You look different," She calls out, pointing at me while smirking.

Uh oh.

"What do you mean?" I ask, feeling the chocolate slide down my throat as I swallow.

"You seem glowy like," She explains with her hands.

Glowy?

"What-" I begin to say but she beats me to it.

She gasps before pointing at me in accusation. "You had sex."

How-

"No," I shake my head in denial, but my face turns against me as I feel it becoming hot.

"Yes, you did! You're turning red," She giggles out.

"Okay I did, will you please shush?" I demanded quietly, looking around.

She sits back in her seat and smiles. "You dirty bitch! How was it?"

I blush just thinking about it and nod. "It was good."

"I remember the first time Landon and I had sex, he put peanut butter on my toes-" She tries to finish but I shake my head quickly.

"Winnie, you're amazing, but please don't tell me about what you and Landon do in private," I whine out and she shrugs.

"Fine," She hums out.

I feel hands on my shoulders and the person gives them a squeeze, I knew the touch very well and I felt myself smile at his touch.

"Hey," Keaton kisses my temple before taking a seat beside me.

"Hi," I smile brightly and I see in the corner of my eye Winnie staring at us in a daze.

Landon takes a seat besides Winnie and wraps his arm around her shoulders.

"Where were you guys at?" Winnie asks, looking at the boys.

"Coach wanted to give us a proper goodbye and we ate with him," Keaton explains, rubbing his chin.

"Was Reece there?" She asks.

Keaton shakes his head. "He wasn't allowed."

"Good," She sassily states.

Landon sits up in his seat and lays his arms on the table and nods behind us. "There goes the fucker now."

Before we knew it, we were all looking back and in comes Reece with a black eye and a swollen lip, I look to Keaton who's already staring at me and my eyes catch onto his lip that looked to be almost healed already.

Landon starts talking to Winnie about having a date tonight and Keaton lays his hand gently on my thigh and squeezes, I wince.

"Shit, are you sore?" He asks, rubbing my inner thigh.

"A little," I answer, nodding.

A little? I'm sore all the way up to my cooch.

Winnie giggles and we both look up to see her watching us, Keaton raises an eyebrow at her and she waves it off.

I look at the time on my phone and grab my trash from the table getting ready to leave, Keaton grabs my wrist.

"Where are you going?" He asks.

"Going to the nurse," I say without whispering it or trying to hide it from Winnie nor Landon.

I was happy that I wasn't living in a bubble anymore, maybe it was a good thing Reece found out and let the whole school embarrass me.

I felt stronger in a way.

"Let me come with you," He says, his eyes were full of passion.

"I'm not stopping you," I smile at him as he stands up from the chair.

I look towards Winnie to see that she's already staring back at me with a smile and Landon mimics her actions.

"I'll see you in class," She tells me.

I nod and Landon waves a little. "Don't worry, we're not going to think differently towards you, we still think you're a book nerd and a control freak."

My mouth falls open and Keaton pushes the small part of my back and Winnie giggles but waves at us.

"I can't believe he said that," I laugh out as we exit the lunch room.

"Not saying I agree to I, but he isn't wrong," Keaton says, holding his hands up in surrender.

I gasp out before shoving him as he chuckles.

We get to Nurse Pattie's office and knock before entering, we're greeted by Nurse Pattie's gorgeous smile and she rolls around in her rolly chair.

"Tae Lambert and Keaton Davis," She greets, waving us in and Keaton shuts the door behind him.

"How are you guys doing?"

"Good," We both say in sync.

I hop on the table like bed and sit while she takes out my medicine.

"When was the last time you went to the doctors?" She asks me.

"Back in November," I told her.

"Mhm..." She mumbles. "You should've already had to go back, when's your next appointment?"

"I have no clue, my dad talked with the doctor, so I'm guessing he knows."

"Talk with him about your next appointment because you took your last bit of medicine and I should've gotten some more in before you even ran out," She explains and I furrow my eyebrows.

I nod. "I'll talk with him."

She smiles and nods along with me. "Okay, well you're good to go, but Chris and I are thinking it's gonna be a beach wedding, but I kinda want it to be in the mountains."

"You should do the beach," Keaton states, putting his hands in his pockets.

"You think so?" She asks.

He nods and she thinks quietly. "Good to know."

The bell rings just then and I hop off the bed. "I'll see you next time."

"Okay, come visit me sometime even when you don't have to take your medicine," She states.

"I will," I smile while nodding.

We leave her office and enter the filled hallways with screaming freshman's and tall seniors.

Keaton sighs. "Meet me after class?"

"Of course," I tell him, nodding.

"Alright, I love you," He says, pressing his lips onto mine and before I could melt to his touch he lets go with a smirk on his face.

"I love you too," I tell him and he smiles brightly at me before turning around and walks off towards his locker.

I watched him walk off and some guy fist bumped him which only made me smile harder, I walked off to class with a smile.

****

"Why can't I take you home anymore? It's like Winnie and Georgie are always racing to get to you first," Keaton crosses his arms like a kid pouting and I laugh.

"I'll let you pick me up next time, I promise," I tell him, holding onto his shoulder as I look back to Georgie's old mustang with his windows rolled down trying to yell something at me but I ignore him.

"I won't even get to see you tomorrow cause I gotta go get a tux with Landon," He blows out a breath and I awe at him in cuteness.

"It's not the end of the world if we don't see each other for one day," I roll my eyes playfully at him.

"Say that again," He points at me, playfully glaring.

I hold my hands up in surrender and he huffs out before wrapping his arms around my shoulders bringing me in for a hug.

"Be safe and call me soon," He mumbles against my head.

"I will," I nod, letting go of him.

"I love you..." He trails, pushing a piece of hair out of my face as I stare up at him.

"And I love you," I said in a daze.

He grabs my face and kisses my lips softly before letting me go to my brother who keeps honking for me to come on, I wave towards Keaton and turn back around to Georgie and glare at him before flipping him off and he smiles sweetly at me.

"Hey," I say to him as I enter his car.

"It feels so weird being here after all this time," He mumbles, looking up at the school like he's never seen it before.

"It hasn't changed," I tell him truthfully.

He pulls off out of the school. "I bet."

"Anyways, I was thinking of staying longer, if you want me to, of course," He adds, explaining.

"Of course, I want you to, Georgie, have you told dad?"

He nods. "Yeah, I'm thinking of getting a job down here too if I do stay longer."

"You getting a job? Not happening," I laugh out.

He glares at me before looking off towards the road, frowns then look back at me, he looks me up and down before looking back up at the road.

"What?" I ask, annoyed.

"You got dicked down, didn't you?"

"What? No," I quickly deny.

How is this happening?

Chapter Fifty-Two

Keaton's Pov.

"Do these suit pants make my ass fat?" Landon asks, turning around in the mirror as I sit back on the comfy sofa chairs.

I close my eyes and shake my head. "Bro, come on."

"Fine, whatever," He waves me off before walking back to the dressing room.

I stare at my lock screen and a smile appears on my face, it was off guard on our date at the movies, she looked the other way with a serious look on her face while her bottom lip was sucked in.

She was the definition of beautiful and nobody could say otherwise, Tae was the smartest person I knew and that's what attracted me the most and because she was a challenge.

She was so hard to get that made me want to chase her, she was worth the wait, she was worth the chase.

Landon walks out of the dressing room with regular clothes on with his tux hanging on a hanger ready to check out.

"Dude, you've been looking at your lock screen since we got here," Landon calls out, sucking his teeth.

I shake my head. "No, I haven't."

"Mhm," He hums sarcastically.

Winnie taught him so much.

We just might have to thank Winnie for Landon's sassiness.

"Wanna go eat somewhere?" He asks, waiting in line as I stand behind him.

"Sure," I nod.

We check out before walking out of the tux shop, we hop in Landon's truck and take off to get something to eat.

"So, a little birdie told me that you and Tae went frisky," Landon speaks as he drives and I tap my fingers on my knee looking out of the window.

I turn my head to look at him. "Winnie told you, didn't she?"

"Yep," He said, popping the p.

"I should've known," I rolled my eyes.

"So... How was it?"

"Stop acting like a girl," I fix my hair before laughing out.

"Tell me," He says impatiently.

"It was actually pretty good," I tell him truthfully.

He smirks. "What? You didn't think it was gonna be good?"

"No, I did, I just thought I had to worry about going slow and shit and that really gets you out of your pleasure you know?"

"Which I'm not saying it was bad with Tae because I had to go slow cause once, I slipped through she was clawing at me like-" I begin to add but he coughs awkwardly.

"Too much?" I ask.

He nods. "Yeah, a little."

We both laughed before getting out at Greenhouse Diner, which was no surprise there, it was busier than usual and I was glad at that. Ally and Tommy finally have a full house.

"What's up Ally," Landon calls out and Ally turns her head at us and her face lights up.

"My boys," She exclaims, pinching his cheeks.

"Wow, fake," Tommy calls out through the window as he stares at his wife.

She waves Tommy off before turning back to us. "Come, I'll bring you to your seat."

We take a seat at our usual spot and Ally tells us she'll be back with our drinks.

Landon leans over the table. "Remember Caleb?"

"Caleb Erwin?" I raise an eyebrow. "The one that was a senior while we were freshmen?"

"That one," He nods.

"What about him?" I shrug.

"He's here," He states, nodding in front of him.

"You're kidding," I raise up.

"I'm for real."

"Ain't he famous now?" I ask, furrowing my eyebrows.

"In our town maybe, but he didn't go far in football cause his wife got pregnant and he had to focus on that," He explains.

Damn.

"Speaking of pregnancy," Ally cuts in, setting our drinks down before taking a seat beside me.

I perk up hearing the news, but the sad smile on Ally's face told me something else.

"I was pregnant but not for long, we lost another one," She tells us, fiddling around with her fingernail.

I rub her back. "I'm sorry to hear that, Al."

"Everything is so perfect so why can't this one thing happen for me?" She asks, tearing up.

"Shit happens, why don't you adopt?" I ask, shrugging.

"I want my own, not that I wouldn't love to adopt a kid, but it's not the same as having your own," She explains, before looking around. "I best get back; it was nice seeing you two and I'll be at you two's graduation."

"Great," Landon smiles at her.

"Wait," She turns around. "Where's Reece?"

I look at Landon before nodding at him for him to tell her.

I knew we were gonna be here for a while.

****

Tae's Pov

"It feels so damn good to be home," I hear Georgie call out as I pour the popcorn into one big bowl.

I smile as I walk into the living room to see Georgie made a pallet of blankets for us and our favorite movie to watch together.

Grease.

Even though Georgie claims he doesn't like it, he watches it with a smile.

"I'm glad your home, I worried about you night and day," I tell him, popping a piece of popcorn in my mouth.

"I was living the best life back there but here it's different..." He trails, shaking his head looking around. "It's home."

I smile at him. "Does it feel different?"

"Nah, but when I picked you up yesterday that felt weird," He explained. "I miss high school."

"Don't grow up too fast because once you're my age, you're gonna look back and you'll wanna go back," He adds, grabbing a handful of popcorn.

"Is college hard?" I asked, sipping on my soda.

He shakes his head. "Not if you focus and get your work done, it's kinda like high school but you have more freedom."

"I can't wait," I tell him and he smiles.

"Where do you plan on going?" He asks.

"Tri County, I don't want to leave dad."

"You should come to Harvard," He states, nodding.

"I can't just pop up, I have to get a scholarship," I laugh out.

"It's not that hard," He exclaims, and I stare at him like he's got three heads.

"Okay," I laugh out, letting him win the conversation.

"Where's mister Keaton Davis going?" He asks, smiling.

I frown, looking down at the popcorn. "I actually don't know."

"How is that?" He raised an eyebrow. "He should've told you."

"He doesn't know really, his dad wants him to go to Ohio but he acts like he doesn't want to go but then again he does, he never really told me where he wanted to go," I say, shaking my head.

"Ohio's a good school, but it's pretty far," He states, giving me a serious look.

Would I be okay with him going to Ohio? I never really thought about this.

I want him to go if he wants to, but I don't think I'd be happy that he's gone.

"Next topic," Georgie laughs out knowing I was thinking too hard and I give him a sad smile.

Were we going to break up if he left?

Of course not. *Right?*

Chapter Fifty-Three

Tae's Pov.

A month later and everything was still the same, everything was great and Georgie was still here. Days were counting down till prom and then Keaton and Landon graduating which is still crazy to me.

I hold onto the gift I got for Winnie for her birthday and wait by her locker.

She walks towards me with her red binder against her chest. "Hey."

"Happy birthday, you're finally not sixteen anymore," I tell her, smiling sweetly.

She smiles. "Thank you, I hated being sixteen, it was god awful."

"Here, I got something for you," I handed her the bag with the gift inside and she frowns.

"Tae, my gift to you was horrible," She whines.

"No, I love chocolate," I tell her, waving her off. "Open it."

"Okay," She is hesitant, but opens it and gasps.

Diamond earrings are what were in the bag and inside a tiny box, they were knock offs of course, because real diamond earrings were too much for this broke girl.

"Tae," She gasps, looking up at me.

"Yes?" I bite my lip, stopping myself from laughing.

"Thank you so much, these are beautiful," She says, hugging me tightly.

"You're welcome."

She takes the earrings out of the box before placing them in her earring holes in her ears, she opens her locker and sticks the bag in there before staring at her ears in the mirror on her locker door.

"I feel so bad that I got you chocolate," She turns around, whining to me.

"It's fine, I loved it," I wave it off.

I really did, it's the thought that counts.

"No, I'm getting you something even though it's not your birthday," She states. "And I don't want to hear you say no."

"Winnie-"

She cuts me off. "What did I say?"

"Sorry..." I mumble.

The bell rings and the intercom starts to come on and I lean on one of the lockers beside Winnie's.

"Students please join Principal Myers and the faculty for our afternoon pep rally, thank you," The woman at the front desk in the school's office announces and everyone starts walking towards the gym.

"Let's go hear people scream and jump around for an hour, then we'll be out of here," Winnie states, causing me to laugh.

Winnie and I make our way to the gym with everyone else and I look around for Keaton and Landon who are walking with the football team wearing they're jock jackets. I look away from the golden boy and proceed to enter the gym and sit down on the bleachers beside Winnie.

Keaton takes a seat at the bottom of the bleachers looking up and around at the students looking like he was looking for someone.

His eyes latch onto mine and he smiles and I mimic his actions.

"Y'all two are something else," Winnie yells over the yelling students.

Principal Myers walks out holding a microphone and everyone goes quiet.

"Good afternoon, are you guys ready for an amazing pep rally?!" He asks and all the fresh-man's jump up and yell.

"We'll start it soon, but first I want to give some guy's credit for their hard work this year, will the senior football players come up here," Principal Myers waves to the boys to come and they do as they were told.

Everyone starts to clap and cheer and I do a little clapping myself.

"These boys have worked so hard to get here, to get on their spot and to be the best role models for you guys, I'm so proud of these guys and you should be too. I'm actually probably going to cry when I watch them graduate," He explains, laughing a little.

A smile reaches my ears as Keaton makes eye contact with me and he bites his lip.

"I just wanted to say a final goodbye to you guys and a trophy because you were one of our best senior football players so far."

Keaton and all the others smile and nod at Principal Myers.

"And a big shout out to Coach Lambert for teaching these boys manners and correction during these times because they're gonna need it when it's time for college," My dad smiles at Myers when he shouts him out.

"Thank you for coming up here, you can be seated now," He lets the boys sit down before yelling out at us that the pep rally was starting.

Keaton turned around and looked at me, it looked like he wanted to climb the steps to get to me, but he had to walk all over people to do that, so with the flick of his head, he told me to leave the gym.

I waited a few seconds before getting up and telling one of the teachers who looked at me in confusion that I was going to the bathroom, I stepped down the steps before passing by Keaton who smirks.

I exit the loud gym and enter the quiet and deserted halls, I walk towards the bathroom which is not far away from the gym and enter it, I wipe the sweat from my hand off and for some reason I was nervous when I had no right to be.

I pace the bathroom back and forth and wait about a couple of minutes, the sound of the bathroom door opens and I turn around seeing Keaton, I walk quickly towards him and cup his face with my hands and bury my lips against his.

"You look beautiful today," He tells me in between the kiss and I smile.

He grabs the back of my thighs and lifts me up, I wrap my arms around the back of his neck and my hands go straight to his hair, he grunts before taking both of us into the big stall, he lets me down and we split apart.

"What was that?" He asks me, his lips were tinted red. "I never seen you like that."

"I'm feeling weird again," I tell him, shrugging.

"It means you're horny," He takes a piece of my hair out of my face and I blush.

"Yes..." I mumble as his lips attack mine again.

His fingers go down to the button of my pants and undoes them before zipping down the zipper, I push my pants down with my hands and gasping out as Keaton's lips attack my neck.

I feel Keaton's hand go to my core but my hand stops him and he looks up at me in concern.

"I don't want to be touched, I don't want the little bits and pieces, I don't want the tease, I want it," Before I could stop myself from telling him, I already did the damage and my face goes red as he looks down at me with a surprised look.

"Yes ma'am," He says after a while and undoes his belt and helps me back up on his waist again after he slips on a condom.

He slides my underwear to the side and enters me with no question, I gasp out with it only being my second time and I smile through it, grabbing onto Keaton's shirt.

I look down at him and cup his jaw in my hand and connect lips with him, moaning into his mouth.

I couldn't believe we were doing this on school grounds, matter of fact, we were doing it inside the school, with my dad under the same roof.

But I didn't care.

Just then I pause, hearing girls laughing and I smack Keaton's shoulder telling him to stop, the bathroom door opens and what sounded to be like three girls were talking amongst each other, Keaton raises his head and looks at me and smirks before going slow in me, not stopping and not fazed by my weak hits.

I close my mouth and eyes, holding in a moan and suddenly the girls go quiet, and then Keaton stopped finally.

The girls start back talking again and then they exit the bathroom, I smack Keaton's shoulder before unwrapping my legs around his waist.

"Are you crazy?" I ask him as he continues to laugh, pulling my pants up.

"A little bit," He answers, buckling his belt.

"If those girls caught us, we'd be in detention and my butt would be grass and you'd be dead and my dad would be in jail," I explain, making Keaton laugh more.

"You can't tell me that wasn't funny," He ask, following me out of the bathroom.

I turn my head away trying to stop myself from smiling but I crack and let out a laugh.

"It kinda was," I agree with him.

Some people would call us crazy, maybe mad, or stupid, we were all of those things.

We were stupid in love.

Chapter Fifty-Four

Tae's Pov.

"Hi," I mumble, hopping into Keaton's Jeep.

Keaton smiles as I face him with his hand on the wheel. "Hey."

"You ready?"

"Ready as I'll ever be," I sigh out, buckling myself in.

"Are you nervous?" He asks, pulling out of my driveway.

I shake my head. "Not really."

"Only because you're here," I remind him, smiling.

He gives me a gentle smile before laying his hand across my thigh.

We get to the doctors within thirty minutes, I blow out a breath before entering the place and seeing a girl walk out with no hair and a bandage across her arm.

My heart drops to my stomach seeing that the girl didn't look but eleven or twelve, she didn't deserve this, nobody deserves having cancer.

Keaton squeezes my hand for reassurance and we take a seat in the waiting area. A random nurse calls out for my last name after a couple of minutes and she smiles at me as I stand up with Keaton, she takes us back and sets us in a tiny room.

"Dr. Simmons will be here in a few," The nurse states before heading out of the room.

I looked around sitting on the table like bed as Keaton watched me while he bounced his leg up and down getting impatient by the minute.

"You good?" I raise my eyebrow.

"Yeah," He nods. "I just hate hospitals."

"We won't be here long, they'll probably take a few X-rays again and we'll be gone," I tell him and he nods.

The door opens after a few minutes and Dr. Simmons is in full sight as he closes the door.

"Ms. Lambert, how are you?" He asks with a smile.

I smile sweetly back. "I'm good, how are you?"

"Good," He answers.

"How's everything with school? Good grades? Partying any?"

"You know me I don't party," I lie a little. "And my grades are great."

Keaton smirks at me and I mouth for him to shut up, Dr. Simmons turns around and smiles at Keaton.

"I didn't see you there for a second, how are you?" Dr. Simmons says to Keaton.

Keaton nods. "I'm pretty good, thanks."

"Good, now Tae, I'm sure your dad has told you the news and I know you're not excited about doing chemo, but it's going to be a breeze if you follow the steps correctly-"

Woah wait-

Did he just say chemo?

I shake my head completely confused. "What do you mean chemo?"

"You'll be taking chemo treatments, did your father not speak with you on that?" He asks, confusedly.

When did this become a decision?

How come my dad didn't tell me?

My hands start to shake and I almost fall off the table but Keaton is quick to my side and turns to Dr. Simmons.

"When will she have to be taking the treatments?" Keaton asks, rubbing his hand soothingly across my back.

I take deep breaths as Dr. Simmons gives me a concerned look.

"As soon as possible, I didn't know that your father didn't discuss with you by now, but he should've. You're getting weaker by the moment and your system is very bad and if you don't start getting your treatments soon, I'm sorry I have to say this, but you won't be here much longer Ms. Lambert," He explains, shaking his head while giving me a sad look.

I nod feeling tears prick to my eyes, my throat became dry and all I wanted to do was to go home and scream into my pillow.

"Oh my god," Keaton mumbles, Un attaching himself from me and covering his mouth with his hand.

Dr. Simmons knew we were in complete shock, so he let us leave with his sorries and goodbyes, the ride home was intense and silent, neither of us said a word and by the minute, I was growing angry at my dad who didn't tell me, yet he let me go to the doctors knowing they were going to tell me.

"Tae, I'm sure your dad had a good reason for not telling you," Keaton tries to defend my dad, but I ignore him and keep looking out of the window.

Once we get to my house, I slam Keaton's jeep door closed and he stays quiet as he chases me inside the house, my breathing is heavy as I stare at the man that hid this secret in front of me and I break down.

"You must've found out," He points out.

I scoff. "Obviously, how could you not tell me?"

"Because, you were so happy I didn't want to ruin that," He explains, holding back his tears.

"Dad, it's chemo!" I yelled out, hearing footsteps run down the stairs and in comes Georgie.

"I just didn't know how to tell you!" He fights back.

"So instead, you let me hear it from my doctor? You know how embarrassing that was for me that I didn't even know when they were talking about it?" I glare at him.

I was so shocked that he didn't tell me.

"I'm sorry, I knew this was going to end badly," He rubs his face with his hand.

"If you knew it was gonna be bad then why keep it from me, dad? I've got to do chemo, this is life changing for me," I yell out, tears dripping down my face.

"It's life changing for us too, we have to go through the pain just as much as you do," He bites back, pointing his finger at me.

I look at Georgie then back at my dad, I look back at Georgie to see him staring at the floor with a guilty look written on his face.

Wait-

Did Georgie come down here to see us or was it because he knew the cancer got bad and he was scared and came down here.

This is mind blowing and crazy.

It was too much to think about.

"You knew, didn't you?!" I ask Georgie who looks away, locking his jaw.

I scoff. "I thought we were better than this, we used to not keep secrets."

"Don't be mad at Georgie, be mad at me, I was the one that told him to keep quiet," Dad states, shaking his head.

I shake my head. "Neither of you speak to me."

I walk upstairs completely forgetting that Keaton was watching us the whole time, I hear footsteps behind me trying to catch up with me.

"I have to speak to you, I'm your dad!" Dad calls out and I ignore him.

I walk in my room and wipe the tear that was dragging along my face, the door of my room shuts and I turn around and burst into tears.

"Why does this have to happen to me? What did I do to deserve this?" I ask, knowing I'm ugly crying but I didn't care.

I was hurt.

And by my own family at that.

"Come here," Keaton demands sadly, opening his arms.

I walk into his arms wrapping mine around his waist.

"How am I gonna get through this?" I whisper but in question, closing my eyes tightly hoping I would just fall asleep and not wake up.

"You will," He says against my head. "I'll be there through everything, I promise."

I promise...

Chapter Fifty-Five

"Now that's what I like to call a masterpiece there!" Landon exclaims loudly after he drew a stick figure on the poster in which Winnie tears it saying it was trash.

I smile sadly at the two and feel a hand at the lower side of my back, I turn to see Keaton.

He knew I was still upset about the whole chemo treatment and he didn't argue or wonder why I was still sad, he understood why I was mad with my dad and upset about the chemo.

"You alright?" He asks lowly in my ear.

I nod, continuing to draw on the poster. "Yeah, I'm fine."

"Nowadays I don't believe you when you say you're fine," He playfully glares at me.

I shake my head. "I'm for real."

"I know you're lying, but I'll let it go for now," He sighs out. "I gotta take a leak."

He kisses my cheek before heading towards the bathroom, I smile watching him leave the class and wonder how'd I get so lucky when it came to him.

He was a blessing from up above.

"I'm proud of the person he's becoming," I hear Landon in my ear and I raise an eyebrow before turning to look at him as he's at my side staring at the same place I'm staring at.

"Sorry," He laughs out. "I know that was sudden, but seriously, you've changed him."

"He changed himself," I shrugged.

"I've seen a change in him and I started seeing it when he met you, you're his goal getter," He explains, pointing at me.

"What are you saying to that poor girl?" Winnie asks from across the room.

"Mind your business woman!"

She scoffs. "You are my business!"

Landon rolls his eyes before looking back at me. "I'm telling you the truth."

"Was he a handful back then?"

"Hell yeah," He laughs out. "He was worse than Reece."

"I never really knew Reece..." I trail, looking down at the poster.

"Reece was a closed-up guy, he never told anyone the way he was feeling or what was happening at home."

"Mhhh," I mumble.

"Hey, you kinda look pale, you good?" He asked and I touched my face.

It was hot.

I walk towards the mirror in the classroom and see that I really was pale.

"I'm fine," I tell him with a smile.

"You sure?" He asks as I sit back down in my seat.

"I'm sure, but thanks for being concerned," I really was thankful, he was very observant.

Like *always*.

Hearing footsteps step back into the room, Landon slips away from me and I turn to look back at Keaton but instead of seeing Keaton I feel a slimy wet substance get placed on my face, I jump up from my seat and gasp.

Keaton had splattered paint on the side of my face thinking it was cute.

"Oops," He shrugs, placing the paint brush in the paint bucket.

I glare at him. "You son of a-"

"Language Ms. Tae," Keaton mocks me, backing up from me as he holds up his finger.

Winnie giggles at us and I grab some red paint from the ground and grab a paint brush before dipping the brush into the slimy paint and wiping it on Keaton's black shirt quickly, before running around the table as he stops his movements to glare at me.

"Payback!" I stick my tongue out at him and laugh.

"Cute," He sarcastically says, smiling.

"Thank you," I flip my hair from my shoulders.

"Don't come near me with that!" I demand at Keaton who grabs a blue bucket of paint forgetting about the paint brush.

"You think you're funny, I'll show you something funnier," He laughs out, walking towards me.

I quickly made a run for it but it was too late when the blue paint got on my back side.

"Keaton," I gasped out, but couldn't help but laugh.

His smile touches his ears and I couldn't believe how gorgeous he was just by standing there.

Grabbing a bucket of yellow paint, I quickly throw it on Keaton's front side as he gives Landon a thumbs up like he had won or something.

Keaton slowly gives me a playful glare and smirks and opens his arms out.

"Come on, babe," He orders for me to hug him. "I only want a hug."

"You better run Tae!" Winnie squeals out, but then gasps as she gets splashed with paint by Landon whose smirk never leaves his face.

Arms wrap around me as I get distracted by the couple throwing paint at each other like Keaton and I were doing.

"You're a handful," I tell him, playfully rolling my eyes at him.

"Oh, but you love me," He sings out, connecting his forehead with mine.

"I do," I whisper out, smiling up at him.

"What is this mess?" Mrs. Hyde asks, looking around the room with wide eyes.

I looked around awkwardly to see that all the posters were a mess and the ground was covered in paint.

"A paint fight?" Landon says confusedly and Winnie slaps her forehead only bringing yellow to it.

"Well, nah shit!" Mrs. Hyde cusses out and I have to cover my mouth with my hand to cover my laugh up.

"You guys this is not a playground, this is your school's art room, what are you gonna do when principal Myers sees this?"

"I'll stay behind to clean this up," Keaton says, looking around at the place. "After all, it was my idea."

"No, I'll hire someone to come and clean, but I don't want to see any more messes from you kids," She gives us a pointed look and we all nod.

"Damn it, I always gotta clean up after kids," She mumbles to herself, leaving the classroom.

"Dude, I thought our asses were grass," Winnie says with her eyes wide.

I laugh out. "Me too."

"I've never seen Mrs. Hyde cuss so much," Landon says surprised.

"She's having a rough time with her husband," I shrug.

"Ouuu what if we get your dad and Mrs. Hyde together?" Landon asks like he said the most brilliant thing.

"Landon, she's still married," Keaton shakes his head at him.

"Not for long though," He points at us.

My dad and Mrs. Hyde together? I don't see it.

Chapter Fifty-Six

Tae's Pov.

"Tae, you need to hurry up, Keaton's here already and I need to take your pictures," My dad yells at me from downstairs.

"I'm coming!" I yell back, walking to my mirror.

I pull the hair out of my face before looking over myself one last time, I sigh out but jump as the door of my room opens revealing a suited good-looking Keaton. His eyes traveled down my body giving me a look that caused me to shiver, he coughs nervously.

"Your dad wanted me to check up on you..." He trails as his eyes stay on me.

"My dad wanted you to check on me even though I could've been naked?" I question him, because there was no way my dad told Keaton to come into my room.

He tugs his bottom lip between his teeth ignoring my question. "Damn."

"What?" I blush, looking down at my dress.

"Give me a twirl," He instructs and I give a confused look, but comply.

As I turn around for Keaton and face him, he's smiling.

"You look absolutely breathtaking," He compliments, causing me to tug a piece of my hair behind my ear.

I watch him walk closer towards me, his shadow appearing on the wall from my lamp being on.

"Thank you," I say quietly, as my breath get caught in my throat.

"You don't know how happy I am you're going to prom with me," He tells me and I smile as I feel his hands barely slide against my arms until he stops at my hands to caress them.

"It's not my thing, but it's for you," I squeeze at his hands for reassurance.

"I promise you; you will have the best time, I will make sure your first prom is your best prom," He promises me, his eyes never leaving mine.

"I'm looking forward to it," I bite my lip.

"Let's go see your dad before he has a heart attack and thinks I'm planting kids in you," Keaton jokes and I giggle out as he takes my hand and leads me downstairs.

I feel myself frown at the sight of my dad staring up at me with a smile, I put on a fake smile just for this night because I know he's been dreaming of it and I really didn't want to end up fighting.

"My little girl..." He mumbles, tearing up a little.

"Take the damn pictures, dad, so we can go out," Georgie complains, waiting at the door with his jacket on.

"Hold on a damn second," Dad glares at him and Georgie rolls his eyes.

I actually smile for once at the two getting annoyed at each other.

"You look more like your mom every day, I can't believe you're growing up on me," He takes a hold of my hands.

"I love you dad," I tell him.

"I love you," He whispers, a tear falling on his cheek and he backs up to take our pictures.

Keaton's arm wraps around my waist and my hand falls on his back and we both stare at my dad's camera and place smiles on our faces, two photos came then three, six, then ten, Georgie had to photo bomb of course.

"We've got to go or we're gonna be late," I state to everyone and my dad nods.

"Okay, have fun and be safe, I love you," Dad says, kissing my cheek.

"Love you," I smile at him.

Keaton's hand stays behind my back as we leave my house, he follows me at the passenger side of the Jeep and opens the door for me.

"Thank you," I smile at him and he winks at me, waiting for me patiently to hop in the car.

He shuts the door before running over to the driver's side and gets in and pulls out of the driveway to get to our destination.

We jam out to Whitney Houston, but more like me doing all the singing while Keaton gazes from time to time with a smirk.

We get to the school which had bright lights coming from the inside, nervous bubbles form in my stomach and I felt sick to my stomach.

"What's with the look?" Keaton asks, observing me from the side.

I bite my lip. "I'm nervous."

"Don't be, you're gonna be here with me."

"I know," I tell him, nodding while smiling as he grabs my hand and kisses my palm. "This is my first prom so of course I'm gonna be nervous."

He nods and a truck pulls up beside us with lights underneath it, Landon pops out with Winnie on the other side jumping out. Literally.

I open the door and Winnie runs to me holding the bottom of her dress.

"Hi babe," She squeals, looking down at my dress. "You look so gorgeous!"

"Thank you, but you..." I trail, looking at her as she twirls. "You look so hot!"

"Well thank you," She flips her hair before hugging me. "I'm so glad you're here."

"*Always*," I tell her, smiling.

"I never had a girlfriend that went to prom with me," She shrugs.

I hit her arm playfully. "I'm here now, so don't worry."

She wraps her arm around my shoulders and I smile at her.

"Landon, get your girl because she stole my girlfriend," Keaton demands Landon as he points to us.

Landon shrugs. "She's gone."

Keaton shakes his head at his best friend and we all head into the school which was filled with students who were dressed in dresses and suits with punch in their hands and some dancing.

Winnie lets go of me and Keaton takes the situation and wraps his arm around my waist.

"Are you feeling better now?" He whispers.

I nod, looking up at him. "Yeah."

"Wanna dance?" He asks, holding his hand out for me to take.

"I'm not good at dancing," I tell him, shaking my head.

He rolls his eyes playfully. "Come on, you only live once."

"Fine," I whine out, letting him drag me to the dance floor.

A slow song starts to play and I recognize it from me playing it in my bedroom when I go to read my books.

You Are the Reason by Calum Scott

I smile up at Keaton as he takes my arms and wraps them around his neck and takes his and wraps them around my waist, we sway to the beautiful song and a twinkle in his eye brings tears of joy to me.

"Why are you crying?" He asks, lifting my head up with his finger.

"I love you," I whisper out, smiling up at him.

He smiles gently, kissing my lips before saying. "I love you too."

"I don't want this to end," I tell him, and not talking about the prom ending.

His smile fades and a frown takes place.

"I don't care how many doctor visits we go to or bills I have to pay in order to get you better, I'm *always* gonna be here Tae Lambert," He states, giving me a serious look.

"You mean the world to me and to see you upset about chemo is making me upset, hell, I'm already upset about it, but I don't want to be constantly reminded that you have to take it," He explains, letting go of me.

I grab his arm. "Keaton, I'm sorry, but can you see where I'm coming from? Anyone would be upset that they have to take it."

He closes his eyes and presses his hand into them and sighs out. "Are we seriously gonna talk about this at prom?"

The sadness in his eyes was clear and the happiness was long gone, I felt hot and sweaty and we only danced to one song. Winnie runs up to us on the dance floor and swifts me away.

"I know that look in his eyes, he's angry," She says, looking at Keaton then looking back at me.

"Yeah..." I mumble, feeling dizzy.

I closed my eyes before shaking my head and opening them back, I tell Winnie that I was going to head to the bathroom, she nodded asking me if she needed me to go with her because she knew how boys were and I told her that I'd be okay.

I walked to the bathroom and when I got inside, I leaned against the sink and let out heavy breaths, the room seemed to spin and I was in and out, I shook my head and tried to splash water on my face but it didn't seem to stop spinning.

The door of the bathroom opens and I turn my head to see Lydia, I roll my eyes and look back down at the ground to stop the dizziness.

"Hey..." She trails.

I look in the mirror to see her slightly behind me. "If you've come here to make fun of me, don't, please do it another time."

"I'm not here for that, I wanted to say I'm sorry..." She says, sighing.

I give her a confused look and she continues.

"I've been a bitch to you and Keaton-" I couldn't hear the rest of what she was telling me, I closed my eyes and my ears started to ring.

"Tae, it'd be really nice if you listen to me because it's kinda hard-" I hear before blacking out and falling backwards onto the floor.

"Tae!" I hear as I open my eyes and close my eyes then back, feeling them get heavy.

"I'm going to get some help!" I hear before losing conscious completely.

Keaton's Pov.

"Winnie, where's Tae?" I ask the redhead who was sipping on her punch.

Her eyebrows crunch up and she looks around. "She said she was going to the bathroom; she should've been back by now."

"Shit," I mumble under my breath, looking around for the dirty blonde.

Just then I see Lydia running towards me with her messy curls dangling from her head, I roll my eyes annoyed as she grabs my arm.

"Lydia, I don't need your shit right now," I tell her, slinging her off of me.

She shakes her head. "No, I'm not here for that, Tae..."

She couldn't get her sentence out and my eyes went wide and she swallowed.

"Something's wrong with Tae," She explains quickly.

"Where is she?" I ask her.

"Bathroom," She points and I rush quickly to the bathroom.

I almost knock the door off the hinges to get in the bathroom and I hear footsteps run after me. Tae lays on the floor on her back unconscious and my heart drops.

"Tae!" I yell even though I know she can't hear me.

The bathroom door opens and I turn around to see Lydia, Winnie, and Landon looking down with wide eyes and a teary face.

"Is she okay?" Winnie asks, covering her mouth.

"Call the ambulance!" I order to whoever.

Winnie nods wiping a tear off her face before dialing the police quickly as she could, I give my phone to Landon.

"Call Tae's dad and tell him that something's happened and she's gotta go to the hospital," I demand of him and he nods with shaky hands.

"Hi, I'm at Westside High and I need an ambulance here fast, my friend is unconscious," Winnie stutters out.

I rub Tae's head as I look down at her. "*Please be okay.*"

****

I watch as they lifted Tae up on a stretcher with her dad hanging onto her like a puppy on a leash with tears in his eyes, fear was all the look he gave to me as the doors shut of the ambulance. Kids from prom filed out of the gym to see what happened, but didn't Tae passing out give them enough information?

A tight hand on my shoulder caused me to come undone, everything seemed like it was in slow motion, tears flooded down my face, and worry filled my heart.

I turned around and my sights landed on Landon's worried face and him trying to talk to me but all I heard was the sound of my heartbeat, his lips moved but nothing seemed to come out. I had worried looks from Winnie and as she tried to touch me, I moved away.

I moved away from everyone, I wiped my eyes with the back of my hand before racing towards my Jeep with Landon and Winnie hollering for me. I yanked my tie off around my neck as I got settled in the car.

Screeches were heard as I pulled out of the parking lot, my phone buzzed in my pocket and I didn't seem to look at who it was when I answered.

"Yeah?" I said into the phone.

"Keaton honey, where are you? Landon called me and said you were heading to the hospital," I hear my mom's soft voice ask me.

"Tae's in the hospital," I couldn't even barely get a word out. It was above a whisper and I then proceeded to let a few tears out.

"What is it? I can't hear you, speak louder," She tells me and I focus myself on trying to tell her and trying to keep my eyes on the road.

"Tae's in the fucking hospital, tell dad to meet me at Glenn-view hospital and get the best doctors he can find," I yell out into the phone before hanging up.

I couldn't deal with their shit today; something was wrong with Tae and I wasn't about to deal with my dad's shit.

This was supposed to be a good night, one of the best nights according to what I told Tae. I told her that this was going to be the best prom she would ever have, and this had to happen.

I didn't care about my scholarship to Ohio or about my dad or my mom, all I cared about was how much time I had left with Tae.

The last moment I spoke to her was when we had a little argument, I hit my fist on the steering wheel and clenched my teeth together and screamed before flooring it behind the ambulance.

Please be okay.

Chapter Fifty-Seven

Keaton's Pov.

Watching Tae still not woken on the hospital bed drove me insane, none of us heard from the doctor yet after he ran a few tests, Bo left to get coffee to calm his nerves and Georgie sits on the sofa biting his fingernails as he watches his sister.

Georgie must've couldn't take it much longer when he gets up and leaves the room to breathe.

I brush Tae's hair out of her face and grab her hand and lay a kiss on her palm lightly.

"Please don't leave me, Tae. If I can't breathe without being with you for a second then how am I supposed to live without you forever?" I ask her, feeling tears come to my eyes.

"From the moment I met you, I knew you were something special and when you didn't want anything to do with me, I knew you were going to be a hard one to crack, but you were worth every minute, every second, every night and day, you were worth the fight and the wait and I loved the chase, so do me this favor and fight through this for me," I explain but begin to ask her, feeling the one tear drop from my eyes.

I didn't even know if she heard me or maybe I just wanted to say this stuff to get it off my chest, but damn did it feel good.

Just then Bo enters the room and I give him a sad smile as he hands me a cup of coffee.

"Have you talked to your parents?" He asks, taking a seat beside me.

I nod. "I talked to them last night when I was on my way here."

"Are they coming?"

"I have no idea nor do I care," I tell him truthfully, taking a sip of the warm coffee.

"I barely made it with her mom..." Bo trails suddenly, staring at Tae. "I don't know how I'm gonna make it if something happens to her."

I stay quiet not knowing what to say, Georgie comes back in the room with a tear-stained face as he wipes his nose, he sits down in a chair and stays quiet as he looks down at the floor.

A knock on the door causes us to look up in alarm thinking it's the doctor but reality was Winnie and Landon giving us a sad smile.

"I'll talk with them," I tell Bo who nods and waves at the couple.

I get up from my seat that I haven't moved from only to take a leak and walk towards my best friends. As I get outside, they are quiet at first as they look at me to see me in my state of shock.

"How is she?" Winnie's the first to speak.

I shrug. "Still the same from last night, the doctor hasn't come back since he ran some tests."

"We can come back another time-" Landon starts off, but with the shake of my head he stops.

"No, you guys are here for support, Tae would be thankful," I tell him who nods.

"Has anyone said anything? Like the nurses?" Winnie asks, looking in the room to see Tae.

"All they do is come in and put iv's in her to start her chemo treatments and when we ask them about the tests all they do is shrug," I explain, putting my hands on my waist.

Landon shakes his head. "That's bullshit."

"They started her chemo treatments?" Winnie's eyes were covered in tears.

I nod staying silent hearing Winnie's soft cries and she shakes her head.

"Keaton, she's only got us and her dad and brother, she needs all the support she can get if she's going to beat this," She states.

"She'll beat it, babe," Landon tells Winnie as he holds her shoulders giving them a squeeze for reassurance.

"Bo Lambert?" A manly voice calls out and I turn my head to see the doctor.

"Yes, that's me," Bo instantly stands and walks towards him.

"The tests came back and it's bad news, the cancer has spread throughout her body and she's just getting weaker and weaker, so that's why we started giving her the chemo treatments, she'll wake up around tomorrow, and she'll need to take these treatments with Dr. Simmons once a week," The doctor explains as Bo shakes his head.

"It's going to get nasty, so please bear with her. She will lose her hair which she probably already knows from the others that have taken it and she will be very weak so don't stress her or make her lift any heavy objects," The doctor adds.

I didn't notice until I stopped hearing what the doctor was telling Bo that I was biting my fingernails.

"We'll come back tomorrow when she's awake to see her," Landon tells me, giving me a hug.

"Thanks for coming," I say, giving them a sad smile as I hug Winnie.

"Keep us updated on how she's doing," Winnie reminds as she walks down the hall with Landon.

"Will do," I tell her, waving.

I sigh out before going back inside the room but before I go back, a voice calls for me.

"Keaton," I turn around and instantly frown.

I look around before shoving the still bruised up boy to the wall. "What the hell are you doing here?"

"I heard what happened with Tae, I wanted to check on you," Reece explains, holding his hands up in surrender.

"I don't need you here, what I need is for you to leave and stay the hell away," I hissed out quietly.

"Look man I'm sorry, I wanted-" I cut him off short.

"Are you seriously trying to apologize to me when my girlfriend is in the hospital?! I exclaim in confusion.

The nerve of him.

I let him go and he backs away.

"I just wanted to say I'm sorry," He defends himself.

"You've done enough," I accuse, shaking my head.

"I'm moving," He tells me as I go to enter the hospital room.

I turn back around and laugh out in sarcasm.

"Do I look like I give a fuck? You screwed me over and now since Tae's in the hospital you suddenly feel bad? Get the fuck away from me, leave I don't care," I exclaim, giving him a disgusting look.

"Okay," That's all he says and he turns around and leaves.

I felt like punching the wall but then again, I don't want broken knuckles or a broken hand, how did everything become so good, then to bad, then to worse? In just a year?

Why does shit like this happen to me?

First my mom getting sick, and me acting out almost getting kicked out of school, then me fixing myself and getting a second chance and getting on the football team, second, I meet Tae and everything goes well- no I mean great, then Reece backstabs me, and third Tae gets even more sick.

My life was falling apart in the blink of an eye and there was nothing to do.

But I needed to be strong for Tae.

And that's what I was going to do.

Chapter Fifty-Eight

Keaton's Pov.

I hear a tiny cough thinking it was in my dream but then I hear another loud one which wakes me up, I open my eyes to see Tae's big doe ones staring straight at me.

"Hey," I quickly sit up in my chair and take a hold of her hand.

"Water," She pointed towards the water jug and I instantly grab it and fill her cup and gave it to her.

She takes a few sips and hands it back to me. "How are you feeling?"

"Drowsy," She answers, licking her lips.

I smile down at her while combing her hair with my fingers, Bo wakes up and almost falls out of his chair seeing that his daughter was awake.

"You don't know how happy I am to see you up," Bo tells her, kissing her head.

"Tae, oh my god!" Georgie states, chuckling.

"I'm happy to see you guys too," She laughs out.

It felt good to see her smile again.

"I'm so sorry about me not telling you had to take chemo," Her dad apologizes and she shakes her head.

"It doesn't matter anymore," She smiles up at him and he kisses her forehead one more time.

She looks back at me. "You still have your tux on?"

"Yeah, I haven't changed yet, I was waiting for you to wake up," I explain, rubbing my thumb across her hand and hearing her sigh.

"I'll go get you some food," Bo states, pointing his thumb behind him at the door.

Tae nods telling him a quick thank you.

Before I could get a word out a small hey was heard in the room and my eyes go into a glare, why do these idiots keep coming into my life?

"Leave," I warn Lydia who gives me a pleading look.

"I'm not here to fight," She defends, shaking her head.

"So, leave," I ordered her.

Tae grabs my hand, grabbing my attention. "Let her talk."

What the hell?

I huff out, sitting back down in my seat before leaning back and crossing my arms.

"How are you feeling?" Lydia asks with a soft smile.

I've never seen her this nice and it's making me uncomfortable.

Tae shrugs. "Tired, but I'm better."

"You took quite the fall the night before," Lydia says back and Tae laughs.

"I know."

"Look Tae, I'm so sorry for causing pain towards you and Keaton," She begins and I roll my eyes, not buying her lies.

"I'm leaving for college soon and I didn't want any bad blood between all of us before I went because now, I'm looking back and all the popularity and stuff really wasn't it," She explains to us.

"I thought you didn't get that scholarship to Ohio?" Tae asks, confused.

"Oh, I didn't," Lydia states, shaking her head. "I actually am going to one where nobody really knows of, they were the only ones that will let me in, so I took it."

"Oh," Tae's bottom lip pokes out.

"I'm glad to see that you're doing good, I have to go, but again thank you for letting me talk with you and apologize," Lydia thanks her and Tae waves her off.

"I'll see you," Lydia waves, smiling brightly at Tae.

"Bye," Tae smiles at her until she's gone.

I can't believe what I just witnessed.

My ex and my now girlfriend got along.

How?

"That was strange," Georgie butts in, I nod along with him.

I totally forgot he was in here with him being so quiet.

"Why would you let her talk when you know she's going to lie?" I asked Tae who was playing with her fingers.

She scoffs. "You could see straight through her and could tell she was sorry."

"Oh, come on," I sarcastically laugh out.

Georgie gets up and leaves the room to let us have our privacy but more like argue in peace.

"You are so bothered by her," She tells me.

"You were too," I accused, pointing my finger at her.

"Keaton, it got old with us all hating each other and starting things," She explains, sitting up in the bed.

"She was the one starting things, not us," I defended us and she shakes her head.

"You need to let go of your past with her, or are you still hooked on her?"

I pause and glare at her. "Did you just seriously ask me that? Am I still hooked on her? What kind of question is that? Tae, I love you, how could I still be into Lydia when I'm in love with you?"

"You need to let go of the past if you want it to let go of you," She says, rolling her eyes.

Shit.

She was right.

She *always* was.

I sigh out and grab her hand. "I'm sorry."

"And?" She raises an eyebrow and I give her a bored look and she cracks a smile.

"I'm sorry too," She lets out, nodding.

"I just don't want her hurting you," I state, rubbing my thumb on her hand.

"She won't," She says, shaking her head.

"Everything good?" Georgie pops his head back in and asks.

Tae nods with a smile. "All good."

"Phew, I was thinking Tae was gonna get up and whoop that ass," Georgie says to me and I laugh.

"I wouldn't doubt it," I look at her who smirks up at me.

Cheeky little thing.

Chapter Fifty-Nine

Keaton's Pov.

I watched as Tae's doctor put in treatments for Tae as she sat calm on her bed staring at the wall in front of her, her hair was up in a bun and her pale lips were pouting as my hand held onto her petite ones.

"We're all done Ms. Tae," The doctor tells her who smiles.

"Thank you," She mumbles quietly, her voice a rasp.

The doctor leaves and I kiss Tae's temple. "You did good."

She sadly smiles at me before squeezing my hand.

"She's done?" Bo asks as he exits the bathroom.

I nod. "Doc just left."

"How are you feeling?" Bo asks his daughter who shrugs.

"Tired," She answers.

A light knock on the door makes everyone in the room head turn, my mom and dad stood at the door with a sad smile on their face but I could see my dad faking it for Tae.

I stand up, giving them a confused look. "What are you guys doing here?"

"Honey, you haven't returned our calls, you haven't come home since prom, we're worried," My mom says, walking towards us.

My dad follows along behind her.

"You knew where I was," I shrug.

"Keaton, look at you, you look like you haven't slept, have you eaten?" She asks, giving me a concerned look.

"I'm fine, I'm watching over Tae," I tell her, giving Tae's hand a squeeze again.

I could see my dad getting irritated by the minute and that's when Bo stands.

"I'll be out in the hall if you need me," He tells Tae as he kisses her forehead.

"Okay," She lets out.

Georgie gets up in a hurry and walks behind his dad as they exit the room, I haven't heard him speak or eaten in days which was weird.

"Son, you have to come home, your mother and I need our son at home," My dad speaks out.

"I'm staying here with Tae," I tell him in a demanding tone.

My dad sighs loudly and my mom puts her hand over his chest but he shoves her away.

"I've been waiting for you to pick a college and I've been very patient with you, but there's no more time for that anymore, I'm sick of the waiting and I'm tired of being patient, tell me your decision," He says aggravatedly.

Was he serious right now?

Was he going to pick a fight when Tae was in the hospital and right in front of her?

I scoff. "I can't believe you're doing this here and right now."

"Oh, you best believe it, now choose," He sarcastically laughs out before getting serious.

My mom gives him a disapproving look as she stands away from him, crossing her arms.

"Can we do this later?" I ask him, glaring a bit.

"No," His tone was hard and raspy.

"Please?" I beg.

"No!"

"Fine, I choose Tae!" I scream out, flying my arms all over the place.

"What?" Tae asks, with wide eyes.

"Keaton," Mom begs, with teary eyes.

"What the fuck is wrong with you?" My dad glares.

"I'll go to school here, I'm not leaving Tae," I shake my head, giving him my final decision.

"Keaton, no, don't do this," Tae shakes her head up at me.

I sit down and grab her hands with mine and trail kisses on them. "I want *this*."

"It's what you think you want, Ohio is your dream, don't throw it away because of me, I'm sick and *always* probably will be, please go," Tae begs me with teary eyes.

I can't.

There was no way I could leave this girl behind.

"I can't. I physically can't and I won't leave, I can stay here and still do what I want for the future," I explain, shaking my head. "Ohio is not what I want, what I want is to be here with you."

"Please go," She whispers out, a tear dropping down on her cheek.

"No," I tell her, shaking my head again.

"Listen to the girl, Keaton, she wants you to go so do it!" My dad exclaims, pointing towards Tae.

I look up at him and glare. "Just shut the fuck up! Ohio was your idea *remember*? Not mine!"

"Tae, I want this, I really want this," I beg her with my eyes.

"Just let him be Randy, you can tell he wants to stay," Mom interferes, giving me a sad smile.

Tae looks at my mom before looking back at me. "Are you sure you want this?"

"Yes," I say with no hesitation. "I want this. I want *you.*"

"I choose you, Tae," I finish, nodding.

She wipes the tear off her face and smiles. "Then stay."

My dad sighs. "If you do this, Keaton, you're going to regret it."

"I know I won't," I answer him, keeping my eyes on Tae.

Dad blows out a breath before walking out of the room angrily and my mom gives us a sweet smile. "I'm so happy that you've woken up and I'm so happy to see that you've made my son this happy, keep him this way."

"I will," Tae says, biting her bottom lip.

My mom winks at Tae before coming around the bed to my side and kisses my head.

"I love you, my sweet boy," She whispers.

"Love you, mom," I tell her, smiling.

She leaves the room and Bo comes back in whistling.

"You're really staying?" He asks and Georgie stares.

"Yeah," I answer.

"Oh, thank god, I was about to have a heart attack if you didn't," He looks up and prays up above.

Tae's laughter filled the room and I couldn't help but stare.

"What?" She blushes, pushing a piece of hair behind her ear.

"I love you," I mumble, biting my bottom lip.

She blushes red even more. "I love you."

Chapter Sixty

Tae's Pov.

My dad sits in the pickup truck happy as he can be that I was getting to come home, we sing along to some eighty's music and let the windows roll down feeling the cool breeze come in the truck, finally Keaton let me off his chain, but I knew it wasn't for long.

He left the hospital about an hour before I got signed out, I was wondering what he was up to.

We pull up to the house and I sigh out as I'd miss home too much since I was gone.

"We're home," I mumble, smiling at myself.

"Let me help you out," Dad states, exiting the truck quickly and running over to my side of the truck.

He opens the door and lets me out and takes my hand, I hop out of the truck and without any hesitation, dad and I were heading for the front door.

He sticks the key into the keyhole and we hear it unlock, he opens the door slowly with a smile and I walk in carrying my bag.

"Surprise!" I hear a crowd say.

I look up in confusion and my face goes red from seeing a crowd of people standing at the front door, standing in front of me with smiles on their faces. A huge sign hung in front of the stairs that says 'welcome home' and my heart warms at that.

My eyes catch onto familiar ones and I smile at the different faces.

Winnie stood there covering her mouth with her hand trying to not cry and Landon stood there with a smile. Georgie was sitting on the counter eating an apple giving me a big welcoming smile, Mrs. Hyde stood there wearing a beautiful dress with open arms.

I wrap my arms around her waist.

"Welcome home," She says, smiling.

"Thank you," I tell her.

My heart warms as the people stood in front of me, all these people cared when I didn't think they did, and half of them were because of Keaton Davis.

"Tae!" Winnie screeches, bear hugging me.

"Hi!" I greet her, laughing out as she squeezes me.

"I'm so happy to see you," She tells me.

"You look so beautiful!" I compliment her, looking over at her white dress with rose petals all over it.

"Thank you, so do you! I wish I looked like that when I came from the hospital," She laughs out, rubbing my arms.

"Happy to see you're alive," Landon jokes which only makes Winnie slap him. "Kidding!"

I giggle at the two and a pair of arms wrap around my waist and a head lands on my shoulders.

"Hello beautiful," Keaton's voice says in my ear and I snuggle into his touch.

"You did this?" I ask him as I turn around in his arms.

He nods. "Georgie, your dad, and I did."

"Thank you..." I mumble, kissing his lips as he smiles.

"I wanted to give you this, Tae," Winnie tells me and I turn around to see her holding a burgundy box.

"What is it?" I take it gently in my hands.

"It's something to make up for since I only got you chocolate for your birthday," She explains and I gasp as I open the tiny box to reveal a tiny diamond necklace which had to cost a fortune.

"Winnie-" I begin to say, but her shaking her head cuts me off.

"Don't say that you can't take this because you are, it's yours," She states, pointing at me.

I smile gratefully at her. "Thank you, really."

"It was no problem," She hugs me.

A hand lands on my shoulder as Keaton unwraps his arms around me and I turn to see Bonnie.

"Hi," I greet her sweetly.

"Hi sweetie, how are you feeling?" She asks, raising an eyebrow.

I nod. "I'm doing good."

"I was so worried about you, I'm so sorry that happened to you at prom," She frowns at me.

"I'm just glad that I'm out of that hospital," I smile at her.

"Me too," She says, before giving me a stack of books. "These are yours to keep, I saw you eye them a couple of times but never checked them out."

"Bonnie, I love these," I tell her gratefully, knowing I couldn't argue with an Adams. "Thank you."

"You're welcome, sweetie."

Ally and Tommy make their way towards me and I noticed Keaton slipped off away from me and I focused on Ally who hugs me.

"Babygirl, my heart dropped when I got that call from Keaton, ask Tommy, I couldn't cook until I knew you were okay," Ally tells me with her country accent.

I smile at her. "I'm okay now."

"Thank the lord you are," She nods. "I got you something."

"You didn't have to," I whine.

"I wanted to," She reminds, bringing out a pie. "I made it, it's apple."

"Thank you so much," I take it gently, smiling at the married couple who mimics my actions.

"There's a young fella waiting for you," She points out behind me.

I turn around to be faced with Georgie and I smile.

"Thank you for making this happen," I went in for a hug and his arms wrapped around me.

"Anything for my little sister," He says as we pull apart.

I put my hands on my hips. "But what I wanna know is why didn't you speak to me a lot at the hospital?"

"I'm sorry, my mind was messed up, I kept thinking you were mad when you forgave dad and if I had talked to you, I would've started crying," He explained, sighing out.

"I'm sorry for overreacting, but you had to see where I was coming from, you guys shouldn't have hidden that away from me," I remind him, poking at his stomach.

"I know," He says, nodding. "So, that's why I got you something to make up for it."

"Not another present," I roll my eyes playfully.

"Yep," He says, popping the p while holding up car keys and jiggling them in my face.

I raise my eyebrow. "What?"

"It's yours," He says, handing them over to me and my eyes go wide.

"No," I shake my head. "You've got to be kidding me!"

"I put my money and dad chipped in and helped me pay for it," He says, shrugging like it was nothing.

"Georgie, you got me a car!" I exclaimed, almost yelling.

"Yes! Go see it," He orders, pushing me out of the house to see a little grey Honda sitting in the drive way that I didn't even notice was there and scream.

"Oh my god!"

"Nice right?" He laughs out.

"Thank you," I tell him, side hugging him.

After moments later of looking over at the car, Georgie and I got back inside while my dad made a toast to everyone and thanked them for being here. We ate, laughed, and cheered, and I showed Winnie my car and she fell in love with the car as much as I did.

I was incredibly grateful for what my brother and dad did. I didn't know how to repay them.

As Winnie and I were talking with a punch in our hands I couldn't help but notice someone staring at me from afar, I looked to see Keaton's eyes piercing through me and I smiled at him which only caused me to smirk.

"I love you," I mumble, biting my bottom lip.

A wink was sent my way which only made my heart race, everything seemed to be a disaster, but sometimes when life gets down, it'll eventually turn itself back around and good things will happen.

Chapter Sixty-One

Tae's Pov.

"Woah, calm down blondie," My dad orders me as I slide around the house with my socks on in a hurry to get to Keaton's graduation.

Oh my god.

Keaton's graduating today.

He's not a high school student after this.

I was so beyond thrilled that Keaton was finally graduating, but kind've sad because he wouldn't be going to school with me anymore, after he made that decision of staying here and not going to Ohio, I was happy he wanted to do what he wanted, but his dad said he would regret it and I was nervous for the outcome of that.

I hurry and put my shoes on and grab my blue jean jacket.

"Georgie!" I yell out. "Dad!"

"We're gonna be late if you guys don't get your butts down here," I demand at them and I hear Georgie footsteps running down the stairs in a hurry and my dad stands next to me coming from the kitchen.

"Sorry," Georgie apologizes and we head out of the house quickly and right on time for the graduation.

We arrive at the school and we walk towards the back to the football field to see the graduation set already set up. Winnie and Bonnie walk towards us and while Bonnie and my dad speak with each other, Winnie and I take our seats with smiles, Georgie sits next to me.

"I bet you miss this huh?" I ask Georgie who stares around at the place.

He nods. "Hell yes."

Winnie giggles and I smile at her.

I look around at the people to see Keaton's parents sitting with Ally and Tommy, and Chris and Pattie are sitting together alone.

Ally stares back at me and motions a gun with her hand and pretends to shoot herself in the head while Tommy speaks with Randy, I laugh out and she winks at me before looking up at the stage as Principal Myers taps the mic.

"Hello everyone! I've been dreading this day to come because this was honestly my favorite senior group and to see them graduating breaks my heart, but also makes me happy because they're going to be something someday," He tells the crowd of people.

I chew on my gum that Winnie gave me in boredom as Myers cries about the memories he shares with everyone and he ends it off with calling a girl to walk up there and give out her graduation speech.

"Hi, I'm McKenna Gurley, in my previous ages I got into some trouble, I was smoking, drinking, and vandalizing the school which I should've went to jail for, all thanks to Principal Myers, I was at a tough place and felt like nobody wanted me or even loved me, until Myers called me into his office and said if you stop doing these bad things, I can make your life turn upside down, I was confused but I did it, I don't know why, but I did. He was true to his word and Myers made me class president of the school because of my good behavior and told me he seen something in me, now here I am today graduating, which I didn't think I was gonna do and going into Harvard University, life is so little, but the world is yet so big and so is your dreams, so please follow them, thank you, forever a Ram!" She explains her life and her long journey with Principal Myers.

Everyone yells a chant at her like they always do in graduation after they say '*always* a ram.'

I clap along with everyone putting a smile on my face.

Principal Myers stands up and gives McKenna a hug before going back to the mic.

"Now a word from our team Quarterback, Keaton Davis," He announces and my heart races.

Everyone claps and cheers and even whistles were heard in the crowd as Keaton walked the stairs in his cap and gown.

Never have I ever seen a guy look so good in a cap and gown.

"As some of you know, I was a troubled kid, I got into drinking real bad and fights were my main priority, when I wanted to change my act, I got into football, all thanks to Principal Myers and Coach Lambert, they seen that I could change and be somebody, that's what life's about, when it gets hard, don't do stuff that distracts you to get through it, toughen it out and get through it, thank you for listening to me talk class of twenty - twenty and the crowd to watch us as well, I'll forever be a ram and *always* will be," After Keaton finishes his speech, he smiles up at the crowd and they do the same chant.

He walks off the stage but not before giving Myers a hug and taking his seat.

"Now it's time to call out our twenty - twenty graduates to come up here and take their diploma," Myers tells us and we cheer.

"Landon Barnes," Landon stands up at his name being called and Winnie stands up yelling 'that's my boyfriend'.

We all clap and cheer for the blonde boy as he takes his seat with his diploma in his hand.

"Lydia Brock," I hear myself clap with some other few people and look at Winnie to see her roll her eyes at the girl walking up the steps.

"I hope she trips," Winnie mumbles and I couldn't help but laugh.

"Next we have, Keaton Davis."

Keaton's parents, Ally and Tommy, Chris and Pattie, and my dad, Bonnie, Georgie, Winnie, and I stand up clapping and cheering for the golden boy who waves down at us before grabbing his diploma.

I cover my mouth before letting out a few tears, my heart leaps for joy as I watch my boyfriend walk down the stage with his diploma, no longer a high school student.

"Mandy Moore."

People clapped and cheered until one familiar name gets announced.

"Reece Paul."

We all stayed silent as a crowd of people yelled out for him and he looked to not be happy as he retrieved his diploma.

"Thank you so much for a wonderful year and I can't wait to see what you guys are up to in the future, you have been great and the most amazing team, I'll miss you forever, class of twenty - twenty, you may now move your tassels over to the left!" Myers calls out and everyone whistles and air horns are heard from all around.

The graduates throw their hats in the air and I smile up at the moment and couldn't wait to be in their seats next year.

As I see Keaton and everyone else leave their seats to go see their families, I stand up and run for dear life into his arms as I'm whipped up and spun around in his arms.

I let out a tiny giggle as he put me down. "I'm so proud of you."

"Thank you," He gives me one of his brightest smiles.

I push his hair out of his face as he lets his lips crash down onto mine, I hear screeches of everyone else coming towards us behind us, I pull apart from Keaton who gets tackled by his family and his friends.

Landon finally joins us and I give him a hug to congratulate him on graduating.

"Thank you, Tae, really means a lot," He says, bumping his shoulder with mine.

Winnie attacks him with kisses and he groans playfully.

"Well, I'm hungry," Georgie calls out, squinting his eyes from the sun.

Keaton wraps his arms around me and I smile up at him.

"You guys wanna head to the Diner?" Tommy asks, raising an eyebrow.

Everyone shrugs and agrees, except for Keaton's parents.

"We have a lot of work to do at home, but Keaton we're so proud of you and go have fun," Keaton's mom says with a sad smile.

I felt bad for Keaton's mom, I felt like she was being pushed into Randy's world, Keaton's dad was pushing her to do the things he wanted and never seeing her side to let her be happy.

Keaton's smile doesn't fade, but I know he's hurt that they aren't eating out with us, I give his hand a light squeeze to let him know I'm there for him, he gives me a smile, one I knew was fake and kisses my head lightly.

I wish he had different parents. More like a different dad.

Graduation was a success and hopefully everything else goes as perfect.

Chapter Sixty-Two

Tae's Pov.

"Babe, you ready?" Keaton calls out entering my bedroom before entering the bathroom staring at me who was holding onto my brush which held a bunch of hair.

I look up at him with teary eyes and give him a soft smile. "It's happening."

His shoulders slouch and I grab the strands of hair and throw them in the trashcan near the toilet, I wipe a fallen tear hoping Keaton wouldn't catch me, but I knew he saw it when he walked towards me.

"Tae-" He starts, but I cut him off by putting my hand up.

I wipe another fallen tear. "I knew this was going to happen, but not this soon."

"I don't want to be bald," I laughed out, watching a smile appear on Keaton's face.

He wraps his arms around me pulling me in for a hug and I lay my head on his shoulder as he rubbed my back.

"It won't matter because I'm gonna love you no matter what," He lets out, causing me to smile against his shoulder. "You're beautiful with or without hair, nothing could change that."

"You really do know how to make a girl feel special don't you?"

We pull away from the hug and he shrugs. "I'm your boyfriend, it's my job."

I playfully push at his shoulder before looking back at myself in the mirror, I slightly touch my hair with a frown causing nothing to happen, I sigh out and Keaton moves in behind me wrapping his arms around me, he leans his head down to my neck and gives me light kisses.

"You can always wear a wig if that will make you feel comfortable," He tries cheering me up and I scoff.

"Like I know how to put on a wig," I retort, turning around in his arms to face him.

"Yeah, but Winnie can teach you, she's good at that stuff," He says, and I feel his hand rub down my back, lifting my shirt a little to touch my skin above my bottom.

"Okay," I give in, shivering at his touch.

"I love you," He whispers as his eyes drop down to my lips.

I lean forward, pecking his lips. "I love you too."

"*Always?*"

I nod. "*Always.*"

Keaton and I walk out of the bathroom and on our way out of my room, something catches my eye.

Mom's letter.

I never read it.

My hands get a hold of it and Keaton turns around giving me a confused look.

"My dad gave my mom's old photo book on my birthday and it had this letter addressed to me, but I never got the chance to read it," I explained to him and he raised his eyebrows.

"Read it," He points to it.

I nod before carefully opening it.

I read the words on the front and blow out a breath before going back to reading it.

My dearest Tae,

You're probably reading this when your seventeen or eighteen, God, I bet you're gorgeous! I hope you're not giving your daddy a rough time; I'm writing this letter to you because I know you've got leukemia. I knew all along you were going to get it, but I was hoping and praying you didn't. I wanted to write a few things to you about life cause I wish my mother had done the same for me, but live life to the fullest, life is so short and in the blink of an eye it's gone, never lose faith or hope because that's the most greatest thing you could have, I never wanted to leave you and Georgie, but my time was coming to an end just don't forget I'm watching, I love you so much, sweetie, and to my son in law or my daughter's boyfriend if you hurt her I will come back and haunt you or her daddy and brother will take care of it, if you ever miss me please go to Lincoln's tree near Westside high, that's where I used to write my poems at, just sit under it and think of me and take your husband or boyfriend if you want, I know your daddy enjoyed those moments. I love you, forever and always.

Love, mom.

I wipe from under my eyes and smile at Keaton.

"You good?" He asks, with concerning eyes.

"Never been better."

I stared at the boy in front of me as he stared right back at me, it was crazy to know that I used to hate Keaton, but look at me now, hopelessly in love with him. Beginning of the year, I thought I was going to get through this year just like every other face in the crowd, but it all changed that day on the football field.

I had lost faith in myself when it came to me beating cancer, but Keaton was worth fighting for. Taking treatments is a scary thing to think about, you have your ups and downs, the downs were; you would get weak and lose your hair, the treatments couldn't work and you eventually have to fight it off by yourself or *die*, the good was that you kick the hell out of cancer.

Keaton taught me one thing in this life, you don't get to choose for the ones close to you, you don't push people away, you love instead of feeling bad for yourself and not taking control of *you*. When you leave this world, the people that were close to you will cherish and never *forget* the moments they spent with you.

I missed my mom, terribly at that, but I have memories and I'll cherish them as I grow up, because that's what my mom wanted me to do. Keaton made me *forget* that I was sick, dying even, he made me *forget* all of my doubts and that's what I'll *always remember*, I'll *remember* him.

The end.

Made in the USA
Coppell, TX
15 June 2022

78886972R00341